Sherlock Never Lies

New Sherlock Holmes Mysteries
Collection Eight

The Horror of the Bastard's Villa
The Dancer from the Dance
The Solitary Bicycle Thief
The Adventure of the Prioress's Tale

Craig Stephen Copland

The four stories in this book are tributes to the following four in the original Canon by Arthur Conan Doyle:

The Hound of the Baskervilles
The Adventure of the Dancing Men
The Adventure of the Solitary Cyclist
The Adventure of the Priory School

If you have never read these original stories or if it was a long time ago, your enjoyment of the New Sherlock Holmes Mysteries will be enhanced by first. reading the original stories again. They are available free from several sources on the Internet.

Welcome to New Sherlock Holmes Mysteries

The first six novellas are always free to enjoy in ebook format. If you have not already read them, go the the site now, sign up, download, and enjoy. www.SherlockHolmesMystery.com

Contents

The Horror of the Bastard's Villa 1

The Dancer from the Dance 156

The Solitary Bicycle Thief 270

The Adventure of the Prioress's Tale 396

About the Author 557

More Historical Mysteries by Craig Stephen Copland 558

A NEW SHERLOCK HOLMES MYSTERY

THE HORROR OF THE BASTARD'S VILLA

CRAIG STEPHEN COPLAND

The Horror of the Bastard's Villa

A New Sherlock Holmes Mystery

Chapter One
Mr. Sherlock Holmes

"'MR. SHERLOCK HOLMES WILL BE BACK WITHIN THE HOUR' is what I said to him," said Mrs. Hudson. "He was terrible consternated and said it was highly important that he see you straight away. I told him he could wait in your rooms, seeing he was a clergyman, one of those Scottish ministers, so I wasn't worried about him making off with anything of value. Not that there is anything, but he was so upset I wanted to do something to put his mind at ease whilst he waited."

"Is he still here?" I asked.

"No, he sat for a minute, and then he began to pace back and forth and then they left saying they would be back before long."

"*They?* Mrs. Hudson," said Holmes. "There were two of them?"

"Oh, no, Mr. Holmes. It were just the minister and his dog. I told him he could tie the wee thing to the lamppost but the next thing it follows him up the stairs and sits down right beside him on the sofa. And when he gets up to pace doesn't the dog get up and hop along beside him back and forth."

"Holmes," I said. "I am so sorry. I fear I may have caused you to miss a possible client."

It was a lovely spring day in late April of 1890. For the past month, Sherlock Holmes had gone with little sleep and insufficient food whilst relentlessly following the clues related to the death of the elderly spinster, Miss Entwhistle, who, though spry, had died unexpectedly of heart failure as a result of an apparent attack by a flock of starlings. Holmes had uncovered the truth and her nephew and only heir was now on his way to the gallows. Having done so, and with no cases in his docket until the following week, he had lapsed into one of his moods of lethargy and melancholy. I feared the actions he might take to relieve his dreaded boredom.

As his friend and personal physician, I had prevailed upon him to get out of the haze of his tobacco smoke and take a brisk walk with me in the Park. I had attempted to engage him in conversation about the events of the day, but he was not interested. It never ceased to amaze me how his acute mind could be so completely engaged when in pursuit of a complicated criminal case and yet so vacant when his calendar was void.

Now, to my disappointment, it appeared that an interesting potential client had come and gone. Agitated members of the clergy often brought interesting cases to test the skills of London's now quite famous detective, although there had been a few issues in the past with their capacity to pay Holmes's fees. Those from Scotland were, predictably, the most problematic in this regard.

Holmes looked around our front room and turned to me with a smile.

"Do not be concerned, my friend. He will be returning soon."

Then he turned to our ever-accommodating landlady.

"Mrs. Hudson, would you mind awfully describing this clergyman chap. And kindly keep to an accurate description and avoid conjecture."

"Very well, Mr. Holmes. That I can do. Well, to begin with, he was a big fellow. That's what I noticed first off. As tall as you and as thick as the doctor. When he took off his hat, his head was as shiny as a mirror, except for a fringe above his ears. Not young. No, not young at all. I would say he had his three score and ten behind him, but he looked healthy enough. A gentleman, too, he was, and pleasant, for a Scot that is. Smiled when I brought his tea.

Not one of those dour Scots whose face would crack in two should they dare to grin. Wore his black suit and clerical collar. Talked all the time to his dog. A regular conversation with the cur is what he did."

"What was his name?" I asked.

"Who? The dog or the minister?" replied Mrs. Hudson.

"Both," said Holmes.

"He left his card. Here it is. Name was Reverend Donald Fraser. He kept calling the dog Mister David Hume."

"What?" I sputtered. "That is a ridiculous name for a dog."

"Perhaps not," said Holmes. "Peculiar, maybe. However, I suspect there is a good reason behind it. Was Mr. Hume by chance a border collie?"

"That he was," said Mrs. Hudson. "And attached like glue to the minister. If he ever comes back, you can see for yourself."

With that, Mrs. Hudson departed, and I turned to Holmes.

"How did you know what breed of dog it was?" I asked.

"Mr. David Hume left a generous sample of his hair on the sofa. Observe the piebald colors. It is also one of the most intelligent breed of dogs, claims a heritage in the Borders of Scotland, and is appealing to those men who are prone to carrying on conversations with canines."

I looked and noticed the mixture of black and white dog hair.

"Very well, Holmes. If you say so. But you seem rather certain that the fellow will return."

"Within the quarter hour."

"How can you possibly predict that?"

"Please, Watson, observe the end table beside the sofa."

I did and saw a small leather-bound black book.

"Kindly hand it to me," said Holmes. "It is a pocket-sized New Testament and very well-worn. Our good clergyman took it out whilst waiting and was so agitated and distracted that he left it behind. He will soon notice its absence and return to retrieve it."

He took the small testament and sat down in his usual armchair. I sat on the sofa and regarded him carefully. Over the next few minutes, he opened the covers and flipped through the pages. Then he smiled and handed it to me.

"Watson, my friend, you know my methods. What do you make of this accidental souvenir that was left behind? Kindly tell me what can be known about the Reverend Fraser by glancing through his New Testament."

I took the small book in hand and, attempting to use the methods of my companion, made some observations.

"His name is inscribed on the fly-leaf inside the front cover. He has owned this Testament since he was a boy."

On the fly-leaf, I had read the words, written in a feminine hand: *To Donny Fraser, for perfect attendance all year, December 31, 1830. Fort William Presbyterian Church Sunday School.*

"The man," I continued, "still owns and regularly reads it and has done so his entire life. He must be a confirmed believer and has never ceased to be."

"Excellent!" exulted Holmes. "Not entirely accurate, but a fine start. Pray continue."

I was somewhat piqued by his qualifying remark but soldiered on all the same.

"He wrote his name on cover page when he was given this book. I can tell that by the obvious juvenile penmanship."

"Quite so. Keep going. Reconstruct the man."

"He has written his addresses on the backside of the flyleaf. There are over a dozen, no doubt an old one crossed out and a new one added as he progressed through his life. They are all, however, in towns and villages in the Western Highlands, right up to his current address in Kyleakin, with three exceptions."

"Precisely. And those exceptions are?"

"He appears to have attended a boarding school, the Glasgow Academy, and then to have taken his degree at St. Andrews before going on to seminary in Aberdeen. Except for those fifteen years, he has lived his life in the Highlands. For the past twenty years, he has resided nigh to or on the Isle of Skye."

"Correct. Anything else to add?"

"There are scribblings in the margins on every page, along with dates when those notes were added. He has been a faithful reader of the scriptures for his whole life. The dates begin in the 1830s and continue until this current decade."

I closed the worn soft-leather covers and put the book down on the coffee table.

"Ah ha, there you are wrong," said Holmes, yet again smiling in his condescending manner.

"Nonsense," I replied. "There are dates jotted beside underlines and comments all the way from 1832 to 1890."

"Indeed, there are. But there is a gap between the years 1837 and 1841. There was not a single note inscribed between those years."

I thought for a moment, doing the arithmetic in my head, and then smiled.

"When he was studying at the university."

"Precisely," said Holmes. "You excel yourself. Thus, we may conclude that when faced with the arguments of science and the philosophers, our good minister temporarily discarded the dogma of his childhood and youth. But then he managed to recover his faith and integrate it with his enlightened studies. Therein is the significance of his naming his beloved dog after one of the great skeptics of the Scottish Enlightenment. I am presuming that we are about to meet an educated, honorable, and solid gentleman who, for some unknown reason, is in a state of great distress."

He smiled, relaxed in his favorite armchair, lit a pipe, and picked up the morning copy of *The Times*. No more than five minutes had passed before the bell on Baker Street rang.

"Mrs. Hudson," shouted Holmes. "Would you be so kind as to welcome the Rev. Fraser and Mr. David Hume?"

The good woman stuck her head inside the door of our room, gave a queer look to Holmes, rolled her eyes, and proceeded down the stairs. She re-appeared two minutes later.

"Allow me, Mr. Holmes," she said, a note of whimsy in her voice, "to present the Reverend Donald Fraser and his distinguished companion, Mr. David Hume."

The imposing visitor let out a hearty laugh, as did Holmes and I. Holmes immediately rose and strode over to greet them. The clergyman held out his hand in greeting, but Holmes ignored him and quickly squatted until he was facing the dog. Then he held out his hand.

"Ah, Mr. Hume, so glad to meet you."

The dog let out a soft bark, wagged its tail and lifted a paw in response. Holmes took it and gave it a gentle shake.

"And the children," continued Holmes, "Demea, Philo, and Cleanthes. I trust they are well."

The dog barked again, and the clergyman laughed. Whereupon Holmes stood up and shook the large hand that was extended to him.

"Please, Reverend Fraser," he said. "Sit down and relax yourself. Your New Testament is waiting for you and a hot cup of tea will arrive shortly."

"Auch, Mr. Holmes, Thank you. That's the first time I have laughed in this past month. I rather think my dear Mr. David Hume has been ready to take me by the cuff and drag me into hospital."

"Then it is most opportune that you have come here," said Holmes. "For you shall have the services of a doctor as well as a detective; both of which I assume are needed this morning."

"Aye, you have me on that one, Mr. Holmes. That they are."

"Then, my good man, take a minute over tea and then explain your situation to me and Dr. Watson."

Mrs. Hudson had arrived with a tray bearing a pot of tea and a plate of warm scones. The three of us took a few minutes to enjoy them whilst making inconsequential chat about border collies and the weather. The dog curled up contentedly on the hearth-rug beside his master.

"Now then, Reverend," said Holmes. "Forgive me, but I am assuming that prior to entering this room you have composed the words you are about to deliver to me down to the last jot and tittle, much as you do your sermons. If so, please proceed."

"Thank you, Mr. Holmes, for putting an old man at ease. And aye, you are quite correct. I have written out my words inside my mind. Allow me, though, to begin by asking a question of you."

"Ask whatever you wish, sir."

He did not immediately respond but put his cup of tea on the side table and stood and began to pace back and forth through the length of the room, circumnavigating Holmes's table of chemical paraphernalia at the far end. Mr. David Hume followed at his heels, adroitly managing to hop aside and not be trampled each time his master made an abrupt one hundred and eighty degree turn.

"Please do not think me disrespectful in any way, Mr. Holmes. But my question bears directly on what I about to tell you. Are you, sir, a man of faith? Are you a believer?"

Holmes leaned back in his chair and slowly and deliberately lit his pipe. In all my years with him, I could recount no more than a few instances when matters related to his spiritual beliefs had been raised. A full minute passed before he responded.

"If, by faith," he said, "you accept that I believe there is a divinity that shapes our ends, rough hew them how we may, then yes. It is unthinkable that the universe is ruled by chance. If you are asking whether I believe in the immortality of the human soul, I do. Although our destination after death forever remains the undiscovered country from whose borne no traveler returns. If you are asking if I have, for one second in my life, attributed human behavior and, in particular, criminal behavior, to be the responsibility of a supernatural power, then my firm answer is no. I have no need of any hypothesis that fails to place all blame for our actions on the head, heart, and hand – the mind-forged manacles – of man."

Here he stopped and took another slow draught on his pipe.

"That, Mr. Holmes," the reverend said, still pacing, "is rather what I expected and had assumed I would hear. With that in mind, I shall inform you of my situation. I need to preface my account with a brief record of myself. Although I am a man of the cloth, I have no truck or trade with religious enthusiasts, healers, tongues speakers, self-proclaimed doomsday prophets, or visionaries. I dismiss reports of incidents that cannot be reconciled with the settled order of Nature. With regard to alcohol, I am and, except for some wayward times in my youth, have always been an abstainer. I am also a reasonably learned man and have read the work of the scientists from Isaac Newton through Charles Darwin. I have studied mathematics and am thoroughly familiar with the writings of the philosophers and in particular the works of our brilliant empirical thinkers from Scotland. I admit of no conflict between faith and reason. I trust you will accept my account of myself and consider it before rendering judgment on what I am about to say."

Holmes took another slow draught on his pipe and replied. "Sir, I perceive that you are making these statements prior to telling me your case out of concern that what you are about to say would contradict your account of yourself. You fear that I might conclude that I am speaking to someone who has departed from his senses and quite gone over to the supernaturalists. Am I correct in that assumption, sir?"

"Auch, yes. I fear you are," he sighed. He sat down and took a generous gulp of his somewhat cooled tea.

"Then allow me," said Holmes, "to assure you that I have a respectful regard for your sanity and competence and will listen to the fantastic account that I suspect you are about to deliver without departing from that regard."

"Very well, Mr. Holmes. Then kindly allow me to begin with another question. Are you familiar with the stories from Gaelic folklore regarding the appearance of the *banshee*?"

"I am," said Holmes. "It is a superstition held by Irish peasants. They claim that in the nights prior to a death, a ghostly female figure hovers over the house of the one who is about to die and moans and screams and generally terrifies them. Its appearance, as far as I am concerned, is invariably preceded by an over-indulgence in copious amounts of cheap Irish whiskey and records of its activities are of interest to those who collect fairy tales."

Reverend Fraser nodded and smiled back at Holmes.

"Your description matches mine, Mr. Holmes." Then he paused, rose to his feet, resumed his pacing, and added, "At least it did up to a few weeks ago. We Scots share more of a common Gaelic heritage with our cousins in the miserable sodden isle across the North Channel than we care to admit. In Scottish folklore, there exists a version of the same superstition, although we know it as the *Ben Shee*. In keeping with our obsession with industry, the female ghoul has occasionally been accorded a vocation and may appear as a washer-woman. Nevertheless, the apparitions likewise are accompanied by unholy moans and screams and followed soon after by the death of someone in the village."

Here he paused and gazed intently at Holmes as if attempting to discern his reaction. Holmes was as inscrutable as the Sphinx.

"Keep going, please, sir," he said.

"I am not given to foolish superstitions, Mr. Holmes."

"You have already so said, Reverend Fraser. Please, your account, sir."

"Beginning several weeks ago, several of the folk from both the Kyle of Lochalsh on the mainland and Kyleakin, across the water on the Isle of Skye, reported hearing the horrible moans and screams of the Ben Shee. These are good Scottish people, sir. Fishermen and their families mainly. They are not given to strong drink overly often and although a wee bit superstitious are not prone to wild fantasies. Yet, to a person, they are all making the same claim. They all say that they heard the same terrifying sounds and it frightened them to the marrow of their bones."

Here he paused and stood still.

Holmes interjected, "I am quite certain, sir, that you have not come all the way to London in such a state of distress and sought me out to tell me about a spectral event in the Western Highlands."

"Auch, no Mr. Holmes. Would that were all that happened. Within a few days of the reports, two people, a man from Kyleakin and a woman from Lochalsh died."

"And are you telling me, sir, that you, a learned man, believe that those deaths were in any way connected to the reports of moans and screams? Perhaps a comet appeared in the sky as well. Or did an eagle fly by carrying a cypress branch? Come, come, sir. No end of natural phenomena have been claimed as portending deaths and such claims are all utter poppycock."

"I agree, sir," he said, now once more on the move. "And if it were only the passing of two older members of the villages, I would not be here. The man who died, Mr. Hamish Mackinnon, was the laird of the area. He was in good health and of sound mind. The woman, Mrs. Annie Wallace from the Kyle of Lochalsh, was likewise. Within three days of each other, both of them disappeared. Their bodies were swept out by the tide and found by fishermen. Both of them had lived their entire lives close to the channel and knew every step and rock along the coast. It is hard to believe that they merely fell into the water and were swept away without anyone hearing cries for help."

"It is," replied Holmes, now looking somewhat interested, "a tragic and unusual coincidence of events, but nothing you have said so far indicates foul play and certainly not any connection to supernatural forces. Drownings happen all too frequently amongst those who have lived by the sea but have become careless in their familiarity with its dangers."

"They did not drown, Mr. Holmes. They were murdered."

That caught Holmes's attention. He laid his pipe aside and leaned forward. His eyes were now focused on our visitor.

"That is a serious charge, sir. What is the exact nature of the grounds on which you make that statement?"

"I was called upon to conduct both of their funerals. After the second one, our local mortician took me aside and informed me of the condition of the bodies when they were brought to him. They were in rough shape and covered with seaweed and such, but as he prepared them, he observed that they had not only been stabbed but had been, in the words of the Bard, *unseemed from the knave to the chops.*"

Holmes's eyes were now glistening. For a moment he instinctively began to rub his hands together before catching himself and placing them back in his lap.

"Might you, Reverend, describe what happened in a manner more anatomical and less poetic?"

"Aye, the mortician claimed that both of them had been stabbed in their nether regions and then, with what must have been a large, sharp knife, ripped open all the way to their throats. He said it was the most horrible treatment of a body he had ever encountered."

"Surely," said Holmes, "he reported that to the local police. Yet there has been no such report in the press or the records of Scotland Yard, to which I am privy. Please explain, sir."

"He did indeed report to our local constable."

"Yes, continue, sir," Holmes instructed our visitor, who had parked himself briefly in front of the bay window and was now directing his speech to the traffic of Baker Street.

"I do not wish to speak ill of a man behind his back, Mr. Holmes. However, it is fair to say that our local constable has a high regard for himself and may have deliberately failed to file a report so that he can claim all the credit for himself when he solves the crimes."

"Did you challenge him on his actions?"

"I did. He is a bit of a belligerent chap and berated me for being a foolish old man. He muttered several vile curses and told me to mind my own business. Now, sir, I have spent my entire life dealing with the minor transgressions of common folk and encouraging virtuous actions amongst the flock, not with murder. But I know full well that it is folly to refrain from making such a report. I know of your reputation, Mr. Holmes, from the stories in the *Strand*. That is why, after several sleepless nights, I have made my way to London to meet with you."

"My good sir," said Holmes. "A wire to Scotland Yard would have sufficed. There must be more to your visit than just rendering your report of two murders."

The man turned to face us and placed his hands on his hips. He closed his eyes and nodded, and his answer came in a whisper, accompanied by a quiet whimper from Mr. Hume.

"There is, sir."

"Then please, Reverend Fraser, do tell. I assure you that my respect for your mind and character will not be diminished in the least, regardless of what you say."

"It is about the Ben Shee, Mr. Holmes." He had resumed his perambulations.

"I expected as much. Pray speak of it."

"It has not only been heard by the people of the villages, sir. There are a half dozen folk who claim to have seen her. The word has spread of their sightings, as has the report of what was done to the bodies of Laird Mackinnon and Mrs. Wallace. All of the villagers are filled with dread and terror. Their common sense has fled, and they are attributing the horrible events to the Ben Shee. Every last soul is frightened to the depths of their being."

"I am sure that they all would be sorely distressed having heard such accounts. But forgive me, sir. Surely, you are aware that in conditions of terror it is not uncommon for people to imagine apparitions, to convince themselves that such specters are real, and to spread their reports. These things do happen."

"That was my conclusion exactly, Mr. Holmes, until three nights ago."

"What happened?"

The man took a slow, deep breath and sat down on the sofa. He looked directly into the eyes of Sherlock Holmes.

"I saw her."

He spoke in a whisper. The man's face had gone white, and his hands had begun to tremble. The dog raised its head and looked up at its master. Holmes replied in quiet, measured tones.

"Go on."

There was a thrill in the man's voice as he continued his story.

"It was night. Dark as pitch before the moon had come up. Damp and raw. I was walking along the lane from the village up to the house of Clan Mackinnon. I have walked that path a hundred times and need no torch to find my way. As I approached the final hill, I heard the low plaintive moan. It was like unto what is sounded by the keening of mourners at a wake. It increased in volume until it filled the small valley. Then … then she appeared, lit up and glowing at the top of the hill, and uttered a scream like unto nothing I have heard in my entire life. I was frozen with fear, my blood ran cold within me, and it is a wonder my heart did not fail. The feeling of evil and terror pervaded my body. Then the light went out … and she vanished."

"Can you describe what you saw?"

"Aye. At first, it was a figure of a human body but covered in a cape and a hood from head to foot. Then she turned toward me. Her cape was open, and her breasts were exposed. Her flesh was as white as chalk, except for those parts that were blood red."

"And her face?"

"Mr. Holmes, it was the face of the messenger of death from Satan's Hell."

Chapter Two
The Apparition of the Isle of Skye

"IF YOU CAN, SIR," SAID HOLMES. "Please describe what you observed without reference to any supernatural place of origin."

The poor old fellow was shaking and took a few moments to get control of himself. His dog, sensing the distress of it master, stood up and laid his head across the powerful thigh of the stricken minister.

"Of course, I will try my best to do that. Aye. I can describe her all right. Her face was white but streaked with black lines as if it were a skull that had been cracked in several places. There were no eyes, only black holes in the skull. The mouth area was brilliant red and dripping with blood. When she opened her mouth, there was another recess of blackness."

"And her hair?"

"Her hood concealed it. I cannot say for certain."

"Did her scream come directly from her or from another location?"

"Oh, it was from her. Nowhere else. When she opened her mouth and shrieked, the source was unmistakable. It was horrible."

Holmes paused his questions, and I stood and made my way to the decanters on the mantle.

"Reverend," I said to our visitor. "I know you are by habit an abstainer, but we do have a small supply of Scottish water of life. I do not believe that the good Lord would object to a wee dram given the circumstances."

He gave me a blank look and then a thin smile. "No, I do not suppose he would. But no more than one finger. Well, perhaps two, if you can spare it."

I poured three glasses of two fingers each – well, perhaps three – and served them to Holmes, Rev. Fraser and myself. We sipped in silence for several minutes, and the reverend calmed himself with the single malt whilst stroking his beloved collie. Then Holmes returned to his questions.

"I shall need data concerning the victims. Kindly begin with this Mrs. Wallace of the Kyle of Lochalsh. Who was she? Is there any reason anyone would wish her dead?"

"None that I know of. She was a pleasant lady of a certain age. A grandmother. Her husband was the ferryman who shuttled people across from Lochalsh to Kyleakin. Aye, he did so for years. They lived by the dock and owned a few acres up by the narrows. They have a son and a daughter, but both of them are up and grown and gone to live in Glasgow. Her daughter just had a son, and Mrs. Wallace was all a-flutter about her first grandchild. She was a bit of a quiet one and kept mostly to herself, unlike some of the more gregarious women of the village. But not an enemy in the world."

"And her husband?"

"Teddy? The poor fellow fell apart when she died. The word was out that her death was foretold by the Ben Shee. He was beside himself, and on the afternoon after the funeral, he packed up his clothes and a few belongings and left to go and live with his daughter. For twenty years he has had no other job than taking folks across the water, chatting and telling stories and listening to their woes and complaints. When he isn't working his boat, he has tried his hand at cultivating his few acres, but he has never had much success. The land is too hard. There is no value in it. I heard he put his land and his boat up for sale, and it may be sold by now. But it could fetch no more than a few pounds."

"Thank you, Reverend. Now, about the victim in Kyleakin. You said he was the laird of the area. Was he beloved of his crofters or hated?"

"No laird is beloved. But hated? Nay so much. Any hatred was inherited. Before the Clearances, all the local crofters shared the land but first the grandfather, and then the father cleared most of the crofters and sent them packing. Quite a few made their way to the colonies, but many made it no farther than the miserable Gorbals in Glasgow. With the recent passing of the Crofters' Holding Act four years back, the old manorial and communal laws were repealed and those crofters remaining on the island are protected. There's nothing Laird Mackinnon could have done now to dispossess them. He was never much of a one for doing so anyway, what with the fortune he already has. He was more concerned with keeping his seat in parliament and being thought of as an enlightened nobleman."

"Who was heir to his land and holdings?"

"Aye, there's a rub to that one. He had a younger brother. Lionel was his name but he was the prodigal son of the two and when he was no more than twenty years old – that would be thirty years ago – he quarreled with the father and up and took himself off to London and then to America. The story was told that he joined up with the Confederate army and was killed at Antietam. No one in the village had heard hide nor hair of him for decades, but he must have kept in touch with his brother. The Laird and his lady had no children and, in the will, the Laird wrote that his estate should be divided between his wife and his brother and a handful of much smaller beneficiaries, mostly near Kyleakin, including your humble servant. An address for the brother in Paris was contained in the will. A telegram was sent off, and a week later the fellow shows up."

"And was it the brother?" asked Holmes. "Or was it an opportunistic imposter?"

At this point in the cross-questioning, the reverend had drained his glass of single malt and once again rose to his feet. His steps had, I noticed, slowed somewhat from his earlier exercises.

"Or it was Lionel all right. Even with all the years gone, the folks of the village recognized him straight away. Smaller in stature but same eyes and nose and eyebrows as the father and grandfather. Lady Mackinnon was quite delighted to see him. She had no interest in trying to manage the estates all by herself, and she has enough money from her half to keep her in a comfortable way until she dies. Lionel was a strange one when he was young, but he appears to have accepted his fate and seems willing to settle down and be responsible for the remaining crofters and those in the village who depend on the estate for their wages."

Holmes closed his eyes for several seconds and slowly moved his lips as if having a conference with his inner self.

"Ah," said as his eyes opened. "What of the past? Any dreadful secrets? Legends of iniquity? Sins to be found out?"

"Adultery," said the minister, "is a sin according to the scriptures, but if it were a hundred years back, it is hard to make a case against it."

"Yet there is a story to be told, is there not?" said Holmes.

"Oh, yes, and a good one. You know the story of Bonnie Prince Charlie who fled after his miserable defeat at the Battle of Culloden, do you not?"

Holmes did not reply but gave a smile and a nod in my direction.

"Of course," I said. "He fled the mainland and persuaded Flora MacDonald to help him escape. She disguised the prince as her maid and took him over the sea to Skye. Is that the story you refer to?"

The horror of the Ben Shee having momentarily passed, the imposing clergyman sat down yet again and seemed willing to stay down.

"Aye. Now he is a bit of a hero to the Scots, what with his being so tied to the Jacobites and the struggle against the English. But the truth is that he was mostly a poor leader of his troops, and in exile in Paris, all he did for the rest of his pathetic life was to gamble and father children by numerous women. So, it has long been claimed by the Clan Mackinnon that one of their direct ancestors was the offspring of Miss Flora Macdonald and the Bonnie Prince and that it was him what built the sprawling stately house that looks across the narrows from the hill beside Kyleakin. The family gave the house the high-sounding name of Bethel-by-the-Sea. But the local folk, as local folk will do, gave it a different title. To them, it has long been called *The Bastard's Villa* in honor of the illegitimate offspring of the Bonnie Prince Charles Stuart."

I smiled to myself. The working class of every country, it seemed, had a delightfully wicked way of taking the pompous winds out of the sails of the local nobility. To have a lordly estate house assigned a moniker that tied it to a lecherous event of the past century was ironically fitting. Holmes must have failed to see any humor in the story. Instead of smiling, he leaned forward and continued his questions.

"And these astute local folks to whom you refer, what are their imaginings about the events that have taken place?"

"They are fearful but divided. It depends on whom you ask and on which day. Some are convinced that we have been visited by the devil in the form of the Ben Shee as punishment for grievous past sins. Others claim it is the spirit of Lady Macbeth what with her bloody dagger. And yet others say it is the return of Saucy Mary."

"Who?" I blurted.

"It is a legend from our local folklore. Back around the year 900 the local lord kidnapped a Norwegian princess by the name of Mary and made her his wife. She proved to be a spirited handful. It was she who convinced him to lay a great chain across the narrows to snag any ship that was passing through. A toll was demanded before the chain would be lowered. Once it was paid, the ship sailed on past the castle where the princess was staying. According to the legend, she would wave at the sailors, and as a token of her appreciation for the toll they had paid, she would open her robes and expose her breasts to them. It was said that such a cheerful sight of Saucy Mary made the payment of the toll bearable."

I laughed. Holmes did not. He was in a severe state.

"Enough of racy legends. This Lionel Mackinnon fellow – what protection does he have from anyone seeking to do him harm?"

"Good gracious, Mr. Holmes. Why, none that I know of. Who would want to hurt him? He has not even been anywhere near the village for years. He has only been back a week and could not have acquired any enemies in that short time."

"If my memory is correct," said Holmes, "the Laird Mackinnon not only owns the traditional clan lands in Skye and Mull but also has properties and assets throughout England, the colonies, and in America. Is that correct?"

"I have heard some talk to that effect," said the reverend. "The value of his properties on the island cannot be much. The lands are good for grazing sheep, but not much else."

"The man," said Holmes, "also owns vast herds of sheep in New Zealand, several factories in the north of England, and a plantation in Virginia."

"Does he?" responded Fraser. "That is news to me. How is it you know about that?"

"It is my business to know things," said Holmes. "I also know that when a very wealthy man is murdered the motive may occasionally be revenge, but the probability is in favor of money. If a long-lost brother has suddenly appeared, he now stands in the way of whoever may be after the wealth of the laird. His life may also be at risk."

Here Holmes paused and closed his eyes. When he opened them stood up and spoke severely to our guest.

"Please, sir, return at once to the Isle of Skye and keep an eye out for any possible danger to the man."

The old fellow looked thoroughly uncomfortable. "Mr. Holmes, I have no skill in giving protection. I have never held a gun in my hands let alone fired one. I may have been a decent pugilist whilst at school, but I have not struck another man for over forty years."

Here he paused and looked directly at Holmes.

"If the danger is as you fear it is, Mr. Holmes, can you not arrange to come to Skye yourself? Is there no way you could do that, sir?"

Holmes paused and again closed his eyes in silent concentration. Then *he* began to pace.

"I cannot. I have accepted a case under instructions from Whitehall and have an unavoidable obligation beginning in a few days. However, I believe I might be able to find a capable man to go with you."

"That would be greatly appreciated, Mr. Holmes. Who, may I ask, have you in mind?"

To my utter surprise, Holmes stopped and turned to me.

"My dear doctor, your lovely wife is still abroad in America, is she not? Would it be too much to ask for you to reassign your patients to your medical colleagues for the next week or two and take a journey north to the Isle of Skye?"

I was stunned. I had accompanied Sherlock Holmes on many of his adventures and had even been willing to put myself at risk when joining him in the pursuit of dangerous criminals, but he had never sent me out on my own without him. I was at one and the same time flattered and nonplussed.

"I suppose I could if you truly think I would be of use."

"You would be invaluable, my friend. When could you be ready to depart?"

"I would need a day or two to re-arrange my affairs, but I could be set by Wednesday evening."

"Capital. Then I advise that Reverend Fraser return north today and that you follow him as quickly as possible after. Would that be acceptable to you, Reverend?"

"Aye, that it is. I sense that you perceive the possibility of more horrible events to come."

"Someone has already gone to considerable lengths to terrify the population and to murder two people. When large amounts of money and property are involved, and an unexpected heir emerges, evil deeds are likely to continue. Beyond knowing that fact, I cannot say more. But that is enough to warrant immediate action. I will do what I can to follow within the fortnight."

The poor old clergyman had arrived at 221B Baker Street in a state of distress and was now leaving in the same way, if not worse. I walked down the stairs with him, followed by a whimpering Mr. David Hume, and placed my hand on his arm as we stood on the pavement.

"Sherlock Holmes," I assured him, "is inhumanly capable in his perceptions. Please be careful both for this Lionel Mackinnon fellow as well as yourself. I shall see you in Kyleakin in a few days."

He thanked me and, with his dog at his heels, walked south toward the Underground station.

Chapter Three
The Road to the Isles

I RETURNED TO THE FRONT ROOM OF BAKER STREET to find Holmes still pacing back and forth. Before I could utter a word, he began his dictation.

"Watson, I shall need a report daily from you. Be as thorough as possible and, I beg you, do not fail to report any incident that strikes you as curious and unusual. Do not neglect those obvious things which nobody by any chance ever observes. I shall need a full description of the villages on either side of the channel and of the villagers. Find out and report everything you can about the Wallace couple and any recent happenings to them or their family. And get me as full a report as possible on the murdered laird and his wife. And investigate his relationship with the crofters. And by all means, learn everything possible about the newly-arrived brother. There is no doubt a story behind that fellow. He could be a villain, or he could be in line to meet with an evil fate. And, finally, a full report on the belligerent constable who has violated his responsibilities of reporting the murders. I will not bias your mind by suggesting theories or suspicions, Watson. If I think of anything else I need, I shall inform you."

He had not ceased pacing whilst dictating his instructions. I had, on numerous occasions in the past, known Holmes to exhibit agitation, but this degree of concern was far beyond normal for him. He was shaking his head and looking very grave.

"You clearly believe," I said, "that something untoward is still to happen."

"I am certain of it."

"Very well. I shall do what I can. When do you expect to join me?"

"I cannot free myself for at least the next week, possibly longer. As soon as I can do so, I shall be there. Oh, and one more thing. I shall need a full report on any recent visitors to either of the villages. Do have a good day and send my regards to you dear wife."

With that, he waved his hand as if he was shooing me out the door. I departed 221B and made my way quickly to Marylebone and the nearest Royal Mail office so I could send a wire off to my wife. In as few words as I was capable of using, I wished her to know of my feelings of both thrill and apprehension at being sent off on my own without Sherlock Holmes to a situation fraught with danger. I must confess that the sensation of blood coursing through my body was something I had not felt since my days in the Afghan wars when I knew that within hours my regiment would be engaging the enemy in deadly combat. Had I been asked if I felt fear, my answer would be affirmative. What sane man would not? If asked if I felt utterly and completely alive, with every cell and fiber of my body tingling with anticipation, my answer would be the same.

The following morning, I received a reply from my beloved. She assured me of her love, of her undying support for my spirit of adventure, and of her insistence that I remember to keep my service revolver by me day and night and my socks dry.

From my days in the medical corps, I had acquired the discipline of being able to pack quickly and lightly and making myself ready to depart in short order. Assigning my list of waiting patients to various medical colleagues took longer. The medical profession is notorious for letting the entire population of the rest of the world wait, our fellow doctors being no exception. By Monday evening, however, my schedule had been cleared. Those patients in true need of medical attention had been assigned to a competent colleague, whilst those whose complaint was either imagined or exaggerated were encouraged to get a good night's sleep before deciding if they truly needed to see a doctor.

Travel arrangements were somewhat more complicated, A journey from Euston or King's Cross to a remote corner of Scotland was far more complicated than booking a cabin from Victoria to Southampton. The capable agent at Thomas Cook's gave me a choice between the West Coast Main Line, through Birmingham, Liverpool and then on to Glasgow, and the competing East Coast Main Line that stopped briefly at Leeds, York, and Newcastle before arriving in Edinburgh. I chose the latter, even though it would add several hours to my overall time to the Kyle of Lochalsh.

There was method in my madness. For the past month, the Press had been filled with stories about the opening of the magnificent bridge over the Firth of Forth. The miracle of modern engineering had been called *the eighth wonder of the world* and had accomplished a span that was by far the largest in the world. The Prince of Wales had officially opened it on the forth of March, and the cheeky Press had confirmed that if it had supported his weight, it could be counted on to carry a fully loaded train and a string of powerful locomotives.

I made a brief stop at the library of the British Museum and asked for the loan of whatever books they might have that touched on the legend of the banshee as well as Ordnance maps of the Isle of Skye and the adjacent mainland. The dear, bespectacled librarian gave me a very queer look until I identified myself and explained that I was conducting research for writing a story for the *Strand*. Then she became thoroughly animated and highly energetic. I assured her that should I ever publish the story, I would give due credit to her. Therefore, dear reader, kindly note that the diligent efforts of Miss Dorothy (known to her friends as 'Dot') Barron were most useful in the writing of this story, even though at the time the fine woman had no idea that it was to be a true tale of horror, terror, and gruesome death.

Tuesday evening found me three-quarters of the way along the ninth platform of King's Cross, waiting to board the overnight train that had been dubbed *The Flying Scotsman*. My booking assured me of a stopover of several hours in Edinburgh the following morning before connecting to a local train through the Highlands to Skye.

At precisely nine o'clock, the gears of the massive Great Northern Railway's Stirling 4-4-2 were engaged, and the enormous drive wheels began to turn. Slowly but surely the engine and sixteen carriages crept out of the station and began the journey to the North. I enjoyed a cup of tea in the lounge car, adulterated with a pinch medicinal laudanum, returned to my cabin, and promptly fell asleep.

A knock on my cabin door at some ungodly hour in the early morning brought me to the breakfast car at first light. At five in the morning, our train pulled into the great Waverley Station, and I scrambled to check my baggage and find a cab. If I was destined to spend the next two weeks in those lands that a Londoner considers the last stop before the edge of the world, I was determined to indulge myself with a visit to the marvelous new bridge.

A cab sped me through the empty streets from the station to a point on Whitehouse Bay on the Firth of Forth. It was a cloudless morning, and I arrived just before the slanting rays of the morning sun peaked over the eastern horizon. I sat in awe and wonder as the rays of the sun illuminated the Firth of Forth Bridge. The three enormous, elongated diamonds were strung across the water, and their massive cantilevered girders spanned over a mile, connecting the two sides of the Firth. The structure had been eight years in the making.

I had seen photographs of the bridge in the Press but looking at it as the sun rose brought a thrill to my heart. I must have sat and stared for twenty minutes before getting back in my cab. As we drove back in from my vantage place in the bay toward the entry pillar of the bridge, I noticed a small crowd gathered at the base. On the possibility that it was a group of travellers come to see the bridge, I asked the cabbie to stop and allow me to join them.

A smart looking young man was standing on one of the steps of the great pillars, and over the next ten minutes he rhymed off a litany of statistics about what was now the largest bridge span in the world. Not only had it been praised from all corners of the earth for its engineering brilliance, but there had also been a constant stream of inquiries for sharing the plans so that similar bridges could be built across the world's wide rivers and straits. New York City was interested as was the city of Quebec in Canada, and several sites had been proposed throughout the British Isles and on the Continent.

I would have stayed and listened longer but my train to the Highlands was scheduled to depart in just over an hour, and I had to make haste back to the station. As I bounced in my cab whilst the driver hurried back into the center of the city, I felt quite fortunate for having had such a fine morning.

The train from Edinburgh took me across the wondrous bridge and north through Perth. From there we climbed into the Grampian Mountains, the realm of the majestic Ben Nevis and the Cairngorms. Spring flowers might have been blooming in London, but these jagged peaks were still covered with deep snow. Eventually, we left them behind and zigzagged our way back down to sea level in Inverness. I changed trains there, and we chugged and plodded for several more hours through the barrens of Ross and Cromarty. The cows of the south had disappeared along with most of the trees. In their place were endless scattered flocks of sheep, restricted by long fences of piled rocks that served to separate one man's field of rocks from his neighbor's. Eventually the track curved again to the south and led to a terminus in the Kyle of Lochalsh.

The short train and engine worked its way slowly through the fishing village and all the way to the pier. I climbed out along with the remaining handful of passengers and looked around. My first impression was visual. The clouds had taken over the sky, as is common with coastal villages. In front of me was the wide harbor of dark water, surrounded by rugged, rocky hills that were still dull and grey, waiting for the advent of spring. Dotted around the quay, I counted a half-dozen fishing sheds, with small boats tied up beside them and nets spread out to dry. Had I not seen them, I would have known of their presence by the unmistakable smell of fish that pervaded the area. Across the water to the south about half a mile away was the Isle of Skye and towering over the village of Kyleakin on the far shore stood the stark ruins of the Caisteal Maol.

I turned and looked behind me into the village of Kyle of Lochalsh and observed a small gathering of buildings covering ten or so not-at-all-square blocks. To the left of the pier, I saw what I assumed was the small hotel that Cook's had booked me into for the night. I picked up my valise and started on over to it. Suddenly, I felt myself ill at ease. The few people who had exited the train with me had vanished, and I was all alone in a place where I knew no one and where two people had recently been horribly murdered. Anywhere within the boundaries of the great city of London, I would have known where I was and which train or cab to take. Here, I was a complete stranger, and it dawned on me that I had spent almost no time in my life in tiny, remote villages, save those I encountered in the barrens of Afghanistan. I rather wished I had Holmes by my side, but that was not to be. So, I screwed up my courage and entered the front door of the small, dun-colored hotel.

"Are you the doctor?" said the impassive, heavy-featured woman behind the desk, looking up from the book she was reading. She had a stern, set expression of mouth.

"I am," I replied. "I am Dr. Watson."

"Here's your key. You're in room six. Up the stairs to the left. Supper is served at seven thirty. Don't be late."

She placed the key on the counter and returned to her book.

The room was Spartan but adequate and clean. With nothing to do until the supper hour, I took out my notebook and reviewed all the items on which Holmes wished me to send reports. I began to write a few notes but soon realized that, so far, I had nothing to report except my apprehension, which, when I was rigorous with myself, could be attributed to nothing more than a touch of homesickness. I remembered the feeling. Many years ago, I had felt the same desolation in my soul as I lay in a cot on the *Orentes*.

By supper time, the sun was setting, and I found myself alone in the dining room. Another woman of a certain age brought some excellent finnan haddie to start my meal and then a delectable plate of poached salmon.

"That fish was swimming out in the Atlantic Ocean just this morning, doctor," said the hostess of the room. "It is as fine as a man can find anywhere on God's good earth."

I smiled and thanked her. The family resemblance to the woman at the front desk was unmistakable, and I concluded that this one must be the cheerful sister. When she brought a pot of tea, she carried on her pleasant banter.

"Someone of the island must be very sick for them to send for a physician all way from London. I pray you will get there in time to get them back to hale and hearty."

"Oh, no," I replied. "I am not here on a medical call. I am also a writer and thinking of doing a story based on one of the local legends of this area."

"Aye, and which one is that? We are overrun with tall tales from our miserable past."

"The one of Saucy Mary."

The good woman laughed heartily. "Oh, that is one of our best. The tourists who come here cannot get enough of her. Are you going to spin a long tale like our Sir Walter Scott? One that takes a soul a month or more to read?"

"Oh, no. My stories are all quite short. I write them for the *Strand,* so they cannot be more than a few a few pages."

She let out a quick gasp. "Oh, my. You cannot be *the* Dr. Watson, him that writes all those stories about Sherlock Holmes, are you?"

"I am afraid I am."

"A pity you didn't bring him with you. We would be grateful if he would honor us with a visit himself."

"Indeed? Why do you say that?"

"The murders. Have you no heard of what has happened here?"

"Murders? No. Why that's terrible. What happened?"

She did not immediately answer but sat looking at me intently for several seconds. Then a slow smile lit up her face.

"Dr. Watson, almost every man in this village is a fisherman and a liar, and I have been listening to their lies for more than four decades. You don't hold a candle to them when it comes to hiding the truth. You are here for the murders, aren't you? And Sherlock Holmes had been sought out, hasn't he? And that's why the reverend and his pup rushed off to London last week. Ah, ha. Well, now, that is good news. About time someone got to the bottom of what happened to poor Annie and the laird."

I was feeling sheepish and embarrassed at having been so easily caught out trying to deny my identity.

She woman walked over to the door that led to the kitchen.

"Franny," she shouted. "get your fat fanny out here so we can talk to the doctor."

A moment later, the woman who had been sitting at the desk when I arrived appeared.

"What are you wanting?" she demanded of her sister.

"Do you know who our guest is?"

"Aye. He's a doctor from London. Sent here by Cook's."

"Franny, he's not just any doctor. He's Dr. Watson."

"Wilson, Watson, Waterson ... what does it matter? He's only staying for the one night, and he'll be gone in the morning."

"Auch, Franny, can you no be a wee bit less dim? He's the laddie what writes all those stories you keep reading about Sherlock Holmes."

That got the woman's attention.

"No! It canna be true. Here in Lochalsh?"

"Aye. He's pretending that he's doing a story about Saucy Mary, but in truth, he's here about the murders of Annie and the laird. Now sit ye down and see what we can do to help the man."

Without being asked, both of the women pulled chairs up to my table. I was kicking myself for having failed so quickly in disguising my purpose, but I assumed that if anyone knew anything about what had been going on in the villages, these two were sure to.

"Very well, ladies," I began. "I confess that I am here on behalf of Sherlock Holmes to gather information and report back to him. Anything insights you might have would be most helpful. I take it you knew Mrs. Wallace."

"Knew her?" replied the friendly sister. "Aye, we were neighbors for five decades, we were. Saw her most every day of the week from the time we were all bairnies. She was a Rankin before she married Teddy. Now he was a clever fellow he was. Every other boy in the village became a fisherman like his father before him, but no, not Teddy. He saved up his farthings and as soon as he could, he bought the ferry boat and ran it for twenty years. No getting drowned in a storm at sea, for him. As long as he didna try to go out in the spring tides, he had a perfectly safe business. Allowed it to give him enough to send his children off to school and even buy a piece of land up by the narrows. Not that it was any good, but at least it was his and not a crofter's allotment. Annie was a good Christian soul, and we're horrified about what happened. And nobody seems to have any idea what took place."

"Aye," added the unfriendly one. "The worst day the village has ever had. Over the years we have lost a dozen men and boys out in their boats, and a score of wee babies and children who catch something and are gone in a few days. But having someone murdered, that was beyond the pale."

I had my notebook out and was scribbling furiously. I stopped and pondered what question I should ask first, trying to act as I imagined Holmes would had he been in here. I decided to plunge right in.

"Where and when did the Ben Shee first appear in the village?"

They both gave me a queer look in response and then looked at each other as if trying to decide which of them would answer. The unfriendly one, Franny, took the initiative.

"Gie up, and we'll show ye." She stood up and gestured to me to do the same. "The moon's bright. You can come and see for yourself."

I followed her out the front door of the hotel and along the lane back to the road that led from the pier up into the village.

"Here is where it started," said Franny as we stood in the road not far from the pier. "About six weeks back, Gerry Tweedie from up on Church Street, come running into the pub and says he heard a load of screaming down by the docks. Said it sounded like a mad woman. Now everybody knows that Gerry is not one to be taken very serious. The rest of the lads thought right off that he was just trying to get them to run out the pub so he could drink all their ales, so they just gave him a good laugh and a smack on the back and went back to telling lies about fishing and cursing the government. That was the first hearing of it."

"Aye," continued the friendly one, whose name I had not yet learned. "But then, the next night, Jeanie Bruce came into the midweek Bible reading meeting looking like she has seen a ghost. Which is what she says she has. She's trembling and shaking and says she saw this demon woman in the lane close by the Wallace's home and she was holding a dagger like Lady Macbeth and screeching and then she vanished. She must have been walking right along here."

She was pointing to a small lane that led off the main street and over to a modest house.

"Well, we all know that Jeanie is one who is to be taken serious. And she doesn't touch spirits, and she reads her Bible every day and all, and she finished her sixth form in school and is no slouch. So, the group of them, about twenty of them, get up and leave the meeting and come down this way toward the dock and up that lane to the Wallace's house and start looking for it. One of them says that it must be the Ben Shee and soon everyone in the village is talking about the Ben Shee."

"Had a Ben Shee," I asked, "ever been seen or heard in the past?"

"Not in my lifetime," said Franny. "Did you ever hear of one, Bonnie?"

"No. Mind you we all were raised on the folk tales, but we all ken that those stories we only told to children to tingle their wee spines and make them behave. But then it went away, and naught was heard for four weeks, and then another report comes in. This time there were two fellows, Andy McMaster and Angus Pitcairn, both of them sober fishermen. They had been down by the docks tending to their nets until late in the evening. When it was too dark to work the two of them sat down and had a wee smoke and a chat and then, it now being dark and the moon not yet up, they started back toward the pub. They said, both of them, that as they were coming up the road, they first heard the horrible moaning. They looked up to the hill behind the Wallace house where it seemed to be coming from, and suddenly the Ben Shee appears in a glow of light and lets out a scream that freezes them with fear, and then she vanishes."

I asked a few more questions about the apparition, and the women repeated a description of the ghoul in words similar to those used by Reverend Fraser. I moved on to asking about Mr. and Mrs. Wallace as strolled back to the hotel.

"Was there any money in the Wallace family?"

"A little," said Bonnie. "They were Scots, and so they spent as little as they could and saved whenever possible. Annie told me a few years back that the boat was completely paid off and their land by the narrows they had purchased outright fifteen years ago. Altogether, Teddy might have sold the lot for a hundred pounds, but I dinna think it would be a penny more."

With that paltry sum, money, the universal motivation for crime throughout the world and from the dawn of time to the present, vanished. Out of curiosity, though, I asked about the sale.

"Who bought it all? Mr. Wallace was able to sell everything off in short order, was he not?"

"Aye," said Bonnie. "That has been a matter of talk in the village. It were not anyone here or across in Kyleakin. Ozzie Waffle, one of the councilors, says it went to a firm from America."

"Indeed?" I said. "What could they ever want with a boat and a few acres of land in this corner of the globe?"

Having said that, I realized that my comment might be taken as reflecting the prejudice an arrogant Londoner has for the far reaches of the Isles. I hastened to add, "Perhaps they know something about the future potential value that we do not. The Americans are rather clever in that way."

"Clever, you say?" said Franny. "If you ask me they need their head read. Who in their right mind would throw good money away on an old boat and a poor piece of land?"

"Don't forget those tourist people," said Bonnie to her sister.

"Aye, you've a point there. Maybe they have plans to do something with it."

"Ladies," I said. "What tourists?"

"Are ye no going across to Kyleakin tomorrow morning, doctor?" asked Franny. "You'll meet the latest lot of them soon enough. They'll be up and to the ruins and chattering about the Bonnie Prince and Saucy Mary. They canna be missed."

Chapter Four
Over the Sea to Skye

THE FOLLOWING MORNING AT EIGHT O'CLOCK, I was back at the pier waiting for the ferry crossing that the sisters had told me was scheduled for that time. It was a raw, blustery day, with a damp mist-laden wind blowing in from the ocean. I kept waiting for other passengers to appear but none did. At a quarter past eight, a hard-faced, gnarled fellow came walking slowly out to where I was standing beside the small ferry boat.

"You'll have to pay for a private crossing if you want to go now," he said.

"I can wait until the next run," I said. "When is it scheduled?"

"Two this afternoon."

"Good heavens, man," I said. "Surely you can run several trips between now and this afternoon."

"If you can change the tide, sir, I can make the run. Can ye do that?"

I looked out at the channel and must have appeared hopelessly ignorant, for the fellow then offered an explanation.

"The tide is in right now, and the water's still. Within the hour it'll start to flow back out. This time of year, with the snows melting and the rivers raging, the loch fills. When she empties, it goes racing out at nine nauts an hour. I canna take the boat across. We would be swept up into the narrows and like as not flipped over in the whirlpools. So, if ye canna fix the tide, you'll either have to pay for a private crossing or wait until the afternoon when it's all still again."

"Very well, I have no desire to wait six hours. What is the fee for a private crossing?"

"Two pounds."

"What! That is outrageous. That's highway robbery."

"If you say so, sir. So, I shall see you at two o'clock then."

A thought crossed my mind, and I took a different tack.

"Before you go, sir. Are you prepared to consider an alternative offer?"

"Aye. What are ye offering?"

"Three pounds, but with one condition."

That got the fellow's attention, and he gave me a long sidewards look.

"Aye, and what is your condition?"

"As we cross, I am going to stand beside you and ask you as many questions as I want and you are going to answer them all fully and truthfully, keeping nothing back."

He shrugged his shoulders and smiled a semi-toothless smile. "For three pounds, sir, you can ask whatever you want. I'll spill the beans on everybody in both villages past and present."

"Truthfully and completely?"

"Aye."

"You'll swear to it? I will have you take an oath."

"On me dear mother's blessed memory if ye want," he said with a laugh.

"Good, then repeat after me. I ... state your full name."

"I, Allister John Knox Maclean ..."

"Do solemnly swear ..."

"Do solemnly swear..."

"That I shall answer all questions fully and truthfully…"

"That I shall answer all questions fully and truthfully …"

"And should I fail to do so, I invoke upon myself…"

"And should I fail to do so, I invoke upon myself…"

"That the Ben Shee shall visit my home at midnight tonight."

The fellow's head snapped back, and his face took on an immediate look of anger. He let out a string of profanities at me.

"Who in the blazes do you think you are?" he shouted. "I'll no have any man treat me like a superstitious fool. You can get away from my boat this instant. You arrogant blokes from London think you can come up here and treat us like you are our betters. Not for a hundred pounds would I sacrifice my pride for the likes of you. Get out of here. Do not dare come on this boat. Be gone with you."

I had overplayed my hand and could see that an obsequious apology was in order. So, I groveled and assured him that I was only jesting "Oh, very well then. How about if all we say is 'so help me God' and I'll make it five pounds?"

He was still glaring at me, but five pounds is hard to come by in this corner of the country, and his face softened.

"Fine then. I can do that. 'So, help me God.' Now get on board and get this nonsense over."

He stepped on to the small ferry and lit the boiler fire. Within fifteen minutes a head of steam had been worked up, and we were ready to cast off into the Loch Alsh toward Kyleakin. Just before we left the dock, a shout came from the road to the pier.

"Halloa! Hold up just a minute, Mr. Maclean."

A tall, slender young man, carrying a large valise, was running down the pier. The ferryman held the mooring line in his hand and waited until the fellow reached the boat and climbed in. He did not offer to pay and was not asked. Then Maclean pushed away and moved up to the bridge. My not-entirely-friendly look at him elicited a smile and a response.

"He's with the government. They all ride for free. 'Twould seem our taxes are not enough for them."

The new passenger had taken a seat and opened his valise and was already reading a file.

"Good morning," I said to him.

He looked at me. His face was lean. An aquiline nose separated two keen gray eyes. "Oh, good morning. Please do not think me rude but must read this report. Forgive me if I cannot carry on any conversation this morning. And, please, sir, enjoy your crossing."

He returned to his reading.

I made my way to the bridge and stood beside Maclean the ferryman. After spending a minute gazing out over the grey, choppy water, I began my interrogation.

"Who is that fellow?" I asked.

"Him? He would be Mr. Godfrey Thurlow, from the Admiralty. Not that he knows a thing about ships, but he's from their Hydrographic Office and is studying the currents and tides. Not at all a friendly fellow, but that may be more from being shy. You will see him around."

"And he rides for free?"

"That he does. And don't go crying about it. 'Twas not my choice."

The government man had settled into his chair out of earshot from Maclean and me and was busy with his reading.

"I see. Very well. Are you ready to answer my questions?"

"Fire away."

I started off with a few general questions about the villages and the history. Mr. Maclean was quite well-informed and, though sullen as the weather, told me all about the ruined ancient castle that we could see standing on a hill to the left of the village of Kyleakin. He had been a fisherman for over twenty years and had followed in his father's footsteps. He thought he was going to continue to do that trade until he died, but when the former owner of the boat, Mr. Wallace, recently moved away after the death of his wife, he jumped at the opportunity and became the new ferryman.

We were now well out into the loch, and the boat was bouncing with the waves. An occasional spray shot up and fell hard against the window of the cabin. The captain seemed to be pushing the craft faster than I might have thought wise.

"Allister Maclean, my good man, is this *your* boat?"

"Aye. It was Teddy Wallace's, and then he sold it along with his land, and I bought it straight away from the new owners."

"Who were the new owners?"

"I do not know."

"Come now, Mr. Maclean. You had to lease it from someone."

"Are you calling me a liar?"

"Of course not. But you know as well as I that no man does business with a party he does not know."

"This man does," he said, pointing his thumb to his chest. "If you must know, it was handled by a solicitor's office in Fort William. The lawyer acted in trust for the owner. I read an address in New York on the document, but that is all I know. He offered a very good rate, and I wasn't about to let it slip away by being nosey."

"Quite understandable. Very well, then. Tell me what happened to the Laird Mackinnon."

He gave me a hard look, but then nodded and spoke to the bow of the boat.

"He died two weeks ago."

"How?"

"Drowned, according to the constable."

"I am sure that you are telling me the truth and that is what the constable said. Now, a full and truthful answer, please, Mr. Maclean."

"The truth is that no one except the constable and the mortician can say for sure but the word in the village is that he was stabbed before his body was put in the water and swept out with the tide."

"Are you aware that his murder was not reported to Scotland Yard?"

"I have heard that said," replied the ferryman.

"Why would the constable not report it?"

"You'll have to ask him."

"I am asking you for your honest opinion."

"The constable, Murray Craigh, is trying to make a name for himself."

"Is he an honest man?"

"Aye. He's an oversized brute and a swine but not a cheat or a thief. Whatever claims he makes about himself we've learned to doubt, but he does his work fairly."

"Is he from either of the villages?"

"No. He's from Aberdeen. Came here two years back after he got himself appointed both constable and land surveyor."

"A bachelor?"

"He says he is and struts around like a ladies' man."

I asked a few more questions about him, and the goings on in the villages and then, as the dock on the far side of the loch was coming closer and the water had calmed, I moved to the most volatile concern.

"I have to ask you about the Ben Shee."

"I was wondering when you were going to get around to that."

"Have you seen it?"

"No."

"Have you heard it?"

"Aye."

"Where and when?"

"Three weeks ago. Heard it twice. Once by the docks in Lochalsh, and once coming from the manor hill in Kyleakin. Don't be telling me to describe what it sounded like for I am sure you already know."

"I have heard reports," I confirmed. "Now, do the people here truly believe that this apparition is a spirit sent from hell? Or the ghost of Lady Macbeth?"

He turned his gaze from the approaching dock and looked directly at me.

"We are not some group of savage heathens given to wild superstitions."

"I am certain you are not. But it has been very clear to me that this *thing* has brought fear into the hearts of the people, Mr. Maclean."

He turned back to face the shore. "Aye, it has. All anyone can say is that it has been seen and heard. It was hovering around the Wallace's house for a while time and next thing, Mrs. Wallace was dead. It was seen and heard by the Bastard's Villa and next thing the laird himself is dead."

We had arrived at the pier in the small protected harbor, and he eased the ferry into the side of the dock. The harbor was similar to the one on the far side of the loch, with fishing huts, nets laid out to dry, and the inescapable smell of fish. Retired fishing skiffs were pulled up on the shore beyond the reach of the tide. One small building was clearly marked *Office of the Constable*. I took out my wallet, found a five-pound note, and gave it to Maclean. He took it from me and stuffed it into his pocket. Then he put his face just a few inches from mine.

"Now I shall give you an earful of information for free. I do not know who you are, but I can see you are here about the deaths and the Ben Shee. If you value your life and well-being, you will be very careful about what you ask and say to anyone. There is evil in this place. The devil's agents on earth are never anything else than flesh and blood human beings. It could be that one of the villagers has brought it upon us. Or perhaps it has come with one of the outsiders. Or perhaps it is the father of evil himself. You have been warned, sir."

The chap from the Admiralty had packed up his papers and approached the gangplank. He excused himself and edged his way past the two of us. He stepped nimbly on to the dock and turned back to me.

"I am very sorry, sir, if I seemed rude and I thank you for your good manners. It is just that I have a frightful lot of work to do here and the sooner it is done the sooner I will be out of the godforsaken place and it murderous inhabitants."

He gave a shy nod, turned and moved off quickly.

I was about to step out of the boat as well and onto the dock when I noticed a crowd of a dozen people coming toward us. They were carrying their baggage and must have been passengers for the return run across the loch to Lochalsh. I could not resist a final question to Allister Maclean.

"Were you prepared to make all of these people wait until after two o'clock to cross back to the mainland?"

"No. I would not be in business very long if I did that. But I was prepared to let you think I was."

I had to smile back at him before turning and walking down the pier to the embankment. Standing there and waving at me was the distinct profile of Reverend Fraser. At his side was the faithful Mr. David Hume.

Chapter Five
The Usual Suspects

"AND SAE THE LORD BE THANKIT," SAID THE MINISTER. "I am happy to see you here safely. I trust your travels were pleasant."

He held out his meaty hand. As I shook it, I glanced down at the dog. He barked and lifted his paw. I could not resist and bent over and gave it a shake as well. Mr. David Hume gave another friendly bark, and Reverend Fraser offered a friendly pat on my back.

"I never had a dog," he said, "whilst Rowena, my dear wife, was alive. I thought I would die of loneliness when she passed away, but after a year a group of the parishioners got together and gave me this wee collie. He's been a godsend. I cannot imagine now a day without him."

The irony of David Hume's reincarnation as a 'godsend' crossed my mind, but as there were other matters more pressing, I let that thought go and just leaned over and gave the collie a friendly pat.

The big clergyman picked up my valise and gestured toward the street that led away from the dock. "Come, sir. We can get you checked in at the hotel and settled before giving you a guided tour of the village. If we can get these tourists to let us by, we can be on our way."

Standing in the road and effectively blocking everyone's way was a group of about twenty people. By their dress and overheard snatches of conversation, they were Americans. In front of them was a young man with wavy black hair, also an American, who was pointing up to the ruins of the castle and delivering an energetic lesson in local history. Under other circumstances, I would have liked to stay and listen.

The hotel was a pleasant, whitewashed place that faced out to the water and traced its ancestry back to the 1600s. The reverend assisted me with registering and then insisted on our taking an early lunch in the pub on the far end of the ground floor. We took a table, and he went up to the bar to order us both a serving of fish and chips and mushy peas. Whilst he was standing at the bar, a pretty young barmaid with a freckled face and a lovely head of red hair came by the table. She extended a friendly welcome to the Isle of Skye and chatted a bit about the ruins and the story of Saucy Mary. Then she gave a glance over to the bar and saw that the reverend had our plates in front of him and was preparing to pay. She leaned down until her mouth was only a few inches from my ear.

"Dr. Watson," she whispered. "We know you have come about the murders. Please, sir. It is not safe to ask questions. You best get out of here as fast as you can. Go back to London, sir. For God's sake, leave."

I twisted my head to look at her and, in that instant before she turned her face away, I could read the fear in her eyes. She stood up and departed, leaving the room through the door behind the bar.

"I see you had a chance to meet Gracie Burrell," said Reverend Fraser as he returned to our table with the steaming hot lunches. "She's a brave young lass. Lost her husband a year and a bit ago. He caught the cancer and died, leaving her with two wee bairnies. She once had hopes of being an actress, and if you come by this evening, she will entertain the patrons by singing *Flow Gently Sweet Afton and* reciting *The Bairnies Cuddle Doon at Nicht.* She is nae so bad, a young lady of ample attractions. We keep praying that she might find a decent man to marry her, but those that are eligible are not very decent, and the decent ones are all taken."

His eyes took on a somewhat distant look, and a slow smile spread across his face. I decided not to tell him about the warning she had given me.

As we ate our lunch, the pub filled with a score of more people. I quietly asked Fraser to identify them for me.

"The three older men sitting by the window are crofters. They are the few that remain after two hundred years of the Clearances. They have farms between here and Broadford where they try to grow some oats and barley and root vegetables. The two tables with the younger fellows are all men who work for the Clan Mackinnon, tending the sheep, cattle, and swine. It's hard work, but the laird paid fair wages, and Lionel appears set to be fair as well. Most days they eat their lunch out in the fields, but every Friday they come into the village. 'Tis the same for the crofters."

The young barmaid, Mrs. Gracie, appeared to be popular with the farm workers. Their two tables were a constant source of laughter and loud banter each time she paid a visit to them. The older men, the crofters, fulfilled my image of dour old Scotsmen.

"Those young fellows," I observed, "do not appear to have let the murders and the stories of the Ben Shee depress their spirits."

"Auch, they're young," replied Fraser. "Their brains are ruled by their animal spirits, not by reason. Put a pretty lass or a football in front of them, and that is all the distraction they need. But if I were to go over there this instant and ask them about the queer old legend of the Ben Shee, they would become a frightened and cowering bunch of lads straight away."

I looked back around the room and observed the two men who were sitting at tables by themselves. One was the slight, thin young man who came on the ferry with me. His coloring, contrasted with the other denizens of the pub, indicated that he was not a local resident. He sat in a corner, alternating between reading his files and writing in a notebook. I asked Fraser about him.

"That lad? His name if Godfrey Thurlow. He hails from Milton Keynes and claims he went to school in Cambridge. The government sent him here. He's working for the Admiralty at their Hydrographic Office. Here for the past two months measuring the tides and currents. A wee bit of a loner. Cannot say as I blame him. This is not like being sent on a mission to Brighton, or even Blackpool. His work should be done by the end of the month, and he'll be gone."

That left the large man by the window. He occupied the choice table in the pub, had rested his surveyor's theodolite in the corner behind him and was already into his third glass of ale. Each time the barmaid came by he attempted to engage her in conversation without much success. He caught me looking at him and stood up and walked over to our table. He was several inches over six feet in height and must have weighed twenty stone. No doubt he was a very powerful chap when he was younger, but how he carried a full roll of fat around his middle and another smaller roll under his chin. His cheeks, which might have been lean and handsome a decade ago, were now puffy and his nose verged on bulbous. His hair, which hung down over his ears to his collar, was in need of a good wash and his face in need of a shave to remove the scruffy stubble that must have been left untended for the past week.

I now pause my account and refer the reader to my first report to Holmes. My conversation with the chap with the theodolite as well as my subsequent unfriendly chat with the old crofter are recounted therein.

Chapter Six
First Report to Sherlock Holmes

MY DEAR HOLMES: …

[Note to readers: The first two pages of my report covered the events, conversations, and insights I had from the time I arrived in Lochalsh until my lunch in the pub in the King's Arms. As I have already accounted for them in this story, I shall refrain from repeating them here.]

The overly large man lumbered across the pub to our table like a dim-witted but well-fed giant. He moved his bulk right up beside me and looked down.

"So, you're the famous writer, Dr. Johnny Watson, are ye?"

Holmes: As you know, in my years as a battlefield medical officer, I have dealt with all sizes and manners of men, from the latter-day Goliaths to the scrawny mice that roared. Their bravery and courage have nothing whatsoever to do with their corporeal dimensions. I have held the hands of burly men as they cried for their mothers before passing on into eternity and marveled the grit of the chaps we unkindly called leprechauns and they ran once more unto the breach. In my medical practice, I have poked and prodded every orifice of men of every race, religion, size, and shape. As a result, I cannot be intimidated by an unarmed man whose only would-be attribute by which he tries to threaten is his gargantuan proportions. In my mind's eye, I picture them bent over my examining table. I am sure I do not have to elaborate further.

Thus, I did not bother even to look up at him. Instead, I took a final slow draught of my ale and put it back on the table before directing my reply to the empty glass.

"Ah, my friend," I said in faux cheerfulness. "You flatter me, for which I thank you. But please, sir, I must correct you. It is not I who am famous, but Sherlock Holmes. I am merely the scribe."

"What are you doing here?" he demanded.

I continued to address the empty glass. "Just some small research for my regiment, the Northumberland Fusiliers. You must be the constable here. What regiment did you serve in, sir?"

He was not expecting such a question but responded after a brief pause.

"Twenty-two years in the Royal Scottish."

"A wonderful regiment," I responded quickly, before he had a chance to continue. "You chaps were in Afghanistan about the same time I was. Were you at Maiwand as well? Nasty time we had of it there, didn't we? I say, were you there?"

"No…"

"No? Ah, but perhaps you stayed in India. Stationed in Calcutta, were you not?"

"No …"

"No? Well, then where did you serve?"

For a moment, I heard no reply, and then, "I was in the reserve regiment."

Now, as you know, Holmes, there is a rule within Her Majesty's armed forces that says that the reserve regiments must be accorded the same degree of respect and admiration as the active forces. Nevertheless, amongst those of us who were not only fully engaged but who fought in the midst of bullets and grapeshot, the mention of our esteemed reservists is generally accompanied by a wink and a nudge. The weekend warriors who chase each other through the forests, firing off blank ammunition, or who stand guard when the Prince pays a visit do not, in our minds, belong in quite the same company.

"Well then, it has been a pleasure to meet you, Constable Craigh," I said. I stood up and gave him a small nod. "Delighted that both of us could come as visitors to this beautiful island. And a good day to you, sir."

Without waiting for his response or reaction, I turned my back on him and sauntered out of the pub. Reverend Fraser and Mr. David Hume followed me.

Once outside, the clergyman took hold of my arm and was positively giggling.

"Oh, my goodness, doctor. That was brilliant. And in front of the whole pub. The entire village will have heard about it before supper." He giggled a little more. It must have been contagious, for Mr. David Hume was wagging his tail and barking happily.

"I suspect," he added, "That he is quite jealous of your success as a writer. He fancies himself one as well."

"Does he now? And what does he write?"

"Poetry. Mostly it refers to his romantic conquests with indirect allusions to the size of his male appendage. His brief stories are written from the perspective of a soldier at the front, who returns to the village and is fawned over by the ladies."

"The selection of material is not uncommon," I said. "Is his work any good?"

"Utter and complete dreck. He has had a slim volume of his verse published by a small press in Glasgow and is happy to display the book on all possible occasions. I made a point of contacting the publisher, however, and was told that he had paid to have his poems printed."

"Many writers," I said, "have chosen that route. Several of them have written excellent stories."

"Let me assure you, doctor, our Constable Murray Craigh is not one of them."

"Might I inquire as to our next destination?" I asked Fraser.

"We have an appointment in an hour at Bethel-by-the-Sea," he answered. "Both the laird's widow and his brother will be in this afternoon and have agreed to meet you. I have a wee bit of business in the church to attend to. Why don't you relax in your room and I shall meet you back here in forty-five minutes?"

I agreed but remained where I was standing, taking in the view over the loch. It was a beautiful setting, if rugged, barren, gray, and russet can be called beautiful.

"Stranger, a word with you," came a voice from behind me. I turned to see the oldest of the old crofters walking toward me.

"By all means. And whom do I have the honor of addressing?"

"That depends on who is asking."

Oh dear, I thought to myself. Another not-so-friendly welcome.

"I am Dr. John Watson," I said and before I could add anything more, he shot back.

"And what are ye doing here?"

"Well now," I said, "that depends on who is asking, doesn't it?"

He scowled at me but answered. "Garnet Baine is my name. Now, answer my question."

"I am a guest of the Reverend Donald Fraser."

"We got him a dog. What does he need guests for?"

"I suppose that you will have to ask him that, sir."

"Aye. I will do that. You, sir, have the airs of a gentleman. Are ye here to visit with the new laird?"

"I will pay him a visit. It would be most disrespectful not to. I assume you would not wish me to show disrespect to your laird."

"There is no respect given by any crofter to any laird and has not been for two hundred years. This new one seems decent even if he is a dandy, but it is too early to tell. When are you leaving?"

I had gotten impatient with this unnecessarily abrasive interrogation, and my own dander got up and came out in my reply. I spoke quite sharply.

"As far as I am concerned, Mr. Garnet Baine, that is none of your business. I have given you no offense, and frankly, I find your questions disrespectful. Where I come from, we are proud enough of our village to welcome visitors and extend traditional hospitality. It is a pity that you are not so inclined."

That took the fellow aback. He gave a very shallow nod and softened his voice. "This village has been beset recently by the forces of evil. We are merely on our guard against anyone who might be intending to do us harm. There was no love lost between the common folk and the old laird but now he is gone, and our future situation is uncertain. If that makes us come across to you as inhospitable, so be it. The protection of our folk is far more important to us than the feelings of some come-and-be-gone visitor. I trust your business here will be completed soon, and you can then be on your way. Watch what you say to anyone and take care no to be out after dark. Good day sir."

He turned away abruptly and returned to the pub. I had lost most of my time for a short nap but returned to my room for a few minutes before meeting back up with Reverend Fraser.

He and Mr. David Hume were waiting for me at the agreed upon time, and we began our walk to the Bastard's Villa.

At the place in the road where it began to climb the hill, a broad pathway struck off from the road to the right and continued along the edge of the water. There was a man standing a distance away on the path, and I slowed my pace and observed him. It was the same thin fellow who came on the ferry and had recently been sitting in the pub. Now he was acting very strangely. He stood at the edge of the water and tossed a buoy, the type that might be used on fisherman's net, into the water. He then quickly pulled his watch from his pocket, and then he turned and ran along the path for about fifty yards, stopped and again consulted his watch.

I turned to Fraser. "What in heaven's name is he doing," I asked.

"Measuring the rate of the flow of the water. He has been doing that along this stretch for several weeks at different times of day. Some days he has himself taken out to the lighthouse on the island, and on others, he works from the mainland side."

"Have you talked at all with him," I asked. "It seems a very curious assignment."

"He is not the most communicative chap. All he's let on is that it is a study of the currents so that the government can make the channel and the narrows safer. Every year or so another fisherman goes out from here and does not return, so there is a credible cause for his work. But the folks here all think it's a waste of money. They know every inch of the narrows and how the tides move in and out. The men and boys who have been lost capsized in the open sea, not in the channel. We concluded that as it is a project paid for by the government in London, it doesn't have to make sense. And the fellow keeps a room at the hotel and takes his meals in the pub and his money is as good as the next fellow's, so we leave him be."

Holmes had made a point of telling me to take a careful look into anything unusual. There was, of course, nothing more usual on earth than the tides but a visitor from the government who had come to measure them was unusual. So, I asked the reverend, "Could we take a few minutes and chat with this fellow?"

He gave me a questioning look and shrugged.

"Very well, doctor. If you think you can get a word out of him, go ahead."

We walked along the path beside the water until we were closer to him.

"Sir!" shouted the reverend. "A minute of your time if you will."

He did not look at all eager to talk and made a point looking yet again at his watch.

"I can take a minute, but no more. I am in the middle of my research."

"We shan't keep you," I said. "But I am in need of your knowledge. I am a writer and putting together a story about the Isle of Skye. I was about to write a paragraph about the tides, and the reverend here tells me that you are the expert."

He gave a shy smile and said, "I cannot call myself an expert, sir. However, I have a reasonable knowledge. What is it you wish to know?"

"I was told by folks in London," I said, "that the tidal currents here are singularly treacherous. But I do not see any danger. The channel is a bit choppy from the breeze, but it looks perfectly harmless."

His face lit up as does that of a schoolboy when asked a question to which he knows the complete and correct answer.

"Of course, it is calm now, sir. That is because the tide is in. An hour from now it will start to flow out and forced through the bottlenecks on either side of the island. Then it picks up speed, particularly at this time of year. That is when the whirlpools and the haystacks appear in the narrows. If you return here in three hours, it will be in full bore."

Oh," I said, "so this is the most dangerous time of year, then?"

"The second most dangerous. The worst is when the meltwater volume combines with a spring tide. That's when the moon and sun are both pulling in the same direction. *Then* it gets wild. No one dares go out when one of those happens."

"Oh, does that happen very often?"

"Twice every lunar month, sir. Same schedule as has been since time began. Worst of all is the perigean tide when the moon is closest. There will be one in a few days. You can come and see the show it puts on in the narrows."

I asked a few more questions, but then he began looking again at his watch and made it obvious that he could not spare any more time. The fellow threw another buoy into the water and returned to his notebook. I thanked him, and the three of us—two men and a dog—made our way to the road and up the hill.

The Bastard's Villa sat about a quarter mile to the west of the village. From the hill leading up to it, we had a splendid view of the narrows where the Lock Alsh emptied into the sea. The narrows consisted of two channels, one on either side of the island, Elean Ban, a small rocky patch of land that was uninhabited except for a lighthouse at the south end. Boats use the south channel as the north one, I was told, is too shallow for safe passage. The south side can be used safely as long as the tide is not surging.

The house itself is a single-story building, stretching more than one hundred feet, with a balustraded porch along the entire length. It appeared to be in need of a fresh coat of whitewash. The grounds had been allowed to be cared for by Nature alone and the shrubs and trees were stunted and nipped. The rugged setting might have appealed to one of the previous century's Romantic poets, but to the Englishman of today, it was a sign of carelessness.

We trudged on and stopped at a point about twenty yards from the incongruous wrought-iron gates. I looked at the reverend, wondering why we had ceased our walk.

His face had clouded, and his brow was furrowed. With his right hand, he pointed to a place at the top of the embankment nearly ten yards in front of us. For several seconds, with a gloomy face, he held his hand in place and continued to point.

"There, is where she was," he said.

At this point, my dear Holmes, I must end this report as I have only a few more minutes before catching the final post of the day and getting it off to you. The case has become quite complex. I shall continue tomorrow.

Yours very truly,

J.H. Watson

Chapter Seven
Laird Lionel Mackinnon

[Note to readers: I continue on from my report to Holmes.]

THE CLERGYMAN DROPPED THE HAND that he had used to indicate the location of the apparition he had seen recently.

"Have there been," I asked, "any sightings since that time?"

"No. The first reports came just over six weeks ago. Then there was nothing. The most recent, including what I saw, were a fortnight back. Nothing since then."

A man-servant greeted us at the door of the villa. He was a tall, handsome man, with pale, distinguished features.

"Good afternoon, Reverend Fraser," he said, accented by a thick Highland brogue.

"Good afternoon, Hutcheson. I trust all is well in the household."

"Fortunately, all are doing well and their utmost to overcome the recent tragic event. All of the staff were quite attached to the old laird, as I know you were as well, reverend."

He then turned to me.

"And you, sir, must be the esteemed writer of the stories of Mr. Sherlock Holmes. A welcome to Bethel-by-the-Sea, Dr. Watson."

Then turning back to the reverend, he said, "Shall I let the lady and the new laird know of your arrival?"

"Yes, but perhaps just one at a time. Might we meet first with Laird Lionel?"

"Of course, Reverend. I shall inform him of your presence. Kindly wait in the parlor."

Frazer turned to Mr. David Hume and issued a command that the collie was to wait on the doorstep. Hutchinson interrupted him.

"Mr. Hume, sir, is welcome to join you in the parlor. Any other dog in the village would have to wait outside, but yours is so well behaved it is not a problem. Besides, Lady Mackinnon is very fond of him and quite enjoys your visits. Please gentlemen ... and Mr. Hume."

The room into which we were led was a large one, with surprisingly few windows from which to enjoy what must have been a splendid view on a clear day. A row of dark portraits of the ancestors of the Clan Mackinnon hung on the walls, and an uncoordinated collection of artifacts adorned the mantle and side tables. The furniture, although clean and polished, struck me as having been new in 1830.

"Gentlemen, please," came the voice of Mr. Hutchinson as he returned to the room. "Mr. Lionel Mackinnon, Laird of the Isles of Skye and Mull. And Laird, sir, allow me to present the Reverend Fraser whom you have met previously, and his guest, Dr. John Watson, of London."

Into the room stepped a very colorful gentleman. He was attired from head to toe in formal Scottish dress, complete with a high-collared dark green wool jacket, a sash and matching kilt in a pastel tartan of light blue and burnt red squares and lines, plus all the accessories that accompany such a costume, and capped off with a Glengarry bonnet, accented by feathers and dangling ribbons.

The fellow was several inches shorter and at least two stone lighter than I. He was smiling from ear to ear and strode in a lively way into the room.

"Welcome, gentlemen," he said. "What lovely timing you have. My new wardrobe has just arrived from Glasgow and, if I do say so myself, it looks quite bonnie on me, just like it did on my wonderful ancestor. Dr. Watson, you are a man from London and thus must have quite refined taste. Don't you agree?"

I stammered for a moment before choosing my words carefully. "It is a tribute to your family's tradition."

"Oh, yes, it is, isn't is. This is our ancient tartan. Quite subdued, don't you think. Just the thing for yet another ghastly day in the Western Highlands. Our modern tartan is much stronger. Positively cheerful. But as far as I am concerned, it would be suitable for a sunny day, should we ever be so fortunate to see one. Oh, and forgive me for being such a poor host. Please, gentlemen, be seated."

"Thank you, Laird," said Reverend Fraser, "for agreeing to meet with us."

"Oh, but of course, Reverend. I am positively dying for interesting conversation. I have been utterly starved since leaving Paris. I can't imagine how Becky survived for the past thirty years in this god-forsaken place. And this house! Terribly shadowy and gloomy, don't you think so, Dr. Watson? I have already arranged for carpenters to come and knock out the windows. Much larger ones are on their way and within six months you won't know it. I suppose that a hundred years ago when my great-grandfather, the one who claimed to be a royal bastard, built this place, small windows were practical in a house that faces the open water, but you would think that Hamish might have exchanged them for the modern ones now available. I fear that my dear brother, may he rest in peace, did not have an ounce of taste in his body. His did keep in contact with me, for which I am grateful. Filial duty much more than love, but better that than the alienation I endured from daddy."

"I am sure," said the reverend, "that any unpleasantness from the past is over. I have it on good authority that the villagers have been happily surprised by your convivial and generous spirit."

"Oh, nonsense, reverend. Whilst I was a child here, the villagers were positively beastly to me. I could not wait to get away. But now, it seems, I am the richest man within fifty miles, so they treat me with respect. It helped that the day after I arrived here, finding myself the leading employer of the county, was to increase everyone's pay by three shillings a week. The prosperity of the whole, poor, bleak countryside now depends on my presence. It is not as if the estate could not afford it. Hamish kept getting richer and richer, and now we have more money than God. And so, the villagers all adore me. Even the sad old crofters. In the future, I fear I shall have to become an absentee landlord so as not to go mad, but for now I am quite enjoying myself."

"I am glad to see," said Fraser, "that you are recovering from the shock of your brother's death. Your sister-in-law has been much in our prayers."

"Becky? You have been praying for Becky? Honestly, reverend, you might save your prayers for those who truly need them. She recovered wonderfully quickly and has been busy packing her belongings for the past week. She is only still here so that the funeral baked meats might not coldly furnish forth the table of her departure party. Oh, my goodness, isn't Hamlet wonderful? Don't you agree, Dr. Watson? Becky has a sister on Long Island who has been after her for years to move to America. Hamish, of course, wouldn't hear of it. But now she is on her way. She will be a fabulously rich widow living next door to Central Park. And, she has kept herself very well. She needs an entire new wardrobe, of course, but by the fall season, she will be the most eligible dowager on the Eastern Seaboard."

"We wish her well," said Fraser. "Now, if you do not mind, Laird Lionel, there are other matters that we really must discuss."

"Oh, very well, if you insist. But I shall just have to remain in my lovely new kilt. It gives me such a sense of …well … freedom. You want to talk about what happened to Hamish? Oh, my goodness, wasn't it just awful?"

Here I stepped in.

"No, Lionel, we want to talk about *you*. I am concerned that your life might be in danger."

He looked at me in shock and disbelief.

"Oh, you cannot be serious, doctor. You would have me believing I walked into the thicket of a cheap Gothic novel. Who within fifty miles of here wants to do me harm? I am making them all richer. Mind you, that Howard boy from America is also doing his part bringing the tourists. But you know what they say. One should not bite the hand that feeds you. I have felt nothing but fabulous goodwill since I arrived. Or at least since I upped the pay packets."

"Sir," I replied. "I am not concerned about the local people who work for you. I wish to know if you have had any contact with anyone or anything unusual since you arrived here."

"Anything, you say?"

"Yes. Anything."

"Oh, very well, then. Of course, everybody has heard about the banshee. Or, as they insist on calling it here, the *Ben Shee*. The very night I arrived here, a fortnight ago, she came by and let out a great screeching and screaming. At first, I thought it was just a cat in heat. Those poor things are all over Montmartre and forever screeching away. But the cat can keep it up all night. This thing did not last more than two minutes and then disappeared. The next night she came again and did the same thing."

"Did you see her," I asked.

"Good heavens, no. I may have come into my inheritance with a vengeance, but I was already in my pajamas and enjoying my tea in my bed when she started wailing. I wasn't about to be put out and run out into the cold night just to see the thing. If she is serious, she will return when the weather becomes warmer. We'll see about it then."

"But," I said, "she was said to have come by just before your brother disappeared. Were you not concerned at all?"

"Oh, my dear Dr. Watson. I am quite sure that immediate to my dear brother's tragic vanishing a comet was seen in the sky, Jupiter aligned with Mars, and two complete bottles of claret were emptied. He did have a weakness for it you know. As well as for a good single malt, of which there is an abundance all over this poor country, and for Plymouth Gin, but the latter only in the summertime. He did have his principles, after all. I am inclined to believe, my dear doctor, that my brother's death can be quite satisfactorily accounted for by assuming that he got quite drunk one more time, went for a walk down to the water, fell in and, it being a departing tide, was swept away. I find no need for either spectral activity or nasty skullduggery. The true tragedy is that he was such a poor swimmer. I believe you will find that my sister-in-law is of the same opinion."

"Very well, sir. Anything else take place of an unusual nature recently?"

He tilted his head slightly back as if expecting a wave of insight from some external source.

"I suppose you could consider the offer we had to sell the property unusual. One does not receive such an offer every day, does one? Becky says that the first came six weeks ago and then came another one from the same source the day after Hamish's body had been fished out of the sea. Yes, I suppose that was unusual. Becky can tell you more about it."

"The most recent one," I said. "Did you respond to it?"

"Of course. One must answer one's post, mustn't one. It was a generous offer but only for this wretched house and the land around it. No interest in the rest of the lands on Skye or Mull. Becky was ready to let them have it, but I have spent more than a few years in America and learned the art of the deal, as they call it there. I sent a wire back saying that I would be open to an offer for all of the Highlands properties, but not to sell things off piecemeal. No, that would not be wise. If they are serious, they will be back with an offer I can accept. But I must confess that I am becoming accustomed to this place. Here, I am positively *somebody*."

"Who was making that offer, sir," I asked.

"I honestly cannot say. It came by wire from an attorney in America acting in trust for his client. I assume it was a result of a visit by one of the tourists that have come by recently and thought the location just lovely for a summer place given that the Hamptons are full. It is not as if we have the right kind of people here for such a retreat, but then again, it is highly affordable by comparison. Have you been to the Hamptons, Doctor?"

"No."

We chatted on for several more minutes before he bid us a good day and stooped to do the same for Mr. David Hume, receiving an extended paw in return. I had gleaned nothing more of interest from him. My overall impression of him was that he was more than somewhat frivolous, yet every now and then I detected flashes of shrewdness and wondered if perhaps the man was not a consummate actor. More about him will be revealed later in this account. For now, we must move on to Lady Mackinnon.

"Mrs. Rebecca Mackinnon," announced Mr. Hutchinson, "Lady of the Isles of Skye and Mull." He smiled warmly, not at us but at the woman entering the room. She responded by returning a smile of warm familiarity to him.

The woman was quite striking in appearance. She was as tall as I, and even though she might have been somewhat into her fifties in age, she was exceptionally handsome. Her hair was raven black and while most of it was gathered on her head, a ringlet hung down beside each ear and bobbed rather sensuously as she walked into the room. Unlike the rest of the inhabitants of Kyleakin that I had seen so far, her skin was not at all pale but had a slight olive tone. A long winter having only recently passed, her coloring could not have come from spending time outdoors in the sun. Had I met her in London and not on the Isle of Skye, I would have assumed that her heritage was from somewhere in the Mediterranean. She was, as would be expected, dressed in black. Mind you, the cut of her dress struck me as being a shade more stylish than was usual for a widow's garb. She beamed a warm smile at the clergyman.

"Good afternoon Reverend Donald. And welcome, Dr. Watson," she said as she walked confidently into the room. She extended her hand first to Fraser and then to me before sitting down in the small settee that was in front of one of the few windows.

"Your message, Reverend, said that you were bringing the popular author, Dr. Watson, to visit. I am assuming therefore that whilst in London you went to see Mr. Sherlock Holmes and requested his assistance in investigating the recent deaths here and across the channel. Is that correct?"

"Yes, your ladyship," answered Fraser. "That is correct."

"Is it now? Very well, please take no offense, Doctor, but I was rather hoping to meet Mr. Sherlock Holmes himself, not his understudy. Will he be arriving here shortly?"

I sensed I had to be prudent in my reply and said, "That has not yet been established, my lady. I am sending reports off to Mr. Holmes every day and based on what he deduces from them he may or may not decide to come here himself."

"Oh, pity. It would be such a relief to spend time with so fascinating a man. Very well, I shall hope that whatever you discover is so inexplicable as to require his presence. I would very much love to meet him."

"That may happen, my lady," I said. "However, we are informed that you are making plans to leave Kyleakin in the near future. Is that correct?"

"Has Lionel been telling tales out of school? I suppose I should have expected it. Yes, Doctor. I am making plans to leave the Highlands. Within a month, I shall be gone. Lionel is a surprisingly clever man – don't allow his affectations to mislead you –and he seems quite capable of carrying out whatever family responsibilities are owed to the people of the islands."

"You are entrusting your portion of the estate holding to him?" I asked.

"Of course not. We have reached an excellent agreement whereby he shall have sole possession of the properties and holdings in Great Britain and on the Continent. I shall have the New World solely in my name. Our solicitors are drawing up the papers and should have all matters finalized within a few more days. I shall have considerable assets in America, a million or more sheep in New Zealand, and over a thousand acres in the middle of Canada, in the district of Sask … Saska…"

"Saskatchewan," I offered.

"Yes, that's it."

"Madam," I said, "Please forgive my being less than tactful, but why such haste?"

"In part, Dr. Watson. I could say that the tragedy of Hamish's death has been too much for me to bear; that the horrors of what was done to him and the stories of the visits of the Ben Shee were so distressing that I could not stand to live here any longer. But if you are half as clever as your friend, Sherlock Holmes, you would soon learn that such an account was not the complete truth."

"And the complete truth is, madam?"

"The truth is that I have been very unhappy living in Kyleakin for the past thirty years. I was raised in Edinburgh, and throughout my youth, I attended the symphony and the theater with my family and enjoyed the company of a wonderful circle of friends. I married Hamish because he was handsome and very wealthy, not foreseeing that my life would be spent in virtual exile. I am too rich for the villagers to consider me as a friend. As I am a member of the Jewish faith, I did not even have the pleasure of conversing with people after church once a week. Although Reverend Fraser and his wife, my dear friend Rowena, did pay me a visit once a week. It was the high point of my life. The reverend has been kind enough to continue to drop by and chat since Rowena's tragic sickness. For which I am eternally grateful, Reverend.

"Hamish and I had no children, not because I was infertile, but because Hamish was. I was at first horrified at the news of Hamish's death and the suspicions of murder. He was, after all, my husband, and we had spent over thirty years together. However, I quickly realized that his death was my ticket to freedom and I am determined to enjoy what years I have remaining on this earth. So that is the other reason for my haste. You may report same to Sherlock Holmes if you wish."

I thanked the lady for her candor and posed a final question that I thought Holmes would have expected of me.

"Did your husband have any enemies, madam?"

"What wealthy man who has steadily increased his fortune for thirty years does not?"

"Any specifically who might wish to take his life?"

"Dr. Watson, we are in the Highlands of Scotland. Murder is a national pastime. One any given day some skin-clad hairy man might crawl out from a low door and do in a passing stranger with his bow and flint-tipped arrows. Did any patron of the theater ever doubt that Macbeth could have murdered Banquo and Duncan, and all of Macduff's children in one fell swoop? Does anybody question the veracity of the story of the Campbells massacring the MacDonalds? If you gave me a few minutes, I could most likely come up with thirty men, one for each year of his lairdship, who would have happily seen him off. But it is not worth a minute more of my time to try to solve the mystery. I refuse to. That is a problem for you, Sherlock Holmes, and Scotland Yard."

"Are you aware that Scotland Yard was not informed of the murders of either your husband or Mrs. Wallace from across the channel?"

"No, I was not."

"Can you give me any insight as to why that information may have been withheld from them?"

For a moment she paused in thought. "Have you met our local constable?"

"Yes."

"Then you know the answer to your question, do you not?"

"I suppose I do. On another item, if I may; what do you make of the stories, as you called them, of the visits of the Ben Shee?"

"Stories?"

"Your words madam, not mine."

"I suppose I did say that didn't I."

"Yes, madam."

"Dr. Watson, I am not a superstitious peasant. I trust you believe that."

"I do, madam."

"Good, because those stories were all true."

"I beg your pardon, madam. Are you saying that the Ben Shee did indeed visit your home shortly before your husband's death?"

"Yes, Doctor."

Then she turned to Fraser. "My apologies Reverend Donald, I have not told you about this. I greatly value your respect, and I feared that you would think me a foolish woman."

The Reverend reached his long arm toward and put his hand on top of hers.

"No, Rebecca, I would never do that. And allow me to confess. I saw it as well."

"You did?"

"Aye, the same night you did."

For a moment, the lady looked shocked, and then she laughed.

"Well, isn't that good news. Both of us have gone mad."

She relaxed in her chair and smiled at me.

"What else do you need to know, Doctor? I have to admit that hearing and seeing the Ben Shee terrified me. Hamish's death left me shattered. I was ready to put this house up for sale, and when the offer came to buy it, I would have sold it for any price had Lionel not come along. Now it is his problem, and he is welcome to it. I am on my way to start my life over."

I asked several more questions and, before departing, requested loan of the file containing the correspondence between the laird's estate and the firm in New York. Hutchinson furnished them for us, and we bade good day to both Laird Lionel and Lady Rebecca.

"I regret," said Fraser, "that I must abandon you for the remainder of the day and the evening. I have a few matters in the lives of two members of my congregation that Mr. David Hume and I must attend to."

I thanked him for the generous gift of his day and returned to the pub, hoping that it would be somewhat quiet and afford me an opportunity to write my report to Sherlock Holmes.

Chapter Eight
The Broken Tour Enterprise

THE HOTEL DESK FURNISHED ME with several sheets of paper, and I ensconced myself at the window table in the pub and began to write my report.

I had no more than addressed it than my eye caught sight of a man walking toward to pub door. He was walking slowing, and his head was bowed. He entered, took a seat in a back corner, and placed a request with the attentive barmaid. I recognized him. He was the tour leader of the group of Americans that I had observed when I arrived.

I continued to observe him out of the corner of my eye. He sat stone still as if transfixed until his glass of sherry arrived. He took a brief sip and then placed his elbows on the table and buried his face in his hands. Small tremors were agitating his body.

My medical instincts took over, and I rose and walked to his table and sat down across from him.

"Young man," I said gently, "I am a medical doctor, and I know the signs of despair when I see them. I have seen them in innumerable men and I assure you that in almost all cases they have gone away, some sooner, some later. But in all cases, the situation turned out to be nowhere near as bad as first thought.

Why don't you let me join you for a drink and tell me what has happened?"

He looked up at me with a blank gaze. His eyes were glistening.

"Who aw you?"

"I am Dr. John Watson, from London."

"Isn't that wonderful. Never hoid of you. I am from New Yawk, and I am Howard Schapiro."

"I do not wish to presume," I said, "but it is possible if you read *Harper's Weekly* that you are familiar with my name."

He looked at me and repeated my name out loud. "Oy. You are saying to me that you are the schmuck who writes all those stories about Sherlock Holmes?"

"That is indeed who I am."

"*Vunderlekh.* I meet a famous writer but do I meet him on a good day? No, I meet him on the worst day of my life."

I ordered another glass of sherry and placed it in front of him.

"Good day or bad," I said. "It does no harm to tell a doctor what happened. I saw you earlier leading your tour group, and you appeared quite jovial."

"I did, did I? Why did I appear that way? Let me tell you why I appeared that way. It was because I was that way. I was on a roll. I had discovered a gold mine and on my way to *copias pecunias*. Now, I am ruined. So, no, I should no longer appear jovial."

"I am listening. Start at the beginning and tell me about what happened. Start with the gold mine."

"What happened? You want to know what happened? I will tell you what happened. It happens that my Uncle Irving owns a travel agency. A big one. Right smack in the middle of Midtown. In the winter he arranges transport to Miami and, in the spring and summer, he organizes tours to London. It is very popular. London, that is. I want to go to college so I can be a dentist but there is no money, so my mother says to me that I should go and work for a year or two for Uncle Irving and save my money.

"And so, I go to work for Uncle Irving. He pays fair. Why does he pay fair? Is it because he is a swell guy? No. It is because he is my mother's little brother and if he does not pay fair, she will berate him until he does. Uncle Irving gives me a job as his London tour guide, so I bring Americans to London all last summer and fall. Is it good? No, it is not good. London is overrun with American tourists. A thousand of them are already at the Palace to watch the changing of the guards in their big bearskin busbys. Two thousand are wanting a photograph of themselves at the Ten Bells Pub where Jack the Ripper met his victims. Three thousand are waiting to visit the National Gallery. It is not good for our customers, so it is not good for business.

"And then I have an inspiration. I hear of this god-forsaken corner of Scotland called the Isle of Skye. The scenery is beautiful. Americans love natural beauty. This is good for business. There is the story of Bonnie Prince Charlie who rebelled against the English and even if he lost they say he was an inspiration to the heroes of the American Revolution. Americans love this story. This is good for business. They can travel like the brave prince over the sea to Skye. Maybe he did not go by the same exact route but what does it matter? The Bonnie Prince is not only a rebel, he is also a rogue. Americans love rebellious rogues. He dresses up like a maid as he escapes and is helped by the beautiful Miss Flora MacDonald, with whom he has a fling. We love this story. This is good for business.

"And, to make it all the more irresistible, we have the story of Saucy Mary, the beautiful princess who catches the sailors with her chain across the channel and then she pops open her shirt for them after they pay the toll. This story is not so well known, but it is a wonderful story. To make it even better, I tell the ladies in my tour group that the women from the tour from Boston decided that they would achieve oneness with their brave sister Saucy Mary, and so at sunrise, there they were up by the castle and as the sun comes up over the horizon, they all throw their shirts open and bare their breasts to the fishermen, of which there are none anywhere close, but what does it matter? They giggle about this until they get on the boat to go home. This is good for business. They tell all their friends and cousins, of which there are many.

"Soon, I have more people wanting to come on my tours than I can accommodate. I make a deal with my Uncle Irving, and I set up my own company, of which he must be a minority owner, and I become the king of tours to the Isle of Skye. Tours are booked from spring until fall. This is the first tour of the season, and people are loving it. For business, everything is very very good. Then it all falls apart."

"Oh, no," I said. "What happened?"

"The moiders happened."

"You mean the recent murders here and on the mainland?"

"Are there other murders I do not know of? Yes, of course, I mean the recent murders. If murders took place two hundred years ago, it is a good story. So, of course, we stop at Glencoe on our way here. They love the place and the story. If a murder happened three years ago and the murderer has been caught and has been hung, they love it. These murders are good for business. But, if a murder happened three weeks ago in a small village in which you are now sleeping, and no one has even been arrested, this is not good for business.

"This afternoon one of the villagers is talking to one of the ladies in my tour, and she tells her all about the murders. They learn that the laird of the bastard's villa has been done in. And the lady who is the wife of the man who used to run the ferry boat is likewise. They are dead. They are truly and sincerely dead having been stabbed where it hurts, and then had their bellies ripped open. My customers are horrified, even terrified. Why, they ask me, do I bring them to a dangerous place like this? Why do I not give them a warning in advance? Already they are at the post office sending messages to their cousins telling them not to come. They are sending messages to my uncle telling him they want their money back. My business, my gold mine has vanished. My hopes and dreams are shattered. My mother will shout at me for the rest of my life and ask how I could have been so stupid.

"So, Doctor, that is why this is the worst day of my life. What medicine do you prescribe to make it better because right now I would rather be dead than have to show my face in front of my tour group knowing that it will be my last tour forever? Maybe longer than forever."

He emptied both glasses of sherry and returned his face to his hands. I was about to give the poor lad a pat on the back when an inspired thought flashed through my mind.

"Howard, my good man, I may have a way of saving you."

"If you do, Doctor, you had better tell me about it quickly, because I am on my way to drowning my sorrows in what passes for an aperitif in this place which is the last stop before the end of the world."

"What if… ?" I said. "What if rather than being defeated by the murders, you could help Sherlock Holmes solve the crime and bring the murderer to justice? And, of course, you would be given credit when the story appears in *Harper's Weekly*. Might that be of use to you?

He raised his head and looked me in the eye.

"Would that be useful? Of course, that would be useful. But you better not be playing games with me because I am not in the mood for playing games. I am in the mood for getting drunk, but I will now cease from doing so and listen to you, Doctor."

"You said you were from New York?"

"I did say that. Did you not believe me? Do you think maybe I am from Oshkosh?"

"I assume that you have relatives in New York City?"

"Do I have relatives in New York City he asks. Do we fly the flag on the fourth of July? Is haggis unfit for human consumption? Of course, I have relatives in New York City? How many of them would you like? I have many more than I need … or even want."

I pulled out of my case the file about the firm in New York that had offered to buy the Bastard's Villa and explained to him the possible connection to the murders. It might amount to nothing, I told him, but it was the only clue I currently had that could not be explained. Could Howard contact one or more of his relatives and find out who the principals of the company were? Could they do it quickly? If it turned out to be a useful quest, I would most assuredly give him full credit in the story about this case.

He turned both of his hands palms up and shrugged his shoulders.

"What can I say? It is worth a try. My day cannot get worse. Give me the address in Manhattan, and I will proceed directly to the telegraph man and send off a dozen wires to New England. It is for certain that I will get you your answer immediately if not sooner."

I though about that for a moment, trying as always to act as I thought Holmes might in such a situation.

"Perhaps it would be better if you hired a trap and ran up to the Royal Mail office in Portree."

"And why should I do that? It is two hours up and two hours back whereas the office here is almost next door if not closer."

"This is not New York, Howard. It is a small village and there are no secrets. Any telegram that arrives here is read by the postmaster and there is a danger that its contents would become fodder for the village gossip machine and soon known by all including the villain we are trying to identify. That is why it would be better to have them sent and returned to Portree."

Now Howard thought for a moment and then smiled. "This man, your postmaster, he speaks English, doe he not?"

"Of course, he does."

"As do I and as does everybody in the village at least some dialect of it which is more than somewhat close to unintelligible. However, I am willing to bet my shirt that he does not speak Yiddish, which it so happens I do because my grandparents live with us and only converse in that language. It also happens that everyone to whom I will send a telegram also speaks Yiddish. Therefore, it is in Yiddish I will send my telegrams and instruct those who receive them to reply in the same tongue."

"Howard. That is a brilliant solution. Please proceed accordingly."

"That I will do. I will have the answer to you by tomorrow morning. Or maybe by noon hour as we are five hours ahead of New York and you cannot expect even a New Yorker to be working before seven o'clock in the morning. Better still, make it one o'clock."

I thanked him and suggested a time to meet the following afternoon, expecting that he would have to attend to the members of his tour, regardless of their now diminished opinion of him.

"I shall be available. Tomorrow morning is their final morning. It is the morning when the women of the group, or at least most of them, walk to the top of the castle hill before sunrise and pay their homage to Saucy Mary by repeating her famous performance. Obviously, the men are not invited, and they remain in their beds."

I confess that I found the escapade highly amusing and could not resist asking about it.

"Was it truly a few women from Boston who started this ritual?"

"Boston, Schmoston," he replied. "What does it matter? If you want to know the truth, it was a group of Swedish women from Stockholm. For them, it was not in the least daring or naughty since I am told that is what they wear to go shopping. But the story worked. It has been good for business."

As we parted, I chortled and shook my head. Then I returned to my task of writing my report.

Chapter Nine
Second Report to
Sherlock Holmes

MY DEAR HOLMES:

[Again, I shall refrain from including in this copy of my report to Holmes a repetition of information I have already imparted in this account.]

You now have possession of all of the data I have acquired so far. I am acutely aware of your prohibition of conclusions before sufficient information can be considered. Nevertheless, I have formed a few initial thoughts that I feel I have a duty to share with you.

To a man – or a woman for that matter – there is not a one here who is unaware of the visions of the Ben Shee. I have chatted in a friendly manner with many of them, and they are quite prepared to talk about the weather, or the latest football match between the Rangers and the recently formed Celtic Club. Any chat which allows them to curse the government in London is always met with friendly enthusiasm. When I steer the conversation to the Ben Shee, however, they close up tighter than a drum and usually find an excuse to depart.

There is no doubt in my mind that something evil this way hath come. In the night ahead and the ones to come, I plan to go out looking for it. The Irish say that you can catch a leprechaun by leaving a gold coin inside a trap. Somehow, I doubt any self-respecting Scottish apparition would be so foolish as to fall for such nonsense, but if I do catch it, I shall let you know.

One of your methods that I have, of course, observed time and time again, is the priority of following *cui bono.* This is especially necessary when excessive amounts of money are at stake. In this situation, an enormous estate worth well over a million pounds has now passed from the former laird, Hamish Mackinnon, to his widow and younger brother. I do not claim to have anything close to your insight into the character of a man or a woman, but neither of them strikes me as having been capable of murder. They are, I will admit, very composed individuals who could lie to your face and tell you that two and two was five without disturbing an eyelash.

Lionel Mackinnon's existence and his living in Paris do not appear to have come as a surprise to Rebecca Mackinnon even if it was to the rest of the village, including Reverend Fraser. So, there remains the possibility that the two of them colluded to their mutual benefit.

The shortcoming with any hypothesis involving them is the death of the Wallace woman across the channel. She had no connection that I can see to the Mackinnon fortune and no one appears to have benefited from her death. This leads me to wonder if perhaps she was not a mistaken victim, killed by mistake when another had been the intended one.

These hypotheses may be foreign to the mission on which you sent me but they cannot be banished from my mind.

I leave these thoughts with you. My soul is full of vague fears.

When do you expect to be here? Please advise with a firm date as soon as possible. The fact that I am associated with Sherlock Holmes has become widely known, and several folks are anxious to meet you.

Yours very truly,
Watson

Chapter Ten
Toss and Fetch and Tragedy

I ROSE EARLY THE FOLLOWING MORNING and entered the breakfast room in time to see the women of the tour group gathered and about to leave on their journey of emancipation. One does not wish to be uncharitable in one's thoughts, but it occurred to me that whilst several of them might indeed brighten a sailor's day, others would more likely frighten them off. Gravity had not been a friend to them.

As I was finishing my breakfast, Reverend Fraser entered, accompanied as always by Mr. David Hume.

"I had hoped," he said, "to spend the morning with you, doctor. It is not to be. I have had a call to visit one of the elderly members of my congregation. She will not be much longer with us on this side of eternity, so I need to spend an hour or two reading her favorite psalms. I have made a list for you of some places in the village that you might wish to visit and folks you might wish to speak to."

He handed me a sheet of paper, for which I thanked him.

"I trust," I said, "that you shall have a peaceful visit."

"That," he said, "it is not at all likely to be. The dear lady has cats, seven of them at last count. They do not take kindly to sharing their territory with a dog, even one so well-trained and Mr. David Hume. It could be a wee bit of an ordeal."

I allowed my imagination to see the scene he just described. 'Peaceful' was not how it would be described. I proposed a solution.

"Why don't you let me take Mr. David Hume for the morning," I said. "He and I can stroll through the village visiting your list. I would be sure not to get lost."

"Indeed? You would not mind, Doctor?"

"Not at all. I kept a bull pup for a while quite a few years back and miss the company. I would enjoy the morning."

"Very kind of you, sir. Here then, I shall put his leash on him, and you might want to put this in your pocket."

He reached into his pocket and handed me a well-worn tennis ball.

"Mind you, if you start throwing it, he will keep bringing it back forever. Your arm will fall off before he tires of it."

With Mr. David Hume now walking along beside me, I began my self-directed tour of the village. Whilst I had the reverend's list of suggested stops, my own itinerary had been formed by the question I had put to myself – *If I were a Ben Shee, where would I appear next?*

My first destination was the ruins of the Caisteal Maol on the hill to the east of the harbor. We followed the road to where it ended on the far side of the bay and then took the footpath up to the ruins. Along the way, we passed the troupe of women from the tour who were on their way back down after greeting the sunrise and titillating any fishermen who might have been gazing in their direction. They were all talking and laughing somewhat raucously as they trotted their way, sans selected undergarments I suspected, back to the hotel.

Mr. David Hume and I continued to the fabled ruins which were, upon seeing them, somewhat of a disappointment. There are many impressive ruined castles all over the British Isles. This one consisted of no more than portions of two thick walls, one with an archway through it. It had a commanding view of the village but seemed to me to be too far away from the village for any specter to have a terrifying effect on a dark night. For that matter, it was much too far away from the water for any passing sailor a thousand years ago to have enjoyed much of a reward from his distant view of Saucy Mary.

On the way back down, I stopped on the small Obbe Road bridge that crossed the estuary at the southwest edge of the harbor. Yes, I thought, this would be a good place to make a terrifying appearance. A traveler crossing the bridge would have little choice but to turn and run if the Ben Shee suddenly glowed and screamed at the other end.

I wandered through the few streets of the village, chatting with those I met. Holmes had expressly said that I should study the neighbors and I attempted to do so. Everyone not only knew who I was but could see that I was walking the minister's dog. The chats were friendly, but after the first fellow abruptly ended our conversation when I asked about the Ben Shee, I refrained from any more questions along that line.

A final stop took me to the graveyard that rose on a hill behind the kirk. The yard was well-kept. Ancient stones had been restored and, where needed, secured with strips of mending plates on their back sides. There was an open space at the top of the hill, and I decided that it was an excellent place in which to give Mr. David Hume his exercise. I had no sooner pulled the tennis ball from my pocket than the collie was bobbing and barking with excitement. I undid his leash and gave the ball a bit of a toss. The dog caught it on the second bounce and brought it back, dropping it at my feet. I began a series of longer tosses, and he returned every one of them. Then I had the insight that I could increase the distance by throwing toward the base of the hill and letting the ball roll and bounce its way to the bottom. I did so, and he had to run almost all the way to the church door to fetch it. But he placed the ball at my feet and immediately ran back part way down the hill to a spot that marked the maximum distance I could throw.

I let go and to my surprise and delight, he leapt into the air and caught the ball just before it hit the ground. Succeeding throws down the hill were met with the same reaction. No matter where among the gravestones I aimed my toss, the collie was at the spot as the ball landed, or at the latest by the first bounce. I am not sure how long I kept throwing the ball, but Mr. David Hume kept bringing it back and wanting more. It did occur to me eventually that during the time with the dog, my mind had forgotten all matter to do with murders and apparitions and had been consumed with the sheer pleasure of playing with an animal. There was a large monument over the grave of a past member of the Clan Mackinnon so, on my final toss, I waited until the collie was distracted by the arc of the ball and hid behind the monument. He returned to where I had been only a second earlier to find no one there. For several seconds he must have been confused before looking behind the large slab of stone.

He then barked happily, and I had to squat done and give his head a friendly rub.

"Did you think I had disappeared, Mr. Hume?" I asked. "Were you worried?"

He barked joyfully, his tail wagging furiously. It was only then that I realized I was having a conversation with a canine.

At a few minutes past noon, I forced myself to put away the thoroughly slobbered ball and make my way back down into the village, much to the obvious disappointment of Mr. David Hume. I stopped by the kirk, knocked on the vestry door, and returned the delightful collie to his master. At the pub, I ordered my lunch meal and sat at a table in the back working on my notes about this case so far. At one o'clock, I put my pencil and paper aside, expecting Howard to arrive.

At a quarter past one, he had not yet entered the pub.

At one thirty he had not arrived.

At forty-five minutes past one, I got up and went outside. Near the door of the hotel, I could see a small crowd of people gathered who I recognized as the tour group for which Howard was responsible. They were standing close together and appeared to be engaged in conversation. I walked up to them and took one of them aside.

"I am looking for Howard Schapiro," I told the chap. "Have you seen him?"

"No, we haven't seen him. Haven't seen him all morning. That's why we're all here. The blighter has disappeared."

From within the gaggle of American tourists came a stream of comments.

"What's happened to him?"

"He's run off because he knows were mad at him."

"Relax. Something must have happened. He will show up."

"He brings us to some village where a murderer is on the loose and then disappears."

"If you ask me, that's all the more reason to demand our money back."

It was apparent that no member of the tour group had seen him that morning. He had not been present, quite understandably, when the women's emancipation troupe marched up to the castle and back. He had been expected to meet with them following breakfast and lead them on a boat tour out to the lighthouse, followed by a picnic lunch on the lovely island. When he hadn't appeared, they told the ferryman to take them without their leader. Allister Maclean provided them with an impromptu lecture about the tides, wildlife, history, and the local fishing industry. Upon their return an hour ago, they had expected to find Howard waiting for them, but he was not to be found.

"I say," said one of the most assertive members of the tour, "that we declare this afternoon a free time and we can all wander wherever we like and meet back here for supper."

"Right ho," came another voice. "Best stay in two and threes. There is a murderer loose you know."

This suggestion was met with murmurs of consent, and the meeting broke up as various small clusters of the wandered off in all directions.

My heart was sinking.

I took the next logical step and walked swiftly to the office of the Royal Mail. I had already chatted with the postmaster when sending off reports to Holmes

"Pardon me, sir," I said to him. "Might I have a word with you?"

"Oh, hello, Dr. Watson. Another report to send off so soon?"

"No. Just a question if I may, sir."

"Aye, go ahead."

"Did a young man, the one who is leading the tour group, come by late yesterday afternoon?"

He had a clear recollection of Howard's visit. "Aye. That he did. Sent off a dozen wires to New York City."

"When did you last see him?"

"Around six o'clock, just before I closed."

"And that was the last time?" I asked.

"No. I saw him again at ten o'clock."

That surprised me, and I asked him to explain how that came about.

"New York is five hours behind us, doctor. It was early in the afternoon when he sent his wires. Three of those he sent to replied before the end of their working day. I live behind the office, and I heard those wires coming in. By nine thirty, those three messages had arrived and seeing as the lad seemed very concerned about them, I took them over to him at his room in the hotel. I knocked on his door, and he was still awake and dressed, and took the wires from me."

"Did he say anything when you gave them to him?"

"He was tickled to get them and he read them as I was standing there. They were in some foreign gibberish as far as I was concerned but he could understand them. Broke into a big smile, he did. Thanked me several times and gave me an American dollar bill. But when he closed the door, I could hear him talking to himself. A wee bit glaikit, if you ask me."

"Do you recall what he said?" I asked.

"Aye, 'Twas if he was reading a newspaper and announcing the headline. Quite pompous like. First, he says 'Tour guide apprehends dangerous criminal,' then he changed it to 'Courageous tour director apprehends murderer.' And that must not have been good enough, so then he says, 'Fearless tour company owner single-handedly brings ruthless murderer to justice.' He may have gone on after that, but I had better things to do than stand and listen to his nonsense."

"Did you see him after that?"

"No. That was the last I saw of him. Has something untoward happened, doctor?"

"I do not know, sir," I said. "If I may, however, I would like to send off a short telegram myself to London."

"Of course, sir. The pad and pencil are on the desk. Just give a wee shout when you are finished, and I will send it."

I quickly imparted to Holmes what had taken place and concluded with a plea that he get himself here at once.

As I walked back to the hotel, I was overcome with the thought that I may have committed the most tragic mistake of my life and I was desperate for the company of Sherlock Holmes.

Chapter Eleven
Then There were Two

ON RETURNING TO THE HOTEL, I went straight away to the top floor where Howard Shapiro's room was located. He had wisely assigned all of the lower rooms with the largest windows to his customers and had taken a small room with a modest dormer window for himself. I knew it was a waste of time, but I knocked on his door. As expected, there was no answer. The front desk confirmed that departed from the hotel late last evening and had not returned.

Again, although I knew it was an exercise in futility, I walked up and down every block of the town, from the Bastard's Villa to the west to the ruined castle to the east. With each passing minute, the fear that I might have sent Howard on a mission that resulted in something untoward kept gnawing at my soul. I came up with a score of other possibilities, innocuous unexpected events that might account for his vanishing, but try as I might, they were utterly overcome by my fears.

At the super hour, I returned to the hotel. The desk handed me a note from Reverend Fraser. He thanked me again for looking after Mr. David Hume for the morning and apologized for not being able to join me for dinner. Laird Lionel and Lady Rebecca had asked him to come over for the evening.

The pub was unusually quiet over the dinner hour. The American tourists were seated together but were speaking in subdued tones. The belligerent constable sat alone at his usual table and tried to make pleasant talk with Gracie the barmaid, but she was unresponsive. I ate only a small portion of my dinner before leaving the pub and retiring to my room. I forced myself to add notes and thoughts to my record of this case, but my mind was not in a condition to concentrate. At ten o'clock, I undressed and crawled into bed.

At eleven o'clock, not being able to sleep, I rose from my bed, dressed, pulled on a sweater and took myself for a walk outside. The moon was not yet up, and it was pitch dark. So, I stayed on the Kyleside Road and slowly walked along the edge of the harbor and out onto the pier. I stood there for a quarter hour or more trying to force my mind to think like Holmes. It was hopeless. Waves of guilt kept sweeping over me combined with an irrational anger at Sherlock Holmes for sending me on this mission. It must have been close to midnight when I walked back to the hotel.

As I approached the hotel, I could hear voices not far in front of me. About fifty yards from the front door, I spotted the telltale glowing orange dots that cigarettes give on a dark night. Soon, I could overhear some of what was being said and reasoned that a half dozen or so of the American tourists had likewise not been able to sleep and were standing on the roadway, chatting quietly amongst themselves.

Then I heard it.

It began like a quiet, mournful groan. The tourists stopped their chatter.

The groan increased in volume until the sound was filing the street and echoing across the channel.

A voice from the small crowd shouted out, "What in God's name is that!?"

Then we saw her.

A glow of light appeared on the peak of the dormer window of Howard's room. A dark figure appeared in the glow. At first, it was a ghoulish black shade. Then she turned around ... and screamed. And she kept on screaming. Her dark robe had opened, and her pale white breasts were exposed with what appeared to be blood dripping from them.

Her screeching continued and was soon matched by screams of terror from the women who were standing in the road.

I knew that I should run into the hotel and make my way up to the roof, but I was paralyzed with fear. I could not move, and I could not take my eyes off of the hideous face with the empty eye sockets and dripping red mouth.

Then, in an instant, the light was extinguished, and the horrible thing was gone.

Now, I took hold of my being and rushed into the hotel. I scrambled up the stairs to the top floor and ran to Howard's room. I did not stop to knock but raised my foot and gave as powerful a kick as I could to the door plate. The door frame shattered and the door flew back. I ran through the room to the dormer and opened the window. As quickly as I could, I worked my way out and onto the roof.

There was nothing.

The pitch on the roof was not overly steep, and I carefully stepped up the slate tiles until I reached the ridgeline. Looking over the roof to the side that faced inland, I saw another string of dormer windows. These were rooms that must have been rented either to travelers who needed the cheapest options available or to resident staff. I considered walking down and along the roof and trying each of those windows but my common sense prevailed, and I realized that if anyone had escaped through them, they could have easily locked the window behind them and I would accomplish nothing more than having myself branded as a peeping Tom.

I struck a match to give me a bit of light and noticed the clear scuff marks on the roof from a recent pair of boots. Ghosts, I reasoned, do not wear boots.

I did not remain long on the roof and within ten minutes had returned to the pavement outside the front door of the hotel. The small crowd of tourists had grown and had been augmented by other hotel guests who were curious about the screaming and commotion. I joined them and was subjected to several rounds of congratulations for my bravery in pursuing the ghoulish apparition.

Whilst modestly deflecting such undeserved praise, I was interrupted by yet another terrified scream. A woman from the group was pointing toward the ruined castle, and soon several others were likewise shrieking in fear. In a distant, glowing pool of light just a few yards down the hill from the castle, we could all see the Ben Shee. In a quiet moment when those who had been screaming and shouting paused to take a breath, we could hear moaning in the distance. Then it changed into a blood-curdling shriek. It was at least three hundred yards off, but there was no mistaking the sound. A minute later the light was extinguished, and the specter vanished.

Pandemonium broke out. It was physically impossible for the creature, whatever it was, to have moved from the roof of the hotel to the brow of the castle hill in the short time between its appearances. To the crowd, it was undeniable evidence of the presence of the supernatural forces of evil. The temptation to allow my own mind to be swept into the same panic was strong, and it was with considerable mental and physical effort that I removed myself from the crowd, walked to the edge of the water, sat on a rock and took many deep breaths.

There was no getting back to normal after that. The entire tour group assembled in the hotel lobby and stayed there, with their baggage for the remainder of the night. They would all be on the first ferry out of Kyleakin in the morning.

I left them and went first to Howard's room and searched it, looking for any clue as to what might have happened to him. Finding nothing, I retired to my room and attempted to catch forty winks with little success.

At five o'clock in the morning, just before first light, I rose and departed and made my way to the pier. About a dozen fishermen had assembled and were preparing their boats and nets so that they could push off as soon as the tide settled.

"Gentlemen!" I shouted to them. "Might I have your attention for just a minute. I am sorry to interrupt but a serious situation has arisen, and we are in need of your assistance."

They all politely stopped what they were doing and turned toward me.

"It is possible," I said, loudly enough for them to hear me, "that a tragic drowning may have taken place sometime in the past two days. Please be watchful for a body that may be floating out in the bay. Thank you, gentlemen. Your assistance is greatly appreciated."

Most of them nodded and went back to preparing for the day. A voice from behind me bellowed.

"What do you think you're doing?" [Note: I have deleted the expletives and will continue to do so.]

I turned and observed the hulking form of Constable Murray Craigh storming toward me.

"If you heard me, Constable, you know what I was doing. Why do you ask?"

"I am in charge of any investigation here. Not you. If a body is missing, I give the order to look for it. Not you. Do you understand that, Dr. Johnny?"

"Most certainly."

I turned back to the fishermen and shouted, "Gentlemen. Please be advised that Constable Craigh has given an order for you to be on the lookout for a body. Thank you."

I smiled and nodded at the brute. "Thank you, Constable, for clearing up that matter."

I said no more and began to walk back to the hotel.

"Stop where you are, Dr. Johnny," he bellowed, adding a few profanities which I have not repeated.

I turned and smiled at him.

"Yes, Constable?"

"Look here. I do not like being lied to."

"Right you are. Neither do I."

"You lied to me."

"I did nothing of the sort," I said.

"You told me that you were doing research for your regiment. That was a lie. You are here investigating the murders."

"Precisely. I always send my regiment advance copies of my stories for their consideration. It is part of my sense of loyalty to my regiment. You would do the same for your regiment, would you not? Out of a sense of loyalty, yes?"

I turned around and started walking again. I rewarded myself by forming a picture in my mind of what his oversized flabby body would look like when … well, delicacy forbids my completing this sentence.

Chapter Twelve
Death on the Water

IT WAS STILL EARLY MORNING, and I plodded my way back up to my hotel room, crawled back into the bed and tried to sleep. It was a futile effort. I was sick at heart, knowing that in all likelihood young Howard Shapiro had met foul play and that I was to blame. It also occurred to me that for the better part of the past decade, I had spent my days either with the company of Sherlock Holmes or with my dear wife. My days and nights of being on my own, as I was when in the BEF, were long ago. I felt profoundly lonely and even somewhat angry with Holmes for having sent me on a mission for which I was obviously not prepared.

I must have dozed off, for when I next opened my eyes the morning sun was well up and the breeze was blowing white caps across the loch. For several minutes, I sat on the edge of the bed asking myself again *what was I doing here?* Then, I took a deep breath and decided that since I was here, I might as well concentrate on the tasks Holmes had requested of me – protecting the new Laird Mackinnon and reporting on whatever I observed in the villages, particularly any activities that seemed out of the ordinary. To those two tasks, I added the third: deducing where and when a Ben Shee would most likely appear next.

I took my desultory breakfast at the hotel and then began a walk up the hill to the Bastard's Villa. I was half-way up when my trek was interrupted. I had stopped to enjoy the view over the lock when my attention was drawn to a single fishing skiff that was being rowed back through the narrows. I could see two men plying the oars and that the boat was tilted off the level, indicating that on the bottom at one end of it was something heavy. Yet again my heart sank, and I turned around and began a downhill march back to the wharf.

I stood on the wharf for several minutes observing the rhythmical action of the oars as the skiff approached. When it rounded the pier, I could see the faces of the men rowing. When fishermen return from a day on the sea with their catch on board, their faces are usually smiling, and they are happily chatting with each other. These men were not. Their faces were grim. They guided the skiff into the wharf, allowing me to see what lay in the bottom. It was, as I had feared the body of Howard Shapiro.

The fellows in the boat shouted to other chaps who were tending nets nearby to come and help. As three of them steadied the skiff, the body was carefully lifted out and laid supine on the wharf. Any blood had been washed away by the water, but it was obvious that the victim had been stabbed. His belly and lower chest were splayed open, and his intestines and organs were protruding. I knelt down over him.

"I am a medical doctor," I said to the surrounding men. "Please give me a minute to examine him."

I bent over the horrible body of young Howard. In a manner similar to what had been done to Mrs. Wallace and Laird Mackinnon, as conveyed by Reverend Fraser, he had been stabbed in his nether region and then had a blade pulled up through his torso until blocked by the rib cage. He would have died within seconds of such an assault. I pushed back his clothing, and then I stopped and starred. Immediately to the left of the sternum was a hole in the body. I knew what it was and using a pocket knife carefully extracted a bullet from his heart. It was a revolver bullet and, on closer examination, I could see a few remaining burn marks surrounding the matching hole in the shirt. The man had been shot to death and subsequently eviscerated.

"Get away from that body!" came a shout from behind me. The voice could not be disguised.

"What do you think you're doing?" shouted Constable Craigh, along with selected chosen profanity.

"I am a medical doctor," I said wearily, without moving. "What does it look like I am doing?"

The brute grabbed me by the collar and hauled me to my feet.

"You have no authority here," he bellowed. "I do!"

"As you wish, Constable," I said. "The man has been murdered. Please carry on and perform your duty."

"There is no proof of murder. How do you know he did not drown?"

I was about to point out the obvious fact that drowning victims do not present with the bowels protruding. Unfortunately, I took a different tack.

"Because this bullet was in his heart," I said, opening my palm and showing him the evidence.

He forcefully grabbed my wrist with one hand and with the other picked up the bullet and put it in his pocket.

"Until I say what happened," he said, "he drowned. Do you understand, Dr. Johnny?"

"Of course, I said. "You have my permission to quote me when you send your report off to Scotland Yard."

"You will keep your nose out of this, and all communication with Scotland Yard will be through me," he said, leaning his large body and unkempt face close to mine.

I merely turned and walked away from him. As I did, he shouted again, "And if you try to interfere, I will smash your face to a pulp."

I was now furious as well as distressed. The walk back through the village to the laird's hill was useful, and I forced my mind to concentrate on the more pressing demands on my time, demands to which I must now turn my unobstructed attention.

The door of the Bastard's Villa was not opened by Mr. Hutchinson but by Lionel Mackinnon himself. He greeted me in a friendly way and explained that the man-servant had been given a few days of leave to spend with family in Fort William. Having done so, Lionel turned to the interior of the house and shouted.

"Becky, darling! We have a visitor! A handsome, educated gentleman to see us."

"The vicar again? Be right there," came the reply from somewhere down a hallway. Lady Rebecca soon appeared in the entryway, and although I would not swear to it, I thought I detected a look of disappointment on her face when she saw that it was me and not Reverend Fraser.

Over a cup of tea in their gloomy front room, I recounted the tragic news of the morning. They were deeply distressed and could see no reason whatsoever for the murder of the American tour leader. I deliberately withheld the fact that I had asked Howard to make inquiries concerning the identity of the party who had offered to buy the Mackinnon property in Kyleakin for fear that Lionel, who had given me the file, would feel a sense of responsibility for the death. That responsibility was mine alone.

Lady Rebecca was not at all surprised by the belligerence of the constable.

"That does not surprise me. Hamish was fond of observing that there is no more tyrannical character on earth than a minor government functionary with a tiny morsel of power. Murray Craigh thinks of himself as the colonial master of the village. I have heard the maid and the charwoman complaining that he is much too free with his large hands and that he has been bedeviling Gracie the barmaid of late. She needs the work, otherwise she would be tossing his beer in his face."

Lionel made no comment about the constable but expressed concern when I noted that Sherlock Holmes had asked me to be on the lookout for his safety.

"Honestly, doctor," he said. "Who in the world could possibly wish me harm. My goodness, I have never hurt a flea in my entire life. Oh, there might be one or two, perhaps three, along the way who thought of me as heartless and fickle but they soon recovered."

"Sir," I said, using my most doctorly tone of voice, "if you were to suddenly die, what would happen to the title to the estate and all its assets."

"It would all go to Rebecca," he replied.

"And Lady Mackinnon," I said, turning to her, "What would you do with this property if you became the sole owner of it."

"Why I would sell it and move. Any fair offer would be accepted in a moment, but I cannot for the life of me imagine who would want to buy it other than some fool from New York. By the way, did you happen to discover who had made that offer?"

"No, but I will continue to search for that answer," I said.

We chatted on for a while, after which they agreed to my request to let me remain in their front room and read and write for the remainder of the day.

A maid brought me a pleasant lunch and, several hours later I joined the laird and lady for dinner. Both of them were far more interested in chatting about the theater scene in London and the latest triumphs on stage of Ellen Terry and Henry Irving at the Lyceum, and the latest clever plays and writing of Oscar Wilde. It was an altogether pleasant evening and, for two enjoyable hours, I was able to push the tragedy of the day to the back of my mind.

Before parting, I advised these two charming people that there was a possibility that the Ben Shee might appear again soon, possibly that evening. They cheerily pooh-poohed the idea and sent me on my way.

Chapter Thirteen
The Man on the Hill

IT WAS STILL TWILIGHT when I walked back down the hill to the hotel. Now was the time for my other task during what remained of the day; trying to deduce the most likely location for the next appearance of the specter.

As I turned the case over in my mind, I began by reminding myself of Holmes's dictum that crime was formed in the mind-forged manacles of man and not in the world of hocus-pocus. Within the depths of my soul, a battle was raging between that primitive part of me that gave in to fear of the supernatural and belief in the forces of evil. Another part insisted that there existed a reasonable and logical explanation, regardless of whether or not it remained unknown.

If so, however, there was no possible way that a physical being, which in the rational sector of my being, I forced myself to conclude the Ben Shee must be, could transport itself from the hotel roof to the castle in a matter of minutes. Nor could it have galloped on a horse. Nor by any other means. Having eliminated these hypotheses, I had to acknowledge the only possible solution, however improbable – there must be two Ben Shees.

One of them might appear again at the Bastard's Villa, but I had already warned Lionel and Rebecca of that danger. As to the second one, I reasoned that it would not reappear at the hotel, perched above Howard's hotel room, as he was already dead. Of course, it could designate my room, but I thought that unlikely as I had no material interest in the village. The location on the eastern hill in front of the ruined castle, where it had appeared recently, was dramatic but somewhat too distant to be seen clearly and give the full horror to those observing it. The roof of the church would be visible and thus terrifying to the entire village but it would a very difficult place from which to beat a hasty retreat. The same applied to any rooftop of one of the village houses as well as the wharf and the pier. I mentally assessed all other locations and arrived at what I concluded to be the most likely – the graveyard.

The place where I had stood and tossed the tennis ball to Mr. David Hume would be an ideal location. It was visible from the main street of the village yet provided numerous places for concealment and avenues of escape. I determined that I would hide myself there that night and wait. It was, I reasoned, an acceptable risk. The Ben Shee was armed with a fearsome dagger, but I would have my service revolver with me.

I had expected to eat a solitary supper in the pub and was pleasantly surprised when Reverend Fraser arrived, accompanied by Mr. David Hume, who recognized me, barked, and held out his paw. I must say that it was a bright moment in an otherwise highly distressing day. The minister and I spoke briefly about the death of the American lad and then, determined to make our meal as pleasant as possible under the circumstances, enjoyed an animated chat about many different subjects, none of which touched on murders or apparitions.

I did not mention to him my plan to lay in wait in the graveyard, not that I did not trust his discretion, but I did not wish either to upset him or to have him try to prevent my admittedly incautious scheme. There were several other men also taking their supper, and I had learned over my years of working with Holmes that strangers and indeed walls have ears.

At dusk, I returned to my hotel room and stripped two blankets off the bed. In the last week of April, spring may have arrived in London, but at the 57th parallel, the temperature descended into the forties or worse at night. Exiting the hotel by the servants' door so as not to be stopped by the front desk and accused of absconding with the blankets, I walked up the laneway behind the church and into the darkening graveyard. In the little light that remained, I worked my way to the top of the hill and sat down on the grass behind the large stone monument which I had used to fool Mr. David Hume. I bundled myself up against the cold and waited, determined to attain my end.

And waited.

The sun had set just prior to nine o'clock, and by ten the entire village was in complete darkness and would remain that way until the moon would rise well after midnight. Half past ten o'clock came and passed, and I was coming to the conclusion that I had given in to foolishness and was accomplishing nothing.

Then I heard something. It rose suddenly out of the vast gloom of the night, distant and coming from the direction of the Bastard's Villa. It was that unmistakable horrid keening, the moan that I had heard the night before both from the roof of the hotel and from the ruined castle. Then, as I expected, it changed into the wail and scream and spread out over the village.

It was the hellish scream of the Ben Shee.

Then it stopped. It had lasted no more than a few seconds. That surprised me. All reports of past appearances and what I had observed the previous night agreed that the terrifying screams continued for several minutes before fading. I was about to get up and walk up to the villa when I reasoned that such a move would be a waste of time and that I was better to continue to lay in wait where I was.

There was no breeze.

I do not know how many readers have ever sat in a field or walked through a forest on a black, still night. Every sound of a mouse scurrying strikes one for certain as a bear or worse. Should a hedgehog of badger wander by, one expects a lion or tiger to appear. Every fluttering sparrow sounds like an eagle about to attack. The fact that I knew these fears to be unfounded did not make them disappear or diminish the volume of the strange sounds.

At eleven o'clock I heard a sound that could not have been a small animal or a bird. I heard footsteps.

They were coming up the path toward the monument but without the aid or any light. Very stealthily, they came closer and closer and then stopped on the other side of the monument no more than three yards away from me. In careful silence, I uncovered myself, laid the blanket down, and painfully slowly stood to my feet.

A broad beam of light appeared, shining on the monument and the empty space that was to my right side. I leaned my head around the left side and could plainly see that a dark lantern had been placed on the ground and tilted and focused to shine up toward the gap on the far side of the monument. A human figure, as black as an ebony statue, was standing in the shadows no more than four yards in front of me, and it quickly stepped into the beam of light and began to moan loudly. It was wearing a hooded cloak and was surprisingly tall for an ancient ghost. I waited in complete stillness until the moan changed to the horrible scream. Then I grabbed my service revolver by its barrel and with two quick steps and a hard swing of my right hand struck a blow on the back of the skull, smack at the base of the occipital bone. The ghoul dropped like a stone to the ground.

I leapt forward and snatched the dark lantern from its perch and directed the light to the body that lay face down in front of me. Grabbing the closest arm and shoulder, I began to roll it over and recognized right away that it was an adult male body that I was moving. In the glimmer of the lantern, I saw two plaster of Paris breasts that had flopped to the side of the man's chest. Each was painted white except for the brilliant, blood red sections. The fake breasts were attached by a strap around the neck and must have hung in the appropriate region when the fellow was standing. The limited light afforded a look at the face. It was horrifying. Like what I had seen the previous night and as described by others who had likewise encountered the apparition, the eyes were completely blackened, as were the nostrils whilst the lips were blood red. Dark streaks lined the cheeks.

I scampered over and fetched the lantern and shone the light directly in the horrid face.

My shock was overwhelming.

Covered in theatrical make-up was the unmistakable face of Sherlock Holmes.

Chapter Fourteen
The Specter in the Graveyard

IT IS POSSIBLE THAT THE SLAP I gave to Holmes's face in an effort to revive him was significantly harder than necessary.

It is possible that the second and third slaps were likewise.

My initial shock had been replaced with anger, and after a fourth hard slap I placed my mouth an inch from his ear and shouted his name. I am not a man that is given to the use of profanity, but it is also possible that at that instant a few choice words that shall not be recorded here slipped past my lips.

Holmes's eyelids flickered, and he made an agonized sigh.

"Holmes!" I shouted again. "What is the meaning of this? How dare you? You deceived me and played me for a fool."

There have been many occasions in the past when I was thoroughly annoyed with Sherlock Holmes. None came anywhere close to the anger with which I now spoke to the man I had considered to be my friend.

"Waaatson? Is that you my good man?" He had struggled to sit up and was rubbing the back of his head.

"Yes, it is me. Now either explain yourself, or I will be on the first boat and ferry out of this horrid place and leave you to it."

"You localized me. You were waiting for me," he said in a tone of disbelief. "Well done. You truly have risen above your natural talents. Congratulations."

I was not in the mood for being congratulated and let him know in no uncertain terms.

"Oh, my dear Watson. Do not be angry. I had no choice."

I demanded an explanation.

"The case for Whitehall, whilst of great importance proved to be remarkably easy to solve, and I was done with it within a few days. If I had sent a wire to you, I was sure it would have been read and known by everyone in the villages. The last thing I wanted was to alert whoever is behind these foul deeds that Sherlock Holmes was on his way to the Isle of Skye. They would have immediately gone into hiding, and the case would have become much more difficult to solve. I am awfully sorry to have distressed you, my friend, but it is a small price to have paid for the progress it allowed me to make. I had to keep my presence here a secret and would surely have found you sometime tomorrow and apprised you of my arrival."

"How did you get here?" I demanded, not mollified in the least. "You did not come on the ferry from Kylealsh."

"No, of course not. I came up the West Coast train through Glasgow and Fort William and took the longer ferry from Mallaig across to Armadale. I found a congenial crofter not far from Kyleakin and have been staying there. I thought I had concealed myself completely, but you found me. I truly am surprised. Again, my dear doctor, well done. Such admirable tenacity. You excelled yourself."

I accepted that there was logic in his actions but was still in a foul mood.

"Very well," I said. "Then get up and come down to the hotel and get that awful grease paint off your face." I grabbed the lantern and started down the hill through the graveyard. Holmes followed chatting amiably whilst now and then rubbing the back of his head.

So as not to alarm any of the hotel staff or remaining guests who might still be awake and roaming around, I led him through the servants' door and stealthily up to my room. He went straight away to the lavatory and washed his face. When he reappeared, I demanded again that he explain his actions and what purpose there was in his impersonating the Ben Shee.

"To sow confusion," he said glibly. "Whoever is behind this scheme has a plan by which he is attempting to lure the villagers into believing that the murders are taking place at the hands of an evil spirit who is the reincarnation of Lady Macbeth. I was hoping that by popping up where he was not planning to have a Ben Shee appear would serve to flush him out."

"But that has not happened," I objected.

"Ah, but it has, at least in part."

I demanded an explanation.

"Did you not hear a Ben Shee earlier this evening?"

"I did. The sounds were coming from the villa. Was that you as well."

"No. But I was lying in wait for it. Unfortunately, I was not near as close to it as you were to me and could not lay my hands on the thing. So, I shone my lantern on myself and screamed back. I am sure I frightened whoever it was out of her ... or his wits, and it suddenly ceased screaming and ran back into the town. I gave chase and followed as far as Olaf Road, but then I lost it. He or she must live in one of the houses on that street, and it shan't be long before we eliminate whoever else lives there and identify the thing."

Then he launched into an interrogation of me, and it became clear that the second report I had diligently written out for his benefit was lying unopened in the post that had been delivered to Baker Street.

I recounted all of the knowledge I had gleaned and the events that had transpired. By the time I finished, my temperament had become more or less steady again, and I admitted the distress I felt in my soul over the death of Howard the American. Holmes listened sympathetically and placed his hand on my forearm.

"My dear friend," he said. "I have felt the same way as you now do more than once. You will recall that I failed both John

Openshaw and Paul Kratides and my failure led to their deaths and many times, in the small hours of the might, my soul has been in turmoil as I realize what I should have done and did not. The temptation to throw in the towel has been strong, but I have forced my mind to accept the fact that doing so would be the worst possible alternative. For then, in choosing to do nothing, I would be allowing evil to go unchallenged.

"Forgive me," he continued quietly, "if I suggest that there must have been many occasions when you were treating men on the battlefield when, in retrospect, you might have used a different procedure and saved a life that was lost. Yet you had no choice but to soldier on and do your best to save so many more who subsequently came into your care."

He was smiling warmly at me, and I had to agree with him. However, it was now well past midnight, and I was utterly exhausted. I told Holmes to use the extra cot in my room and soon fell fast asleep.

Chapter Fifteen
Banished from Kyleakin

WHEN MORNING CAME, I awoke to find that Holmes had departed. I was not surprised and, though still unhappy at his having left me to fend by myself for the past week, I was profoundly relieved to know that he was here on the island with me.

He was nowhere to be seen around the hotel, so I took my breakfast, and with notebook in hand and nothing better to occupy my time, I walked back up the hill to the Bastard's Villa.

The Laird and Lady Mackinnon reported that they had heard the Ben Shee briefly the night before and were perplexed by the sudden curtailment of its performance. Lady Rebecca again opined on her growing terror of the apparition and her desire to get away from the island and Scotland altogether. The Laird Lionel was sanguine and dismissed the occurrences as an exhibition of local culture, somewhat on a par with incessant playing of the bagpipes or eating yesterday's pudding for breakfast. Given Holmes's continued concern for his safety, I attempted, to no avail, to have him take the matter more seriously.

Nevertheless, they were pleased to see me and again enlivened my day with several occasions in which we chatted. Reverend Fraser joined us for lunch, and we talked about all sorts of matter of current importance in the world. Lionel regaled us with stories of the nightlife in Paris and his adventures in the Place Pigalle and Le Marais. Occasionally, his sister-in-law would slap his forearm and remind him that a man of the cloth was in our presence. The minister, to his credit, took no offense and seemed to thoroughly enjoy his time.

I departed around tea time and admonished these good people to please be cautious. Lady Rebecca thanked me for my concern whilst Laird Lionel once again laughed it off.

There were a few customers in the pub and, to my relief, I saw Sherlock Holmes sitting in a back corner by himself. I joined him and inquired as to how he had spent his day.

"Mostly at the post office sending and receiving telegrams," he said. "I have been attempting to acquire data on as many of the players in this drama as possible. Some have fascinating backgrounds. Most, however, have lived their entire lives within twenty miles of where we now sit as did their mothers and fathers before them."

"What did you find of interest?" I asked him.

Any answer he might have given was interrupted by the entrance of Constable Craigh into the pub and his strutting over to our table.

"Are you Sherlock Holmes?" he demanded.

"Indeed, I am," said Holmes smiling at the brute. "And you must be Constable Murray Craigh, also employed by the Ordnance Survey Office. Ah, and a Captain in the Aberdeen Reserve Unit of the Royal Scottish Regiment. Oh, pardon me. A retired captain, as you became too old to continue your service two years back. A good afternoon to you, Constable."

Craigh's face showed that he was not at all pleased that Holmes knew so much about him and responded harshly.

"What are you doing here?"

"Oh, I thought for sure you would already know, Constable. I am investigating the murders of the former laird, of Mrs. Wallace from Kylealsh and, most recently of the leader of the American tour group. I trust that my methods will complement yours and that together we shall solve these horrible crimes."

"You are doing nothing of the sort," he snarled. "I will have you know that I have read every word that your friend Dr. Johnny here has ever written and I know everything there is to know about your methods. I don't need your help and you are not permitted to carry out any investigation."

"Every word my friend has written? You don't say. Have you read his articles in *The Lancet* concerning useful techniques for treating battlefield wounds? What about his fictional stories about that strange character, Professor Challenger? Did you enjoy the operetta he wrote along with our friend, Jim Barrie? By the look on your face, it appears that you are not familiar with any of them. Such a pity."

The look on his face was now one of unconcealed rage. He lowered his large from toward Holmes and muttered, "I do not like being called a liar."

"Oh, my dear chap," said Holmes merrily. "I would never accuse you of lying, only of being ignorant and not knowing what you are talking about. Nothing to be ashamed of though. It is not an uncommon trait among men of your temperament."

That was that last straw. Craigh pointed his large sausage-like finger in Holmes's face.

"I am ordering you, both of you, to get out of this village by tomorrow morning. Do you understand? If I find you here after the first ferry tomorrow, I will arrest you. So, do not dare to cross me or I will beat both of you to a bloody pulp."

As was his wont, he peppered his speech with numerous profanities and vulgarities that cannot be repeated.

As the oaf was walking away from the table, Holmes called out after him in a voice loud enough to be heard throughout the pub, "Oh, Constable, do give my regards to your dear wife, Heather, when you visit her in Aberdeen over Easter. And the children too! I am sure they are looking forward to seeing their daddy!"

A wave of silence swept across the pub. The men were glaring at Craigh with looks of condemnation, the women with utter disdain. He sat at a table and shouted at Gracie, the barmaid for a glass of ale. She brought it to him, and as she lowered it to the table in front of him, she quickly flicked her wrist and threw it in his face. There was a quiet murmur from the rest of the patrons who then returned to their conversations in muted tones.

Holmes leaned back and sighed. "Watson, would you mind if we just picked up our supper plates at the bar and took them up to our room? I shall have to eat quickly and then I fear I have the bothersome task of having to spend another hour or two at the post office."

I agreed, and we both went and stood at the bar. Mr. Godfrey Thurlow was standing there in front of us and Holmes engaged him in brief meaningless conversation.

"Do tell me, sir, you are an Englishman. How do the fish and chips in this corner of the land compare to those in the heart of London?"

"They are not fit for human consumption," said the young man. "That is why I am lined up and waiting for a baked potato. It is impossible even for a Scot to cook one of those badly, but they take much longer."

"But the lamb," said Holmes, "is all locally raised. It must be quite delectable."

"They serve mutton dressed as lamb. The good lamb is all sold down into England where it gets a better price. What else would you expect in Scotland?"

Holmes plied him with a few more questions and received similar answers. Our fish and chip arrived before his special order, and we departed for our rooms.

Holmes wolfed down his supper quickly and departed. I had no inkling as to what he might be up to.

I had already gone to bed and turned down the lamps when Holmes finally appeared in the hotel room. He had brought his valise with him and was soon in his bed and asleep. I smiled for the first time in a week.

Chapter Sixteen
Fixing the Brute

ALSO, FOR THE FIRST TIME IN A WEEK, I slept soundly. I was still fast asleep when Holmes gave me a friendly pull on my shoulder.

"Come Watson, it is past eight o'clock. We have a full day ahead of us."

I gave my head a shake and looked at my watch and then turned to Holmes.

"I trust you slept well," I said. "It was nice to have a peaceful night."

"Peaceful?" he queried. "I fear not. Our Ben Shee, the real one, was out again last night."

"It was?" I asked, astounded. "Where? I heard nothing."

"That is because you were sleeping soundly, as you deserved to. The Ben Shee appeared this time on the far side of the Bastard's Villa. I heard and saw it but was too far away to capture it."

I pondered what he said and took a look at my watch. It was almost eight o'clock.

"Goodness," I said. "The first ferry has already departed. Are we about to have our faces smashed to a pulp?"

"On the contrary, my friend. We are about to enjoy the conscription of Constable Craigh to our unit."

"We are what?"

"Here. Read these as you bathe and dress." He handed me a small cluster of telegrams. The first ran:

REPORT RECEIVED. WILL ARRIVE KYLEAKIN BY LATE THIS EVENING. LESTRADE.

"Ah ha," I said. "You sent a full report off to him?"

"Not only that," said Holmes, "but I confess that I played the snitch on our pompous constable. The chaps at Scotland Yard do not take kindly to having information on three murders concealed from them. Read the next one."

I did so. It ran:

COPY TO MR. SHERLOCK HOLMES.

TO: CHIEF CONSTABLE MACNAUGHTON. EDINBURGH

FROM: CHIEF INSPECTOR LESTRADE. SCOTLAND YARD.

SEE ATTACHED REPORT. ACCOUNT TO ME IMMEDIATELY FOR FAILURE TO REPORT THREE MURDERS IN WESTERN HIGHLANDS. I WILL ARRIVE KYLEAKIN TOMORROW AND TAKE CHARGE OF INVESTIGATION. UNTIL THEN AM GIVING TEMPORARY AUTHORITY TO MR. SHERLOCK HOLMES. INSTRUCT YOUR LOCAL MAN TO PROVIDE WHATEVER ASSISTANCE HOLMES REQUIRES.

"To which," said Holmes, "I must add that Chief Constables of Scotland do not take kindly to being chastised by Scotland Yard. Now, the last one, Watson."

COPY TO MR. SHERLOCK HOLMES.

TO: CONSTABLE MURRAY CRAIGH. KYLEALSH / KYLEAKIN

FROM: CHIEF CONSTABLE ANDREW MACNAUGHTON. GOVERNMENT HOUSE EDINBURGH

SUBMIT REPORTS IMMEDIATELY ON RECENT MURDERS IN YOUR DISTRICT. CHIEF INSPECTOR FROM SCOTLAND YARD ARRIVES TOMORROW PM TO TAKE CHARGE OF CASE. UNTIL HIS ARRIVAL FULL AUTHORITY GIVEN BY SCOTLAND YARD TO SHERLOCK HOLMES. REPORT TO HIM YOUR OFFICE NINE AM. DO AS HE INSTRUCTS YOU. ARRANGE TO COME TO EDINBURGH WITHIN FORTNIGHT TO ACCOUNT FOR YOUR RECENT ACTIONS.

I raised my eyebrows and gave a look to Holmes.

"Our constable will not be happy."

"Better he is unhappy than me," said Holmes.

"But you cannot possibly want to recruit that brute to assist your case. The man's character is deplorable."

"My dear Watson, if all those men who rightly deserve to be despised because of their moral depravity were removed from office, the ranks of our politicians, captains of industry, military, police, press, and schools would be more than somewhat reduced. The same is true for every country on the Continent and most certainly for America. Just because a man is a swine, it does follow that he is entirely incompetent. Our constable may be boorish but still useful to us. Come, we shall enjoy breakfast and then pay him a visit and put him to work."

Chapter Seventeen
The Office of the Constable

THE OFFICE OF THE CONSTABLE was a short walk from the hotel, and at nine o'clock we knocked respectfully on the door.

"It's open," came the reply from within.

We entered a small room that was unfurnished except for a large desk and a single chair in front of it. Behind the desk was a closed door, secured with a padlock. Judging by the overall size of the building, that door must have led into another room of about the same size. There were small windows on two of the walls and a locked cabinet in one corner.

Constable Craigh sat behind the desk, glared up at us, and said nothing.

Holmes nodded at him and then turned to me.

"Please, Dr. Watson, do be seated. As there is only one chair, I am sure the constable will not object if I sit on his desk whilst we conduct our brief meeting."

If a man's head could have exploded, I am sure that the constable's would have done so. A look of absolute rage swept across his face but, to his credit, he held his tongue.

"Now then, Constable," said Holmes, "am I correct in assuming that you have devoted significant effort in the recent past to the case of the murders and their association with claims of seeing and hearing this Ben Shee. Is that correct?"

"Aye," he muttered.

"Very good sir. As we have no choice but to work together, I am requesting that you apprise us of all relevant information you have gleaned and we shall do likewise in return."

"What do you want to know?"

"How many credible reports of sightings of this Ben Shee have you received?"

"Six people reporting in Kylealsh, two with multiple sightings for a total of eight. Twenty individuals in Kyleakin, with total reported sightings of thirty-two. Ten of those reporting were American tourists."

"And were the reports consistent? Did they all say they saw and heard the same thing?" asked Holmes.

"Aye, except for those who heard the one up on the hill two nights ago. All others were said to sound like a practiced keener. That one they said sounded like a sick cow."

Holmes was for a moment speechless, and I bit my tongue.

"Did you speak to any of these people? What did those who heard and saw the Ben Shee think that it was?" asked Holmes.

"I spoke to every one of them. There is a written report on every conversation in the files."

"Excellent, constable. Thank you. Would you mind summarizing what you were told?"

"The superstitious ones say that it is the demonic evil spirit of Lady Macbeth sent from hell."

"And the others?"

"What others? These are fishing villages, Holmes. Have you ever met a fisherman who wasn't superstitious?"

"An excellent, point, constable. Very well, what say *you*? Has a diabolical apparition been visiting your villages?"

"We have been visited by something or someone that is diabolically clever. I have no use for belief in anything supernatural."

"When it comes to criminal activity," said Holmes, "nor do I. In which case, we have no alternative but to conclude that the role of the apparition is being played by a human being. Would you agree?"

"Aye."

"Do you have any suspicions as to who it might be?"

"No."

"Would you agree that it is most likely being carried out by a woman?"

"No."

"And why not, sir?"

"The folks who have heard to Ben Shee say that they thought it had been a woman's voice but then the sounds that came from the ruins and the graveyard were a man's. It is hard to disguise the difference."

"Ah, yes of course. But other than those two occurrences, did the moans and screams sound as if coming from a woman?"

"Aye, they did."

"You are acquainted with all of the women folk in both villages, constable. Have you formed any suspicions as to who it might be?"

"Why confine it to the villages? There have been scores of visitors coming and going over the past two months."

"Another excellent point. Then permit me a rather blunt question. Have you had any reason to believe that the woman impersonating the Ben Shee might be Mrs. Gracie Burrell?"

A look of rage swept across Craigh's face. He leapt to his feet and moved towards Holmes.

"How dare you?" he said and added some rather vulgar curses and profanities which ended with his instructing to perform a solo sexual act which, as a medical doctor, I can confirm is anatomically impossible.

To my surprise, Holmes meekly apologized and assured the brute that he was only seeking to remove any possible suspicion that might arise. Craigh resumed his seat, and Holmes then gesticulated towards the locked storage cabinet.

"Very well, then, sir, if you will kindly open the locker, I shall review your notes, for which I thank you. Now, perhaps, Dr. Watson, could you kindly inform the constable what we have learned concerning the interest in the properties on either side of the narrows?"

I told what I had learned about the purchase of the boat and property from Edward Wallace in Lochalsh, and about the offer made to Lady Mackinnon for the property in Kyleakin. Constable Craigh listened attentively. I then recounted the assignment I have given to Howard Schapiro and my conclusion that his murder was directly connected to what he had discovered. That led to a sneer from Constable Craigh.

"Congratulations, doctor," he said. "You led a man who had nothing whatsoever to do with this mess to his death."

I had no response, and the pain of what he said was like a nail driven into my soul. Fortunately, Holmes interjected.

"For your accusation to be correct, Constable," said Holmes, "it would have to be true that the telegrams received by Mr. Schapiro contained the identity of the murderer. Would you agree?"

"Aye."

"As do I. Therefore, might I impose upon you to use your good offices as constable for the area to acquire copies of those telegrams from the Royal Mail. Is that possible?"

"Aye."

"How long would that take."

"An hour at most."

"Excellent. However, the messages will be written in the Yiddish language. Could you find a way to have them translated?"

"Aye. I can have that done. There is a Hebrew jeweler up in Portree. I can have them back here by this afternoon."

"Excellent, sir. Could you also speak with Mr. Maclean, the fellow who has leased the ferry and ascertain the name of the solicitor through whom he leased the boat? And then send off a telegram to that man demanding that the name of his client be made known? May I suggest that we meet in the pub at six o'clock? Chief Inspector Lestrade of Scotland Yard will be here by that time. Would that be acceptable?"

"Aye."

With that, Holmes thanked the man for his valuable service, and we departed.

"Where to now?" I asked.

"To have a chat with the terrible Ben Shee."

Chapter Eighteen
The Problem Barmaid

"AND JUST WHERE, HOLMES, are we going to find said frightful Ben Shee?" I asked.

"In the closet, I suspect, of Gracie Burrell's house."

"*She* is the Ben Shee?"

"Precisely."

"But," I protested, "Craigh was sincere, fiercely so, in opposing that suggestion."

"Precisely."

"Enough Holmes."

"Ah yes. His reaction merely proves that she has kept her secret hidden from everybody, including the oaf who was expressing his affections for her."

"So, how did you deduce that it was she?"

"Elementary, my dear friend. Reverend Fraser reported that the Ben Shee had red hair, as does Mrs. Burnell. You reported to me that she sings and recites poetry and had aspirations once for the theater. She fits the description of whoever it is that is playing the role of the Ben Shee."

"Good heavens, Holmes. We are in the Highlands of Scotland. Half of the women in this village have red hair, and they all have loud voices."

"Quite so, Watson. Therefore, I was led to my conclusion without the use of any logical deduction whatsoever. I merely waited for her to appear. Whilst you were sleeping soundly, I spent the hours close to midnight near the Bastard's Villa. When she appeared, I did not, as I had previously, interrupt her. I merely waited until she had finished and then surreptitiously followed her back to her house. I waited until six o'clock this morning when she again departed. She had her two small children with her and left them in the care of a neighbor and subsequently made her way to the pub to prepare for the morning breakfast shift."

"Then why are we now going to her house. She will still be at the pub."

"That shift ends at ten o'clock, allowing her almost two hours break before returning for the lunch service."

"Holmes," I said. "Are you saying that we are about to unlawfully enter her home and wait for her."

"Precisely. But we are doing so in the best interests of the young woman and her children."

There was no point in arguing with him, and we walked to a street two blocks back from the harbor. I kept looking around to see if anyone was observing us.

"Do relax yourself, Watson," said Holmes. "The men from this street are either out in their boats or at work in the pastures. All of the women are attending their weekly sewing and prayer session at the kirk, more commonly known amongst them as their weekly gathering of stitch and snitch."

At a small cottage halfway down the block, he turned through the gate and entered a well-kept front yard. A cheerful display of crocuses had forced their way up through the soil, and a few shoots of daffodils were poking into the daylight. Holmes went directly to the front door, turned the unlocked handle and entered.

The tiny house was a neat as a pin and spotless. A box in the corner held a small collection of much loved stuffed dolls and animals.

"Please, Watson, have a seat at the table in the kitchen whilst I make a quick search."

I did so and less than a minute later he came to the table bearing a long, dark green, hooded robe, which he laid across the table. He then made his way to the lavatory in the back of the house and returned with several jars of what appeared to be theatrical make-up. His last effort at foraging took somewhat longer, but eventually, I heard a triumphal "Ah ha!" coming from the bedroom.

"Here it is," he said. "The fearsome prop."

On the kitchen table, he placed a theatrical *biodag*, the long Highland dagger beloved of those actors who strode across the boards in *The Scottish Play*. The steel blade was gleaming, but the tip had a small steel ball affixed to it, and the sides of the blade were rounded. It had been fashioned so that it appeared realistic but prevented any untoward accidents in the staging of fights and murders.

I looked at my watch and ascertained that we likely had fifteen minutes or so still to wait. Holmes leaned back in his chair and by force of habit reached for his cigarette case.

"Holmes!" I snapped at him. "This young mother has children and does not foul the atmosphere of her home with tobacco smoke. Please be more considerate."

"Oh. Oh, yes. Of course. You are quite right." He put away his case and, having nothing to occupy his hands, he fidgeted constantly with his pen and nail file. He put them away quickly when we heard the front door open.

Mrs. Gracie Burrell shut the door behind her and moved rapidly into her kitchen. She stopped in her tracks when she saw Holmes and me sitting at her table. Her face first displayed shock and then anger.

"Get out of here this instant!" she shouted, and she lunged for the dagger on the table.

"Mrs. Burrell," said Holmes, "my name is Sherlock Holmes. We are here not to do you any harm but for the protection of yourself and your children."

"I know who you are," she said. "And you will get out of my house or so help me I will run this dagger into your guts. Now move!"

Holmes remained motionless and spoke calmly. "My dear lady, you know perfectly well that your dagger would leave no more than an unpleasant bruise on me. I assure you that if you will sit down and speak with us, it will be for your own good as well as your economic benefit."

As he spoke, he withdrew his billfold, took out a pound and laid it on the table. That caught her interest.

"You will have to do better than that, Mr. Holmes, to better the payment I already have."

"Ah, as I suspected," said Holmes, smiling. "You have been employed to put your dramatic talents to effect. Very well."

He laid two more pounds notes on the table. She looked at him and shook her head. He produced yet two more, and still she shook her head.

"You will have to do much better than that."

He reached out and withdrew the pile of currency and replaced it with a fifty-pound note.

"Mrs. Burrell, that is my final offer. Either you accept it and agree to answer all the questions I pose to you fully and truthfully, or I shall leave you to your fate."

Her eyes went wide looking at the note in front of her. She laid down the dagger, picked up the money, and sat down at the table across from us. Then she smiled. Perhaps smirked would be the better word.

"Auch, you may be a famous detective, but you no can bargain worth a toot wi a Scot. I'd have settled for ten. What is it you need to know?"

Holmes smiled back at her. "I need a truthful answer to this question. Who is paying you to perform as the Ben Shee and frighten the living lights out of the villagers?"

She laughed. "Oh, and do you like my performance? A wee bit proud of it myself. Haven't had so much fun since I played Lady Macbeth in high school."

"Madam, an answer, please."

"I do not know who is paying me."

"Mrs. Burrell," said Holmes, sharply.

"That, sir, is God's truth. For sure I would tell you if I did, but I don't. All my instructions have come by notes that are not signed and what I am paid comes the same way. I do not even have an address to send a note back. Whoever it is must be from the village as he knows every time I perform and sends another message. The notes are all in the drawer, you can read them yourself."

"I shall do that. Would you mind bringing them to me?"

The woman stood and walked over to a set of drawers beside her stove. From a lower drawer, she withdrew a stack of letters and handed them to Holmes.

"Most recent on the top. Earliest on the bottom."

Holmes quickly flipped through them. "These began about two months ago, is that correct."

"Aye, out of nowhere comes a letter asking if I could do a bit of theatrical work, that's what he called it."

"Why did you accept?"

"Because there was a five-pound note attached. I work all week to earn that much. If someone wants me to dress up and pretend and is willing to pay me five pounds, then I am all for it."

"Did he give you explicit instructions as to how to dress and what to look like?"

"Aye, that he did. He made it clear I was to seem like Lady Macbeth. The wee bit of fun adding the Saucy Mary action was my own doing, I admit."

"Does he say why he wanted you to frighten the villages with this horrid apparition?"

"Aye, he says so in his second letter. You can read it. He says he has secret information that someone is out to kill people in the village, and I am to play the Ben Shee as a way to warn them."

"Did it not occur to you that he could have just sent them a note directly telling them to take cover?"

"Aye, but he says that for some secret reason he canna do that. Who was I to argue? I would have been out my five pounds, wouldn't I? That's what he paid for every time I got up in the night and played the role. So far, I have earned thirty-five quid. That has been a boon to my bairnies. I am not about to bite the hand that's feeding me. Would you?"

Here I interjected. "Why did you warn me to leave when you first saw me in the pub?"

"I was paid to do that too. In his instructions, he said that I had to try to frighten not only the villagers as the Ben Shee of Lady Macbeth but any strangers who came into the village and seemed rather suspicious. And that, Doctor Watson, would be you."

I was not particularly flattered. Holmes resumed his cross-questioning.

"Why did you not inform Constable Craigh? You were quite closely acquainted with him, were you not?"

"Aye, I was. Thanks to you Mr. Holmes, that is over. Murray Craigh lied to the village about having lost his wife and child in a terrible accident in Aberdeen. He was a bit sweet on me and was useful. Came and fixed my gate and my roof, he did. But we all knew that he was only ever after one thing, and he certainly did not get that from me."

"What are your current instructions?" asked Holmes.

"I am to keep appearing up by the Bastard's Villa as often as I can, taking care not to let myself get caught. Almost happened a couple of nights back. Some scoundrel chased me all the way back to the houses. Was that you, Mr. Holmes? Well, you will just have to learn to run a wee bit faster in the dark if you are going to catch a Ben Shee."

She laughed and seemed to be enjoying her repartee with Holmes. He was not and came back on her sharply.

"Mrs. Burrell, this is not a laughing matter. Three people are now dead. Murdered. And their deaths can be directly connected to your actions, which would make you an accomplice to murder. If you are so accused and convicted, you will face at least ten years in prison, and you can bid goodbye to your children. Do you understand that, Mrs. Burrell?"

That caught her up short. The smirk disappeared, and color drained from her face.

"Sir, when I first received the messages I honestly believed that the sender was trying in his way to warn Mrs. Wallace and the Laird that their lives were in danger. When they were found dead, I feared that I had been too late. That is what I believed, sir. It was only when I received a note to appear over the window of the young American chap that I realized, to my horror, that whoever was sending me the notes and paying me might be doing the killing. When they brought the lad's body in we all could see that he had been killed before I was told to give the warning. Now, sir, I am quite certain that either the new laird or Lady Mackinnon is to be the next victim. I had determined that I would never appear again, but then I feared that if it was the killer sending me the messages and the payments, he might turn on me. My flippancy, Mr. Holmes, has been an act. I took it on as soon as you started offering me money. It worked for that. But, in truth, I am frightened."

"And with good reason," said Holmes. "Now, tell me truthfully, Mrs. Burwell, do you have any suspicions as to who in the village might have recruited you for this task?"

"As I said, it must be someone in the village. Else, how could he know my every move? But I cannot imagine who. Some say that there are no secrets in a village, but except for you and him what's paying me, no one here knows what I have been up to. Maybe it is one of the outsiders. We have a handful of them coming and going. Now it seems that him that's doing the killing has fixed on the laird or the widow Mackinnon. There's several here that might want him dead but none with enough hatred to do murder. None that I can see, sir."

For several seconds Holmes did not reply. Then he spoke to the young mother in a firm voice.

"Mrs. Burrell, for your sake and for your children, you should continue to do what you have been told to do. Otherwise, we would be sending a signal to the murderer that your disguise has been found out, and he would be likely to bolt. If you were told to appear again at the Bastard's Villa, then you must do that tonight and keep doing it if so instructed. May I have your word on that, Mrs. Burrell?"

"Aye, I will do that. Can you make sure that the folks up at the villa are not harmed?"

"I will act on that now," said Holmes. "I am also concerned at their situation. Perhaps you can recommend a few of the local men who can be trusted to stand guard and, if necessary, fight to protect those who are depending on them?"

"Are you willing to pay them?"

"Certainly."

"Auch, then any one of the men here will do it. If you need brawn, you can go and ask among the fishermen. They are all strong lads and live with hurt and pain every day. They will all be coming back in soon from their morning's work. Down at the dock is where you will find them."

Chapter Nineteen
Posting the Guards

AS GRACIE BURRELL HAD SAID, the fishing boats had returned to port by the late morning, so Holmes and I walked down to the wharf where the boats had been pulled up on the shore. We spied two boats close to each other, around which six men were now standing and chatting. Given their weather-beaten faces, it was hard to tell their age, but all of them looked sinewy and fit. Holmes approached them.

"Gentlemen," he said, "I am in need of your assistance and will pay a good wage for your service."

They looked at him and gave him a queer look indeed.

"Aye," said one, "and what is it you are offering, sir?"

"Tell me truthfully what you would earn from your catch on a good day, and I will pay that and half again."

The same man spoke again. Going by the leathery look of his countenance, he must have been the oldest of the group. "You're talking a good line, sir. On a good day, we might clear six shillings, if you're saying you can make that nine, then keep going."

"I will pay ten shillings a day," said Holmes. "You will work in shifts of eight hours each. Two at a time, around the clock."

"Keep talking, sir. What'll ye have us do?"

"Someone has threatened Lady Mackinnon and the new laird. I need brave guards to watch over the Bastard's Villa and make sure no harm comes to them. You may read whilst standing guard but no sleeping. If you wish to eat, you must bring your meal with you."

"And that's all? Just stand guard?" They were all now looking at us as if they had spotted a couple of city fools.

"Yes."

"And who has threatened the laird and the lady?"

"The Ben Shee."

Oh my, but didn't that set the cat amongst the pigeons. A flush of vexation passed over their faces and every one of the involuntarily backed away from us and cast furtive glances at each other. The senior man spoke for the group.

"Now that, sir, is a different kettle of fish. Every one of us risks his life every day at sea, but we don't risk our souls. If we perish at sea, then we go straight to the pearly gates and hope for a sympathetic hearing before St. Peter, the fisherman. But it is said that the Ben Shee will drag your soul kicking and screaming right down to hell. Of that sir, every one of us is terrified."

"Gentlemen, I assure you that the Ben Shee who has appeared around here recently is nothing more than a flesh and blood human being who is pretending to be a Ben Shee in order to frighten all of us."

That assurance did not go very far, so Holmes continued.

"I will improve my offer to twice your daily income. A pound a day."

"Can we bring a wee bit of liquid courage with us?" one of the younger men asked.

"No more than a hip flask. I need you to remain alert," replied Holmes.

"Any objection if the missus sits with us?"

"That is acceptable," said Holmes. "Now then. What do you say? Or shall I make my offer to your colleagues?"

The men looked at each other and carried out a silent round of shrugs and nods, and then the senior fellow announced their decision.

"Fine. We'll do it on those terms. When does the first shift start?"

"Now."

They quickly assigned themselves partners and allocated the rotating shifts. Just before our meeting broke up, the oldest fisherman put his hand on Holmes's shoulder.

"You seem like a decent lad," he said. "So, let me give you a wee bit of advice. When you're hiring a Highland fisherman, be sure to do your homework and learn the tides and the weather before making your offer."

Holmes looked straight at him, thoroughly perplexed. The man continued, smiling.

"There is a storm coming in, and the moon and sun are about to deliver a perigean spring tide. That combined with the high water from the thaw will make the narrows a death trap for the next few days. Not a man in the village will be doing any fishing until it all passes. We thank you for paying us handsomely when otherwise we would have been sitting on the shore earning nothing."

I made a mental note not to forget that a Londoner could lose his shirt doing business in the Highlands.

With our troop of guards hired, we walked back up the hill to the villa and waited near the gate for the first unit to arrive. Two of the fishermen soon appeared, having doffed their heavy wool sweaters and warm trousers, for their kilts. Both of them carried a Hercules club and had a dirk tucked into their belts.

"I would not," I said, "put my wager on a Ben Shee up against those two."

"If all goes well," said Holmes, "will never see such an encounter."

It was not necessary to introduce the guards to Lady Mackinnon or Hutchinson. They knew each other already. Laird Lionel was another matter. Again, he protested and assured us that no one would ever wish him harm, but he agreed to have the guards remain, noting how fabulous they looked in their kilts.

We were treated to a pleasant lunch on the long porch. Part way through the meal, I felt the wind change direction and become noticeably cooler. The weather was still damp and mild, but on the distant horizon, I could see the cumulonimbus clouds gathering on the horizon. Our guards were in for a wet night and would more than earn their wages.

At mid-afternoon, we began the descent back to the hotel. "Lestrade," said Holmes, "should be arriving sometime around supper. We can further review the constable's notes before he gets here."

Chapter Twenty
Lestrade Appears

TO MY SURPRISE, INSPECTOR LESTRADE had already arrived and was waiting for us at the pub. With him was Inspector Stanley Hopkins, a young policeman and one of the few of whom Holmes consistently spoke highly. At the table and conversing with them was Reverend Fraser. To be more accurate, Hopkins was chatting with Fraser whilst Lestrade was obviously enjoying the company of Mr. David Hume.

"Good heavens," I said as we approached their table. "You made it here awfully quickly."

"Dr. Watson," said Lestrade, smiling, "over the years I have learned that when a case becomes highly perplexing, *I* call in Sherlock Holmes. When Sherlock Holmes call *me* in, then I know that something bloody dangerous is in the works. Would you agree?"

"Quite so, Inspector. Nevertheless, you did make it in what must be record time."

"I hired a private car all the way," he said. "A bit of a dent in my budget but, as I said, I knew it was urgent. Had the ferryman do a special crossing too. Just as well. He said that with the super spring tide and the storm and such, the current would be so fierce over the next two days that there would be no crossings at all. Good thing I arrived when I did, or we would be standing on the shores shouting to each other. But now I am here, so best you get to work, gentlemen, and bring me up to snuff on this case."

Over the next hour, Holmes, Reverend Fraser and I informed the inspector on every detail we have managed to glean. Holmes concluded by making reference to the telegrams that were to arrive at six o'clock care of Constable Craigh, and which might shed light on the party trying to purchase the properties.

"The only thing," Holmes said, "that cannot be explained is why anyone in his right mind would wish to purchase the properties on either side of the narrows."

"It perfectly explicable," retorted Lestrade. "In a few more weeks those properties could take off like a shot. They will be worth ten, maybe even twenty times what they are now."

"How is that possible?" I asked.

"The bridge."

"What bridge?" I said.

"Ever since they finished the bridge in Edinburgh, the firms that designed and built it have been looking for other places that could use one."

"I know that," I said, having learned such just a week ago. "But they are talking about Canada and New York."

"And the Isle of Skye," said Lestrade. "The distance is less than across the Firth of Forth. There's an island conveniently in the middle of the gap. It could be done. Not surprised you have not heard about it. All still under wraps. But at the Yard, we had to investigate the parties involved. There was a whiff of fraud, so the file was referred to us before going to the Cabinet. All those whose fingers are in the pie are clean, and it is not up to us to comment on what is economically imbecilic. That is the province of politicians."

Holmes slowly leaned back and smiled.

"Thank you, Inspector. We now have a strong motive. Fast, easy money to be made with no effort. It is not the first time we have seen it. And the method? Terrify the current owners into selling and if they do not come around quickly, murder them. And the means? Shoot them, and then run a knife up through their torsos to invoke the spirit of Macbeth. All we need now is a prime suspect. And that data should arrive at six o'clock when our boorish but competent constable reports on the ownership of the American firm making the offers. He should be here in half an hour. Until then, gentlemen, I suggest a round of brandies as perhaps a small down payment on an event soon to be celebrated."

We ordered a round, and a couple of us continued chatting about various aspects of the case. Inspector Hopkins, zealous young police officer that he was, plied Holmes with question after question about his methods and experiences. Lestrade, Fraser and Mr. David Hume went outside and played fetch and catch.

Six o'clock came and passed.

At a quarter past the hour, Lestrade and his sporting companions entered the pub.

"You said," said Lestrade, "that this constable fellow was reliable, Holmes. Where is he?"

"Please be patient. I have been wrong before," said Holmes. Under his breath, I heard him mutter, "Once or twice."

At six-thirty, Holmes checked his watch yet again and began those movements of impatience that led him to get up and look out the door. Seeing nothing, he returned. At six-forty the chap from the front desk of the hotel walked up to our table.

"Mr. Holmes," he said. "I was just now informed that you were in the pub. I apologize for not getting this to you sooner."

He handed Holmes a small envelope out of which he drew a handwritten note.

"It is from the constable. It reads: *If you want to apprehend your murderer, I am holding him in my office. Come at once.* Very well, then. Let us remove ourselves from here and pay a visit to our confident constable."

The five of us—six counting Mr. David Hume—departed the pub and walked the few yards east along the water's edge to the constable building. Holmes knocked on the door.

There was no answer.

He opened it and stepped inside. I followed close behind him. Both of us stopped in our tracks.

"What's wrong?" shouted Lestrade behind us.

The stench was overpowering.

Lestrade, Hopkins and the reverend entered and without speaking all of us except for the clergyman exchanged horrified knowing looks with each other. We recognized a stench we had been assaulted by all too often in our lives spent in medicine or the pursuit of criminals. It was the horrible smell that a man's body makes soon after death as his bladder and bowels lose control and void themselves.

The front room was empty. Holmes slowly moved to the door into the room used to confine those who had transgressed the law. As he opened it, a much strong odor swept across us. The source was now obvious. Lying prone on the floor was the large body of Constable Murray Craigh. Wet blood soaked his chest area. His intestines and organs had spilled out of his abdomen. He had been *unseamed from the nave to the chops*. The smell was nauseating.

Lestrade and I both snapped out our handkerchiefs and held them to our faces as we knelt down to inspect the body. Inspector Hopkins rushed to unlock any windows in the building that could be flung open. Holmes began a furious search through the drawers and cabinets for whatever documents the constable might have obtained that day. Reverend Fraser, accompanied by a whimpering Mr. David Hume, retreated entirely from the building, announcing that he would fetch the mortician.

"He was shot directly in the heart," I observed.

"Yes," agreed Lestrade, "and from point-blank range. You can see the powder residue and burns along with the blood."

Holmes walked over and looked down on us. "We may as well wait outside. Any useful documents have been removed."

He turned and exited the building. The rest of us followed. Standing out on the pavement, Holmes turned to Lestrade.

"I have made the same error in judgment as Dr. Watson did with Howard Shapiro. Having secured the information that identified the murderer, Howard foolishly must have tried to apprehend him by himself. Constable Craigh also took it upon himself to arrest the villain rather than wait for the arrival of Scotland Yard. Both underestimated the cold-blooded character of a man who apparently does not flinch either from killing or desecrating his victim's bodies. We need to find him and stop him before he kills again."

"And you believe that he will try to murder the laird, is that right?" asked Lestrade.

"That is my expectation at this time," said Holmes. "Very well then," said Lestrade. "We shall proceed with systematic police work the way we professionals have to. Sorry if that does not appeal to you, Mr. Holmes. But we shall just have to make an exhaustive list of suspects, round them all up, and give them all the third degree. Whoever this monster is, he cannot leave the island what with the ferry stopped and the narrows in a maelstrom. Shall we get to work, gentlemen?"

"My dear Inspector," said Holmes, "with great respect, allow me to suggest that there might be a more efficient and effective method to consider."

"I am listening, Holmes. Make it snappy."

"The local ferry service may be temporarily curtailed, but we are on a very large island. There are several score of villages of comparable size to this one as well as towns such as Portree that are more substantial. A large-scale rounding up of the men of the village, all except one of whom are completely innocent, would not only tip our hand to the villain and send him packing to some remote corner of the Isle, but it would needlessly antagonize the local population whose help we may seek to enlist."

"Then you better have an alternative to suggest, Holmes," said Lestrade.

"I do," said Holmes. "And may I request that we proceed immediately to the Bastard's Villa to have a chat with Lady Mackinnon and Laird Lionel?"

Chapter Twenty-One
The Trap is Set

"NOW LET ME TRY TO UNDERSTAND what you are saying," said Lionel Mackinnon, looking oddly both confused and eager. "You are telling me that some demented madman is intent on killing me so he can gain title to this obscure parcel of rocky property."

"That is correct," affirmed Holmes.

"And," continued the laird, "you want Rebecca to set the trap by telling whoever it was who wanted to buy the property that she would truly love to sell it but that *I* am standing in the way of her doing so."

"Correct as well," said Holmes.

"And you want me to serve as the bait for the trap and to leave my now well-protected home—for which I thank you—and go out walking along the paths of the town so that someone as yet unidentified can try to kill me."

"Precisely."

"Somehow, this does not strike me as being a particularly fabulous idea," said the laird. "Can any of you dear chaps give me a good reason why I should agree to such a plan?"

"Because," said Holmes, "if we do not stop this villain now he is going to keep on trying to kill you until he succeeds."

"Oh, very well. I suppose that is not a bad reason. Capital. Quite so. So, say again how this is going to work."

Holmes explained proposed scheme. Straight away, Lady Mackinnon would send a wire off to the party who had expressed a desire to purchase the property. She would inform them that while she was eager to sell for any reasonable price, her brother-in-law was not. He was the only obstacle standing in the way of a successful transaction and appeared rather adamant in his resolve.

Although this wire would be sent to America, Holmes reasoned that within an hour or two it would be forwarded back to the killer by a circuitous means that had been established to protect the identity of the recipient.

Next, beginning this evening, Laird Lionel would take an evening stroll down the hill and along the waterfront. He would be carefully watched by the rest of us, who would be hidden at strategic points along the way, armed and ready to pounce should any suspicious body be seen approaching the laird.

The identity of Lestrade and Hopkins as inspectors from Scotland Yard would not be revealed to the villagers. The local councilors and the mortician would take care of the body of Constable Craigh. No official statement would be made as to the cause of death, allowing the rumor mill to manufacture another visitation of the Ben Shee.

"Quite frankly, Holmes," opined Lestrade, "this sounds utterly ridiculous. It is beyond praying."

"An element of hoping against the odds is admittedly present," said Holmes. "Do you, Inspector, have a better alternative that can be implemented quickly and will not tip our hand to the killer?"

"No, Holmes. I do not."

"Neither do I," said Holmes. "Thus, are we agreed to give it our best try?"

"Agreed," said Lestrade and Hopkins concurred.

"Just a moment," said Laird Lionel. "What about me? Do I not get to voice my opinion?"

"Of course, sir," said Lestrade. "What might be your concern?"

"Well," he said, adding a touch of drama, "I will have you know that when it comes to taking walks in the evening, and after dark, in Paris, New York, London, or even Chicago, I am quite fearless. I have found my way home in the wee small hours of the morning countless times in those great cities. But, as we say in France, *J'ai peur de la nature.* I find the experience of being all by myself in the woods or along a river altogether just too frightful. I do not believe I could do it. At least not alone."

He was sitting with his shoulders rounded and wringing his delicate hands as he spoke; his fingers as agitated as the antennae of an insect. There was no doubt as to his sincerity.

"It would not do, sir," said Inspector Hopkins, "for one of us to be with you. No villain acting alone is going to attack two men walking together."

"Well," continued the laird, "that just will not do. You will have to come up with a better idea."

For a minute, none of us said anything. All were pondering an alternative solution. Then the reverend spoke.

"What if Mr. David Hume were to accompany you. He's good company. His bark will scare off any menacing rabbit or mole that might threaten you."

"Oh, yes, well, that might work," said the laird.

He knelt down in front of Mr. David Hume and extended his hand. The collie returned the gesture. A conversation ensued.

"So, my pretty puppy," he said, "are we going to be friends and go for nice walks together. Yes, we are. Yes, we are, you pretty puppy." The dog moved forward and gave a friendly lick to the laird's face.

"Excellent," said Holmes, "then that is settled. Lady Rebecca's telegram shall be sent off forthwith. At dusk, we shall have a trial run. Oh, and one more thing. Laird Lionel, I strongly advise that you and Lady Mackinnon make out your wills immediately. Your doing so will significantly lessen the appeal of your deaths to any currently unknown kin."

Holmes, Hopkins, Lestrade and I departed from the villa. The reverend, having been invited to stay for an evening tea and chat by Lady Rebecca, remained behind. The four of us casually sauntered down the hill towards the town and, on reaching the fork where the path along the water branched off, turned and followed it back towards the narrows. Making an effort to avoid giving away our purpose, Holmes and Lestrade selected six different locations where a man could hide and yet be close enough to leap to the rescue if the young laird were threatened.

"But there are only five of us," I said. "And I am not certain how quickly the reverend could run."

"A good point, Watson," said Holmes. "We shall have Inspector Hopkins, the youngest and most nimble of us take the first station. Once Lionel has passed him, he can scramble down the steep face of the hill and also take the last position. Can you manage that, Hopkins?"

"I can do that, Mr. Holmes," said the young inspector.

With that, we parted. Lestrade and Hopkins made their way to the Royal Mail office to send off their first round of reports and Holmes informed me that we would be spending the rest of the evening in the pub.

"Why?" I demanded.

"Elementary, my good doctor. To eavesdrop.".

Chapter Twenty-Two
The Horror of the Bastard's Villa

A SHARED TRAGEDY is one of the strongest forces known to man to bring the members of a neighborhood together. There is something, some part of our souls that knows without being able to express it in words, that we need to be not alone but in the company of our fellow human beings. So, it was that evening in the village of Kyleakin. The brutish boorish constable was not a popular man, not by a long shot. But he was the constable, and he was *their* constable. News of his murder spread quickly from one house to the next bringing the inhabitants out of their cozy front rooms and kitchens and into those places where they customarily gathered. The more pious members of the village gathered on the steps and inside the hall of the kirk. Those less inclined to beseeching the divine with their orisons soon filled the pub.

The mortician had quickly removed the constable's body to his parlor, and no one had issued any public statement as to what had happened. The usual more or less reliable sources of information for the village—the publican, the hotel clerk, the postmaster, the members of the village council, the ferryman, the reverend and, indeed, the constable himself—were either not present or were as completely in a fog as the crofter or the fisherman. In such a void, rumors sprang up quickly.

So far, Holmes's identity was not widely known in the village. Whilst he and I sat in a corner of the pub, we heard one distorted version after another about the events of earlier that evening. Within an hour, however, a consensus appeared to have emerged that it must have been the Ben Shee striking again. A few dissenting voices insisted that such a conclusion was naught but superstitious fantasy but, as is the case all over the earth, fear triumphed over reason, and the Ben Shee won out. The volume of the room slowly diminished as the shouting and speeches collapsed into quiet, fearful whispering.

The usually cheerful and effervescent Grace Burwell was serving the tables but doing so in sullen silence. She approached our table and, in a whisper of intense earnestness, spoke to Holmes.

"Mr. Holmes, must I go and be the Ben Shee again tonight? Can it not be put off? The village is already terrified, and it is my fault. Do I have to do it?"

"With my sincere sympathy, Mrs. Burwell, yes. We must do nothing to give the villain any hint that he has now become the hunted. However, let me assure you that we are doing our utmost to bring this spate of horror to a close. So please, madam, just be brave and carry on."

Later that night, I retired to my bed at a reasonable hour. Holmes did not. The following morning, he reported that the Ben Shee had appeared at around half twelve in the vicinity of the Bastard's Villa. By noon the next day, the entire village was expecting the imminent demise of either the new laird or Lady Rebecca.

Late in the afternoon, our troop assembled at the villa to go over our plan. The reverend attached a short leash to Mr. David Hume and handed the other end of it to Laird Lionel.

"Why is he on a leash," I asked. "You have him so well trained that the laird could play toss and fetch with him and he would keep coming back."

"Oh, yes," said the laird, "that is a splendid idea. Do give me your tennis ball and my pretty puppy and I shall have a delightful time."

No!" snapped the reverend. We were surprised by his rebuke and the stern look on his face. He immediately recovered and softened his countenance.

"You will be walking along the edge of the water," he explained patiently. "If the ball takes a bounce the wrong way and ends up in the channel, my dog, or any dog for that matter, will run right into the water after it. Mr. David Hume may be a smart collie, but no dog can understand that the tidal current would sweep him away. You can play toss and fetch with him in the graveyard until the cows come home, but never beside a moving body of water."

That made complete sense, and I apologized for my foolish suggestion. Holmes explained that he did not expect anything untoward to happen this evening and we were merely conducting a practice run that would not only prepare us but also alert the villain to a new pattern of behavior by the laird.

At dusk, the five sentinels stealthily made their way to their hidden lookout points. Hopkins was assigned the first station, about thirty or forty yards down the hill from the villa. He was also given charge of the last station, along the water's edge path not far from the narrows. He diligently picked out a route down the boulder-sprinkled steep face of the hill which would allow him to move from the first station to the final one whilst the laird and Mr. David Hume traversed the path down from the villa and back along the edge of the water.

Unseen from even a close distance, we silently moved through the copses of trees and bushes of the side of the hill and into our places. Holmes took up the station half way between Hopkins and the confluence of the path up to the villa and the one that led along the channel. Lestrade was positioned where the two routes met. I took my place forty yards farther along the channel path, the reverend another forty yards, and then the final spot would be covered again by Inspector Hopkins.

Just before sunset, Laird Lionel came out of the villa accompanied by Mr. David Hume. From my vantage point, I watched the two of them, and it was not at all clear who was leading whom. The laird and his dog—or perhaps it was more the dog and his laird—strutted and hopped down the hill past Hopkins, then Holmes, and then to the fork in the paths. They turned and walked along the path by the water, passing first myself, then Reverend Fraser, and finally Hopkins one more time. When they reached the spot adjacent to the narrows, they turned around and walked back. Both the collie and the laird seemed to be having a fine time of it and variously ran short distances, pranced around in circles, and stopped so that the laird could catch his breath.

"Brilliant, gentlemen," concluded Holmes, after we had silently returned from our stations to the villa. "We shall repeat the scheme tomorrow night, and possibly a third time. I fully expect that by that point our villain will sense his opportunity and strike. We shall be ready for him."

Throughout the following day, Holmes, Hopkins, and Lestrade confined themselves to their rooms and had their meals sent up. The reverend made a point of announcing in the pub that would be going up to Portree for a couple of days on church business and would be leaving his dog with the new laird, who seemed quite attracted to such a pretty puppy. Of course, he made it no farther along the road north to Portree that the Bastard's Villa, where he seemed to be content to remain and enjoy the food and company.

At twilight, we took up our stations. Laird Lionel and Mr. David Hume took their evening stroll as scheduled.

Nothing happened. Sometime around midnight, the Ben Shee made yet another terrifying visitation not far from the villa.

Our actions the following day were the same. When we assembled in the villa in the early evening, Holmes was quite confident.

"The laird has established a pattern of behavior, and I fully expect that our killer will strike this evening. He will likely appear coming up the road from the village whilst the laird and the dog are walking towards the narrows and then attempt to strike him on the way back. It is also possible he will attack closer to the villa although that is less likely given the visible presence of the guards. We shall be prepared for all possibilities."

Again, nothing happened. And again, the Ben Shee appeared and moaned and screamed. A part of me had to admire the theatrical talents of Mrs. Burwell.

"Look here, Holmes," said Lestrade as we gathered in his room the following morning. "this is not the only place in Britain where a criminal is on the loose. Hopkins and I cannot simply sit around doing nothing in this forsaken corner of the country. The rush of the tide will soon subside, and the ferry will be running tomorrow afternoon. If nothing happens again tonight, we will be on it and back to London."

"Of course, Inspector," said Holmes. "That is entirely understandable. If this evening passes quietly, I shall have to conclude that our prey has taken flight and we will have lost him.

So, we took up our posts for the fourth time. I watched the laird and the collie pass, continue on to the narrows, turn around and come back. They had almost reached the meeting of the two paths when I noticed a dark shape rise up from what had appeared to be a mound of boulders. It was hard to see clearly what it was but it was moving silently behind the laird.

Mr. David Hume suddenly turned and began barking. The laird looked behind him, let out a scream and started to run quickly. The figure was running behind him, and in the darkness, I caught a gleam of what looked like a cutlass being brandished above the head of a hooded figure. The laird was now screaming and running hard, but the hooded man was closing in on him.

I had drawn my service revolver and was running through the copse toward the path. Many years ago, during my rugby days, I was a strong runner. That skill ended when a Jezail bullet hit my leg, and the old wound was screaming with pain. Nevertheless, I kept moving as quickly as I could. In a rush, the long-limbed body of Inspector Hopkins flashed past me. He was moving at a furious rate of speed, leaping over ditches, rocks and any obstacle that stood in his way. Up ahead, I could hear the panicked screams of Laird Lionel and the barking of the dog.

"HALT! Scotland Yard!" Lestrade's voice rang out. He had entered the path and now stood directly in front of the fleeing laird and the hooded villain. I could faintly see him, but he appeared to be holding an electric torch in one hand and a gun in the other. The laird ran past him and collapsed on the ground. The hooded figure stopped and turned around to run in the opposite direction.

"HALT!" shouted Inspector Hopkins, who had now caught up with him from behind. "Drop the knife. Now! You have two guns pointed at you. Drop the blade."

The figure froze in place for several seconds and then the cutlass clanged on the ground.

Holmes had appeared behind Lestrade, and I had caught up to Hopkins. A few seconds later the reverend came lumbering up behind me.

"Mr. Godfrey Thurlow, I presume," said Holmes.

Inspector Hopkins had come up behind the fellow and pulled down the hood exposing his face, now lit up by Lestrade's torch. It was the young man from the Hydrographic Office of the Admiralty.

The young man was looking back and forth quickly. The flashes I saw of his face indicated desperate fear and panic. We had surrounded him. There was nowhere for him to run.

"You are under arrest," said Lestrade. "You do not have to say anything, but it may harm your defense if you do not mention, when questioned, something which you later rely on in court. Anything you do say may be given in evidence. Now, slowly extend your hands."

Lestrade put his gun away and pulled out a set of darbies. Hopkins stepped forward to kick the cutlass away from anywhere within reach of the man who was just arrested.

Thurlow slowly extended his wrists, palms open and up. Then, in a flash, he snapped his right hand back, slipped it inside his cloak and brought it back out, holding a small revolver. He pointed it directly at Laird Lionel.

"Get back!" he shouted. "All of you get back, or I shoot the laird."

"Don't be a fool," retorted Lestrade. "You cannot escape." Nevertheless, he made no attempt to disarm Thurlow, who stepped forward quickly until he was standing directly beside Laird Lionel and holding the gun directly against his chest.

"Move away!" Thurlow screamed. He had now moved behind the laird and put his forearm around the head and neck of the shorter man. The gun had moved upwards so that it was now aimed directly at the laird's temple.

"I am going to the ferry, and he's coming with me. Do not dare follow me or I will kill him."

He began walking backward, pulling the laird quite viciously with him.

"Oww! You're choking me," cried Lionel. "You don't have to hurt me. OWW!"

From down near my feet, I heard a low, menacing growl. Then there was a blur of black and white, and Mr. David Hume let out a sharp bark and lunged at Thurlow. He leapt directly at his upper legs and planted his teeth firmly into the fleshy part of Thurlow's inner thigh.

The villain screamed in pain. He dropped his right hand from the laird's temple, pointed the gun directly at the collie's head and fired. The loud retort echoed across the harbor. Blood and pieces of the dog's skull and brain spattered and it fell dead onto the path.

"Noo!" I screamed in horrified anguish.

The reverend did not scream. As the reflexive cry was coming out of my mouth, he stepped forward and with the weight of his large, powerful body behind it, delivered what the pugilists call a haymaker. He swung his right fist up and into Thurlow's jaw before the gun could be raised. I heard what was either a jawbone breaking or dislocating. The blow knocked Thurlow off his feet and he stumbled toward the edge of the path. As he staggered to regain his balance he lost his footing and fell down the embankment toward the water, ending up in the shallow water at the edge of the channel. He stood up but slipped and fell again. He struggled to stand up again but was now two yards from the edge. He tried to walk back and again fell over. The current was pulling him away and deeper into the channel. Again, he tried to stand only to find that the bottom had fallen away. Now he was attempting to swim back to shore, rendered impossible by the heavy hooded cloak. Desperately, he pushed the cloak off his arms and broke free of its weight. He had been moved by the current more than ten yards from the shore, and the distance was increasing every second. He began flailing his arms in an attempt to swim back to safety.

"Help!" he shouted. "Help me!"

I had learned water rescue in my years in the military and instinctively threw off my jacket and was about to reach down and pull off my boots when a powerful set of hands fixed themselves on my arm and made me immobile.

"No, doctor," said Inspector Hopkins. "You cannot go in after him."

"If the current sweeps him into the narrows, he's a goner," I shouted.

"Yes, and so will you be," said Hopkins. I struggled briefly, but the powerful young police officer held onto me like a vice.

Thurlow's screams of "Help, help!" were louder and more terrified as he was pulled farther and farther away from the shore. Lestrade had his torch light trained on him, and we could see his arms moving like a windmill out of control as he tied to get to shore.

It was no use. No matter how hard he swam, the forceful current was overpowering him and sweeping him closer and closer to the maelstrom of whirlpools and eddies that was boiling in the narrows as the flooded spring tide poured out from the loch and into the sea.

It is a soul-destroying thing to stand on the shore and watch a man drown. I closed my eyes so that I could no longer see his disappearing head and arms, but his cries for help kept coming as he came closer and closer to the narrows.

Then they ceased.

For what seemed an eternity, the group of us stood on the shore and said nothing. I finally turned around to see that the reverend had picked up the limp body of his beloved collie and was sitting on a nearby rock with Mr. David Hume across his lap. The man had buried his head in his hands and was visibly sobbing. Slowly he raised his head and spoke to Lestrade.

"You may as well arrest me," he said.

"Why would I do that?" came the sharp answer.

"Because it is by my hand that the man is dead. You know that," he said, his voice breaking.

"You didn't kill him," said Lestrade. "The water killed him. I cannot arrest the tide."

"Please, Inspector," pleaded Fraser. "I knocked him into the channel. You saw that."

"I saw nothing of the kind," said Lestrade. "I saw him try to take the laird as a hostage and your brave dog come to his aid. He fell into the water after being bit by the dog. That is what you saw as well, Hopkins, is it not."

For a second Hopkins said nothing and then replied. "Oh, right, sir. Right. That is exactly what I saw."

"And," said Lestrade, "Mr. Sherlock Holmes and Dr. Watson will sign a statement saying that they observed the exact same thing. Now, my good man, try to pull yourself together. I am very sorry about the loss of your collie. He was a very brave fellow. You should be proud of him."

Lestrade leaned over the reverend and put his hand on his shoulder for several seconds and then helped the big man to his feet.

I turned to the laird. "Are you all right, sir?" I asked.

"Oh, yes, yes. Quite all right. That man was not a gentleman, but I shall be fine. I am more concerned for our dear minister."

He stepped over to the reverend and took him by the arm.

"Let me take Reverend Fraser back up to the villa. Becky and I can take care of him." He gently steered the much larger man along the path, leaving the four of us standing in silence. Finally, Inspector Lestrade cleared his throat and spoke.

"I need to prepare a statement. Please come with me to the pub where we can sit and talk. Dr. Watson, if you see any of the fishermen there, you might advise them to be on the lookout for another body."

Chapter Twenty-Three
Lined Up for a Baked Potato

"MAY I BRING YOU MEN a wee dram to warm your souls on a cold night," asked Gracie Burwell of the glum quartet of us who had taken a table in the back of the pub."

"Talisker's," she continued, "is just across on the other side of the Isle. It costs next to nothing to transport it here, so the price is no so dear as those from the mainland."

We took her up on her offer and she re-appeared a few minutes later with a round of generous glasses. Holmes looked up at her and expressed his thanks.

"And," he added, "I am sure that from now on you shall enjoy peaceful and uninterrupted full nights' sleep."

She looked down at his smile for a moment and then a warm intensity of feeling lightened her countenance.

"Thank you, Mr. Holmes, I shall do that."

Lestrade turned his ferret-like face at Holmes and gave him a queer look. "And what, Holmes, was that all about?"

"The young woman looked rather weary, did you not observe? I just wished her well."

Lestrade continued to glare at Holmes and then relaxed and shrugged his shoulders. "What am I going to do with you, Holmes?"

"If at all possible, my dear inspector, nothing at all."

Lestrade picked up his glass of single malt, stared at it for several seconds and then took a substantial sip.

"Right. What I will do is demand how you knew it was the chap from the Admiralty who was behind it all."

"I will readily admit," said Holmes, "That until I observed the slender shape of his body under his cloak, I was not certain. Several people had reason to do in the old laird and had the opportunity. Following the reliable principle of *cui bono,* at first, I suspected the belligerent constable who was so self-centered in his refusal to notify his superiors or Scotland Yard of the initial murders. However, getting yourself shot and splayed open serves to remove you from the list of suspects.

"When you so kindly informed us of the potential windfall to be made from the construction of the bridge, I focused on the unpleasant and non-communicative ferryman. He profited substantially from the death of Mrs. Annie Wallace and his claim to have leased the boat through some unnamed solicitor in Glasgow acting on behalf of a firm in New York was suspect. He might well have been the actual purchaser of the boat and property. However, on the night that Howard Shapiro died, the ferry was docked over in Lochalsh. Unless he had an accomplice on this side of the channel, he was ruled out.

"The old crofter, Garnet Baine, might have been a miserable, hostile so-and-so, and the crofters do hold longstanding desires for revenge against the lairds because of the Clearances. But the remaining crofters now have legal title to their properties. The Clearances ended fifty years ago and whilst revenge may be best enjoyed cold, a half a century is a bit long to carry a desire for murderous vengeance, even for a Scot.

"Both Lady Rebecca and the new laird, Lionel, profited enormously from the death of Hamish Mackinnon. I have learned the hard way that a most winning woman can be an evil and vile murderess, and the most gentle-spirited man can be a Mr. Hyde in the darkness. *Cui bono* demanded that they be prime suspects. With these two, however, I had to trust in my emotional response to them. Lady Rebecca struck me as an honest and caring woman, and Laird Lionel is just too … shall we say *light on his feet* to imagine undertaking the disembowelment of several people, even if he has spent time in America.

"My first suspicion of Godfrey Thurlow came when standing behind him here in the pub. He was waiting for his lunch and said that he was in line for his fish and baked potato. Englishmen do not line up, we queue. We do not eat baked potatoes, we eat jacket potatoes. His choice of words was a clear indication that he had spent significant time in America, most likely whilst attending university and acquiring his extensive scientific knowledge.

"But," I protested, "it was reported that he went to Cambridge. No one appeared to question that."

"Ah, careful there, my dear friend," said Holmes. "Those are not the words you recorded and reported of what was said."

I had to wrack my brain to remember exactly what it was I had written. "He said that he had gone to school in Cambridge."

"Precisely. And you know perfectly well that there is another Cambridge where one may attend an excellent school and register an American corporation."

"In Massachusetts," I said, somewhat chagrined.

"Precisely. When I heard his use of American diction, I became suspicious and sent a wire off to my contacts at Cambridge University asking if he had attended. It was returned post haste stating the negative. Thereupon, I sent one off to the Hydrographic Office of the Admiralty asking to confirm his employment. It came back with a positive response, but with an addendum noting that was on short-term leave. The specific nature of his assignment was classed as confidential, but it was disclosed that he had been seconded to assist the firm of Siemens and Brothers."

"Who are they?" asked Hopkins.

"They were one of the major suppliers of steel for the Firth of Forth bridge," said Holmes. "It was a very profitable venture, and they are eager to repeat their success. Mr. Thurlow was not investigating the currents and flows for the sake of navigation safety, but for the sake of building foundations for a bridge. He knew that and, upon arriving here, he cleverly understood the immense value of the land on either side of the narrows. Had he been successful in acquiring the properties and had the bridge gone ahead, he would suddenly become a very wealthy man, and he was prepared to terrify and murder to accomplish his end.

"He quickly did away with Mrs. Wallace over in Lochalsh and bought her family's land from her distressed widowed husband. He nearly accomplished the same by killing the old laird. His widow would have sold everything as well, but the long-lost brother, Lionel, suddenly appeared and foiled the enterprise. He would no doubt have murdered Lionel at the first opportunity, except that such an opportunity did not present itself. Lionel was a homebody and quite taken with his new abode. His butler and staff were always present, and the reverend and Dr. Watson became constant visitors. The two guards added a further barrier. It was only when Lionel began taking evening strolls with Mr. David Hume that he became vulnerable. And we were lying in wait for him."

"*We* were lying in wait?" snorted Lestrade. "You mean *he* was waiting for his prey. We came within a whisker of having him murder and disembowel the laird."

"Yes, Inspector," said Holmes. "Thurlow must have secreted himself under his robe and assumed the form of a small boulder at least two hours before the laird passed by. I had underestimated his determination and patience."

"And what about the banshee?" demanded Lestrade. "How did he arrange that?"

"The *what*?" asked Holmes.

"The banshee. The entire village has been talking about their demonic banshee and how it foretold the coming deaths. They are saying that it was the banshee who came and killed everyone. Surely, you heard all about that."

"Local people will have their superstitions, Inspector. They are attractive to a collector of fairy tales, but hardly to anyone who believes in the science of deduction.".

An Epilogue

LESTRADE AND HOPKINS DEPARTED Kyleakin the next morning and Holmes, and I followed in the afternoon. Lady Rebecca Mackinnon let it be known that she would be on her way to America within the week and Lionel Mackinnon joyfully embraced his new responsibilities as laird of the region. He became inseparable from his kilt, knee socks and sash, and was duly invited to attend all meetings of the local council.

Reverend Fraser resumed his duties to his scattered flock and would soon be seen plodding his way from house to house and village to village in pursuit of his ministerial duties. It was reported to me that his loyal congregation in Kylealsh offered to find him a new collie to replace Mr. David Hume, but the reverend graciously declined the kindness, saying that he would need time to adjust to the loss.

Holmes knew I would soon forgive and forget my anger at him for deceiving me with his frightful disguise as the second Ben Shee. He was right. Although, I confess, I did from time to time smile as I remembered my perfect knock to the base of his occipital bone. Served him right.

Four weeks later, I had a summons from Holmes asking if I could come by 221B the following afternoon as he was expecting visitor and thought I might like to join him. Any request from Holmes for me to meet a client always brought my immediate positive response for it usually meant the beginning of yet another adventure.

I arrived at the appointed time in the late afternoon, was welcomed by Mrs. Hudson and entered the familiar front room of 221B to be greeted warmly by Holmes. I had no more than sat down when another knock came to the door, and a few moments later Mrs. Hudson announced our visitor.

"It is the Reverend Donald Fraser. This time he has come by himself."

Into the room strode the big old clergyman. He was beaming a broad smile, looked relaxed and fit, and even had a bit of a spring in his step.

"So good of you to drop in," said Holmes. "Can we offer you a cup of tea?"

"No, but you can offer me a decent glass of the same fine single malt you did last time I was here."

We both just stared at him in obvious shock. He laughed.

"I have officially retired. The good Lord has seen fit to provide a much younger clergyman to replace me. I am now free and my chief end shall be to glorify God and enjoy Him forever… on my exegesis, for my remaining years on His good earth."

"Have you come to live in London?" I asked incredulously.

"Goodness, no. I am on my way to America. New York, to be specific."

"How are you going to live?" I asked. "It is a frightfully expensive city. Your clergy pension would not cover more than a room in a boarding house in the Bronx."

"I am to be the guest of Lady Rebecca Mackinnon. She has acquired a lovely brownstone on the Upper East Side and a week ago sent me a letter inviting me to come and live with her."

I was shocked. "Pardon me, reverend, but surely you are not telling us that you, an unmarried man, are going to live under the same roof as an unmarried woman?"

"And share the same bed," he added, again with a laugh. "Oh, no. That would be too much. In her letter, she also proposed that we get married. She cannot abide dining out or attending the theater alone in New York but neither can she stand the American men she has been introduced to there. The word has gone around that she is an exceptionally rich widow and she has been beset with no end of fawning, parasitical social climbers. She told me that I was the one man whose company she had consistently enjoyed over the past twenty years and has deduced that our intimacy has ripened into love. As we were now both without spouses and time is marching on, it seemed a good idea for us to be married as soon as possible. Whoso findeth a wife, findeth a good thing, aye? So, I agreed, and I am on my way to be a gentleman of erudite leisure in the new world."

"Are you," I asked, my many years of medical consulting coming into play, "sure that you will be physically and emotionally compatible?"

He paused and then smiled. "No, I canna say that for sure."

"And what will you do," I said in heartfelt consideration, "if it turns out that the two of you do not get along? Forgive me for pointing out that both of you are no longer young and may be quite set in your ways."

He paused and rubbed his chin in thought. Then a sly grin crept across his face.

"One thing I am sure of, doctor, is that if I am not to enjoy marital bliss, auch ... they have border collies in America."

Historical and Other Notes

In searching for a suitable supernatural element for this tribute story, I felt that I could not just repeat a demonic dog, ghosts were too commonplace, and zombies and vampires too far removed from the Canon. I reached back into my childhood and recalled the movie that had terrified me as a child, the Walt Disney film, *Darby O'Gill and the Little People*. The scenes in that movie of the visit of the Banshee frightened me half to death and no doubt left psychological damage from which I never fully recovered. In researching the legend of the Banshee, I was pleased to discover that there was a version of it—the Ben Shee—in the Scottish Highlands and on the Isle of Skye. Therefore, Holmes and Watson are sent there instead of Ireland.

The scandalous tale of Saucy Mary is authentic and there is a pub by that name to honor her in the village of Kyleakin. The references to Bonnie Prince Charlie and Flora Macdonald are historical, except for the fictional suggestion that they had a fling and produced an illegitimate child. It is duly noted that the Bonnie Prince did not escape *over the sea to Skye* by way of Lochalsh and Kyleakin. After the disastrous Battle of Culloden, he fled from the mainland to the Outer Hebrides and it was on the island of Benbecula that he met Flora MacDonald. His fabled return was from South Uist to the village of Kilbride on the southwestern shore of Skye.

The description of the Firth of Forth Bridge in Edinburgh is historically accurate and it was seriously proposed at that time that a similar bridge be built from the mainland to the Isle of Skye. It never happened because there were far too few people living on Skye at the time to warrant such an expense. A stunning new bridge was eventually built and completed in 1995. I drove across it several years ago and recommend the experience.

There are powerful tidal currents that sweep in and out of the Loch Alsh on either side of Elean Ban. The presence of deadly whirlpools is exaggerated but was borrowed from the actual incredible Naruto Whirlpools under the magnificent Onaruto

Bridge in Japan. The tour boat that takes you right up beside them is also recommended.

The poem *The Bairnies Cuddle Doon at Nicht* by the Scottish poet Alexander Anderson was a favorite of an earlier era of Scots. Both my grandmother and mother could recite it. A branch of my family came from Glencoe but were neither Campbells nor MacDonalds.

I duly acknowledge my borrowings from David Hume, William Shakespeare, Walter Scott, Robbie Burns, the Westminster Catechism, and Harry Potter. The Talisker Distillery on the Isle of Skye has been making excellent single malt Scotch for nearly 200 years. The Border Collie is the smartest breed of dog in the world, according to the Scots.

A NEW SHERLOCK HOLMES MYSTERY

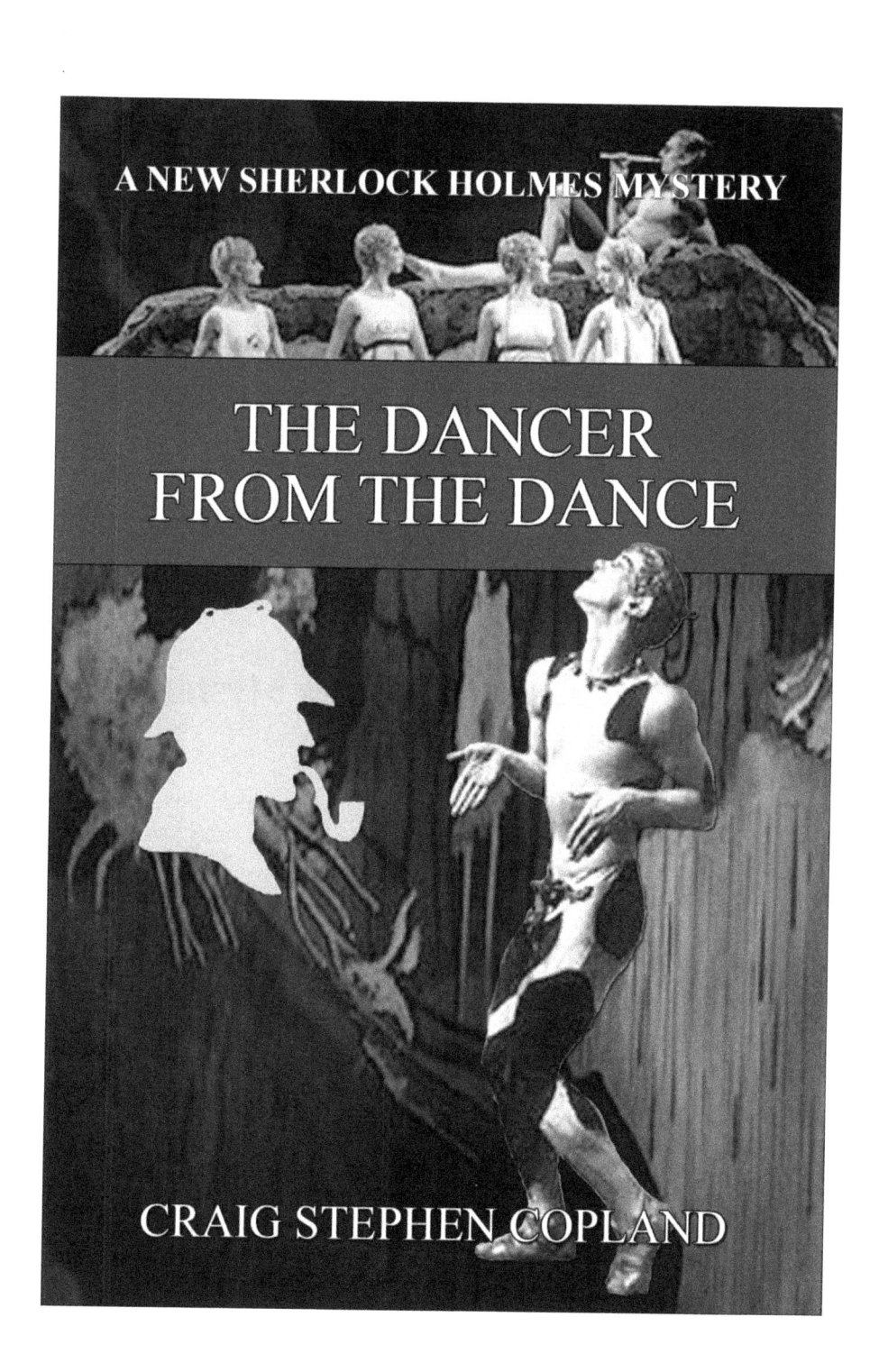

THE DANCER FROM THE DANCE

CRAIG STEPHEN COPLAND

The Dancer from the Dance

A New Sherlock Holmes Mystery

O chestnut tree, great rooted blossomer,
Are you the leaf, the blossom or the bole?
O body swayed to music, O brightening glance,
How can we know the dancer from the dance?

William Butler Yeats, from *Among School Children*

Chapter One
A Murder in the West End

"DANCERS," OBSERVED SHERLOCK HOLMES one late November afternoon, "are just like all other artists. Only ... more so. Unlike the rest of us who merely strut and fret our hour upon the stage, these young men and women display spectacular beauty, form, and athleticism as they gracefully leap and pirouette across the stages of the West End. They are artists of the highest degree, utterly, intensely devoted to and passionate about their art. Their burning passion possesses them not only on the stage but also in every aspect of their bodies and souls. It can be observed in their walk, their speech, their dress, their love lives, their friendships and animosities, and their politics.

"Unfortunately," he continued after lighting his beloved pipe, "it can also be seen in the way, from time to time, they murder each other."

By the late autumn of 1913, when the strange case if *The Dancer from the Dance* took place, Sherlock Holmes and I were no longer young men. Several decades had passed since that day we met as callow young fellows with our adult lives still in front of us and agreed to share lodgings for no other reason than our parlous financial situations. Between us, we did not have two spare farthings to rub together and no means of reliable income.

Now, we are somewhat comfortably well off. Holmes has been the recipient of more awards and rewards than even his prodigious memory can keep track of. I, long ago, substantially reduced my hours at my medical practice and pursued a splendid life as a well-paid writer. We are recognized when walking the streets of London, and we play our role as sixty-year-old smiling public men, expected to deliver wise saws and modern instances.

I am often asked to reflect on the past decades of my life and declare which period of time I consider to have been "the best." The question, of course, is impossible to answer unless the asker is highly specific and phrases it as "the best for *what*?" My days in the military were definitely not the best for anything, but it was my poverty and ill health at the end of those days that led me into my friendship with Sherlock Holmes and so, for that wonderful result, I must be grateful. My early years as Holmes's companion were intense, uncertain, dangerous, and wonderful. Those were the days when together we tracked down Jefferson Hope and Jonathan Small, when Holmes was bested by *the* woman, Irene Adler, and when he sorted out the complicated cases of Jabez Wilson, Mary Sutherland, James McCarthy and the lovely Mrs. Neville St. Clair. It was also the time when I met my first true love, Mary Morstan, and married her. For all those reasons, those early years were good, for *me*.

But what of the rest of mankind?

If I stand back and look at the past, I have to conclude that the all-too-brief years in the early part of the second decade of the twentieth century—before the world descended in the hell of war—were the best any of us can remember. Perhaps they are the best that will ever be.

A new king, George V, had ascended the throne and the British Empire had brought peace, prosperity, the rule of law, and the faith of Christendom to over one-quarter of the earth's population. The nations of Europe were no longer in conflict with each other, and the free flow of capital, goods, and labor gave a boost to the wealth and well-being of all. The rising tide indeed lifted all boats. Science and the application of science to industry meant that experiences, travel, possessions, and health that a generation earlier had been confined to the rich were now within the grasp of a thrifty working man. It was a time of undeniable *progress*, so much so that even the dour theologians were convinced that we had entered the Millennium. These were the final golden years of the Golden Age.

It was also an era in which the arts and letters of Western Civilization exploded with a plenitude of music, painting, sculpture, architecture, research, poetry, creative writing, and, last but not least, dance.

It was this something of a late-comer to the world of the fine arts, dance, that was the focus of the highly unusual case that occupied the genius of Sherlock Holmes during the late autumn of 1913 and the details of which I am now putting to account.

As readers of my records of the cases of Sherlock Holmes will recall, he was quite an accomplished violin player and an enthusiastic musician. The poetic and contemplative part of his spirit led him to a singularly extensive knowledge of the symphony and the opera. Yet his knowledge of dance and specifically ballet remained superficial at best, as was mine. To some extent, this lack was understandable. Prior to 1910, dance was enjoyed mainly within the music halls and on a vulgar and unrefined level. That all changed when *Les Ballets Russes* came first to Paris and then to London.

The involvement of Sherlock Holmes in this rarefied world of the world's finest ballet dancers began on a morning in late November with a phone call to 221B. I answered it.

"Hello, Watson. Lestrade calling. Where's Holmes?"

"And good morning to you as well, Chief Inspector. He is currently here but deep into his chemical investigations. Shall I have him ring you back later? Perhaps this afternoon?"

"No. You can tell him to get himself over to Drury Lane on the double. Corner of Martlett Court. And I mean now."

"Perhaps you would like me to interrupt him, and you can speak to him directly?"

"No, Doctor, I would not. The last thing I need this morning is to endure a round of his arrogance. That is your job. So, you tell him, and I will see him there within half an hour. You should come too."

He hung up.

I looked at Holmes, who was smiling back at me and had already turned off the gas and was placing his test tubes and instruments back in their rack.

"I could hear Lestrade across the room," he said. "This experiment was going nowhere, and we might as well go and see what the old boy is up to."

The days of the Hansom cab were long gone, and we hailed a motor car that was designated as a taxi. The traffic was light, and we made our way along Marylebone, Euston, and Gower in just over twenty minutes. Our old accomplice, now the Chief Inspector of Scotland Yard, was standing on the corner waiting for us.

"They are back here," he said as he turned and started walking into Martlett Court.

"And who might *they* be," asked Holmes, directing his question to the back of Lestrade's head.

"Two dead people. Who do you think? I would not call you in and put up with you if I were dealing with pickpockets. But no way to identify them. Local shopkeepers do not recognize them at all. Nobody heard anything."

A cluster of police officers was standing in the middle of the lane not far in front of us. Through the forest of their legs, I could see two bodies lying prone on the pavement. By their clothing, one was a man and the other a woman.

"Has the site been disturbed?" asked Holmes.

"Good lord, Holmes," said Lestrade. "You have been asking me that question for over thirty years. Of course, it has not been disturbed. Not that it makes much difference. They were not killed here. No blood anywhere except on the backs of their heads where they were shot. Must have been robbed and killed somewhere else and dumped here."

Holmes and I knelt down and carefully examined the two victims. They were both slender and dressed in the height of fashion. The residue of gunpowder on the backs of their skulls and their collars indicated that they had been shot at close range.

We gently rolled them over so we could look at their faces. Both were young and quite attractive, with firm, tight bodies. Holmes conducted an examination of their musculature, facial features, and hands. He removed their shoes and, using his glass, observed their feet. Then he stood up.

"There is a Russian ballet troupe currently in London, is there not? They will be short two dancers for future performances."

"Holmes," said Lestrade, "would you mind terribly explaining how you know that?"

"It could not be more obvious, Inspector. Their faces announce to the world that they are Slavs. Shaped, if you can use your imagination, as if by the forceful application of heavy frying pans."

"Holmes," said Lestrade. "I am not in the mood."

"It is common knowledge, my dear inspector. Whereas the English race is characterized by singularly unattractive puffy faces, untouched by any force of nature, those from the northern part of the Continent have longer, thinner faces, as if two frying pans were firmly smacked together, one to each side of the face, like a pair of cymbals. These two faces are passably attractive but round and lean. It is as if the frying pans were applied one directly to the front, giving them the flattened features and wide-spread eyes, and the other to the top of the head, reducing the height of frontal dome to a mere two inches. Their features announce that they have come from somewhere east of Warsaw. Both the man and the woman have exceptionally hard and highly developed calves, quadriceps, hamstrings, and gluteals. The man's arms and shoulders are likewise strong and firm, but the woman's arms are willowy. Their clothes are somewhat Bohemian in style but expensive. Thus, I conclude that they are from Russian and ballet dancers."

"Good lord, Holmes," said Lestrade. "London is lousy with Russian immigrants now. Half of them ride bicycles."

"Quite so, Inspector. However, if you examine the feet of the woman, you will see that her toes are compacted and bruised. Neither bicyclists nor any other type of athlete bear these marks. On the male, there are specks of a white powder under his fingernails that has the distinct feel of resin. Male dancers apply that substance regularly so as to avoid dropping ballerinas when their hands become sweaty. Now, I have limited knowledge of the ballet but what little I do know leads to the conclusion I have just given you. Were they carrying any travel or foreign identification documents?"

"None of that sort," said Lestrade. "The woman had nothing on her at all. The male only had some papers in the pocket of his overcoat. All their money was taken in the robbery."

Holmes sighed. "No, my dear Inspector, they were not the victims of robbery. Whoever murdered them only wanted Scotland Yard to think that."

"But their pockets were cleaned out."

"Of course, they were. But the man still has his watch and his gold cufflinks. The woman has a necklace and several expensive rings. The total value of their jewelry must be close to one hundred pounds. No thief in London today would leave those items on his victims nor would he murder them and risk the gallows when he could easily have just taken their money and accessories and been on his way. Whatever the reason for their deaths, it was something other than the cash in their pockets."

Lestrade made a sort of grunting sound, summoned one of his police officers, and instructed him to hand over the folded set of papers he was holding.

"This is what the fellow did have in his pockets," he said.

Holmes glanced at them quickly and then gave them to me. They consisted of a single piece of paper and a booklet containing a musical score. On the front page of the score was printed the title, *Prélude à après-midi d'un faune,* underneath which was the name, *Claude Debussy*. The single page contained about twenty lines, all of which contained three numbers each. They were written in this manner:

C.G. 28 – 11 11.00

6 - 4 – x 2

7 – 13 – x 3

8 – 3 – x 9

10 – 19 – x14

"May I suggest," said Holmes, "that you take these bodies to the police morgue and that we arrange a visit immediately to whoever is in charge of the Russian dancers. If you have no objection, Inspector, I shall keep these papers for the present time."

"Fine by me," said Lestrade. "I cannot make any sense of them at all. I will have my office track down the Russians straight away and set up a meeting. You will get a call to let you know when and where. I will see you there."

Having said that, he abruptly departed and walked back out to Drury Lane where his car and driver were waiting for him.

Chapter Two
The Fabulous Impresario

SCOTLAND YARD CALLED in the early afternoon. A woman from Lestrade's office spoke to me in a gracious and respectful manner but stated in no uncertain terms that Holmes and I were required immediately in the lobby of the Savoy Hotel. The Chief Inspector would meet us there in half an hour.

The Savoy, in the Strand, had opened over a decade ago and was the most luxurious hotel in London. It had been the first hotel in Europe to provide every guest with his or her own lavatory, complete with a constant supply of hot and cold running water. The restaurant had become the preferred dining establishment of London's *hoi poloi,* and the rich and shameless could be seen there every evening. Lestrade was waiting for us by the front desk, accompanied by two police officers in uniform and a gentleman whom I recognized from the society pages of the press as Mr. Charles Ritz, the hotel manager. Lestrade introduced us to him.

"We value the patronage of all of our guests," said the manager. "However, the Russian dancers do have a bit of a tendency to exhibit their emotions perhaps somewhat more than an English gentleman or lady is prepared for. Hence, I thought it best that I accompany you just in case you elicit an untoward reaction from them. Their suite is on the south side of the top floor."

The electric lift—the first to be installed in London—took us to the eighth floor of the hotel. Whilst I was enjoying the ride, Holmes turned to Lestrade and queried him concerning the party we were about to meet.

"His name is *Die – og – hi – lev,*" said Lestrade, sounding out each syllable. "He's a Russian but lives now in Paris. Brought a company of Russian dancers with him a couple of years back. Said to be very risqué. The French love them, as might be expected. He comes to London each year now and puts on a few shows at the Royal Opera House or the Drury Lane. The critics here are mixed. The aesthetes adore him; the sensible ones say he and his bunch of degenerates are beyond the pale. I have never seen them perform, so I have no idea. I think he speaks a bit of English. I had one of our artists at the Yard sketch the faces of the victims. There are rather good likenesses. No mistaking them for anyone else."

From the lift, we walked along the beautifully appointed hallway to the door of a corner suite. Lestrade gave several firm knocks on the door.

"Beat it!" came a shout from the other side. "We're busy. Go away and come back in an hour."

The voice was distinctly American. Lestrade nodded to the hotel manager who produced his master key and opened the door. He did not follow us into the suite.

"Hey. You guys deaf or something? Out of here before you get batty-fanged. You want me to call the police?" said a fellow who was standing in the middle of the posh suite. The room was splendidly decorated with fine paintings and furniture and must have had over a dozen large vases of fresh flowers—one on every available surface. The assertive American chap was dressed in a dark double-breasted suit, with a suit jacket cut short as is the style across the Atlantic. Unlike a cultured Englishman, he did not sport a decent set of boots covered with tan spats but instead a finely tooled pair of wing-tipped brogues. His necktie was wide and appeared to have a picture of Niagara Falls embroidered on it. He looked as if he were about to continue his diatribe when he observed the two uniformed police officers enter behind us.

"Jeepers, it's the mutton-shunkers," he exclaimed. Then turning to the other man in the room, he said, "Sergy. What have you done this time? Are your kids stealing the hotel's towels again? You gotta stop lettin' them do that, Sergy. Or we're all gonna end up in the hoosgow."

He then turned to us and spoke to Lestrade. "Whatever it is, gentlemen, I am sure it will be looked after. Allow me to introduce myself. Gerry M. Coghlan is the name, and the Great White Way is the game. And who might I have the honor of addressing, my good man?"

The American fellow was apparently used to taking command of any situation in which he found himself and directing all attention to his presence. Whilst Lestrade was staring at him, still somewhat speechless, I looked at the other people in the lavish suite. I could see that Holmes was doing the same. Sitting in a large wingback chair was a handsome, mustached gentleman clad in a silk dressing gown that covered a fine cotton shirt and colorful cravat. His short boots were stylish and gleaming. In his right hand was a cigarette holder, in which the stub of a cigarette was smoldering. His smile suggested that he found the antics of the New Yorker mildly amusing.

On either end of the sofa were two boys whose age I would have put at around fifteen. The clothes they were wearing would have been appropriate on the ballet stage but hardly what was expected in a London hotel suite in the early afternoon. From the waist down, they wore only dancer's tights that outlined every muscle and bulge in their anatomy. Above the waist, they both wore a short velvet jacket that was flared out about their hips. The front of the jacket was open, exposing their lily-white chests and abdomens. They were both exceedingly attractive, although not in a way that I would call masculine and handsome. They were not saying anything but were obviously smirking, smiling at the American, and trying to suppress their giggles.

Lestrade had recovered from his bewilderment and replied to the American.

"Chief Inspector Lestrade, Scotland Yard. With me are Mr. Sherlock Holmes and Dr. Watson."

"*Bozhe moy,*" muttered the fellow in the dressing gown. The American was more loquacious.

"Sherlock Holmes? You don't mean *the* Sherlock Holmes? Boy oh boy, this is my lucky day. I hit the jackpot. First, I get a deal to bring Sergy and his company to New York, and now I meet the world's most famous detective. In person. I could not have written a better script if I tried. Wait'll they hear about this in Peoria. Did you know, Mr. Holmes that some guy is running all over the United States of America pretending to be you onstage? Tell ya what. Why don't you come yourself and I'll get you onstage on Broadway? The crowds will go wild. Can you see it, Mr. Holmes? *The real Sherlock Holmes. Come and see the world's greatest detective combat the forces of evil.*"

As he was speaking, he slowly waved his open hand in a long sweep from left to right. I assumed that we were supposed to be imagining the lights of a marquee. He extracted a business card from his pocket and walked directly toward Holmes, extending the card.

"No," said Holmes, "I cannot see that. And if you, sir, would kindly step aside, we have business to conduct with Mr. Diaghilev." He walked past Mr. Coghlan and over toward the man sitting in the wing chair. Diaghilev rose to his feet and smiled warmly at him.

"*Godpodin* Sherlock Holmes," he said. "It is great honor to meet so much famous person. *Rad vstreche s vami.* So happy I am to have opportunity to talk with you. But please, sir. In Russia, we never have meeting on empty stomach or without exchanging toast. *Da?*"

He nodded to the boys on the sofa, who instantly sprang to their feet and grabbed two trays off of the side console and came over to us. One tray bore small shot glasses, all filled to the brim with a clear liquid that most certainly was a select vodka. The other had a large plate of small pieces of toasted bread, slathered in caviar. Lestrade, the police officers, and I all partook eagerly. Holmes did not.

"We are not in Russia, Mr. Diaghilev," he said. "We are in London, and I prefer to conduct meetings on an empty stomach and without the interference of alcohol."

"*Bozhe moy*, how you are missing enjoyments of life. *Khorosho,* Mr. Holmes. You are free to deprive yourself, and I shall be free not to." He downed his vodka in one gulp and then consumed one of the caviar morsels. Having done so, he sat back down on his chair and gestured with his cigarette holder for us to take a seat in one of the numerous sofas and chairs that were scatted around the suite.

"It is also custom in Russia, to give small gift before engaging in business. Had I known about your visit, I should have had excellent gift to give to famous Mr. Sherlock Holmes. But I cannot give you nothing. I give all of you tickets to ballet. Today is Sunday, so as good Christians we do not perform but we still have good time. *Poetomu,* how you say, *therefore*, we have reception this evening at Savoy. You must come. Tomorrow is *ponedel'nik,* and is dark night in West End. Next nights we do Tchaikovsky ballet, different each night, after we do *Après-midi d'un faune.* Is short piece. Friday, we do *Le Sacre du Printemps.* First time in London. Will be big event. You will like. You must accept my gift, Mr. Holmes. I am incapable to do business any other way."

I half expected Holmes to tell the impresario that he was not interested but he surprised me and graciously accepted, promising to attend the reception and the performances. He smiled at Diaghilev and thanked him. Diaghilev grinned in return.

"Is not just good for you, sir. Looks good for me to have world's great detective, famous writer, and Inspector Chief at my party. *Da?*" He laughed and downed another shot glass of vodka.

Holmes was not smiling. He gestured to the police officer who was holding the artist's sketch pad. The fellow brought it over and handed it to Holmes, who opened it and placed it in front of Mr. Serge Diaghilev.

"Can you identify this man and woman?" Holmes asked.

The Russian fellow was suave and charming, but he could not hide the flash of recognition that flickered across his face. And it was more than mere recognition. It was fear. If his face could have spoken, it would have said, "Oh, dear God, no."

He recovered his composure immediately and looked over at the American.

"Mr. Coghlan, this does not you concern. Please wait for me in hotel bar. Shall not be long."

"It's okay, Sergy. I don't mind waiting here." He was well into his third piece of caviar-laden toast. Diaghilev's response was more forceful.

"Gerry, you wait in bar. Go now."

"Okay. Whatever you say, Sergy. I will just twenty-three skidoo out of here."

The Russian then turned to the two boys on the sofa.

"*Ubiraysya otsyuda.*"

They jumped to their feet and departed into one of the adjoining bedrooms. He then looked up at Holmes with a forced smile.

"*Da konechno,* of course, I know them. These are two of my beautiful children. Tatiana and Luka. They are members of my *Ballets Russes*. They have been arrested by Scotland Yard, *da?* What wrong were they doing? *Seksom* in Poets' Corner, perhaps? They are dancers. They do these things. I will come to police station and pay fine."

"I regret to inform you, sir," said Holmes, "that if you go to the station, it will not be to pay a fine. It will be to identify the bodies of these two young people. They have been murdered."

For a moment, Diaghilev's face was blank. Then it slowly became contorted with anguish. He gave a desperate glance to Lestrade, who nodded in confirmation. His eyes closed and he brought his clenched fists to his face. His body slumped in his chair and began to sob uncontrollably. Over the next several minutes first Holmes and then Lestrade attempted to have him talk to them but it was to no avail. The man was lost in a sea of pain.

A full five minutes passed before he raised his head and spoke to us in a whisper.

"*Da*, I come to station to identify. Is possible not to tell Press? I must contact families in Russia. Both families wonderful. Trusted me to take care of children. Is possible not to tell Press until I inform families?"

"Yes," said Lestrade. "That can be arranged. But we need your help if we are to find who did this."

He looked at Lestrade and then Holmes.

"*Da*. What to know do you want? Doctor, bring vodka, *pozhaluysta.*"

I took a full shot glass from the sideboard and brought it to him. He tossed it back in one gulp.

"Tell us," said Holmes, "about these two young people. Where do they come from? Did they have enemies? Were they doing anything illegal? You have over seventy people in your company. Is there anything peculiar about these two?"

"*Nyet.* They are beautiful children. Good dancers. Work hard. Not in front line but soon to be. They are friends, lovers. Maybe other dancer is jealous. All dancers are artists. They do crazy things. Tatiana come from Novgorod. My city. Good family. Father is professor. Luka from Perm. Father is mayor. Both families send them as children to St. Petersburg to Imperial Ballet. I ask them to join my *Ballets Russes*. Do anything against law in London? Maybe steal sweets or fruit. Maybe steal shoes. Dancers love new shoes."

He dropped his head back into his hands and began again to sob. A further several minutes passed before he lifted his head again.

"Please. Another favor, I must ask. Is possible not to tell other dancers in company? Not yet. They could not dance if they know this terrible thing. Only four nights left in London. This is end of season for London. Now say them Lukasha and Tanya run off on lovers' holiday. Later, we tell them bad news. Is possible?"

"We cannot promise," said Holmes, "but we will not disclose full information until after your performance on Friday. Now then, sir, pray look at these."

He removed from his suit pocket the papers that the police officer had given him earlier in the day.

"Luka had these in his pocket," said Holmes. "What can you tell me about them?"

Diaghilev looked over the documents and shrugged.

"This is score of *Le Faune* to be played by orchestra this week. Every dancer has copy. These numbers, they make no sense. Maybe leave with me and I try. *Da*?"

"*Nyet*," replied Holmes and held out his hand for the return of the papers.

"I do what you want. We go now to station. I do what I have to do. Do not forget, you are come to reception. We all try not to look sad, *da*? Like you say, show must go on."

The group of us departed the suite and returned to the hotel lobby. The two police officers discreetly led the impresario through a back door to a waiting police car. Holmes, Lestrade and I found a table in the Savoy Grill.

"He knows more," said Lestrade, "than he's letting on."

Chapter Three
A Wisconsin Countess
at the Savoy

HOLMES AND I MET AGAIN at the end of the afternoon in 221B and relaxed in front of the hearth with a round of sherry whilst waiting for the ever-faithful Mrs. Hudson to prepare our supper. Holmes's dear landlady was now elderly but still spry and devoted to looking after her famous boarder.

"You are planning," I asked, "to speak to the other members of the company?"

He nodded.

"But you do not speak Russian," I said.

"I have called in reinforcements."

"Indeed? Who, may I ask?"

"Countess Elizaveta d'Eau Claire," he said.

"You mean Big Betsy from Wisconsin?"

"The one and only. Regardless of her eccentricities, she is a fluent native Russian speaker and always eager to assist me."

"Which I translate to mean, eager to help as long as you pay her well."

"Which I am more than happy to do. She will conduct interviews and provide translation for me as required and will accompany us to the theater. We will be attending from Tuesday through Friday. I trust you will enjoy it."

"It will be a most interesting experience," I said. "Cannot go wrong listening to Beecham conduct Tchaikovsky. He's doing *The 1812* as well, isn't he? And the Russians are performing both *Swan Lake* and *The Nutcracker*, right? Yes, that should be quite enjoyable, even if the new ballet is a bit of a way down queer street."

"More than a bit," said Holmes, "Friday may be a somewhat novel experience."

"Oh, yes, indeed. Then we shall have to sit through *The Rite of Spring*. Is not that the one that drove the French to riot when it was first performed a few months back in Paris?"

"Of course the French staged a riot. What would anyone have expected? They are French and are always either on strike or staging a riot."

"How do you think it will be received by Londoners?" I asked.

"We will listen in silence, give polite applause, and complain about it for years afterward. We are English. That is what we do."

I might have challenged his ethnographic generalizations but was interrupted by the bell at the door on Baker Street.

Mrs. Hudson appeared a moment later and handed Holmes a gilt-edged card.

"The Countess has come for a visit," she said. "You are welcome to ask her to stay for supper, but there might not be enough food for you and the doctor if she fills her plate first."

She gave me a wink and departed to fetch one of Holmes's favorite informants.

"Sheeerlock ... daaaahlink!" said the woman who appeared in our doorway. "*Bozhe moy,* and Doctor Watson. Two of my favorite men in all the world. How lovely of you, my dear, to ask me to call on you. Are we going to Simpson's for dinner, darlink? Or shall we be dining here in elegant privacy? Your dear Mrs. Hudson is such a divine chef. Not quite up to my lovely Pierre at the Savoy but makes up for it in her devotion to you. How are you anyway, dahlink?"

The woman who had entered the room and who bore the legal name of Betsy Burkovsky was of the same vintage as Holmes and me and, like a fine wine, had become more fabulous with each passing year. She was wearing an ermine stole, a gigantic hat, and a gown that provided enough yards of fine cloth to flatter her ample endowments. Under her arm, she swaddled a dog that was about the size of a well-fed rat. Upon entering the room, she immediately put the tiny beast down on the floor.

"There you go, Pépé," she said as the pathetic excuse for a canine scampered away. "Go and explore but try not to leave an indiscretion on the carpet. Ah, Sherlock, my dearest. How sweet of you to ask for my help. I do so love rescuing you one more time. Well, frankly, I love the way I live for two weeks after you pay me for rescuing you. What is it you need this time, dahlink? An introduction to a member of the Czar's household? London is utterly crawling with the excrescence of St. Petersburg. You would think they were fleeing Russia for their lives. Or do you need to know who has been smuggling sable stoles into London? Do tell me, dahlink?"

"Translation services."

"Translation? That is all? Sherlock, my sweet man, any one of a thousand poor Russian students can translate for you. Who is it you have to speak to? The third mate from a Russian fishing trawler?"

"The members of *Les Ballets Russes*."

"Oooh, why didn't you say so!" She clapped her hands together in front of her massive bosom. "Well then, I must tell you the secret for interviewing any cultured Russian. You can learn *everything* you need to know by asking him … or maybe her … only *one* question."

She stopped, obviously expecting that we would demand to know what that question was. I did not want to disappoint her and demanded with feigned eagerness that she tell us.

"My dears, you merely look them in the eye and ask them 'Do you prefer Tolstoy or Dostoevsky?' If they give a truthful answer, that is all you need to know. Everything else follows from that."

I complimented the Countess on her profound knowledge of Russian literature.

"*Bozhe moy,* Doctor. There is nothing at all to understanding the great literature of Mother Russia. The plots of every one of our stories can be summarized in only five words."

Again, she expected us to plead for such a revelation, and again I did not disappoint. I took out my pencil and notebook and posed myself as if ready to write down the answer.

"And what," I asked, "my dear Countess, might those five words be?"

She lifted her head and spoke to the light coming in the bay window. "They are 'And then … it got worse.'"

Both Holmes and I laughed, and I thanked her again for such insight and wisdom. Holmes assured her that he would remember her counsel when speaking to the dancers.

"And, of course," she said, "we shall be attending the performances at the Royal Opera House?"

"For four nights running this week," said Holmes.

"*Zamechatel'no*! Preceded by dinner at Simpson's, of course. And followed by drinks and desserts at the Savoy. How lovely."

"Except for tonight," said Holmes. "We have to attend the reception for the company where we shall join with the excrescence of London."

"Brilliant! If I were only forty years younger, I would have that Serge Diaghilev on his knees proposing marriage to me before the night is over. I am quite sure—as we used to say in Wisconsin—I could straighten the boy out. Now then, what is your dear Mrs. Hudson serving for dinner?"

* * *

At eight o'clock that evening, Holmes, the Countess, and I met on the pavement in front of the Savoy Hotel. Lestrade had refused the invitation noting, wisely, that Chief Inspectors of Scotland

Yard should not be seen in public enjoying the crumbs that fell from the tables of the principals in a case he was investigating.

A string of large, luxurious motor cars was puttering up, discharging cargoes of shirt-fronted men and beshaled and bediamonded women. In our early years together, I had to admonish Holmes on numerous occasions when he failed to conceal his contempt for, as he called them, the *crud de la crud*, who lived idly but well off the rents of their inherited lands and firms. Now, he was so famous that receiving an insult from Sherlock Holmes was worn as a badge of honor amongst this ostentatious crowd and was bragged about in the clubs of Pall Mall or the high teas of Mayfair.

We entered the hotel and were directed to the Lancaster Ballroom where a small throng had already gathered beneath the glittering crystal chandeliers and were, as duty required, engaging in bantering inconsequence and forced laughter. Holmes moved directly to the far corner of the room where his tall stature permitted him to survey the crowd.

"Kindly make a note," he said to the Countess and me, "of any of these pompous people who have a finger in the theater."

"Sherlock, my dearest," said the Countess, *sotto voce*, "do you think any of these lovely people could be involved in something criminal?"

"If you are asking me if one of them might have committed or commissioned murder, then *yes*. We have to start our investigation somewhere, and those connected to the victims are the logical place to begin."

"Shall we engage some of the dancers in conversation?" I asked.

"What dancers?" replied Holmes.

"Those who have been pressed into service to distribute the champagne and *hors-d'oeuvres*."

Some twenty young men and women were attending to the refreshments of the guests. They were all clad in their ballet costumes. The lads were dressed in a similar manner to the boys we had seen earlier in Diaghilev's suite. They were wearing nothing but tights below their waists, and short, black velvet jackets, buttoned in the vicinity of their navels. The young women all bore the famous costumes of the *petits cygnes* of *Swan Lake*. Instead of skirts, they wore *tutus* that hung just shy of horizontal, exposing their legs. On their torsos, they were covered in form-fitting corsets made of thin material that hugged every mound and bulge in their young bodies. I assumed that they were all members of *Les Ballets Russes*.

"They are not dancers," said Holmes. "They are employees of the hotel who have been costumed for the occasion. That is obvious and quite unfortunate as I had been hoping to observe any signs of passionate feelings amongst them that might be strong enough to lead to murder."

"They look like dancers to me," I said in rejoinder.

"Watson. Please. Observe. Whilst they may have been selected because of their attractive faces and bodies, most of the males have legs that are positively spindly compared to a dancer's. The same is true of the females, in addition to which several of the girls are blessed with ample breasts that would topple them off balance should they attempt to stand *en point*. They are all balancing large trays on their spread palms and by experience remove champagne glasses first from one side and then the other so as not to render the tray unbalanced and crashing to the ground. Add to that the obvious observation that all of them are quite self-conscious of their grossly immodest costumes and do not appreciate being leered at by the aging Lotharios who surround them. The only reason I would have to speak to them is to advise that they meet together tomorrow morning and form a union so that they may never again be treated in such a degrading manner."

"Oh, Sherlock dahlink," said the Countess. "There is reason you are still a bachelor. Why do you think all those noble ladies rave about attending the ballet if it is not because they are entranced by the parade of gorgeous *gluteus maximus* that prance across the stage? You are a lost cause, my dahlink. But come now, I shall introduce you to someone I see and whom I consider a dear and intimate friend. She is my fellow American."

"What," I asked her, "does she have to do with the theater?"

"She owns several of them. Her husband, may he rest in peace, had more money than God and theaters were his playthings. She has turned them into machines for making money."

"Ah, then she must be quite popular amongst the dramatic crowd."

"*Au contraire,* my dear Doctor. She has banished the serious playwrights and actors from half of her real estate and turned the theaters into splendid music halls filled with vulgar vaudevillians. That, I fear, is where the money is to be found today. Come, we shall engage her. Do not be put off by her accent. She is American, and we cannot help what we do to your precious English language."

Chapter Four
We Meet Nijinsky

THE COUNTESS SAILED across the portion of the ballroom between where we were standing and where a blonde woman of a certain age was momentarily alone having recently disentangled herself from a cluster of similarly gowned and bejeweled dowagers.

"*Ellssieee*," cooed the Countess and we approached the lady. "How lovely to see you again. Why, I have not seen you since Epsom, or was it the party for Henry Ford at the American ambassador's? And ... oh my ... your gown is stunning. From the House of Worth? Did Jean-Phillipe design it for you? It is so much his style. His signature is all over it. Utterly maaavellous, my dear."

The lady was looking at the Countess in a manner that had words been attached to it might have said, "*Who is this?*" She obviously did not know who had accosted and was now gushing all over her. Our Countess carried on undaunted.

"Oh, my dear, Elsie, you must forgive me. Allow me to introduce you to my two gentlemen escorts for the evening. Really, my dear, how lucky can a lady be to have not only one but two famous gentlemen by her side for such a fabulous occasion. This is the famous writer, Dr. John Watson, the best-selling author now in the entire Empire and this, if you can believe it, is Mr. Sherlock Holmes, and I am sure you know who he is. Gentleman, please meet my compatriot, Mrs. Elsie Cubitt of North Walsham."

Holmes, the woman, and I all said nothing, frozen momentarily on the sport. The elegant woman recovered first.

"Well, we meet again, Mr. Holmes. How nice to see you."

"Goodness, gracious," exclaimed the Countess. "You two know each other?"

"We have," said Mrs. Cubitt, "met before. Unfortunately, I was unconscious at the time, a bit of a bloody mess, and had a splitting headache. I have been told that it was thanks to you, Mr. Holmes, that I was not sent to the gallows."

"Good heavens!" said the Countess. "What did you do?"

"Murdered my husband; at least that is what the police first assumed. And then I tried, rather unsuccessfully, to murder myself. But thanks to Mr. Holmes, no charges were ever laid. A pleasure, sir, to renew your acquaintance under much more favorable circumstances than the previous occasion." The lady's facial expression changed to a smile, and she extended her hand. Holmes, remembering his manners for once, graciously accepted with a gallant bow.

"Your recovery," he said, "and your many accomplishments since that dreadful day are greatly admired."

"Yours as well, Mr. Holmes. I and every one of my friends wept when we read of your demise at the waterfall and were in ecstasy when you returned from the dead. But I had the impression that you rather disdained effete affairs like this."

"It seems, madam," said Holmes, "that I have reached the time of life where a man is required to participate in the events of the social stratum which I appear to have, in spite of my diligent efforts, attained. Thus, I find myself at this elegant event and with the pleasure of meeting you once again."

Mrs. Elsie Cubitt laughed pleasantly. "Oh my, Mr. Holmes. Who would have guessed that you had such refined and gracious manners?"

"Ah, but what can I say, my lady? There are occasions, such as when standing in front of a respected and elegant woman, that such behavior comes naturally."

She laughed merrily again. "And who would have guessed that Sherlock Holmes is such an accomplished liar." Now she laughed heartily. Holmes looked quite taken aback.

"I beg your pardon, madam!"

"Oh, my dear Mr. Holmes. I spend every working day administering funds for charities and the arts. I meet with countless do-gooders, theater impresarios, and lawyers. They smile graciously and flatter me, and then proceed to tell me all manner of lies. Surely you do not expect me to believe for a minute that Sherlock Holmes has come to a gala event at the Savoy because he enjoys doing so? I noticed you several minutes ago standing at the edge of this room peering over it like an eagle looking for his lunch. You are here because, as your friend, Dr, Watson, might write, *the game is afoot*. Would you deny what I am saying is true, Mr. Holmes?"

She did not give Holmes time to respond before continuing.

"However, my dear sir, your presence has just made this event so much more interesting. Now we are no longer at yet another pompous evening attended by England's parasitical nobility and those who wish they were. We are present at a party in which there is some sort of criminal activity taking place. That is so much more interesting. Positively intriguing. Now then, what could it possibly be? You cannot be here on behalf of the creditors of Mr. Diaghilev, that much I know for sure."

"Do you, madam?" asked Holmes. "May I ask you how you know that?"

"How? Because I am one of them and nobody told *me*. Serge owes me a fortune as he does several others here this evening and *we* certainly did not hire Sherlock Holmes to investigate where all of the money has gone. So, pray tell, Mr. Holmes, why are you here?"

Holmes did not answer her question but responded with one of his own.

"Pray tell yourself, my lady. Why, if he does not pay his bills, do you continue to allow him to use your theaters?"

That brought a hearty laugh from the woman. "Oh, my dear, dear Mr. Sherlock Holmes. You may possess the finest mind in the Empire when it comes to bringing criminals to justice, but it is apparent that you know nothing about the business of running a theater. Let me give you your first lesson. Anyone who can fill the house with rich people is welcome to put on his production. As long as we come within thirty percent of covering our costs from the ticket sales, we are satisfied. The profit is made on the truly criminal amounts we charge for champagne at the intermission, for souvenir magazines, for copies of the musical score, for anything that people who have more money than sense will buy. The profit on our concession sales allows us to live quite well, thank you very much. And Serge Diaghilev fills our houses night after night. The last thing we want is to put him in prison for non-payment of his debts."

Holmes nodded slowly. "I see. Very well, I assure you that I am not present this evening on behalf of his creditors. The truth is, madam, we are guests of Mr. Diaghilev."

"Oh! Well now, that does make it more interesting. Why would *he* want to hire a detective? Is somebody blackmailing the man? Has someone threatened to expose his utterly degenerate private life? I cannot imagine what purpose there would be in that. Perhaps if he were the Archbishop, there would be profit in blackmailing, but Serge's private life is public knowledge. He positively flaunts his young playthings in front of us. The word on the street is that any young man with a slender body is advised not to turn his back on him for if he does then Serge the Impresario may become Vlad the Impaler. We all know the man is depraved and his ballets are likewise. Why do you think the English are flocking to see them? If you come to see his *Après-midi,* you will see what I mean. Are you planning to attend, Mr. Holmes?"

"I am," said Holmes, "and I look forward to seeing you there. It has been a pleasure."

He offered a shallow bow and retreated from Mrs. Cubitt. She was grinning at him as he did so.

"The lady," I said, "makes a good case for not equating the creditors of Mr. Diaghilev with his enemies."

Holmes tilted his head a bit to the side and raised an eyebrow. "Do you truly think so?" he said.

"It makes sense," I said.

"I claim," said Holmes, "neither expertise nor sufficient data concerning the business of the theater. Such instincts as I have, however, lead me to doubt what I have just been told."

"Well, my dahlink," replied the Countess, "I have no doubt that it is certainly *not* true with those creditors whose sole business is loaning Diaghilev money."

"He has been borrowing money?" asked Holmes.

"Well, dahlink, I cannot say for certain," said the Countess, "but I know of no other reason for Mr. Abraham Slainstein to be here."

She was discreetly nodding in the direction of a smallish, well-dressed man who was loading up his plate at the food table. Without further comment, she walked over to him. Holmes and I obediently followed.

"Abe, my dahlink," she said as she sidled up to the fellow. "How lovely to see you here. Have you suddenly developed a cultivated interest in the arts, dahlink? Wonders never cease."

The man did not look up from his plate of food. His answer seemed as sour as the cabbage roll on which he was gnawing.

"Hello, Betsy. You know I have no more interest in the arts than you do. I am here for the same reason you are. The food and wine are free, and the prospects for new clients are promising."

"Oh, Abe, you are always working, working, working. The day is over. Time to relax and enjoy yourself. Let me introduce you to the two gentlemen who are escorting me this evening."

He briefly looked up from his plate before returning his gaze to his free supper.

"Don't bother, Betsy. I know who they are. Just tell me why you are bringing Sherlock Holmes and Dr. Watson to a reception put on by pompous poseurs for the benefit of a bunch of Bohemian degenerates. And do not try to tell me that England's most famous detective and highest-paid writer have suddenly developed an interest in watching young men in stockings prance across the stage."

"I assure you, sir," said Holmes even though the request had been made to the Countess, "that I have no interest in either the artistic merit or the moral depravity of a ballet company. My interest has arisen only because of rumors that a criminal element that may have become attached to them."

That got the fellow's attention. He put down his full plate of delectable food and looked directly at Holmes.

"Well, now, this boring evening has suddenly become interesting. A pleasure to meet you, Mr. Holmes. I am Abraham Slainstein, and as I have some pecuniary interest in these dancers, your comment demands my attention as I would not want my investment in them to go down the drain even more than it already has."

"A pleasure to meet you, sir," said Holmes. "Am I correct in understanding that you are one of the financial backers of this artistic enterprise?"

"If by that you mean am I one of the fools that was sweet-talked by Serge Diaghilev into loaning money for his extravaganzas, you are correct. I thought he was bringing *Swan Lake* to the West End, which he does. But he also brings his afternoon of a salacious faun along with his bizarre *Rite of Spring*. And yesterday I am hearing that Nijinsky the flying fairy is about to cut and run. What should be a gold mine of profit appears to be a bottomless pit for expenses as long as Diaghilev is in charge. And now Mr. Sherlock Holmes is telling me that there are criminals connected somehow to my investment. Is there any more bad news you wish to tell me, Mr. Holmes, before I slit my wrists?"

"Your comment about Mr. Nijinsky is very interesting, sir," said Holmes. "Would you mind awfully explaining it to me?"

"An explanation? You need an explanation? Why do you not just ask him yourself? Here he comes now."

He nodded toward the doors of the reception room where it was evident that someone significant had just entered. Swirling around me, I could hear the whispered name "Nijinsky" being passed from one patron to the other. As crowds do on such occasions, the inchoate mass of people began creeping and politely elbowing in the direction of the doorway. Countess Betsy turned and pushed her way through the crowd like a powerful ice-breaker. We followed in her wake.

Several indignant comments and glaring rebukes later, we found ourselves in the front line of a small circle that had surrounded a young man and an attractive woman who was firmly attached to his arm. He was surprisingly short, although strikingly handsome, with soft, refined features. He was elegantly dressed in a fine suit that I thought had been somewhat padded in the shoulders so as not to let them appear so narrow. The cut of the trousers, however, was disproportionately large and loose, indicating powerful pairs of thighs and calves.

The young man, who I concluded could be none other than Vaslav Nijinsky, the most famous male ballet dancer in the world, was not looking at all comfortable in the situation. A string of elegantly dressed women of all ages and sizes were bumping and shouldering each other to put their bodies in front of him. Once they achieved that strategic position, they were offering the poor fellow their gloved hands and speaking to him loudly, with elongated vowels, about how much they simply *adoored* his *daancing*. It was obvious that he did not understand what they were saying and the woman, who was clinging to him like ivy to a lamppost, had her mouth a few inches from his left ear and appeared to be translating.

While she smiled graciously back at the well-wishers, he was oblivious to them. He took a few of the hands extended to him and gave the fingertips and very short shake. The rest he ignored. His eyes were wide and were darting about the room as if he were a cornered animal looking for a rapid means of escaping a predator. This odd spectacle went on for several minutes during which the woman who was affixed to his arm steered him in a brief circle around the room. We shuffled and elbowed our way close behind. At one point, I observed that his gaze suddenly stopped flashing back and forth and had become fixed. My own glance in the direction in which he was looking revealed that Serge Diaghilev was standing in the line of sight and was looking directly back at Nijinsky. It was hard to describe what I read in the look they were giving to each other. Diaghilev was angry, but the anger seemed tinged with condescension and sadness. In Nijinsky, I read defiance but also fear. Something had transpired between the two of them, and it was far from resolved.

Holmes grabbed my elbow and, with his other hand on Betsy's arm, led us away from the madding crowd and over to the bar where we could refresh our glasses of Champagne.

"Countess," said Holmes. "Doctor Watson and I shall remain here. It is not advisable for me to encourage even more speculation regarding my presence. Would you be so kind as to mingle amongst the guests and find out, whether it is in English, Russian or Polish, just what is going on here? And then come and report back to us. I shall look after your food plate whilst you do so."

Countess Betsy smiled warmly at Holmes and ploughed her way back into the crowd. Holmes discreetly worked his way to the back of the bar until he was standing beside the well-starched waiter who was tending to the libations of the gentry. He removed his wallet from his suitcoat pocket and extracted a five-pound note and slipped it into the hand of the barkeep. Without looking at each other, Holmes quietly asked questions about certain of the guests who had caught his attention. The barkeep whispered back, displaying a rather impressive knowledge of the upper crust of London. I stood behind the two of them, within earshot, and scribbled notes.

We kept up this exercise for over a half-hour. The barkeep provided extensive data, some factual and some mere gossip, concerning the various personages and pretenders on the floor.

"You see those two chaps by the wall on the left," he said. "The ones in the suits that do not fit properly?"

Our gaze was directed to two tall Slavic looking fellows standing apart from the crowd.

"I do," said Holmes. "And who, pray tell, might they be?"

"The Ambassador of Russia and his deputy, who is also the head of the Okhrana for all of Britain. They like to keep an eye on their citizens to make sure they behave themselves. And do you see the three young chaps by the food tables who are trying to fill their pockets with pieces of meat and cheese without being noticed?"

I now looked in that direction and, sure enough, noticed three young men standing with their backs to the food table. Several times as I was watching them, one of them slipped his hand behind his back, grabbed as many slices of cold meat as he could hold and surreptitiously deposited them into his trousers pocket.

"They are," whispered the barkeep, "members of the Autonomie Club up on Windmill Street. Anarchists, all three of them."

"What, in heaven's name," I demanded, "are they doing here?"

"Other than stealing tomorrow's lunch, it is hard to tell. We overhear some of them saying that they hate the dancers because they are tools of the Czar and he is using them to burnish his image abroad. Others, particularly the younger fellows, seem to think they can recruit new members. They foolishly believe that because a dancer has an independent spirit when it comes to the arts or personal morality, they will also lean toward revolutionary politics."

"And do they?" I asked.

"Perhaps. Mind you, one of the leaders of the anarchists who used to live in London referred to such artists as *useful idiots*. Unfortunately for those starving revolutionaries, the dancers are not here tonight."

I watched as one of the anarchists, his pockets now bulging, sidled up to an attractive young woman. He leaned his head toward her ear and appeared to be saying something. She responded by giving him a look that could have frozen a volcano and walked away.

The barkeep was struggling to repress his laughter. "Better luck next time, Igor," he muttered.

"Why," I asked, "does the hotel allow mashers like that to enter the premises?"

"The fellow in charge, that Diaghilev chap, says we must not create a fuss and throw them out. Such an incident would then become the story in the Press the following day instead of the opening of the ballet. So as long as they do not start shouting their slogans, we ignore them. And they know that the Okhrana fellow will send his thugs to give them a thorough beating if they embarrass Mother Russia. Mind you, we do not trust any of them. But all I can do is keep the bottles of vodka under the table where they cannot be pilfered by either party."

As the crowd began to thin, Countess Betsy returned to us, beaming like the cat who swallowed the canary.

"*Yolki*, Sherlock, do I have a story? *Da*, what a story I have. It is juicier than even I could have imagined and, I assure you, my imagination is not lacking in degeneracy."

"We are all attention," said Holmes.

"Oh my. Where to start? Nijinsky. *Da*, I start with Nijinsky. Everyone here calls him "our Vatsa." He was a poor boy from Kiev but an exceptional dancer and so, when he is seventeen years old, he is made a member of the Imperial Ballet in St. Petersburg. What does he find there? He finds that there are rich, older men who, to use their words, "adopt" pretty boys from the ballet. No less than Prince Lvov adopts Vaslav. The Prince looks after Vaslav every day and the boy looks after the prince every night, if you know what I mean. The Prince passes off Vaslav to his friend, Serge Diaghilev, and Serge adopts Vaslav. He recruits him away from the Imperial Ballet and into *Les Ballets Russes* and makes him a the most famous male dancer in the world. He can leap and show passion with his body like no other man has ever done on the stage. Serge tells Vaslav to be a choreographer. So Vaslav Nijinsky creates *The Faun* and *The Rite of Spring.* Some say these ballets are brilliant, the work of a genius. Others that they are terrible, the work of a depraved madman.

"Serge is worried about the reaction of audiences, so he takes the choreographer job away from Nijinsky and gives it back to Fokine. Our Vaslav is upset. The whole *Ballets Russe*s company goes on tour this past summer to South America. Serge does not go with them because some gypsy told him that he will die on the water, so Serge does not like long boat trips. But this young woman, the one you saw attached to Nijinsky, Miss Romola de Pulszky, does go along. She is in love, utterly besotted with Nijinsky. She adores him. She pesters him all the way to Brazil and convinces him that he is in love with her even though they have no language in common. In Rio, they buy engagement rings. In Buenos Aires, they find a church, San Miguel Arcangel, and they get married. Our Vaslav is happy.

"When Serge finds out, he is not happy. He does not like to lose his pretty boy. Now there is a rumor that he will fire Nijinsky. Throw him out of *Les Ballets Russes*. The whole company hears this rumor. They are in turmoil. They will still perform here in London because many tickets have already been sold and Nijinsky will be on the stage. But after that, who knows? The company is like a swan. Gliding smoothly across the water but beneath, the feet are going crazy.

"Now, I ask you, my dear Sherlock, is not that a good story? What else do you want to know?"

Chapter Five
Diaghilev Comes
at Midnight

HOLMES AND I LISTENED, wide-eyed and fascinated.

"Indeed, my dear Countess," said Holmes, "a very good story. All is not well in the land of Russian ballet dancers, it seems. I now have several other avenues of inquiry to make."

Our gala evening ended. The two of us returned to Baker Street and a late-evening glass of port.

"Any thoughts or insights, my friend?" said Holmes to me after I had lit the hearth and stretched out in my customary padded chair. I took a long slow sip of port as I mentally prepared my considered response. I was about to commence my dissertation when I was interrupted by a loud ringing of the bell on Baker Street, followed by a forceful banging on the door.

"Merciful heavens," I said. "it is almost midnight. Who in the world could be coming at this hour?"

Holmes merely shrugged. I rose and, Mrs. Hudson having long retired for the night, descended the stairs and opened the door. Mr. Serge Diaghilev rudely pushed past me was a curt *"Dobryy vecher"* and began climbing the stairs. I followed him.

He positioned himself in the center of the room and looked directly at Holmes.

"Mr. Holmes, I thank you for coming this evening to reception for *Les Ballets Russes*. I am most grateful. I am never forget your kindness."

"And I," said Holmes, "will never believe that you have come here at this hour merely to express your gratitude."

"Ah. You are very smart man, Mr. Holmes. Yes. I am here because I need help from you."

"Then kindly be seated and state your case, preferably with a minimum of dramatic flourishes."

It was difficult to look at the man seated on the sofa and think that just two hours earlier he was smiling and joking with his adoring fans and sycophants at the Savoy. Mr. Serge Diaghilev now appeared deeply distressed.

"Forgive me, Mr. Holmes, when we met earlier for not saying to you everything I should have."

"Agreed. Please get on with what should have said."

"My company … my dancers … my *children* … we have big trouble come upon us."

"Go on."

"Where to start? My company, my *Ballets Russes* is tearing apart. How does this happen? It starts with Nijinsky. Vaslav I discover in St. Petersburg. He is brilliant dancer. Genius. I invite him to join my *Ballet Russes*. I make him famous. He is now most famous man dancer in entire world. I make him choreographer. He creates new ballets. He is genius but very modern. Too modern for audiences. We argue. I give next assignment for choreographer not to Nijinsky but back to Fokine. Vaslav is hurt. We argue. We cannot reconcile. He is dancer, so very … how you say? … very passionate. He say to me that he will quit *Ballets Russes* because of differences. Now whole company is in turmoil. Someone is trying to steal company from me …"

Holmes quickly stood up and pointed a finger at Diaghilev.

"Get out!" he ordered. "Get out of here this minute and do not dare to come back!"

Diaghilev looked shocked. "Mr. Holmes ..."

"You heard me. Get out of here!"

"Why you say me this?"

"I have no use whatsoever for men who tell me lies to my face. The entire West End knows that you have dismissed Nijinsky because he married and now prefers to spend his nights in his wife's bed, not yours. What you just told me was a pack of lies. Now get out."

Diaghilev remained seated on the sofa. He raised both hands, palms facing Holmes.

"I am sorry, Mr. Holmes. I am sorry ..."

"I have no use for your apology. I will not deal with liars. Now leave."

"Mr. Holmes, I beg you. Two of my children are murdered. I come here because another one of them, just a child, her life is in danger. She will also be murdered. You must help. I will tell truth and only truth. I promise."

His utterance demanded Holmes's attention and he sat down and crossed his arms across his chest.

"Very well. State your case. And if you lie to me again, I will throw you down the stairs. Is that understood?"

"*Da*. I understand. You are right, sir. I tell Nijinsky to leave *Ballets Russes*. This upsets whole company. Someone, I do not know who, someone sends messages to my dancers saying that they are invited to join new company. Nijinsky will come with them they are told. New company will give better pay. They are told, forget Diaghilev and come to new company. But must be kept secret from Diaghilev. Two dancers, Tatiana and Luka. They are loyal to me. They love me. I introduce them to each other and they become lovers and so they love me. They come to me and say me about this attempt to steal my company. I say them please, be my spies. Pretend to want to join new company and report back to me. They agree. Next thing ... next thing, they are murdered. Whoever does this knows they are spies. I am sorry, I should have said you this before. Because they are loyal to me and I make them spies, now they are dead."

He stopped, closed his eyes and clenched his fists and took several deep breaths. Then he continued.

"They are not only dancers who come to me. Also comes Veronika Vinokurova. She is mere child. Only has sixteen years. She is niece, daughter of my brother in Novgorod. On mother's side, has important relatives. I promise my brother and his wife I protect their daughter. She joins company and is good dancer. Plays swan, or maybe servant, or maybe child. She has promise. But she is my niece and loyal to her uncle. She also comes me and says me what she overhears about secret invitation to join new company. I also ask her to be spy. She agrees. Now I fear whoever found out Tanya and Lukasha and killed them also knows Veronika is spy and will kill her. Please, Mr. Holmes. I am beg you. You must help me find killers and protect her."

For several moments, Holmes said nothing. He was looking at our visitor very intently. I was reasonably sure that Mr. Diaghilev was telling the truth now and I assumed Holmes thought the same.

"Why," asked Holmes, "have you come to me? Why have you not gone to Scotland Yard?"

"If necessary ... if you not help me, I go to Scotland Yard. But if I go and say all to them, they make order that all remaining shows in London be canceled and *Ballet Russes* sent back to Paris. Then *Ballets Russes* is bankrupt. Creditors seize everything. There is no performance in Paris. We are over. Everyone is ruined and goes back to Russia. Whoever killed Tatiana and Luka is never caught. Whoever killed them gets away with murder and can now form new company. I do not want this. I need help of Sherlock Holmes."

"Arresting murderers," said Holmes, "is a prospect that attracts me. Preventing another murder of an innocent young person compels me. Saving your company from bankruptcy is your concern, not mine. Besides which, I am informed that *Ballets Russes* is already bankrupt. Is that not true?"

"*Nyet.* Not at all. We are in debt. *Da.* But bankrupt? *Nyet.* Is opposite. We are sold out all this week in London. We are sell out until Christmas in Paris at Opéra. We lose money on tour of South America because Czar tell Diaghilev that we must take Russian culture to world and we lose money. But now we are most famous ballet in world and we are ... how you say? ... a gold mine. Everywhere we are sell out to big houses. By end of London we pay off all debts and in profit. *Ochen' vygodno*! Why you think someone want to steal *Ballets Russes* from me? Is not any good if bankrupt. Only worth stealing and murder if profitable."

"How much profit?" asked Holmes.

"*Mnogo.* We go to Paris. We double price for ticket. Accountant and banker agree that by Christmas we have half million French franc. We go to America; we make ticket three maybe four times. They agree we have one hundred thousand dollar profit every month. Now you see why someone want to steal and murder."

"Ah," mused Holmes. "That does cast things in a different light. Much more interesting. Yes, Mr. Diaghilev, your case is of interest to me."

"*Spasibo,* Mr. Holmes. I pay you well. Very big money if you find murderer and protect my niece."

"You will pay me nothing," said Holmes. "I have already been consulted on this case by Scotland Yard. They are my client. I cannot serve two masters. Therefore, I cannot also work for you. If you have any further information about your case that would be useful to me, kindly furnish it now."

The impresario produced a photo of his niece. She looked no more than fourteen years old and all innocence. He had a full list of the members of his company and had marked off those who he suspected might be willing to abandon him and join a competing enterprise. He also had a complete schedule of all upcoming performances both in London and on the Continent. Holmes took these from him and asked many questions. I furiously scribbled down his answers. By one o'clock in the morning, I had tired and Diaghilev seemed exhausted. Holmes was utterly awake and alive.

Our visitor departed leaving Holmes and me to one final glass of port.

He looked over at me with a friendly smile.

"My dear doctor, I fear I must impose on your generous spirit."

"Yes?"

"My knowledge of the universe of dance is severely limited. In order to gain useful insights into this case, I must acquire far more expertise than I now have and do so rather quickly."

"Yes?"

"Beginning at opening hours tomorrow morning, I shall present myself to the desk of the library of the British Museum and request a cartload of books, ancient and modern, on dance and ballet. Therefore, I must ask a favor of you."

"Yes?"

"Would it be possible for you to rearrange your schedule and provide a close shadow to this Miss Veronika and see that she comes to no harm during the course of this week? She is living, as you just heard from Mr. Diaghilev, in a rooming house in the West End. Given that she keeps the hours of the theater crowd, it is highly unlikely that she will rise any time before noon, but between that time and her showing up at the stage door of the Royal Opera Theatre, she could wander anywhere in London. She will need to be closely followed and kept from harm. Might I beseech you to take on that task."

"Yes," I said. "Of course, I will."

"It may be deadly boring and utterly meaningless."

"That is what a book and a notepad are for," I said

.

Chapter Six
I am Not That Old

THE FOLLOWING DAY was a Monday. I rose early and hastened to my medical office and made arrangements for my colleagues to cover appointments with patients whose ailments were serious and to postpone those—the majority of them—whose complaints varied between hypochondria and malingering. By eleven, I was seated at a table by the front window of a café on Mercer Street, immediately across from the rooming house in which Miss Veronika Vinokurova was residing during her week in London. I had brought with me a newly purchased copy of the latest novel by a promising young writer, a Mr. David Lawrence. It was titled *Sons and Lovers,* and the reviews had been mixed. Some critics complained that it was indecent whilst others praised its modernity and brilliance. Just in case, I wrapped it in the paper jacket of an older novel, *Paul Clifford,* which might lead to questions as to my literary maturity but assuredly not to rumors about my seeking sensuous titillation in my now advancing years.

By noon, not a single soul had emerged from the rooming house, and I began to wonder if the location we had been given was correct. But then a pair of young women appeared, followed by three more sets of twos and threes but none of them looked at all like the Miss Veronika I had been instructed to follow. At twenty past noon, a group of six girls appeared all laughing gayly as if they had just been let out of school. Miss Veronika was a member of the pack, and I quickly thanked the café owner and began to follow them. All of them were young and exceptionally beautiful, and I knew that under no circumstances could I be seen to be following them, as a gentleman of my vintage being so observed would arouse far more unkind speculation than being caught reading a racy novel.

The squad of them were chattering loudly in Russian and giggling incessantly, so much so that I felt a pang of profound sympathy for the school teachers who had to endure such an age every day. They walked up Mercer, turned left on Earlham, and then left again on Shaftsbury Avenue. Within ten minutes they were standing by the fountain in Piccadilly Circus and soon could be seen chatting in English and smiling coyly in the company of some lads dressed in the blazers of King's College. I could see that my Russian ballerinas was quite comfortable and confident in the language of flirtation. Most likely, they could do the same in French. Some fifteen minutes of smiles, admiring looks, and charming laughter passed before the entire lot of boys and girls departed Piccadilly and walked en masse toward Leicester Square. Just past the Prince of Wales Theatre, they entered a select restaurant in which, I was quite certain, the bewitched students would soon be parted from their monthly allowances.

I stood across the street and read a copy of the *Times* and constantly checked my watch so as to give the look of a gentleman who was waiting for a tardy friend. An hour later, the group emerged, and I was quite shocked on seeing the young women plant friendly kisses on both cheeks of the lads before sending them back to their afternoon classes. I concluded, much to my dismay, that the morality of convenience, so notorious amongst the leading dancers and other artists of this age had been passed down all too quickly to this unchaperoned troupe of girls. Had I more time, I might have reflected on that thought but they set off quickly in the direction of Regent Street, and once they were finished with their window shopping, they descended on the select stores of Bond Street. They did not dare venture into any of those retail establishments but soon found their way into Fortnum and Mason.

For two full hours, they wandered the departments of the great store, picking up and putting down endless articles of clothing, hats, gloves and the like. I watched from a distance with my newspaper in hand. I was approached by several shop-ladies asking if I needed assistance. I smiled and replied with the universal response of gentlemen trapped in such a situation.

"I am waiting for my wife," I told them, accompanied by a weary sigh. They gave a well-practiced word of solace and left me alone.

Finally, the young women departed F & M. As I exited the store and stepped back on to the pavement, I noticed a large maroon-colored motor car parked across the street. I had seen the same car parked not far from the door of the select restaurant where the girls had enjoyed their lunch. It was in all likelihood a coincidence—those who patronize fine restaurants also shop in expensive stores—but I made a note of its registration number all the same.

Several stops were made along the way at food carts and pavement merchants, all accompanied by shrieks and giggles. At one point during the slow meander back to the rooming house, it struck me that these dancers were running late for their call for tonight's performance, but then I remembered that Monday is a dark night throughout almost all of the West End. They could wander until midnight, and I would still have to follow them; a prospect that I found too exhausting to think about.

Fortunately, by seven o'clock they had returned to Mercer Street, and I returned to my seat in the café opposite the door of the rooming house. To my great relief, they did not re-emerge that evening.

The following morning, I returned to my table at the same café and waited. Again, sometime after eleven o'clock, twos and threes of young Russian dancers came out of the rooming house door and made their way up Mercer Street. However, it was eleven thirty before Miss Veronika Vinokurova emerged. She was very smartly dressed and made up and was, even to an aging eye as mine, quite the beauty. To my surprise, she did not walk north toward

Shaftsbury, but south toward the Strand. She was walking quickly and even seemed to have a lively spring in her step. Then she began to run, interrupted with an occasional skip. Had I been a twenty-year-old and not well past sixty, I might have been able to keep up with her. Wisely, I stopped a cab that was going in the same direction.

Cab drivers are understandably loath to assist a man of mature years in the pursuit of a pretty girl who is more than forty years younger.

"Driver," I said as I hopped into his cab. "My name is Dr. John Watson. I write the stories about Sherlock Holmes? Are you familiar with them?"

"Well, of course, I am, Guv'nor. Read every one of them. Honor to have you in my cab but I would have given you a good ride even if you was a nobody."

"I am sure you would, sir. I identified myself so that you could help Sherlock Holmes and me prevent a terrible crime. Do you see a young woman in a black cape up ahead on the right? She's walking quickly. See who I mean?"

"Right. I sees her, doctor. What are we to do with her?"

"Please," I said. "Just keep up with her and do not let her get out of sight. Keep close. Can you do that?"

"Sure and I can. As long as it's for Sherlock Holmes, it will be no trouble at all."

He was as good as his word. Miss Veronika zigged and zagged her way south until she was skipping down Southampton Street on her way to the Strand. Then I saw her wave. At the corner, a man waved back. As we drew closer, I could see that it was one of the young men from King's who had been with the group for lunch yesterday. I relaxed. Obviously, they had been attracted to each other and had made a plan to meet again today. Possibly, they were going for an elegant lunch at the Savoy. I could not fault the young man for his taste in either dining establishments or lovely young ballerinas. He was, after all, a university lad.

I watched and smiled as he greeted her, reaching for her hand and bowing gallantly. I could not see her face, but he was all smiles and laughter. It had all the trappings of a blossoming affair of young love and rather brought a warm feeling to my heart. I was about to tell the driver that he could take me back to Baker Street and then decided not to.

A large maroon motor car pulled up along the Strand just behind the young man. It stopped. Suddenly a thick thuggish-looking fellow jumped out. In two steps he was standing behind the lad and gave him a hard sucker punch to the side of his head. He dropped sideways, almost falling into the traffic turning from Southampton on to the Strand. Then he lunged forward toward Veronkia. She turned to run, but it was too late. He had his arms around her, lifted her off the ground and moved rapidly back into the motor car. The car took off straight away and sped along the Strand.

"After him!" I shouted to the driver. At the corner, I flung the door open and shouted to the student who was staggering back to his feet.

"Get in!" I screamed at him. "She is in danger!"

He stared at me for a split second and then took two running steps and dove into the car through the open door.

"Can you catch them!?" I shouted to the driver.

"Just you hold on there Dr. Watson, we'll be on him in no time."

The young fellow had managed to get his body off the floor and up on to the seat of the cab beside me. He looked at me, eyes wide.

"Dr. Watson? *The* Dr. Watson who helps Sherlock Holmes?"

"Yes. Now, listen and listen carefully. Veronika was grabbed and dragged into that maroon car up ahead. See it. They likely do not know that we are following them. When they stop in traffic, we both get out. Veronika will still be on the left side, as that was the way she was dragged into the car. The thug will be on the right. When I say *go*, we both fly out of the car and run up to that one and open doors on both sides. You go to the left. Grab the thug by the hair and go for his eyes. Gouge, hard. No mercy. I will go to the right and pull Veronika out. Do you understand?"

"Uh … yes. Yes, sir. But why would anybody try to kidnap her?"

"Questions later, young man. Get ready to move."

The car we were following had moved east along the Strand, past the Savoy, and into the turn lane that would take it over Waterloo bridge. It stopped at the intersection waiting for a break in the oncoming traffic. We were still several cars behind, but I estimated we had a good fifteen seconds to make our move.

"Now!" I shouted.

I leapt out the left side, and my newly acquired accomplice did the same on the right. He was faster on his feet than I was and in a flash was at the target, had the door open, and had the thug's head most of the way out of the car whilst driving his fingers into his eyes. I opened the other door, leaned in, and wrapped my arms around the girl's legs and pulled.

Our monster was not about to give up easily. He kept his one arm locked around Veronika's neck whilst defending his eyes and fending off his attacker with the other. We had only a few more seconds before traffic would clear and the car would start moving.

Then Veronika took action.

She turned her head to the side, forced her mouth forward along a burly arm, and sunk her teeth deep into his thumb joint. The blood spurted from his hand across Veronika's mouth as he screamed with pain. By instinct, he pulled his hand back releasing his grip on her neck. I pulled hard on her legs and, using my own, braced against the running board to give me leverage. She came sliding out, and the two of us ended up in a tangled heap on the road.

The maroon car roared off through the intersection, turned and raced toward the open expanse of Waterloo Bridge.

The ballerina sprang to her feet, and I soon felt multiple sets of hands on my arms lifting me up off the roadway and partly leading, partly carrying me back to the pavement. Suddenly, I had become the victim, and these two absurdly fit young people and my cab driver were intent on rescuing me.

"The Savoy is just ahead. We can take him in there," said the lad. He paid the driver, and then he and Veronika half-carried me along the pavement to the door of the Savoy.

Once through the door, he shouted at the bellboy.

"Oscar, some help here please."

The uniformed bellboy shouted at one of the maids who ran over to us bearing the tray of damp scented towels that the hotel had on hand for greeting weary guests. The maid offered one straight away to Veronika, whose mouth and chin were covered with blood.

"No!" she shouted. "It is not me. It is this poor old man. Help him!"

By now, I was back on my feet and, having disentangled from the helpful hands and arms of my rescuers, I reasserted my dignity.

"Please. Enough," I said. "Kindly, follow me through to the bar. We need to have a few words." I began moving immediately toward the bar before either of the two of them or the now three bellboys could grab on to my arms and steer me as if I were a common drunk.

I led them to a table in the hotel bar. A waiter in starched black and white appeared immediately at our table.

"Good morning, Master Stapleton-Cotton. Lovely to see you again," he said to the student. "Some refreshment? Perhaps something warm on a November morning?"

"Thank you, Ronnie," said the lad, whose name I now knew. "Dr. John Watson, the best-selling writer in all of England, and a frightfully brave man as well is my guest. What will you have, Doctor?"

"Just a brandy," I said.

"Would Hennessey be acceptable, sir?" asked the waiter.

Before I could reply and opine that I was not in the habit of paying a month's wage for a snifter of brandy, my Viscount-to-be interrupted.

"An excellent suggestion, Ronnie. And the young lady would likely enjoy a chilled glass of fruit juice."

"*Nyet*," came the immediate reply from Veronika. "*Molodaya ledi khotela by vodki na l'du.*" She smiled coyly at the waiter.

"*Bezuslovno,*" replied Ronnie with a pleasant laugh. "Coming up right away, miss."

"Forgive me," said the young man, "for failing to introduce myself properly. Please, Doctor, ignore my last name and just call me Tom. And you appear to already know who this young lady is. I do not wish to be rude, but you really must tell us what this was all about. It is not every day that some thug knocks my block off, and kidnaps the girl I am with, only to be rescued by the partner of Sherlock Holmes."

"Sherlock Holmes?" gasped Miss Veronika. "The man who is famous detective?"

"Yes, my dear. And this wonderful gentleman is the one who records all of his adventures. This is Doctor Watson, the famous writer."

"*Bozhe moy.* Then please tell me why it is someone grabs me and tries to kidnap me and what does Mr. Sherlock Holmes have to do with any of this?"

I took a small sip on my over-priced brandy and looked solemnly at one then the other.

"I am of the opinion that both of you are people of sterling character and I have to demand that whatever I tell you must never leave this room. Will you agree to that?"

"What does he mean?" Veronika demanded of Tom.

"He means that we have to keep it a secret."

"*Da.* I can do that."

"You as well?" I demanded of Tom.

"Sure. I can keep a secret. This is getting to be quite the jolly adventure, I must say."

"Very well," I said. "Miss Veronika Vinokurova, an attempt was made to kidnap you because some party has learned that you agreed to work as a spy for your Uncle Serge."

"My golly!" blustered Tom. "You're a spy. Wow. Isn't that just bang up the elephant. The boys at King's will be in a stitch when I tell them that you're a spy."

"No, Tom," I said quite sharply. "They will not be because they will never know. You may never say anything to them. If you do, Miss Veronika's life could be in danger."

"Oh. Yes. Sorry. I will keep it a secret. I promise."

"That's better," I said. "Your uncle knows that someone is trying to take *Les Ballets Russes* away from him and whoever is trying to do so is prepared to do very evil deeds to get what he wants."

"Like kidnap people?" asked Tom.

"Or worse."

"Is it so?" asked Tom, incredulous. "Here I thought these music hall folks were all nanty narkers."

"We are not music hall," snapped Miss Veronika. "We are artists. If you think I am music hall girl, you leave right now."

There was a spark of fire in her eye. Whilst she gave the nonplussed Tom a hard look, I looked closely at her. On her head, she had perfectly arranged golden blonde hair. Her face was pale but without a single blemish. Her eyes were set wide and had a faint hint of the oriental to them. She was breathtakingly beautiful. Tom was struggling for words.

"Oh no, no, I know you are an artist, my dear. Of course, you are. It's just that … well … the people in the business of looking after our theaters, both artistic and vulgar, always seemed like a jocular lot. That's what I meant."

She seemed mollified and continued.

"Your uncle …"

"Her uncle?" interrupted Tom. "Who is your uncle?"

"My uncle is Serge Diaghilev."

"The impresario?" asked Tom. "The chap behind all those ballet shows?"

"*Da*. He is my uncle. My mother is twenty-third cousin to Czar. What of it?"

"Your Uncle Serge," I said, "has asked Sherlock Holmes to investigate and find out who is behind the attempt to take the company away from him."

"Really?" asked Tom. "Why would anyone want to do that? Doesn't everybody love him?"

"*Nyet*," said the young woman. "He is difficult man to work with. He thinks that universe should revolve around him. He shouts at dancers. He insults them. He makes them feel bad. Then he does not give wages on time. He is brother to my father, so I must stay with him. He is family. But many are unhappy with him especially after we learn he will get rid of Nijinsky."

"No," exclaimed Tom. "he can't do that. That Nijinsky chap is the best there is. They say he electrifies that stage, *the whole theater* when he dances. Or … or maybe it's Nijinsky that's behind trying to break up the company. Maybe that's who it is."

"*Nyet. Ne stat' glupym.* Nijinsky is unbelievable dancer. We are all in awe of him. As dancer, we worship him. But he is … how do you say … dumb bell. Try to talk to him is like talking to dog. He hears nobody but himself. Maybe now his wife. Maybe in the past, he listened to Diaghilev. Not now. No one will ever leave *Les Ballets Russes* and work for Vaslav. It would be disaster."

"If not Nijinsky," I asked. "who could it be?"

"No one knows," she said. "There is meeting planned sometime, but I have not been invited. They know that Diaghilev is my uncle and that I cannot leave him. I say to him that I will not be very good spy because I will never know anything because I am his niece."

Without revealing anything about the two murdered dancers, I asked her some questions and made oblique references to the score and mysterious page of numbers. She knew the score but that was all. I concluded that I would get no more useful information from Miss Veronika but that her safety was still an issue.

"Tom," I said. "You need to stay with Veronika for the rest of the afternoon. I suggest you remain here at the Savoy. No one is likely to try to kidnap her again as long as she is here. Then, at six thirty, you need to have a hotel car and driver take both of you to the stage door of the Royal Opera House and escort her into the green room. What you do after that is up to you, but I recommend that you find a ticket somehow and enjoy the evening. Can you do all that, young man?"

"I would be happy to, of course, but I have some duties at school."

"You may tell them that you have been requested by Sherlock Holmes to assist in a case. If they doubt your word, you may have them call me at this number." I handed him my card.

"Gosh. Yesterday morning, I was complaining about how dull my life as a student had become now that we were in late November. Guess I cannot do that anymore. You can count on me, Dr. Watson."

I bid the lovely young couple adieu, thinking that they were already starting to look longingly at each other. Miss Veronika would be safe in the care of Thomas Stapleton-Cotton, and I could put in a couple of hours of work. I took a cab back to my medical practice.

Chapter Seven
A Magnificent Swan and a Perverse Faun

THE AFTERNOON PASSED in a desultory manner as I tended to the unending whinges and complaints of the English populace. At five o'clock, I said good-bye to the last old fellow and walked the few blocks back to Baker Street. Holmes was sitting by the hearth, pipe in mouth, and surrounded by small piles of books and manuscripts that bore the markings of the library in the British Museum.

"Oh, hello, Watson. I have asked Mrs. Hudson to prepare an early supper. That will give us time to dress and get to the theater well before curtain time."

I agreed and then asked, "Any insights into the current case?"

"If by that you mean that I am quickly deducing that every party involved cannot be trusted to tell the truth, then, yes. I am holding out some hope for the innocence of the young dancers, but beyond that, I fear that cynicism may overwhelm me."

"Very well, Holmes. On a more cheerful note, are you becoming an expert in matters pertaining to ballet?"

He offered a small smile to that one. "As you know, Watson, my turn to an interest in the arts has been in my veins, thanks perhaps to my grandmother, the sister of Vernet. Unfortunately, art in the blood took the strange form of leaving me ignorant of this exquisite and magnificent form of creative expression."

"You are not alone," I said. "For the past century, all of England appears to have believed that the highest form of dance consisted in making sure that a lady did not accept two invitations to the same foxtrot."

Holmes chuckled. "Yes, and during that time, to our further chagrin, the classical ballet has been sequestered in all places, Mother Russia. All those years, we of the ruling class of the world wrote off the Slavs as no more than a mass of serfs dominated by a French-speaking cabal of Czars and Czarinas and their endless cousins."

"Are you," I asked, "learning anything of use to the case of *our* Russian ballet dancers?"

"All newly acquired knowledge is useful, my friend. But no, nothing has emerged that is immediately applicable. However, I confess to having spent several profoundly satisfying and enjoyable hours in my pursuit, which seems terribly unfair to you when I consider that you have done no more than follow a coterie of mindless debutantes through the shops."

"In truth," I responded, feeling somewhat triumphant, "my day was not in the least boring. I prevented a kidnapping and quite possibly another horrible murder, with some help, of course. I would never wish to take the entire credit."

That got his attention. Down went the scholarly study of the *pas de deux* and he demanded a full account, which, after feigning reluctance and protesting that I did not wish to interrupt his profoundly satisfying studies, I gave. By the end of my account, my old friend was utterly beaming at me.

"Well done, old fellow," he chortled. "Well done, indeed. So good to see that your military training has not abandoned you and you still seize the moment and rush toward the cannon's roar. Well done. Now, did you happen to get a description of the thug or the driver?"

"And a registration number for the car?" I chided.

"Yes, yes. Of course."

"The number, I have. As to the thug, he was young but a thick, swarthy fellow, needing a change of clothes and a shave, but rather like a hundred of those blokes who could be found in an hour in the East End."

"Yes, yes. But did he have any distinguishing marks?"

"He has," I said after a moment of reflection, "a very sore thumb. It is quite likely to stick out, if I may say so, rather like … a sore thumb."

Holmes smiled at my attempt at wit. "Very true, my dear chap. I shall let loose the latest band of my Irregulars and will likely have a report back by this time tomorrow. But now I hear our Mrs. Hudson approaching with what promises to be our supper. Let us enjoy it, and then we shall be on our way to the West End."

We arrived in ample time at the Royal Opera House. The theater had a well-earned reputation for pulling up the drawbridge and shutting its doors at one minute before curtain time, banishing late-comers to the bar until the first intermission. As the first item on the program for the evening was the twelve-minute *Après midi d'un faune,* we would have missed the entire performance had we been tardy. A split second before the doors closed, Countess Betsy appeared and trod across a half a row of feet that were foolishly not pulled back and then took her seat beside us. I am sure she was about to deliver a loud soliloquy and would have had Holmes not silenced her with and brusque "Sssh." The three of us sat back and prepared to enjoy the performance.

The ballet was shocking.

Nijinsky played the role of a male faun waking from his slumber to find a cluster of desirable barefooted nymphs moving about in an irresistibly erotic manner. He chases them about the stage, and the specific desire of his affections escapes his grasp, leaving her scarf behind. The ballet concludes with his performing an act which decency does not allow me to name but may be understood if I refer to the jibe, common amongst school boys, of shouting the augmented biblical instruction to "Go forth and multiply ... *by yourself!*"

When the curtain closed, there was a moment of stunned silence, and then a well-diamonded woman in one of the select boxes leapt to her feet and began applauding enthusiastically. She was followed by several other women in the audience who, I suspect, also made generous donations to the women's suffrage cause. Soon, half of the audience was cheering and clapping while the non-applauding members sat in silence, cowed by the fear of being labeled as degenerate aesthetes. A closer look at the woman who led the response revealed that she was none other Mrs. Elsie Cubitt.

During the brief twelve minutes of the performance, my eyes had been glued to the stage. It was as if the Portland vase had come to life. Holmes, on the other hand, had a copy of the Debussy score open in his lap and kept moving his gaze from the score to the stage and back again. At the final curtain, he had folded up the score and shook his head.

"We may as well join the unruly mob in the bar for the first intermission," he said as he rose from his seat and began to move in that direction. Countess Betsy and I followed.

"Countess," said Holmes, after we had been served our first glass of Champagne, "kindly continue to do the work you do so brilliantly. Please go and chat and listen and report back to me at the next intermission. Thank you, my dear."

She gave Holmes a smug grin and then disengaged herself from the bar and disappeared into the chattering barons and earls and *nouveaux riches.*

The second performance of the evening, *Swan Lake,* was a rapturous joy to watch. The roles of both the beautiful and innocent Odette and the treacherous Odile were danced by Mathilde Kschessinska, and Vaslav Nijinsky danced as Siegfried. Many times, after a spectacular dance—the *pas des quatre danse des petits cygnes* or the *pas de deux*—the dancers had to hold their positions whilst the audience erupted into spontaneous applause. And all of us, even Holmes, were swept into clapping along with the music as Odile danced the electrifying feat that only a Russian ballerina could deliver, the perfectly executed thirty-two continuous fouettés.

By the end of the performance, I could hear the muffled sobs of some of the ladies in the audience as Odette lay dying in her lover's arms and the two of them disappeared beneath the waves. The curtain fell, and the entire house sprang to its feet in a thunderous ovation. The Countess and I were on our feet, clapping furiously and shouting. Holmes was not.

His eyes were closed and his hands were beneath his chin with his fingertips pressed together. He was slowly shaking his head.

"Let us go," he said, once the final bows had been taken. "There is nothing else to be gained here."

We bade the Countess good night and hailed a cab from the long line of them that were strung out along Bow Street. As I climbed in, I happened to catch a glance of the crowd of devotees huddled around the stage door. Master Tom of King's College was standing there, shivering, but clutching a bouquet of roses. I smiled inwardly. My faith in the much-maligned student generation was restored.

Holmes climbed in after me and quickly slouched into the corner of the back seat, tucking his chin into his chest and pulling his hat down. I attempted to make conversation and had only managed to get a few words out when he interrupted me.

"You have a grand gift of silence, Watson. Please be so kind as to exercise it."

Which I did.

And I stayed that way until we were back inside the hallowed cloister of 221B. I poured each of us a glass of port and then decided it was time to poke the bear.

"Am I to remain silent?" I asked. "Or is Mr. Sherlock Holmes now in the mood for civil conversation?"

He did not answer my question. Instead, he took a sip of his port and spread a musical score out on the table.

"The two dancers who were murdered had a copy of *this* score and *this* list of numbers. You reported to me that Miss Veronika heard that some meeting was planned of the potential defectors to which she was clearly *not* invited and that she was not familiar with these cryptic numbers. Therefore, it is possible that some sort of message lies therein, but I can make no sense of it."

"The first line ..." I started to say.

"Oh, yes, Watson. The first line is easy. It states a specific date and time. *C.G. 28 – 11 – 11.00.* That must refer to the twenty-eighth day of the month of November—that would be this Friday—at eleven o'clock in the morning. The lines of numbers that follow are a complete blank. And I have no insight into the possible meaning of *C.G.* Do you?"

I pondered his question for a moment. "Might it be the location of a meeting? Covent Garden, for example. That would be within easy reach of whoever was invited. They are all residing in the West End."

Holmes nodded his head slowly and then replied. "That is good thinking, my friend. It makes some sense. Thank you. But if the first line gives the date, time, and location of the meeting, what is the purpose of the remaining dozen lines of numbers? So, no. It cannot be that straightforward. The cipher must in some way be tied to this score. And it must be something that a member, *any* member of the company would be able to see and solve. Yet to us it is as clear as mud."

It was too much for me at that hour of night. I finished my port, bade my friend a good night, and went to bed. I would not have been surprised had I wakened seven hours later to find him still in his chair.

Chapter Eight
Holmes Fails to
Solve the Code

HOLMES WAS NOT SITTING in his chair come morning. In fact, he was not in the house at all. I had no idea when he departed, but it must have been before I rose at seven o'clock. Mrs. Hudson delivered a nourishing breakfast, which I enjoyed whilst reading the morning newspapers. The reviews of the performance at the Royal Opera House spanned critical opinion from the sublime to the ridiculous. All of the papers gave glowing praise to *Swan Lake*, but the opinions expressed of *The Faun* were nowhere near as consensual. The *Times* acknowledged that it was "innovative and *avant-garde*" but cautioned that families intending to bring their children to see Thursday's performance of *The Nutcracker* were advised to arrive after the short first ballet if they wished to avoid awkward explanations concerning the unseemly actions of the

Faun and the nymph's scarf. The *Daily Mirror* and the *Evening Star,* wishing to retain their pretense of modernity, gave their stamp of approval, noting that the Victorian Age was now well in the past. The *Daily Telegraph* declared the piece to be utterly degenerate, catering to man's basest instincts and bemoaned the diminishing of the power of the office of the Lord Chamberlain, noting that under the Theatres Act of 1853, the current holder of the office, the Lord Sandhurst, still retained the power to banish a production if "it is fitting for the preservation of good manners, decorum or of the public peace so to do."

I was about to depart in order to spend another day serving as the guardian angel to Miss Veronika Vinokurova when a delivery boy brought a note. It was printed on a very fine stock of paper, addressed to me, and bore the return insignia of a house in Mayfair. It ran:

My dear Doctor Watson:

Words cannot express my gratitude to you for your prompt and courageous actions yesterday as you rescued such a beautiful, brilliant, and spirited young woman, Miss Veronika Vinokurova, from certain peril. Whilst I assure you that I have repeatedly given all credit to you, she insists on treating me as her hero and bestowing such affection upon me as might be the stuff that dreams are made of.

I fear that she may still be in danger and wished you to know that, following the performance last night, I insisted on having her come and reside at my family's home. I have assigned two of our drivers to serve as her bodyguards until she is safe on the ferry back to France. Both of them are retired Royal Marines, are armed at all times, and will never let any harm come to anyone under their care.

She asked me to send her apologies for not being entirely forthcoming in her conversation with you. In truth, she is not only the niece of Mr. Serge Diaghilev. She is also a distant member of the Czar's family and for reasons of state cannot allow her true identity to become known. Her passion for ballet is overwhelming, and her mother agreed to allow her to join Les Ballets Russes only if Diaghilev agreed to keep her safe from all harm.

Please, sir, do not consider it required of you to follow her again today or during the rest of the week. She will be safe.

Again, my thanks and please know that I am honored beyond all I could ask or imagine to have been able to assist in a case of Mr. Sherlock Holmes and Dr. Watson.

Yours very truly,

Thomas Stapleton-Cotton (Tom)

I leaned back in my chair and enjoyed a slow sip of my morning coffee. I could return to my medical practice with a clear conscience knowing that Mr. Diaghilev's niece was in better hands than I could ever hope to provide. I might even find an hour or two to do some writing.

At five o'clock, I returned to Baker Street to find Holmes, yet again, poring over a cluster of texts and papers whilst gazing blankly at the score by Claude Debussy.

"Have you learned anything, Holmes?" I asked.

He sighed. "more than I ever imagined there was to know about this most unusual form of artistic expression."

"Indeed? Do tell."

"The ballet was invented centuries ago in Italy. It was adopted by the French, who provided it with an entire dictionary of terms, confirming my prejudice that the French do not care a whit what one does with one's body as long as one pronounces it properly. But nearly a century ago, the art form was adopted by the Russians, and they have continued to nurture it and train the world's finest ballet dancers up until the present day. And they did so not just in the Court in St. Petersburg or the mansions of Moscow. Every Russian village and town lays claim to its own ballet school, local company, and performance hall. The same is true for their orchestras. It has been quite the revelation to such as I who must humbly admit to thinking that all those Slavs, only recently released from universal serfdom, were only a small rung above cave dwellers."

"That makes," I said, "for interesting history, but what about those strange numbers. Where do they fit in?"

"*That,* I do not yet know. We know that the numbers in the first line give us a date and time. If the letters 'C' and 'G' refer to Covent Garden, as you suggested and I take as a distinct possibility, then the following numbers may give directions from Covent Garden to a meeting place somewhere else in the West End. But ... the numbers in the first column range from one to twelve. Those in the second from one through twenty-four. And third from one through ten. Obviously, they cannot be linked to basic ballet positions. There are only five of those. Several of the more difficult moves, such as the *arabesque* have numbered variations, but again they do not rise above five. The human body only has four limbs, and thus there are a limited number of contortions that even the most advanced dancer can assume. The stage has eight designated locations, beginning with the center of the stage at the front and moving in a clockwise direction to stage front-left, half way back the stage on the left and so on. But there are only eight. So, it cannot be them."

"What about to a repetition of the movements?" I suggested. "We watched Mathilde Kschessinska do thirty-two fouettés, did we not. Wasn't she magnificent?"

"Indeed, she was. But she did them all in the same place. Now, some of the moves, those that involve running leaps, a *grand jeté* for example, may take a dancer some distance, but only two or at the most three are performed in succession before he or she runs out of room on the stage. The standard stage for ballet is only forty feet wide and thirty-two feet deep. No, there must be some other code to these numbers."

He said no more and returned to his books and the score.

"I regret," he said, "having agreed that we would dine with the Countess at Simpson's. I would have preferred to spend more time trying to deduce the meaning of the code. Nevertheless, it is possible that, given the unpredictable directions of her brain and conversation, she might spark an insight in my mind. We can always hope."

Holmes's hope was futile. Countess Betsy was radiant and charming and predictably banal. The dinner, however, was excellent. We departed the restaurant and walked over to Bow Street with sufficient time to spare for Holmes to ensconce himself in seats provided for us by Mr. Diaghilev in the Dress Circle. He spread the score of *Après Midi* on his lap and took out a set of opera glasses. Several sharpened pencils could now be seen protruding from the breast pocket of his suit.

As soon as the curtain lifted, he began to scribble furiously on to the score. As a decent musician himself, he was fully capable of reading music and following along in the score with what he was hearing from the orchestra. In the limited light, I could make out that he was recording the body positions of the dancers as they changed with the progression of the music. His concentration was intense, and at one point I saw him using two pencils at once, one in each hand. Fortunately, the ballets as choreographed by Nijinsky did not entail many rapid changes in body position. Most of the movements were intended to be slow and sensual, emphasizing the subtext of sexual attraction. Holmes appeared to be capturing every movement of all of the eight figures on the stage.

The response of the audience on the second night of this unusual ballet was more enthusiastic than the opening night. I assumed that those who had read the reviews and concluded that the performance would be offensive had decided against coming, leaving those who considered themselves to be amongst the self-appointed clique of the progressive and enlightened.

My second viewing of *Swan Lake* was every bit as thrilling as the first. This time around, I knew what was going to happen and was able to watch the dancers more closely as they positioned themselves for the moves they were about to make. Whereas the previous evening, my attention was captured by the extraordinary display of the lead dancers, this time I marveled at the precision uniformity of the *corps de ballet*. Sixty swans all moved as if they were a single being. Watching them was truly an awe-inspiring experience.

As on opening night, there was a short intermission after the end of *Après Midi* and a longer one part-way through *Swan Lake*. At the beginning of the second break, Holmes leaned toward my ear.

"Enjoy the rest of the evening, my friend. I must get to work on what I have recorded."

With that, he quickly made his way up the stairs to the upper lobby and vanished.

In spite of my vain protests of the late hour, the Countess prevailed upon me to join her for an after-theater repast at the Savoy. I had resigned myself to listening to her flamboyant nonsense but, to my surprise, she was all business. Not so much that it diminished her appetite, but in between mouthfuls of baked egg cocotte, rare breed sirloin, and lemon tart, she held forth on what she had been doing over the past few days.

"Doctor, my darling, Perhaps, you think I am nothing more than an amusing diversion for your brilliant friend …"

"Not at all, Countess," I interrupted. "You are a woman of the world with a rare set of exceptional gifts."

She laughed. "I hope you are more honest with your patients than *that*. Otherwise, they would all be dead by now. No Doctor, what I am is a farm girl from Wisconsin who is not afraid of hard work and willing to give diligent service to my employer, regardless of who he or she may be. Doing so has gotten me where I am now while my cousins are still milking cows and making cheese."

Now I laughed. "Somehow, Countess, I just cannot see you in that role."

"Neither can I. But now I must be serious. Our mutual friend, Mr. Sherlock Holmes, hired me not just to be his translator but also his informant. And so, I have spent all day, every day, trying to pry information out of the dancers and the other members of the company that might give me something to bring back to Mr. Holmes. I pretended to be the travel agent responsible for booking their passage back to Paris. That way I can ask them very personal questions about the food they will and will not eat, and who they will and will not share a cabin with, and which of the hunters is sleeping with which of the swans, and so many other things. Once a young girl tells me about her intestinal digestive problems because of foods that do not agree with her, it is easy to get her to tell me about everything else as if I were her mother fussing over her. I have worked faithfully at this task since I met with you and Mr. Holmes earlier this week."

"Excellent. And what have you learned."

"Everything and nothing."

"You will have to be more explicit."

"Well ... since you asked ... every time I pay a visit to the rooming house where the young women are living I spot one or more of those people who were at the reception. They are also watching the place or attempting to be nonchalant while they chat with the girls."

"Yes, as in?"

"There are at least a half-a-dozen Russian men whose suits do not fit them properly. They are either diplomats or spies—which are, of course, one in the same—or members of the Czar's secret police. Then there are those anarchist boys, who quite frankly seem far more interested in flirting with the swans than in recruiting for the revolution. And to my surprise, Mrs. Cubitt has dropped in twice along with a translator, a priest borrowed from the Dormition Church."

"Goodness, what would she want with the ballerinas?" I said.

"You tell me, doctor. But even stranger has been Romola Nijinsky. You know, that former Miss de Pulszky who married Nijinsky in Argentina. She's been chatting up both the young men and the young women for the past two days."

I sat back, bewildered. "This is becoming utterly indecipherable. I am tempted to suggest to Holmes that he should declare a plague on all their houses and send them packing. It all makes no sense whatsoever. But then there is the matter of the two murdered dancers. What to make of them?"

"You tell me. You're the doctor."

I could not. We enjoyed the rest of the late dinner, and I bade her good night. When I returned to Baker Street, Holmes was nowhere to be found. So, I went to bed.

Chapter Nine
Running Out on The Nutcracker

THURSDAY EVENING marked our third night in a row at the ballet. This time, however, as it was now less than a month until Christmas, at least in England if not in Russia, *Les Ballets Russes* put on a performance of *The Nutcracker*. It was again preceded by the short ballet, *Après midi d'un faun,* and I suspected that the scores of young mothers who were standing around in the lobby were waiting for that performance to end before bringing their little darlings to watch the joyful celebrations of Clara and Fritz.

I had not seen Holmes all day, and he was not even present at supper. I met Countess Betsy in the lobby, and together we waded our way through the throngs of children and to our seats in the Dress Circle. To my surprise, Holmes was already sitting in his seat with Debussy's score yet again open on his lap.

"Good evening," I said pleasantly, but before I could add anything to my greeting, Holmes raised his hand, palm facing me, and made it clear that he did not wish to be disturbed.

"Sorry, my friends," he said, speaking to the score, not to us. "Kindly do not disturb me. I may be on to something."

Throughout the short performance, he scribbled furiously, constantly drawing small lines with arrowheads at one end in the space above the staves. It made no sense at all to me, so I watched the strange ballet for what I hoped would be my last time.

At the first intermission, the Countess and I rose to make our way to the bar. Holmes remained seated, looking intently at the score that was now covered with arrows, stick men in various contorted poses, and written notes. I offered to bring him a glass of Champagne.

"No. I need my mind to be completely clear." Then, as if, remembering his manners, he hastened to add, "But I thank you all the same. Please enjoy yourselves."

After the intermission, the families swarmed into the hall. Little girls in pretty dresses could be seen, and heard, everywhere. The decibel level rose accordingly. Holmes was oblivious to the cacophony and, at the beginning of the *Ouverture miniature,* he unfolded what appeared to be a map of London and spread it out on one knee whilst still balancing Debussy's score on the other.

He continued to ignore what was taking place on the stage. The children dancers did their delightful entrance, and he did not bother even to look up. The same for the entrance of Drosselmeyer, then toy soldiers, and then the waltzes of the parents and the grandparents.

Just as the stage darkened and the audience was hushed, watching Clara rise from her bed and return to the Christmas tree to retrieve her cherished Nutcracker, Holmes suddenly spoke a loud "Yes!" and pounded his thigh with his palm. Several heads turned to look at him. Several minutes later, as the hungry mice were terrorizing poor Clara, he let out another "Yes!" but even louder and highly inappropriate, considering what was taking place on the stage.

Fortunately, we were in the front row of the balcony, so could not disturb anyone sitting directly in front of us, but several mothers sitting behind us muttered their "shuuuush" in his direction.

The tableau faded and opened again with Nijinsky appearing as the nutcracker who was transformed into the handsome prince and our local princess, Miss Hilda Munnings, born and bred in the suburbs of London, appearing as the grown-up Clara. The audience burst into applause, and the dancers began their lovely *pas de deux*. Just seconds before the number ended, with the orchestra fading and the prince lifting Clara high above his head, Holmes let out a very loud,

"AH HA!!"

It could be heard throughout the theater. Now even those who were sitting in the orchestra section below us turned around to look up.

Holmes was on his feet.

"Watson. Come. Now," he commanded.

"Holmes," I pleaded, in a stage whisper. "Sit down. There are only the snowflakes to come before intermission."

"No! We have to go now." He had grabbed my arm and was forcefully tugging on it.

"Countess," he said to the horrified Betsy. "Tomorrow at Baker Street at nine. Be there. Oh ... and enjoy the rest of the evening. Watson! We have to go now."

If looks could have killed, we would have been slain several times over by half the mothers and matrons in the audience. Once we climbed up the steps in the dark, pushed our way past the ushers and through the doors, and entered the upper lobby, I turned to Holmes.

"Holmes! Are you mad? What has gotten into you?"

"I have solved it! Come. We need to get out of here and up to Covent Garden."

He was already moving toward the staircase, and I followed him down to the street level and out on to Bow Street. It was a clear, cold, early winter night and I struggled to pull on my coat, gloves, and scarf on as we walked quickly—Holmes was nearly running—down Bow to Russell Street and then turned right into Covent Garden.

"St. Paul's is around the other end, facing the main entrance," Holmes shouted back at me. "That is where we start."

That much made sense. The first line of the cryptic numbers told us that. So, we pushed our way through the flower girls and food carts that were waiting for the exodus from the surrounding theaters and, a few minutes later, we were standing at the main door of Covent Garden, looking across the piazza at the pediment front of a church.

Holmes was on fire. He was still carrying his coat over his arm whilst looking at the score in one hand and his map in the other. It was cold enough that I could see the vapor from his quick breaths as he stood. I caught up to him, forcibly removed his coat from his arm, and held it out behind him, ordering him to pull it on.

"Right. Thank you, Watson. Now look, this is where we go from here."

"Holmes," I said. "For pity sake, slow down and explain yourself."

"It finally became clear. Look at the score. See the numbers? Those are rehearsal numbers, references that the conductor, musicians, and dancers use to find their way around the score quickly. They're printed at the top of the page and again above the first violin staff. There are twelve of them."

He held the score open in front of me and quickly flipped through the twenty or so pages.

"Each section contains anywhere from four to seventeen bars of music. You may need your eyeglasses, but you can see that I have put a small number at the top of each bar."

I quickly pulled out my glasses and looked closely. Holmes had written a tiny number above each bar. His numbering started over with each section. Some sections were longer, others quite short.

"Last night, I tracked the ballet positions that the dancers assumed with each bar of music," he said. "But it made no sense. Their positions were utterly non-traditional, and many were altered whilst standing in the same position on the stage. The only dancer who was moving about the stage was the faun. This evening, I marked his movements from one location on the stage to another. At various times he moves from upstage to downstage, or stage left to stage right. And occasionally diagonally across either a portion of the stage or the entire expanse. I have recorded each direction and distance on the score."

"Yes," I said, not at all sure what this meant.

"Let us begin. Here we are at the front door of Covent Garden, where the code tells us we start."

"Yes."

"That first set of numbers reads 6 – 4 – x 2. We turn to section six, the fourth bar. At that point in the music, the Faun moves forward from center stage and dances downstage to stage location One, the front and middle, just before the apron. Had he come much further he would be in the orchestra pit. He moves a distance of thirty-two feet."

"How do you know that?"

"Elementary, my dear Watson. Remember, the standard stage is thirty-two feet deep by forty feet wide. Thus, the distance from the center to the front is sixteen feet, and doing that distance twice is thirty-two feet. Now, if we walk forward that same distance from the front door of Covent Garden, it brings us out to the pavement of the west piazza, just in front of the church. Our second instruction reads: 7 – 13 – x 3. If we look at the score, I have noted that beginning at the thirteenth bar of the seventh section, he began in location seven of the stage, at the front and far stage right. He then turned to his right—and bear in mind that stage right and stage left are according to how they are seen by the audience, not by the actors or dancers—and traveled all the way from there across the entire front of the stage, a distance of forty feet which, when multiplied by three becomes one hundred and twenty feet. If we now turn to our right, we traverse the piazza and end up at the edge of King Street. It makes perfect sense."

"Holmes," I protested. "It may make sense, but it took you days to decipher. How are those dancers going to follow the code? They will not have all your scribbles and arrows in front of them."

"They will not need it. The map of the short ballet is written in their memories. Do I need a copy of a musical score to play Barcarolle one more time on the violin? Did any of the dancers during the past three evenings need a page of instructions telling them what steps to take, what positions to hold? Of course not. Do you need a medical text to tell you how to deliver a baby? Those dancers have danced *Après Midi* dozens of times. They know exactly who moves from place to place and when in the music they do so, and they can all read music. Their bodies retain the memory of the dimensions of the stage. For them, it is like reading a nursery rhyme. For anyone else, it is meaningless. Really quite ingenious. Now follow me."

The next set of numbers took us right along King Street to the corner of James. There we turned left and followed the code up James to Long Acre. From there it was right to the odd-shaped intersection of Long Acre with Bow and Endell Streets.

"Here," said Holmes, "we do as the Faun did and move on an angle, just as he did when dancing from stage location six back to center stage front, location eight."

"How do we know how far to go?" I asked.

"One of two ways can be used. We may, if we choose, make us of Pythagoras's theorem as moving from location six to position eight involves a hypotenuse. The one side is half the depth of the stage, therefore sixteen feet. The other side is twenty feet, being half the width of the stage. The sum of the squares is six hundred and fifty-six. The square root of that is twenty-five and six tenths plus an inch, perhaps."

"You are putting a tax on my brain, Holmes. It has been a very long time since I struggled through my maths back in school."

"Well, then we could do it the easy way, if you insist."

"And what is that?"

"Just look at the short section of road in front of us. It stops not far ahead and then turns. We go to where it stops and then follow the next direction."

"Right. That is somewhat easier."

Doing so took us through the intersection, and then we turned left on to Long Acre and subsequently followed it all the way out to Drury Lane. The next instruction had a high multiple, and we turned left on Drury Lane and followed it all the way to High Holborn. Another right and another high multiple led us to the intersection of New Oxford Street. We followed that to the east as far as Southampton Row, where we were instructed to turn back south two short blocks to Gate Street. Moving as the Faun had during the eleventh section of the musical composition, we walked a short block and a half along the narrow Gate Street.

We were now out of instructions but had found ourselves standing at the door of an old ale house whose sign proclaimed *The Ship Tavern. Founded in 1549.*

"Capital. Just capital," exulted Holmes. "Had we known the movements we could have found our way here in under fifteen minutes. I think we can be quite certain that this is the location of the meeting tomorrow when the fate of Mr. Diaghilev's company shall be determined. Come, let us investigate the place."

He walked in as he spoke. The place was very old and lined with dark oak panels and heavy tables. There were a few windows at the front of the main room, but the remainder was well lit with relatively new electric light fixtures. At the back of the room was a set of doors that opened into a smaller room in which chairs were set up to accommodate up to forty people."

"Most likely," said Holmes, "a favorite place for meetings of union locals or branches of fraternal organizations. Mark my words; tomorrow at eleven o'clock, it will be filled with Russian dancers. If we disguise ourselves, we should be able to sit at this table right beside the door and overhear everything that is said."

"They will be speaking Russian," I said.

"That is why the Countess will be with us."

"In disguise? Her?"

"It will take some application of imagination, but I am certain I can provide something appropriate."

"She will die before she lets you dress her as a buxom madam."

Holmes nodded and sighed. "Some bribery may be required."

Chapter Ten
Eavesdropping on the
Secret Meeting

AT TWENTY MINUTES past nine the following morning, the bell sounded on Baker Street followed by the yipping and yapping of a small dog and a set of slow, deliberate footsteps.

"Sheerlock, daahlink. You know, I really should not even be speaking to you," said Countess Betsy as she strode into the room and let down her tiny beast, assuming it would not run off in search of the nearest RSPCA officer.

"It is utterly unacceptable to run off and leave a lady sitting alone in a theater. And *you*, Dr. Watson. You did so too. I might have expected it from Sherlock, but never from you."

I smiled in return. "My dear Countess, matters of great importance to the Empire were at stake and had we been so indiscreet as to inform you of same, the Foreign Office might have deported you back to Wisconsin. And we would not have wanted that, now would we?"

She laughed back at me. "No, Doctor, anything but that. Even English cuisine—an oxymoron if ever there was one—is better than cheese three times a day. Very well, I forgive you both. Now, what is it we have to do today that required me to rise at such an ungodly hour in the morning?"

"You will be joining us, and we shall be spies," said Holmes.

"Impossible," she replied. "Nothing in London worth spying on happens before three o'clock in the afternoon."

"We shall be spying on Russians."

"Then make that four o'clock."

"Young Russians."

"They do not even go to bed, at least to sleep, before six o'clock in the morning. They are too busy with ... well ... you know."

"The young Russian dancers from *Les Ballets Russes.*"

"But Sherlock, dahlink, they all know me. I have been engaging in intimate chats with them for the past two days."

"That is why all three of us must be in disguise. Please wait a minute."

Holmes got up and retreated to his bedroom. A minute later he reappeared with a red velvet gown over his arm, and he laid it out over the back of the sofa. Even to my eye, I could see that the front of it was daringly low cut.

"Sherlock! I will not! Not even east of Aldgate would I be caught dead wearing something like that."

Holmes laid a wig of flaming red hair down beside the gown and then withdrew his wallet and added two ten-pound notes beside it.

"No one will recognize any of us. However, your utmost extended concentration shall be required. I trust we are in agreement."

"Is an elegant lunch included?"

"We shall be in a pub just off Holborn."

"Horrors ... Very well. I shall do it, but only because I adore you, dahlink."

We arrived at the Ship Tavern at ten-thirty and took the table Holmes had selected adjacent to the meeting room in the back of the pub. Holmes had dressed himself and me to match the Countess. The three of us could have passed for two sketchy pimps dividing the income from the previous evening with the local madam. The front section of the room was occupied by retired chaps who were still devouring their full English. A few of them looked up at us, ignored us, and returned to their sausage and baked beans.

"As we have a few minutes before they arrive," said Holmes, "would you mind, Watson, entering the meeting room and speaking a few words from the front as if you were addressing a full room of listeners?"

I did and recited a few familiar lines, beginning with "Friends, Romans, countrymen ..." and then returned to our table.

"Excellent," said Holmes. "You could be heard loud and clear. Now, if the two of you wish anything to eat, kindly order it now. Our young friends should be here by eleven o'clock."

The young friends did not arrive.

Eleven o'clock came and went, and not a single young Russian dancer had appeared.

Holmes was visibly agitated. At twelve minutes past eleven, he rose and walked back out the door to the pavement and stood and stared in the direction of the Kingsway for a full minute. He returned to our table, shaking his head.

"I appear to have failed in my deduction. But it seemed the only possible interpretation."

He sat down and lit a cigarette in an effort to calm his spirit. At twenty minutes past the hour, he extinguished it and pushed his chair back from the table as if to stand up and depart. Then his facial expression changed. He was looking in the direction of the door and smiling. I turned and looked as well and noticed two young men, both tall, slender, and Slavic-looking who had just appeared.

"Ah ha," said Holmes, quietly. "Eleven o'clock was not the hour at which they were supposed to arrive here, but the hour at which they departed Covent Garden. Likely, all the departure times were staggered so that they would not walk together and arrive en masse. Quite astute on behalf of the organizer."

Over the next half-hour, twos and threes of the members of *Les Ballets Russes* came through the pub and made their way into the meeting room and began to chatter amongst themselves.

"What are they talking about?" Holmes demanded of the Countess.

"They are young," she said. "What do you think they would be talking about? They boys are bragging about how much they had to drink after the performance last night. The girls are talking about their costumes and their sore feet and wondering what has happened to Tanya and Lukasha. They are all complaining about the food here in England and telling stories about where you can find a decent meal of zakusky and bliny. They are teasing each other and flirting. They are not old and serious like you, dahlink. Just be patient."

By eleven-fifty, nearly sixty people had gathered in the room. All the seats were taken, and several of the young men were standing along the wall at the back. Holmes was seated so that he could see who was still entering the pub. Countess Betsy and I had our backs to the door. At eleven fifty-five, Holmes's eyes went wide, and his lips parted. The other two of us adjusted our chairs and bodies nonchalantly so we could see what had grabbed his attention.

Three adults were entering the room. I recognized them from the reception Sunday night. They were the Russian Ambassador, the head of the Okhrana, and Mrs. Elsie Cubitt. They walked purposely through the pub and entered the back room. All chatter ceased, and the entire room stood up as they made their way to the front and sat in chairs that had been left vacant. One of the older male dancers came over to them, bowed, leaned over, and chatted briefly. Then he turned and stood to face the silent room. He addressed them in Russian. Betsy leaned in to the middle of the table and began her whispered translation.

"Brothers and sisters of Ballets Russes: Congratulations, I can see that you were all able to understand the code, follow my instructions, and come to this meeting. Now, my friends, it is my honor to introduce our Ambassador, His Excellency, Graf Sergey Semionovich Uvarov."

His words were followed by polite applause. Then there was a pause before the next speaker began. I could not see the speaker, but his voice was older and confident.

"Children of Mother Russia, I address you in the name of Nicholas the Second, the Emperor of All Russia …"

"And then," said the Countess, "he says all the required things about the Czar and the glorious country. You know. Ah, now he starts …"

"You have all been brilliant emissaries for your country. You have introduced first the French and now the English to the great culture of Russia and in particular to our magnificent tradition of classical ballet, for which Russia is by far the most developed in the entire world. You have done this well. All of France and England and now even in the Americas they speak with great respect and admiration of the culture of Russia. The Emperor, all of his family, and all of Russia are very proud of you."

She paused. "He is just flattering them. That is what diplomats do before they ask you to do something … ah, now he is getting to the point."

"We know that you have experienced great trials and tribulations over the past few months. We understand that Sergei Pavlovich Diaghilev is at times a difficult man to work for. This is common with many men of genius. We are, like you, very disappointed that he will not allow Vatslav Fomeech Nijinsky to continue to be a member of Les Ballet Russes. And we also understand why some of you, with nothing but loyalty to Mother Russia in your hearts, have come to us and said that the Emperor should recall Sergei Pavlovich Diaghilev to Moscow and let Les Ballet Russes continue with Vatslav Fomeech Nijinsky as the director…"

Again, the Countess paused. "Are they crazy? Nijinsky as director? He is now saying many nice things about Nijinsky. Now he stops and has to speak truth again"

Whilst she was listening, her eyes widened, and she muttered, "Oh no, that is sad."

"We all agree that he is the best dancer in the entire world but just because he is the best dancer it does not mean that he is a good choice to be director. And there is something else we must, with great sadness tell you. We have had Nijinsky examined by doctors. Good doctors. French doctors, English doctors and even we brought a Russian doctor. They are all agreed that Vatslav Fomeech Nijinsky is not well in his mind. His behavior and the things he says are not just because he is a passionate artist, it is also because his sanity is failing him. The doctors agree that madness is slowly overtaking him. It is possible that he will recover, but it is not likely. We all pray for a miracle, but we cannot act responsibly hoping that one will take place."

The fellow stopped speaking for a moment, and we could hear murmuring and then the quiet sobs of some of the young women. Then came the awkward muffled sounds of young men trying to hold back their tears.

"For these reasons, we want you to know that we have heard and sympathized with your concerns and your suggestions. For the time being, however, we have decided, and Emperor and Empress themselves support this decision, that we must allow Sergei Pavlovich Diaghilev to continue to lead Les Ballets Russes. We will have words with him and remind him that he must not show disrespect to his dancers and that he must pay your wages on time and that he must keep his private life private. However, it is best at this time that his decision not to have Vatslav Fomeech Nijinsky continue as a member must be respected. It is better for all of you, and it is better for Mother Russia if we do this. We have also met with the very great lady, Mrs. Cubitt, and we thank her for coming to this meeting. And we thank Anyushka for translating for her. She has assured us that one of her theaters, either the

Royal Opera or the Royal Drury Lane will be available again for use by Les Ballets Russes next year at this same time."

He stopped and again we could hear a growing volume of murmurs and whispering.

"Da. Yes. You wish to say something, young man. Speak. And speak freely. You may say what is in your heart. Your loyalty to the Emperor is not in question. Speak."

"It is," said the Countess, "one of the male dancers who now speaks."

"Excellency, we thank you for meeting with us and for your understanding and sympathy. We are all saddened to hear the news about our friend and brother Vaslav. There is, however, another matter of great concern to us and we need to make you aware of it."

"Da, speak. We are listening."

"We have received messages, bad messages, threats, from someone we do not know but they are all saying the same thing. They are demanding that we abandon not only Sergei Diaghilev but the company itself. They have said to us that after the performance this evening, there will be no more Ballets Russes. It will be gone, destroyed. These messages have nothing to do with the health of Vaslav or the behavior of Sergei. We cannot say for certain, but we think they sound like they come from someone who is criminal. We are all dancers, and we will perform because that is not only our duty but our passion. But, Excellency, please understand, we are also afraid. Already two of us have gone missing. Sergei has said that Tatiana and Luka have run away back to Paris because they are lovers but we do not believe this. We see the fear in his eyes when he says this to us. We know Tanya and Lukasha. They are our friends. We know they are lovers but they are also dancers and they would never run away from their duties to Les Ballets Russes. We fear for them. We fear for ourselves. Please understand us on this matter and do not say think that we are being cowards. Many of us have fathers who served the Emperor's army and who proudly wear the medals for their courage. But we know that something evil is taking place here in London. We need to know that we have not only your sympathy but your protection."

The young fellow stopped speaking. Various versions of *"Da"* could be heard from the gathered crowd. The Ambassador called for their attention.

"We have heard rumors of these threats and we are very troubled as well. My Deputy, **Nikolai Nikitich Demidov**, assures me that he will have men at the theater this evening. He will have men to guard you at your residences. You will be protected until you depart on the ferry back to France on Sunday. You will be safe. We make this promise to you. Now, please, continue to be brave and be great dancers. Tonight, you perform a very difficult ballet. It is brilliant. **Vatslav Fomeech Nijinsky and** Igor Fyodorovich Stravinsky have created a masterpiece. It is very modern, and Russia needs for you to show England that we are not only the greatest in the music and ballet of the past but also will lead the world into dance and music that is new. And after you give a great performance, we can all relax and listen to the English musicians, and their orchestra do their best to play The 1812. It will be a great evening."

"He is now calling," said the Countess, "for a meeting with the leaders of the company to come and talk to him and the Deputy. He is telling the rest of them to go and enjoy a terrible English lunch of fish and chips, and mushy peas served on yesterday's newspaper."

There was a burst of laughter and a round of appreciative applause. Then the room broke up into general conversation. I took a quick peek inside the room and could seek that the crowd had stood up and had formed into clusters of friends, all chatting. A small group was at the front, standing around the Ambassador and his deputy. Another small group, almost entirely young women, had formed around Mrs. Elsie Cubitt and, with admiration written all over their lovely young faces, were happily bantering back and forth with her.

Within a few minutes, the dancers began to leave the room, generally looking cheerful. I was prepared to do the same. His Excellency's mention of a hot pub lunch, even if in jest, had aroused my appetite. Holmes, however, was not moving. He had brought his hands up in front of his chin and assumed a very familiar pose. His fingertips were pressed together, and he was scowling.

"This is not what I was expecting," he said. "I had hoped that we would be able to listen in on a meeting between the villains and those dancers who were thinking of throwing their lot in with them and defecting. Instead, we have a group of earnest young patriots who appear to care as much about their country as they do for each other and an Ambassador who, on the surface at least, cares about his young citizens."

"Sherlock, dahlink, do you think the Ambassador is being truthful?"

Holmes paused before answering that one. "One does not reach the elevated position as Ambassador of the Imperial Court of St. Petersburg to the Court of St. James's by spending the past twenty years telling the truth. He may have ulterior motives and certainly is privy to some facts of which we know nothing. He did appear genuinely concerned about the threats to the dancers. Of course, it would reflect badly on him if something untoward were to happen to them, the pride and joy of Russia, and it took place on his watch."

"Will he be able to protect them?" I asked.

"Possibly. Possibly not," said Holmes. "So, come now. We need to find Lestrade and make sure he has trained officers guarding them as well."

Chapter Eleven
Break a Leg, May the Sets Fall Down

AT SEVEN O'CLOCK that evening, Holmes and I met with Chief Inspector Lestrade at the Sir John Falstaff pub in Covent Garden.

"I would hope," said Lestrade, "that your predictions about tonight are right, Holmes. I have twenty men, half in uniform and half not, who will be scattered throughout the theater waiting for something to happen because Sherlock Holmes says it might. You better be right."

Holmes smiled back at his old compatriot. "My dear Lestrade. You really should be hoping that I am completely wrong and that the evening passes without anyone, citizen or foreign, receiving a scratch."

"Cut it out, Holmes. You know what I mean."

"I do, and I sincerely wish I had more specific suspicions to give you, but I do not. Only that it makes sense that whoever it is—and we do not know who they are—will do something—and we do not know what—this evening. If nothing happens, they will have lost their chance to destroy *Les Ballets Russes,* and we are operating only on very questionable evidence of their intentions.

The alternative, however, to stand by and let them do something horrific, is not permissible. Is it, Inspector?"

"And where," asked Lestrade, "are you going to be all evening?"

"Unless required elsewhere, I shall be in my seat in the Dress Circle enjoying the performances."

Lestrade grunted. "From what I've heard that new ballet they are doing is like having alley cats screeching in the orchestra pit and the inmates of Bedlam going wild on the stage."

"I fear something close to that is how the critics will report it. However, Beecham's rendition of *The 1812* should be stirring. If nothing else, your men will enjoy that. Please remind them not to arrest the chaps sent by the Russian Embassy. They are supposed to all be on the same side."

At fifteen minutes before curtain time, we met Countess Betsy outside the Royal Opera House and entered the house yet again, our fourth consecutive night at the theater.

"Sherlock, my dear, you had better not abandon me again this evening," said the Countess, "or I may never speak to you again. And if you say something smart like 'Is that a threat or a promise?' I might just impale you with my hat pin."

Holmes looked at her warmly. "I shall consider myself a most fortunate gentleman indeed if I am honored to sit beside you throughout the entire performance."

"That's good, dahlink. Of course, I might get up and walk out if the new ballet is as horrendous as rumor has it."

"Ah, but will you return for Tchaikovsky?" replied Holmes.

"Only if you promise to finally take me back to the Savoy for my dinner afterward."

"I promise. Sometime after the performance, it is for certain that you shall be my guest."

We took our seats, and Holmes quietly opened the small valise he had been carrying and handed me a cloth bag, pulled tight at the top by a drawstring.

"Please use these," he said.

I opened the small sack to find a substantial set of field glasses, such as might be used by the Royal Navy.

"They are not," said Holmes, "as elegant as small opera glasses but these binoculars are much more powerful. Once the house lights are lowered, no one will notice you anyway. Kindly keep scanning the audience, the stage, and the orchestra and alert me if anything seems unusual."

The audience was much livelier than normal, and I could hear snippets of animated conversation, all talking at once about the *avant-guard* and quite risqué ballet we were about to watch and the reputation of the music which *"that Russian, Stravinsky"* had composed. Soon, the house lights were dimmed, and the audience fell silent. A round of applause was given as Thomas Beecham entered, gave a practiced bow, and assumed his place in front of the orchestra. Then there was silence.

In the dim light, I could see the orchestra conductor make a small movement with his outstretched hand. Then a quiet, almost imperceptible sound could be heard. Some single instrument that I could not identify was playing an eerie melody. It was joined by first one and then several other instruments, but they were not playing in harmony. They were in discord, yet there was something about the discord that made it compelling. The music became louder and louder, and then the curtains opened.

On stage were several clusters of men, some standing together, others sitting or crouched together on the ground. The accented strings began to throb, but not in any consistent rhythm. I could hear three beats, followed by two beats, followed by nine and then five. The timpani pounded. The group of standing men started to jump up and down in time with the beats. A female dancer, dressed as an old crone started making wild and awkward movements. She roused the rest of the huddled men, who joined the others and jumped and flailed their arms in unison. From the back stage-right wing, a string of females entered, also dressed as primitive peasants but not performing any dance step I had ever seen before. They were also jumping and stomping and flailing.

And it did not stop. The drums kept beating. The music was all in discord. And the dancers kept jumping and stomping, and falling down, and embracing the ground, and getting up and stomping some more.

"Holmes," I whispered. "What is *this*?"

He was gazing at the stage, positively enthralled. He whispered back without looking at me.

"My friend, you are witnessing the arrival of the future. They are *making it new*."

I took up my binoculars and kept scanning the house and the stage. I could not resist the temptation of looking at some members of the audience. Some were horrified. Others radiant.

The intermission mercifully arrived. Kissing the earth and becoming one with it and the strutting of a bearded old man had ended. I could not imagine what they would be doing in the second half. I was about to get up and make my way to the bar for a much-needed drink when I felt Holmes's hand on my forearm.

"Sorry, my friend. But I need for you to continue to watch this crowd especially now. If anyone is going to do something, it will most likely begin to unfold whilst the audience is up and moving around. Please keep looking for anything unusual."

The drink would have to wait. I picked up my binoculars and began watching all the antics that people carry on whilst they think no one is watching. Husbands were arguing with their wives, who in turn were either laughing with or arguing with other wives. One lady was fixing her hair whilst an overly large gentleman was conducting excavation operations on his left nostril. It was getting rather tedious, and the heavy navy binoculars had become a burden to my arms and wrists. I was about to set them aside when my gaze was frozen.

"Holmes. Front left corner of the orchestra section. Going through the door. See him?"

I handed him the binoculars and he looked in that direction but doing so was futile. The man I had tried to point out to him had exited through the door that leads to the off-right wings.

Holmes put down the binoculars and looked at me, wanting an explanation.

"I cannot say for certain," I said. "I may be imagining things, but that chap, even though he was wearing decent clothes, looked for all the world like the thug who grabbed Miss Veronika."

"Did you see where he came from?"

"No. I just caught him in my sight as he crossed the hall in front of the orchestra pit. He was walking purposefully but not in a hurry. He just worked his way through the crowd who were standing in that corner and exited through the door. Nobody took notice of him."

Holmes stood up. "Come with me. Bring your binoculars."

He then turned to Countess Betsy. "My dear, in all probability we shall return shortly. Certainly, in time to enjoy *The 1812*."

She gave a loud, haughty harrumph and did not bother looking up at him.

We made way back up the stairs from the Dress Circle, across the upper lobby and down the theater's far stairwell. I followed Holmes as he took me all the way to the basement, through a labyrinth of hallways and back up another narrow set of stairs. When I recovered my bearings, I found myself standing in the far corner of the off-right wing. A few dancers were standing around along with a dozen or more stagehands. Back against the wall, two large Slavic-looking fellows were leaning back against the brickwork, their arms folded across their chests. There were also four of London's police force in uniform, standing more or less at attention.

"Is Lestrade here?" I whispered to Holmes.

"Somewhere," he whispered back.

I followed him until we were standing beside one of the policemen. Holmes leaned his head near to the fellow's ear.

"Constable. My name is Sherlock Holmes. Is Inspector Lestrade back here with you?"

The policeman beamed a cheerful smile at Holmes. "An honor to meet you, Mr. Holmes. And you must be Dr. Watson. An honor, gentlemen. Yes, the Chief Inspector was here a few minutes back, but he went through the crossover to the other wing. You can probably find him there, but I warn you, he's in a foul mood. Didn't like the music he had to listen to. Not one little bit, he didn't."

"Thank you. Excellent advice. We shall leave him in his crankiness. Now then, constable, did you happen to see a chap come back here who was not one of the Russian bodyguards and did not seem to fit in with the company?"

"They are all a bit odd back here, Mr. Holmes. What might he have looked like?"

Holmes looked over at me.

"He was about your height and size," I said. "He was wearing a black suit and a dark shirt. Black hair and had the look of a nasty chap from Whitechapel."

The policeman gave me a blank look. "Sir, you are describing almost every one of these blokes back here. Only difference is that the stagehands are a bit undernourished and the bodyguards all look like they served as foot soldiers under Ivan the Terrible. Can't say as I noticed any one of them acting strange. They are all running back and forth and not making a sound. Up and down the ladders they go pulling the ropes and dropping the sets and getting ready to hop out on the stage and change things around. But that's what all these fellows do, sir."

As we were standing there, a voice far above us shouted. "Heads! Large, heavy set flying down to center stage."

A chorus of "*Thank you* and *spasibo*" was returned by the dancers and the stagehands. I looked up into the fly tower and watched as an enormous thing was lowered slowly to a spot somewhat upstage of the center. Several chaps gathered around it as it descended and guided it into place.

"What in heaven's name is that?" I asked one of the stagehands.

"It's the altar," he said. "That's where they sacrifice the Chosen Virgin. They put her right up on top of it and leave her there. After the curtain, we bring her a ladder so she can climb down."

The set, now that I could see it, was painted to look like a pile of rock and boulders. The top of it, sitting about seven feet above the floor, was flat. That made sense to me. You cannot very well have sacrificial virgins rolling off.

"All these fellows," said Holmes, "seem legitimate. Come, we shall investigate the other wing. Stay out of their way on the stage. We can use the crossover behind the cyclorama."

Holmes appeared to be thoroughly familiar with the activity and arrangement of the backstage world. I reminded myself of an observation I had made many years ago, that the stage lost a fine actor when Holmes became a specialist in crime. I followed him behind the enormous painted canvas that hung just in front of the back wall of the stage, and we moved over to the other wing. Lestrade was standing there, looking unhappy.

"If this," said Lestrade, "is what music and dance are becoming, I have no hope for the next generation. Making my lads watch and listen to this nonsense is beyond belief."

"*The 1812*," said Holmes, "is coming. Only one more act to endure. Have you or your men observed any unusual activity back here."

"If you had asked me, Holmes, if I had observed anything *usual*, it would be easy to answer. The answer would be 'no.' But no one has been waving a gun or a knife or tossing dynamite, if that is what you are asking me."

The dancers were moving into a definite line-up, obviously about ready for the second act to start. As they did so, a young man took his place behind one of the leg curtains. He was dressed in a fine suit and climbed up onto the top of a small podium, rather like one of the preachers who stand on their soapbox at Hyde Park Corner. A closer look at him indicated that it was Vaslav Nijinsky.

"What's he doing there?" I asked Lestrade.

"He stays there right through the whole act. He gives directions to all the dancers and when the music is too hard to follow he shouts out the beat so they can keep in time. Seems to know what everybody is supposed to be doing out there."

"He should," said Holmes. "He created it."

The general dull roar from the house suddenly went silent, and I assumed that the house lights had dimmed. A minute later, I heard a polite round of applause and concluded that Beecham had again entered and given his bow to the audience. In the darkness of the wing, a group of the young women dancers silently moved from the wing and onto the stage.

The music began.

Again, a strange instrument played an eerie solo. It was joined by a few strings and woodwinds, again in discord.

The main curtain parted. The stage was dark. Then the lights brightened ever so slightly to reveal a circle of young women in peasant dress standing in front of the stone altar. In unison, they started to move around the circle, all swaying their arms, heads, and legs in coordinated movements but unlike any ballets moves I had ever seen. Every so often they stopped, went up *en pointe* all together and back down again, and returned to their strange circling routine.

They kept this up for several minutes. Now and again, I could see one of them and then another cast a quick look at Nijinsky who was gesticulating constantly with his hands and arms, indicating the type of movements the dancers were supposed to be doing. He then stopped making circles in the air and started to weave his hands back and forth. The dancers complied and started to weave in and out and exchange their positions in the circle. They then kept this up for another several minutes.

Then the stage lights brightened. The weaving stopped, and there was just one beautiful, slender young woman standing in the middle of the circle. The rest of them were dancing, if you can call it that, in place and directing their movements in her direction.

The audience gave a round of applause.

"What was that for?" I whispered to Holmes.

"It's for the local girl, Hilda Munnings. She is the Chosen Virgin," he whispered back.

"What happens to her?"

"She is sacrificed on the altar."

Merciful heavens, I thought to myself. But then I remembered that in almost every ballet and opera, some young woman has to die before the finale.

The drums began to beat. In time with them, the dancers began to jump, and stomp, flail their arms, slap their thighs, and drop to the floor and pop up again. The music became louder and louder.

Then the men reappeared, some were dressed as peasants, but several had added bear skins, with the animal's head sitting on top of their own. Slowly, in time with the incessant beating of the drums and thrumming of the other instruments, they moved, menacingly, around the Chosen Virgin.

She did not move. She stood, frozen in place as if transfixed with fear knowing that she would soon be ritually sacrificed so that the earth would give forth an abundant harvest and sustain the tribe through another year.

All of the dancers, men and women, were dancing around her, stomping and threatening. Again, this continued for several minutes and again became louder, insistent, disconcerting. And then the Chosen Virgin began to move. She did so with non-stop jumps and twists, bends, and stomps. At times she turned and turned like a whirling dervish but flailing and contorting at the same time. And she kept going and going and going.

"How can she keep it up," I whispered to Holmes. "She's going to dance herself to death."

"Precisely," he whispered back. "Please keep observing those who are backstage and not just the dancers."

Meanwhile, he was transfixed by the performance.

I raised the binoculars once more to my eyes and scanned the fly loft and rigging and the high catwalks that allowed the fly men to walk back and forth far above the action of the stage. Nothing up there, I concluded. So, I shifted my gaze to the fly gallery on the far side of the stage and, in the limited light, perused the distant catwalk adjacent to the locking rail whereon all the manila ropes had been tied, securing the dozen or more batons and dangling sets that were stored in the fly tower.

I was not at all sure of what I was seeing and in a familiar if non-sensical move, I lowered my binoculars and looked in the same direction with my naked eye.

"Holmes," said, loud enough to be heard above the clamorous music. "Look."

I pointed to the catwalk high above the other wing and handed him the binoculars.

There was a man up there, and he was acting very oddly. Twice, I saw a tiny flash of light, as if reflected off of a small polished object.

"What is he doing?" I said.

"I cannot tell," Holmes replied.

"Should we do something?"

"Not yet. It may be nothing, and it would not do to interrupt the finale."

On the stage, the Chosen Virgin was continuing to dance like a crazed person. Turning, jumping, turning, dropping, rising, leaping. It was exhausting to watch her. Then, in time with a crash in the music. She dropped her body to the stage and lay prone. Then, one last convulsion and finally motionless. Dead.

The male dancers circled her, bent down and slid their hands under her limp body. Together, they slowly lifted her up and up until the men's arms were stretched out above their heads and the woman was being borne high in the air toward the altar. All of the dancers moved in and did slow movements indicating worship and obeisance. The Chosen Virgin was laid, lifeless, on the high altar.

I felt Holmes's elbow in my ribs. He was pointing to one of the largest sets held by the rigging above the stage. Unlike all the other units up there, it was no longer hanging level. One end had dropped several feet, and it was swaying and jerking.

"Dear God," gasped Holmes. "He's cutting the lines."

The same massive set was now bouncing up and down like an off-balance teeter-totter; first one end dropping and bouncing back up and then the other.

"There's only one line left," shouted Holmes.

He ran the short distance until he was beside Nijinsky on his podium. The brilliant dancer was utterly absorbed with the action on the stage and Holmes swatted him on the leg to get his attention. Nijinsky glared down at him and shouted something in Russian which I was certain was a rather abusive oath. Again, Holmes hit him and pointed up into the fly loft. For several seconds, Nijinsky looked up, completely confused. Then a look of horror came over his face, and he began shouting at the dancers.

The music of the finale was too loud. They could not hear him. I looked again up to the far fly catwalk. Whoever it was up there was moving his arm back and forth. He was cutting the final line that was holding up a massive set.

Holmes rushed up beside me and drove his hand into my pocket and pulled out my service revolver. He stepped out of the legs and onto the stage, pointed the gun at the altar set and began firing. The sound of the retorts exploded through the theater and were more than loud enough to be heard by the dancers. They all looked over at what appeared to be a madman shooting at them. On mass, they turned and ran toward the other wing.

Screams came from the audience, and people were jumping out of their seats.

The Chosen Virgin was still lying on the altar.

Nijinsky saw her.

With inhuman speed, he leapt off of his podium and ran across the stage. I watched as he did a shallow crouch whilst running and then, like a tremendous gazelle, he jumped. It was a *grand jeté*, his one leg stretched forward and well above the level of his head. His foot hit the top of a painted boulder some six feet above the stage. His forward momentum carried him on up to the top of the altar.

He stooped over and put his arms around the waist of the Chosen Virgin and yanked her up off the altar. Her face was a picture of shock and disbelief.

The audience was now screaming.

Nijinsky leapt off the altar to the stage floor, landing and somersaulting forward, the Chosen Virgin in his arms.

A split second after he landed, an enormous set, the forest scene from the *Nutcracker* of the previous evening, came smashing down onto the altar, crushing it. Pieces of wood and paper maché and wire mesh exploded across the stage. Some of it landed in the orchestra pit. Some hit Nijinsky and the young woman as they were staggering to their feet.

Pandemonium had broken out in the house. Women were screaming. Men were shouting. Bodies were already running toward the exit doors.

Nijinsky had lifted the ballerina to her feet and as I watched he shouted something in her ear. She looked completely bewildered. He shouted again.

Then Hilda Munnings of Wanstead, England, the Chosen Virgin, walked as only a ballerina can toward the apron of the stage, dropped to one knee and bowed gracefully. Nijinsky walked up beside her and bowed. Then he shouted to the far wing of the stage. Several seconds later, the entire troupe of dancers stomped and jumped their way to the front of the stage and bowed.

The screaming in the house suddenly vanished. After a few moments of stunned silence, the audience broke into a thunderous roar. Cheers, whistles, and endless loud shouts of 'bravo' filled the theater. I shook my head in disbelief.

Meanwhile, Holmes and Lestrade had gathered several of the police officers, and together they ran across the stage to the other wing, trying to reach the bottom of the fly loft ladder before the man who had cut the lines could descend and escape. He must have seen them coming. I could see several of them pointing up into the fly tower and shouting. A dark figure was running across the fly tower catwalk back to the wing where I was standing.

A larger group of officers now rushed back across the stage, accompanied by several of the Russian bodyguards.

It must have looked extremely strange to the audience, who were still cheering and clapping for the dancers. The decibel level increased to deafening when the second charge came back across the stage.

The desperate villain had descended the ladders and now jumped the remaining ten feet to the floor by the far wall of the wing. The Russian bodyguards who had not crossed with the first charge swarmed upon him and would have beat him half to death had not the London Police officers arrived, pushed the Russians aside, surrounded the would-be assassin, and put a set of handcuffs on him.

I recognized him. For certain, it was the same thug who had tried to kidnap Miss Veronika. I shouted my observation above the continuing roar from the house to Lestrade. He did not appear to hear me.

Lestrade made motions with his hands commanding us to follow him out the back exit, along with his perpetrator and several of London's finest. As we worked our way to the back-corner door, we came face to face with Serge Diaghilev.

"*Godpodin* Holmes! What have you done to me!? First, you give me heart attack, and then you make me and *Ballets Russes* most famous act in all London. Good thing I go back to Paris. The French are crazy but not as crazy as what happen tonight. I am never forget this night as long as I live."

"May I assume," said Holmes, "that your satisfaction with my work will mean that you will pay my fee promptly and in full?"

Diaghilev arched his head back with a look of exaggerated shock. "Oh, *Godpodin* Holmes, if only you had accepted me as client instead of tell me is not possible because you work for Scotland Yard. I would pay you ten time what they pay, but you will not allow. I am so sad. But I send you bottle of best Russian vodka as token of my thank you. Whenever you drink it, you think of me."

He laughed heartily, gave Holmes a friendly, hard smack on his back, and disappeared down the stairs to the basement and the dressing rooms where his dancers were now recovering from their shock. We caught up with Lestrade out on the pavement behind the theater.

Chapter Twelve
The Race to Southampton

"THAT WAS A NEAR RUN THING, Holmes," said Lestrade. "Lucky for us that dancing fairy fellow could jump like that."

"He is," said Holmes, "rather famous for that skill."

"Right. Well, I will have this madman taken down to the station and charged. Have to say, I am happy you helped track him down. Glad to have this round of nonsense over with."

"Inspector … I fear it is far from over. Do you truly believe that this monster did all that of his own accord?"

Lestrade glared at Holmes and then shrugged and sighed.

"Go enjoy the rest of the performance. And meet me at the Yard first thing tomorrow morning."

Holmes and I quickly made our way back up to our seats just a moment before the doors were closed. The entire theater was still abuzz with chatter. It would be a long time before they stopped talking about the explosive final scene of *The Rite of Spring*.

Thomas Beecham re-entered and gave his bow. The talking subsided. We took our seats beside the Countess.

"Sherlock, where have you been, darling?" she whispered somewhat more loudly than necessary. "What you missed! I am so sorry darling, that you were not here to watch it. *Oh bozhe,* you would not believe how those crazy Russians ended their wretched ballet."

"Sssshh," said Holmes. "You can tell us all about it after the overture has ended."

The orchestra's rendition of the famous piece of music was stirring, and they even included several house-shaking live canon blasts at the twelve-minute mark and ear-splitting church bells as it ended. On any other night, their use might have been the talk of the town the next day. Tonight, they were met with polite applause. As soon as the clapping had ended and the audience began to stand and prepare to depart, the talk returned to the shared thrill of the end of the ballet.

Over an exquisite after-theater dinner at the Savoy, Countess Betsy delivered an animated and perhaps exaggerated account of the end of the ballet which, so tragically, Holmes and I were not in our seats to enjoy. Holmes smiled at her coyly throughout.

In the taxicab on our way back to Baker Street, I could tell that his mind was elsewhere. Before parting to our rooms for the night, he turned to me.

"Thank you, my dear friend, for all your assistance with this case. However …"

"However," I interrupted him. "It is not over. And yes, Holmes, I shall be ready first thing tomorrow morning to accompany you to Scotland Yard."

"Ah, good old Watson. Have I ever told you …"

"Yes. Many times. Good night, Holmes."

***

Seven-thirty the following morning found us in Lestrade's office on the Embankment.

"His name he says is Jack Ferguson," said the Chief Inspector. "From Sussex, but now lives in London, past Brick Lane. Spent a few years in Broadmoor for being crazy as well as bad. Now he works as a thug for hire. We thought he would be an easy one to crack, but he's a clever devil."

"And why do you say that?" asked Holmes.

"Straight away his makes up a story that he was hired by the Russians to cut the ropes and that the entire thing was staged. No one was hurt, so where is the crime? It's his word against that dandy Russian impresario. Who do you think a jury would believe?"

"Ah, yes. There might be a problem on that front," said Holmes. "Would you mind terribly, Inspector, if I had a word with him?"

"Go ahead. My boys put his arse in a wringer for three hours, so I do not think you can do much more."

We followed Lestrade down to the cells in the basement. A guard opened the door to the cell in which a young man, dressed in a dark shirt and dark suit, was relaxed on a cot, with his back leaning against the wall. He was smoking a cigarette and his free hand was resting on his stomach. He had a bandage on his thumb.

"Good morning, Jack," said Holmes. "It has been a while. How have you been?"

At first the fellow looked puzzled and then a flash of recognition followed by a cold glare of hatred.

"What are you doing here, Sherlock Holmes?' he demanded.

"I need your help, Jack."

"I spent five years in the nut house because of you. You won't get anything from me. I already told the coppers everything. I didn't do no crime, and now they have to let me out."

"Oh dear. That is unfortunate. You see, Jack, it is not just about last night. Do you recognize my colleague, Dr. Watson?"

"Good morning, Jack," I said. "We met down in Lamberley. Your father was an old school chum of mine."

"I know who you are," he snarled. "I remember you."

"Excellent," said Holmes. "However, it appears that Dr. Watson also remembers you as the man who kidnapped a young woman off the streets of London a few days ago and is prepared to identify you as such in a court of law. I understand that your eyes were being attacked at the same time, so you would not have had a good look at the man who rescued the young ballerina."

The thug was now staring at me, but the smirk had gone from his face.

"Kidnapping, as you know Jack," continued Holmes, "is a serious offense and carries a hefty sentence. However, what you did was so far beyond reason that a doctor of the mind would very likely testify that you are still not well in your head and need to be sent back to Broadmoor. You might need another five years. Maybe seven to recover your wits."

The fellow's face changed from insolence to panic.

"You wouldn't."

"Oh, I would not. But a magistrate would. Mind you, if I were to testify that you were merely under contract to someone else, it would likely sway his opinion."

"Blast you, Holmes. What do you want?"

"The identity of whoever hired you."

"I don't know."

"Oh, dear. That is unfortunate. Of course, we might have to charge you with murder as well."

"Bloody hell. No one was murdered. No one even got hurt, except for me when that vixen laid her teeth into my thumb."

"The other two dancers were shot in the head."

Now a look of horror swept across his face. "Shot? No. I had nothing to do with that. He just told me to get them and bring them to him. That's all I did. He said to take their wallets so that it would look like a robbery and I did that and delivered them to him. That was all I did. They were both alive and kicking all the time. I never had nothing to do with hurting them. I swear."

"Where did you bring them?"

"Basement of some place in the West End. Brought them at night. It was dark."

"Who was he?"

"Don't know. No one ever gives a name; you know that. He hired me, and I did the job, and he paid me. No names."

"What did he look like?"

"Don't know. It was dark. Total dark. I couldn't see his face."

"How tall?"

"Can't say. It was dark. Told you that. Seemed about my height, but he could have been on a step. I don't know."

"His voice then. Did he have an accent? Russian? French? Irish?"

"He didn't talk. Just gave me a note with the offer and shone a torch on it. I said 'yes' and then he gives a paper with instructions, lights it up, and it says I have to memorize them, and then he takes it back."

"How much did he offer you?"

"Forty-one pounds, eight shillings, six 'p'. Odd amount, but that was what was written down."

Holmes stopped his questions, stood up and began walking toward the door of the cell.

"Come," he said to me and Lestrade. "We do not have much time."

"Where are we going," I asked as I was almost running behind him.

"Waterloo. If we catch the 8:30 to Southampton, we can get there before she sails."

"Who sails?"

"The *Mauretania*. The murderer is likely getting on it now."

Lestrade disappeared into his office came rushing out a minute later.

"I don't know what you're up to, Holmes, but I know that look on your face. One of our cars will take us to Waterloo," he shouted as he hustled his way out of the building.

We were soon in a powerful police motor car and racing our way across the Waterloo Bridge. Halfway across, the traffic ground to a halt, and we crawled all the way to Southbank. Holmes checked his watch constantly, but to my surprise, Lestrade calmly read a newspaper and seemed oblivious to the increasing likelihood that the train we needed to catch would have departed before we arrived at the station.

At 8:35 we pulled up to the front of Waterloo and sprang out. Holmes ran inside and looked up at the great board where the train times were displayed.

"We are in luck. It has been delayed. Who knows why, but it is our good fortune."

"Good fortune, my arse," said Lestrade. "Your good fortune would be better called a phone call from Scotland Yard telling them to hold the train."

In the first-class cabin, Holmes thanked Lestrade for his foresight and then spent most of the journey pacing up and down the corridor, smoking one cigarette after another. He was not in the mood to explain anything, and Lestrade and I had to content ourselves with speculative chat and reading the newspapers.

At the half-hour mark, the train made a brief stop at Woking Station. Lestrade excused himself and rushed off the train, returning just before the conductor called for all aboard. Lestrade was smiling, somewhat smugly.

"Holmes," he said. "You will be out of time to get on that ship and look for your villain before it casts off."

"We may have to stay on board after it departs. However, it makes a stop at Cobh, and, if necessary, we can disembark there."

"That will not be necessary," said Lestrade. "Departure has been delayed."

Holmes smiled at his colleague of many years. "Am I to conclude, my dear Inspector, that the Cunard Steamship Line has been ordered to delay the departure of their prize ocean liner?"

"Quite legitimate," said Lestrade. "Scotland Yard is going to carry out an inspection of their lifeboat drill to make sure they are complying with the new regulations that came into force this spring because of the tragedy of April of last year. Not going to have that happen again."

The great Southampton Docks were only a few blocks from the Central Railway Station, and a police vehicle was waiting for us. With its bell clanging, it sped its way right out on to the dock and pulled up alongside the gangplank. Once we were out on the pier, the chill wind reminded us that it was late November and even though the sun was shining, it was cold standing out in the open. The ship's captain, Mr. John Pritchard, was waiting for us at the top of the walkway with a cluster of his officers. They were not looking at all happy. His language, as might be expected of an angry sailor, was somewhat colorful and I confess to a bowdlerized account below.

"Since when," he bellowed, "does Scotland Yard conduct an investigation of a ship of state?"

Lestrade took him aside, and I assume confided to him the true reason for our discomfiting him and his crew. The captain nodded, turned to his officers and ordered them to move throughout the ship instructing every one of the passengers to assemble beside their designated lifeboats. His men looked exceptionally puzzled but being good sailors all, went and did as they were told.

"What did you say to him?" I asked Lestrade.

"I told him that Sherlock Holmes and Scotland Yard both suspected that a crazy murderer was on board and either we tried to find him now or he was going to be on board all the way to New York. The captain thought it was rather a good idea that we found him now."

An officer appeared with the manifest of the passengers and Holmes perused it carefully, shaking his head from one page to another. After looking over the final page, he handed it back, saying nothing. I knew without asking that whoever it was we were looking for must be traveling under a false name.

Twenty minutes later, the captain and two of his officers returned.

"They are all assembled," said Captain Pritchard. "We can start at the top with our First-Class folks. Don't want them too inconvenienced."

"Are they sitting on benches?" demanded Holmes. "Do they have blankets?"

The captain, in language that I shall not record, confirmed that they did.

"And no doubt," added Holmes, "are being supplied with Champagne, food and hot chocolate. We will start with the families on the lower decks. Follow me."

He turned and began walking toward the closest set of stairs. The captain looked as if he were about to explode. I happened to catch Lestrade's eye and knew that both of us were biting our lips trying not to laugh.

The lifeboat stations for the third and steerage passengers were a hive of laughter and chatter in every language of Babel. Mothers and fathers were holding their babies and toddlers in their arms to keep them from the cold whilst the older children had managed to all find each other and, needing only the universal language of play, were engaging in tag and hide and seek and endless shrill giggles. When called to attention, however, the entire crowd fell silent immediately and responded promptly and clearly when they heard their names called.

I heard names from every country of Europe. Back before the turn of the century, most of these folks would have come from France, Sweden, Norway, Denmark, Iceland, Germany, and Great Britain, especially Ireland. Now they were overwhelmingly Italians, Greeks, Bulgarian, Romanians, Macedonians, Serbians, and Russians. A least a quarter of them were Jews. I took a moment to gaze at them in profound admiration knowing that they were setting out to the New World to find a life and a future for their children. I could not but be in awe of their spirit and courage.

Within half an hour, we had completed the masses on the lower decks, and now, at the captain's insistence, we moved to the upper deck. The atmosphere could not have been more different. These well-dressed and blanketed folks were chatting amiably. I recognized some of them either from my medical practice or the society pages of the press. They were going to America for a pleasant holiday, much of which they might spend in the warmer climes of the southern states after they had shopped in New York. They generally ignored the officer's request for silence, and he had to shout some names out several times before getting an affirmative answer. As we walked past them, I could not help but hear a few of them exclaim something to the effect of "Oh my God, that's Sherlock Holmes. What is he doing on board?" That question was followed by, "Oh, isn't this a treat. We must have a nasty criminal on board. That will be a welcome relief to the boredom of the next week." A few shouted questions to Holmes as he passed by. He ignored them.

There were about five hundred passengers in the First Class, and we got through them in another twenty minutes. The captain announced that complimentary food and hot drinks would be served in the ballroom and dismissed them from the stations. That left the second class, of which there were another five hundred people.

Many of these passengers were tradespeople, or those with some means and skills and they were traveling to America either to start a new life and business or to engage in some type of commerce before returning to England. A surprising number were men and women of the Hasidic sector of the Hebrew faith. The men were immediately identified by the long dark coats, oversize Bowler hats, and the payots of hair dangling beside their ears. The older men had full grey beards. They were generally quiet and murmured to each other as they stood, huddled together against the wind.

An officer called out names and answers came promptly. We moved quickly from station to station. All the while, Holmes said nothing and merely gave every one of them a quick once over with his eyes.

At the third station we repeated the same drill, but as we were walking away, he turned around and strode quickly up behind one of the Hasidic fellows and, to my utter shock, gave the back of his head a hard swat, sending his hat flying. Shouts of horrified protest came immediately from the crowd, but Holmes then reached up and yanked at the fellow's hair. A close-cropped wig, complete with payots, came off in Holmes's hand. The man immediately began to run but was quickly tackled by two more of the Hebrew men.

"He is imposter," one of them shouted as they wrestled him to the ground. Four of them now man-handled him up to where Holmes and the rest of us were standing.

"Captain, Inspector," said Holmes, "allow me to introduce Mr. Gerald M. Coghlan, a rather wayward Irish Catholic making his return to the Great White Way. May I suggest, Inspector, that if you have your men investigate his activities over the past few weeks, you will have grounds for charging him with murder."

A cluster of burly sailors picked up the disguised American and carried him off the boat and handed him over to the police officers who were waiting on the pier.

Captain Pritchard turned to us and, refraining from any vulgar language, said, "We shall require a half an hour to get everything back in order before we cast off. May I welcome you as guests at my table until then?"

Chapter Thirteen
Elementary,
My Dear Inspector

WE HAD NO SOONER sat down and been handed snifters of a highly select brandy than Lestrade, as might be expected, demanded an explanation.

"We begin, as always," said Holmes, "with *cui bono*. There were several people who could have made a fortune by inducing the members of *Les Ballets Russes* to defect and join a new company in which the brilliant Nijinsky would continue to dance, but the talented yet impossible Serge Diaghilev would have no part. There is a considerable fortune to be made now that it has become so famous."

"Right," interrupted Lestrade. "We all know that. Now get on with it. How did you know it was him?"

"First, one must eliminate the other possible suspects," said Holmes, affecting an air of tedium. "Mrs. Cubitt has the funds and the ability to have a new version of *Les Ballets Russes* become the resident company in one of her theaters. She is an honorable woman who appears to have devoted her life to good deeds, but she is, after all, an American with a very checkered past. Nijinsky's sister, Miss Bronislava, is a brilliant dancer *and* choreographer, as well as a capable business woman and completely loyal to her brother. She might have tried to take control of the company and keep her brother as the lead dancer. Now you may be tempted to answer that both of these women are highly honorable, but I would remind you that the most winning woman I ever knew was hanged for poisoning three little children for their insurance."

"We've heard about her, Holmes," said Lestrade. "More than once."

"You occasionally need a reminder," said Holmes and then continued. "At first I thought the murders could have been ordered by the Russian Embassy if they suspected that the dancers were in league with the anarchists and dissidents. Or by the anarchists, if they suspected the dancers were in league with the Czar. God Almighty only knows what all intrigues that begin in St. Petersburg end up in London, and I suspect that at times even He gets confused. But we learned that the girl they tried to kidnap was a distant cousin of the Czar and royalty are not in the habit of killing family members, at least not recently. And the starving dissidents were more concerned with their empty stomachs than the revolution.

"I fully expected that the secret meeting which we overheard would reveal the identity of the villains, only to have it turn into a sympathetic hearing by the Russian Ambassador and Mrs. Cubitt. That eliminated them. The money lenders had good reason to seize control of the company to protect their investments and that fellow, Mr. Slainstein, remained on my list. But Mr. Coghlan moved to the top."

"Why?" demanded Lestrade.

"He had a very powerful motive in the form of a fortune in profit to be made if he were to poach the dancers, including the brilliant but dismissed Nijinsky, and take them all to America. You heard Diaghilev claim that tickets prices in New York could be quadrupled and an enormous windfall could be made."

"Any one of them," said Lestrade, "could have made a fortune if they took control. I asked you, why the American?"

"Oh, I am sorry. I had thought that was obvious. The amount of the payment offered to Ferguson gave it away."

"Well now," said Lestrade, "I am sorry, but it is not at all obvious to me, so explain, Holmes."

"Why would anyone offer such an odd amount? The reason is that according to the rates of exchange for this week, as given in the early morning edition of the *Times,* forty-one pounds, eight shillings, six *p* is precisely one hundred American dollars. Only an American would offer that amount."

I glanced at Lestrade. He caught me looking at him, and we both rolled our eyes.

Holmes continued.

"Whilst in Diaghilev's hotel suite, I observed an exchange of looks between the two young boys and Coghlan, and it was obvious that some sort of connection existed between them. It is now reasonable to conclude that they were *his* spies and were the source of information to him concerning Diaghilev's spies."

"Right," said Lestrade, "Mind you, I had the impression that they were paid to be … well … affectionate to Diaghilev, if you know what I mean."

"A correct deduction, Inspector. And if you were them, would you not be more willing to work for someone who offered you *more* spending money *without* wanting anything else from you?"

"Well, I am not them," said Lestrade. "But I suppose you have a point there. Keep going."

"Had the disaster at the end of the *Rite of Spring,*" said Holmes, "gone as planned, and several of the dancers either killed or grievously injured, *Les Ballets Russes* would have been in chaos. Bankruptcy would soon follow and poaching the dancers and staff would have been easy pickings. With the failure of the plan, I suspected that the villain, most likely the American, feared that Jack Ferguson could give him away. Therefore, it was highly likely, although not certain, that he would attempt to escape from England on the first and fastest steamship available which, of course, was the *Mauritania*. Thus, we raced to the docks to try to apprehend him before it departed."

"Fine. Just fine, Holmes," said Lestrade. "Not get to the part where you picked him out from two thousand passengers."

"Elementary, my dear inspector. His shoes."

Epilogue

THE MURDERER, Gerald M. Coghlan, was arrested and placed in jail He was, however, a man of means and had access to excellent lawyers. At the time of writing, he is out on bail and his trial has been postponed yet again.

Les Ballets Russes returned to Paris without either Vaslav Nijinsky or his sister, Bronislava Nijinska. They both remained in London and attempted unsuccessfully to form another dance company. Nijinsky and his new wife then moved to Vienna where, I am told, dismal events have overtaken their lives. When war broke out across Europe, Nijinsky, being classed as a Russian and therefore an enemy alien, was placed under house arrest. His mind, sadly, continued to deteriorate and it will not be long before he will be confined to an institution for the mentally ill.

The English girl from Wanstead, Hilda Munnings, has changed her name to Lydia Sokolova, and continues to dance brilliantly, mainly in character roles, with *Les Ballets Russes*.

The handsome and courageous young lord, Tom, (now Sir Thomas Stapleton-Cotton) who helped rescue the abducted ballerina, has completed his studies and is running for a seat in Parliament. The lovely Miss Veronika has been replaced by a sensible if plain-looking English girl, foisted on Tom by his mother, who knew that dalliances with Russian dancers were fraught with danger.

Sherlock Holmes has expanded his appreciation of the arts and is now an enthusiastic follower of the ballet.

Historical and Other Notes

In 1909, Serge Diaghilev brought his company of classically trained Russian ballet dancers to Paris. From then until Diaghilev's death in 1929, they performed in Paris and toured throughout the world. Their impact on the universe of dance is unparalleled. They brought classical ballet back to the stage and introduced modern interpretive ballet to the universe of arts and letters. Many of the individual dancers, such as Ana Pavlova, Bronislava Nijinska, and George Balanchine went on to found schools of ballet and subsequent companies.

Vaslav Nijinsky, now recognized as one of the most brilliant ballet dancers of all time, had a tragically short public career before his break with Serge Diaghilev and his subsequent descent into schizophrenia and a life spent in and out of mental institutions.

The information in this story about *Les Ballets Russes,* Serge Diaghilev, Igor Stravinsky, Vaslav Nijinsky, and the various other historical characters is generally accurate. Some names and dates have been altered to fit the narrative. The Russian dancers did introduce *Le Sacre du Printemps* to an audience in Paris in the spring of 1913 and a riot actually broke out in the Paris Opéra. They also performed it in London but did so before the fated tour to South America, not after.

References to murder, treachery, Scotland Yard and Sherlock Holmes are fictional.

However, while doing the research for the story, I learned that *Les Ballets Russes* had gone on a tour of South America during the summer of 1913. During that tour, Vaslav Nijinsky married Romola de Pulszky, bringing about the rupture of his relationship with Serge Diaghilev. They were married in the church of San Migual Arcangel, located on Suipacha Steet in central Buenos Aires. As I write these words I am living on Suipacha Street, a few blocks north of the church and have been throughout the time of writing the story. Who knew? (I took the photo).

Serge Diaghilev was a brilliant and flamboyant impresario who was openly gay. He was what we would now call a "sugar daddy" to a long line of young male ballet dancers, including Nijinsky. He regularly stayed at the Savoy Hotel and *Les Ballets Russes* performed in the Royal Opera House and the Royal Drury Lane Theatre while in London. (took this one too).

The Ship Tavern is still where it was in 1913, just off of High Holborn. You can walk to it from Covent Garden using the route provided in the story.

The *Mauretania*, one of the great ships of the Cunard Line, held the Blue Riband for many years. Lifeboat drills and adequate provision of life jackets and lifeboats were instituted following the *Titanic* disaster in the spring of 1912.

The ballets and music referred to in the story are still enjoyed by audiences throughout the world.

Simpson's Restaurant is still where it was on the Strand and is still a select dining establishment.

A NEW SHERLOCK HOLMES MYSTERY

THE SOLITARY BICYCLE THIEF

CRAIG STEPHEN COPLAND

The Solitary Bicycle Thief

A New Sherlock Holmes Mystery

Chapter One
The Bicycle Thefts

Daisy, Daisy, Give me your answer do.
I'm half crazy over the love of you.
It won't be a stylish marriage,
I can't afford a carriage.
But you'll look sweet, upon the seat
Of a bicycle built for two.
            From *Daisy Bell* by Harry Dacre, 1892

OF LATE, ENGLISH MEN AND WOMEN, particularly the younger generation, have enthusiastically embraced the joyful sport of cycling.

Just the other day, Mr. A.C. Doyle, my agent for stories about Sherlock Holmes, mused:

> *When the spirits are low, when the day appears dark, when work becomes monotonous, when hope hardly seems worth having, just mount a bicycle and go out for a spin down the road, without thought on anything but the ride you are taking.*

I am sure that many of you agree with him.

I do not.

There was a time, some years ago, when I might have.

Now, I fear that my thoughts and feelings concerning cycling have been forever tainted by a frightful case pursued by Sherlock Holmes in the early spring of 1904.

Of course, one does not expect the joyful sport of cycling to become entangled with murder, a cabal of evil men and women, and crimes too unseemly to name. But that was indeed the nature of this unusual case, with all its ingenuity and dramatic quality of solution, which I now put on account.

It began on an otherwise pleasant March morning with a note from Holmes. It was brought to my door at about half ten, and it ran:

```
Watson: Could you please come by at 11
o'clock? A former client is paying a
call, and it would be valuable if you
could be here. Shall see you then.
Holmes
```

It was a Saturday, and I was concerned about abandoning my dear wife.

"Darling!" I shouted up the stairs. "Holmes has asked me to come over. Would you mind terribly if I am gone for an hour or two?"

She descended the stairs whilst I read out Holmes's note to her. She smiled warmly and came a gave me an affectionate kiss on my cheek.

"Please go. I do love you, and I married you for better or worse but *not* for lunch. I have no end of things to get done, and your absence would be a welcome relief. Do have a jolly time helping Sherlock rid the world of evil and let me know if you are not going to be back in time for dinner."

I started to protest, but she again kissed me, this time directly on my lips, shutting me up. Whereupon, she turned around and went back up the stairs. I followed her and, as it was a Saturday, quickly dressed in a casual manner.

I should have known better.

"Dearest," she said, sighing, "you are not wearing *that*, are you? An old client is very likely coming to see Holmes with the intent of becoming a new client. Saturday or not, you do not want to frighten him away by looking like you just got off the boat from America."

The delay meant that I had to walk briskly to be at 221B on time. Fortunately, it was only a few blocks from our home near Little Venice to Baker Street, and I made it by five minutes past the hour. Although I was in a hurry, I stopped for a second and observed the lamppost immediately across from Holmes's door. Leaning against it and securely protected by a chain and lock was a gleaming new bicycle and not just one of the run-of-the-mill variety that I was used to seeing all over the streets of London. This was a new tandem bicycle from the renowned firm of Pedersen and Company in Dursley and certainly cost the owner a goodly portion of his wages. It did not occur to me that it was ridden by Holmes's client as I was only expecting one person not two.

The door was open, and I climbed the familiar stairs and entered the front room. A very handsome couple rose from the sofa, as eventually did Holmes from his habitual armchair. A beautiful young woman stepped toward me.

"Good morning, Dr. Watson," said the woman. She was tall, graceful and queenly and greeted me with her outstretched hand.

"Merciful heavens!" I sputtered. "Violet Smith ... ah, no, now it is Mrs. Cyril Morton. What a delightful surprise. And you, sir, you must be Mr. Cyril Morton."

I directed these latter words to the broad-shouldered, fine-looking gentleman who stood behind his wife, smiling proudly.

"That I am, sir," he said. "And if it were not for the bravery of you and Mr. Sherlock Holmes, I might never have become the blessed husband of Violet Smith."

He walked over to me and, taking my right hand in his and placing his left upon my wrist, shook my hand in a most collegial manner.

Readers will remember Miss Violet Smith from my account of her case, *The Solitary Cyclist,* several years back. At that time, unknown to her, she was about to be the heir to a great fortune and was horribly abducted by a pair of scoundrels and forced into a marriage. Holmes and I arrived not a minute too soon to rescue her from a fate worse than death. Shortly afterward, her false marriage annulled, she married a very successful young electrician, Cyril Morton and, the last I had heard, they were enjoying the life of a very wealthy young couple.

"My goodness," I said. "What a delight to see you. The two of you look wonderful. Pray tell, what have you been up to? Why, it must be almost a decade since I saw you last."

For the next fifteen minutes or so, assisted by a serving of tea and warm scones brought by the ever-faithful Mrs. Hudson, they recounted the recent events of their life.

Holmes listened attentively and even posed a few questions of sincere interest. He had mellowed over the years, and I remembered how in our early days together I would cringe at his brusqueness with clients, demanding that they "state your case" even before a decent "good morning" could be exchanged.

But on this relaxed Saturday morning, he was all smiles. We learned that Mr. and Mrs. Morton were the proud parents of children (two – a son and a daughter), homeowners (also two – a small estate property in Tunbridge Wells and a townhouse in Chelsea), a dog (only one – a German Shepherd), complete owners of the famous Westminster firm of Morton and Kennedy Electrical Company, and partial owners through shares of other firms (too numerous to mention). He was fully engaged in the management of his firm and, although not wanting for any additional income, she continued to give music lessons for the sheer spiritual joy of doing so and for the relief it brought to the sameness of quotidian married life. They and their children had enjoyed splendid vacations on the Continent and belonged to several clubs and associations dedicated to the healthy outdoor pursuits of cycling, hiking, and shooting.

This last piece of information led me to ask about the bicycle I saw out on the pavement.

"Yes, Doctor," said Cyril, "that is our latest toy. I bought it just two weeks ago as an anniversary present for my wife; and as it was a lovely Saturday morning without much traffic on the streets, she suggested that we pedal to Baker Street from Chelsea."

Ah ha, I thought to myself. That explains the somewhat unusual way they were dressed. Their clothing was obviously custom cut and of a high quality but was oddly casual. He was wearing a short suit jacket of the sort normally used when riding to the hounds and a pair of military-style breeches. His wife sported what I had first thought was an elegant long skirt but could now see was what the fashion magazines called a *split skirt*. It had a row of buttons down the entire length of the middle of the front and a matching row down the back. It allowed the wearer to unbutton it fore and aft and rearrange the buttons so that it became a pair of loose trousers. Frowned upon by the dowagers of Mayfair, it was all the rage amongst the young cyclist crowd, for it allowed a woman to pedal forcefully, unhindered by flowing skirts, and then to make repairs and reappear quickly as an elegantly dressed young lady.

I was about to make further inquiries concerning their passion for cycling when Holmes, as I might have known, drew the idle chit-chat to a close.

"Lovely," he said, "to hear about your recreational activities, but I assume there was a reason for your sudden appointment, and it has nothing whatsoever to do with bicycling. Pray, please enlighten me as to the reason for your visit."

"Oh, Mr. Holmes," said Violet cheerily. "There you are wrong. We are here precisely because of bicycling."

She beamed a radiant impish smile at him, and he smiled back.

"Indeed?" he said. "I have been wrong before, and it appears I am now again. Kindly correct me."

"Why don't you tell him, darling?" she said to her husband.

"No, you, dear," he said. "You are far more gifted in the literary arts."

"But you are the engineer, and much more precise," she countered.

As it was, they both gave their account. She started.

"It all began not long ago," she said.

"Fourteen days," he said. "On the tenth of the month; in the morning."

"Yes, dear," she said. "We were at our home in Chelsea. It was a damp morning, not at all like today. We had agreed to meet some friends, Mr. and Mrs. Fitzroy, who live just a few blocks away …"

"On Shawfield Street," he said.

"Yes, of course, dear" she continued. "We were going for a morning of cycling. I had organized the outing, packed a lunch basket for us, and we had both dressed for the weather."

"The probs," he said, "called for the skies to clear."

"Yes, dear. And when we walked to the back of the house to fetch our bicycles, we were shocked."

"They were gone," he said.

"Thank you, dear. Yes, someone had stolen them. I could not believe it. They were not at all new. Cyril had bought them used, and we had been riding them for five years."

"Six."

"Yes, dear. Our day was ruined. I was deeply embarrassed, having to cancel on Ozzie and Suzie."

"She means Mr. and Mrs. Fitzroy."

"Yes, dear. And instead of having a splendid outing, I spent the day on the High Street in Knightsbridge and Cyril went off to goodness knows where."

"Hoping to find new bicycles to purchase," he said.

Here both of them stopped for a moment, and Holmes interrupted the account.

"I truly hope," said Holmes, "that I am not wrong a second time, but I assume that you have not come to engage my services to search for two stolen, used bicycles."

"Oh no, we would never have come just for that," she said.

"Not at all," he added.

"Why don't you tell them what happened next, dear?" she said.

He paused for a second and appeared about to suggest that she do the telling but thought the better of it.

"The next morning was also damp," he said.

"It had rained during the night," she said. "But only a sprinkle."

"Enough to make the driveway from the pavement through to our back shed quite soft and impressionable. I came out in the morning and was surprised by what I saw embedded in the driveway."

"Cyril saw bicycle tracks. And not just any tracks," she said.

"They were tracks from one of *our* bicycles," he said.

"And they were not there the evening before," she said. "Cyril would have noticed them. Somebody came by late in the evening on one of our bicycles, made those tracks, and turned around and departed."

"They came by at half ten," he said. "The dog barked. I thought nothing of it at the time, but she did not bark again all night. So, that was when the bicycle thief must have pedaled up our drive."

"It made me a little nervous," she said. "It was as if someone was taunting us."

"Actually," he said, "It was quite annoying. And then, it became very unsettling."

"They appeared again, and again, and again. Three times," she said.

"They came by only on damp evenings," he said. "They came between ten o'clock and midnight. The dog would bark, and I would rush outside. Of course, if I was in my pajamas, I could not do so all that quickly. But not once, not once could I catch the rascal. He pedaled in, turned quickly and then departed."

"But last night," she said. "He left a message. He took a stick. We know that because he left it behind. And he scrawled a message in the soft mud. It read …" At this point, they spoke in unison.

"221 B."

"Yes, Mr. Holmes," she said. "That was the message. *221 B*. We knew straight away that it could only refer to you. Your address is the most famous in all of London ... well ... next to Buckingham Palace. Whoever it was must have wanted us to contact you."

"I reasoned," Cyril said, "that someone might possibly be in danger. We had no way of knowing but on the chance that someone was, we felt we had to come to you post haste and let you know. It may be all nonsense, but my wife felt, and I reasoned, that someone was sending us to you. Does that make any sense Mr. Holmes?"

The two of them were now silent and were looking intently at Holmes. He nodded and smiled.

"Perhaps. A small matter to clear up first, however. There must be nearly a quarter million bicycles today in London and the surrounding area. How could you possibly have known that the bicycle was one that had been stolen from you?"

"By the tracks," said Cyril,

"Really, sir," said Holmes. "I have made a study of bicycle tracks and can identify some forty-two different varieties. However, seventy-five percent of those that are seen today are from Dunlop and some twenty percent from Palmer. The other forty brands are seldom if even seen in London. It is impossible to claim that a particular set of tracks must have come from your stolen bicycles."

"No, sir, that was just it," protested Cyril. "Our bicycles are not new, and the tires were quite well worn. I did not want to be troubled with a flat tire when we were out and about so I replaced them just a month ago. I have an interest in the agency that imports a variety of goods from France. Because of that, I was able to order two sets at a much-reduced price. They have a distinct tread."

Holmes eyes suddenly brightened.

"What brand were they?" he asked.

"Michelin. The name is printed right on the tire. You can read it in the track. Their *Superieur Trois* brand. Excellent ..."

Holmes leapt to his feet.

"Come! Immediately," he ordered.

"Good heavens, Holmes," I said. "Where on earth are we going?"

"Scotland Yard."

Chapter Two
A Man with a
New Zealand Accent

HOLMES WAS QUICKLY making his way down the stairs and out on to Baker Street. The three of us followed him, lost in a quandary but doing what we were told.

"We can find a cab down by Marylebone," he said as he started walking south. "Your bicycle will be safe where it is."

He was moving at the speed of a forced march, and we struggled to keep up with him. Fortunately, a closed carriage cab came by, and he waved it down.

"Forgive me," he said as we rattled our way across Oxford Street and down Park Lane. "This may come to naught, but I suspect that your presence at Scotland Yard will be very useful to Inspector Lestrade."

He said no more, and we traveled quickly to the offices on the Embankment.

Lestrade, still sallow and rat-faced but now considerably aged from the first time I met him decades ago, was at his desk reading files and sipping on a cup of tea. He looked up as Holmes barged in.

"Holmes, you know it is generally expected that people call ahead and …"

He stopped in the middle of his sentence, looked at Holmes and then continued.

"Very well, Holmes, I know that look on your face. What is it this time?"

Holmes quickly introduced Mr. and Mrs. Morton and then demanded, "Where is the bicycle that came in three days ago from the Battersea Bridge? These good people may be able to shed some light on it."

"Downstairs," said Lestrade. "Follow me."

I knew that the only significant room in the basement of Scotland Yard was the morgue and that is precisely where Lestrade led us. He opened the door and pointed to a bicycle leaning against a wall.

"That's it," he said.

"Why, that's my bike!" exclaimed Cyril Morton. "How in the name of all that is holy did it end up here?"

"It came in," said Lestrade, "along with the body that was lying beside it."

Violet Morton let out a gasp. "Oh no. Was somebody hit by a motor bus? Was the rider run over? Did he fall into the river? What happened?"

"No, madam," said Lestrade. "*No,* on all counts. There was no accident, and no drowning and no man on the bicycle. It was a young woman … and we are assuming that she was murdered. How she died, we do not know. There are a few bruises on her wrists, so it is possible that she was held down and suffocated. No one has reported her missing. And we have no idea how she ended up beside the river. She's lying in the cold drawer over here. Are the two of you up to taking a look and seeing if you can tell us anything about her?"

Cyril and Violet Morton gave a look to each other; one of those knowing and loving but fearful looks that husbands and wives exchange when together facing a difficult situation. She quietly reached over and took hold of his hand.

"Of course, Inspector," he said. "Not likely that we can be of any help, but we will give it a try and see."

Lestrade led us to a metal drawer that bore the temporary label of 'Battersea bicycle' and a date of three days ago. He pulled it out. Lying inside was a young woman from the Orient, no more than twenty years old. Her face was partially covered by long, silky, straight black hair, but I could see that she was, or at least had been, exceptionally attractive. Her skin, now tinged with blue, was flawless and her lifeless, almond-shaped eyes were perfectly symmetrical. She was wearing a spotless maid's uniform.

"Sorry, Inspector," said Cyril. "Never seen her before."

Violet Morton leaned over the body and looked closely at her. She gently stroked the long hair back from the child-like face.

"Yes, Cyril, we have."

"When?"

"Six weeks ago. Remember when that fellow brought the two girls to our door?"

"Well … yes ... I remember. But we have no idea if this girl was one of them. They all do look alike, darling."

"No, Cyril. They don't. This is definitely one of the two. I remember her."

"Pray tell," said Holmes. "What were they doing at your door and what do you remember about them?"

"It was a Saturday afternoon. Late. Well past tea time. There was a knock on the front door, and the maid came and fetched us. A man I did not recognize—although he seemed strangely familiar—was standing on the porch and with him were two young women from the Orient. He introduced us to them. Their names, if I remember, were…yes… Hatsu … and Kisha. This one is Hatsu. You do remember them, don't you Cyril."

"Yes, I suppose so, now that you remind me, but I would never have recalled their names."

"The man," continued Violet, "gave his name as well."

She paused momentarily and closed her eyes.

"David, yes, that was it, *David*. Last name was McDougall, but I had the impression that it was a false name."

"And how," asked Holmes, "did you form that impression?"

"He changed the way he pronounced it. At first, it was *Mac* Dougall, and when he departed, he said it was *Mic* Dougall. People usually know how their own name is to be pronounced and do not change it."

"Precisely," said Holmes. "Pray continue. Can you describe the fellow?"

"About our age, somewhat past thirty. Average height and weight. Not tall and skinny like you, Mr. Holmes. More thick and bull-necked like the doctor. Face a bit chubby. Dark hair that was plastered down and pale skin. Some freckles. A mustache. Not at all handsome."

"His accent?" asked Holmes. "English? Scottish? Irish?"

"No … none of those. He had a bit of a raspy voice. Definitely overseas but most like someone from New Zealand. Not as broad and coarse as the Aussies but softer. More refined."

"Eye color? Peculiar features?" asked Holmes.

"Hard to say, Mr. Holmes. He wore eyeglasses with thick frames. It was late afternoon, past five o'clock, and already dark."

"Interesting," said Holmes. "Please keep going."

"He said that he represented some charity that was helping refugees find work and asked if we needed domestic services. He was offering the young women to us at a very reasonable rate and claimed that they were industrious workers. He said they were Japanese and their families had been killed by the Shoguns because they had converted to the Christian faith. Missionaries had rescued them and managed to get them to safety in England. I might have been interested but we are already fully staffed both here and in Tunbridge Wells, so I declined. He did not press me at all and seemed almost eager to depart. He thanked us for our time and took each of them by the arm and quickly led them back to a small carriage on the street."

"Yes, of course, darling," said Cyril. "I remember all that now. But how can you be sure that this girl here was one of them? Even the two of them were as alike as Tweedledum and Tweedledee."

"No, dear, they were not. This is the one he called Hatsu. The other, Kisha was a curious thing. Beautiful but quite frightened. Mind you, this one had a defiant look to her. She looked me right in the eye as if challenging me to accept her into service. I could also see that both of them were looking through the door into the study where you have hung our certificates on the wall."

"Cannot see any purpose in that," said Cyril. "What would she learn other than the fact that we are married and that an engineer and a musician lived in the house?"

"She would learn," said Holmes, "your names and your address and your professions."

Violet Morton now looked first at Lestrade and them directly at Holmes.

"Gentlemen, I know that our connection to this horrible event is nothing more than a chance result of the theft of a bicycle, but I feel a strong sense of connection to this poor girl; as if thinking that had I hired them this would not have happened."

"Really darling ..." began her husband.

"No, Cyril. I am not feeling guilty, only a desire to somehow be of help if we possibly can. If there is anything further we can do, please let us know. We are very willing to do whatever you ask, aren't we dear?"

"Oh, yes, of course. Anything to bring a bit of justice for this poor child's death," said Cyril.

"More to the point," said Holmes. "Anything you can do to help us protect *Kisha*. She is one now taking risks, and we had better move quickly."

"How do you know that?" asked Lestrade.

"Elementary, my dear Inspector. The bicycle we have here cannot possibly be the one that left the tracks in your drive. *This* bicycle came in here three days ago, but the latest tracks were left last night. *This* girl is dead, so it cannot have been her. It must be the second girl on the second bicycle, and I suspect she is putting herself in danger."

An hour later found Holmes and me back at 221B, having bade goodbye to the Mortons and seen them pedal off on their tandem bicycle. Holmes had reclined into his familiar armchair and lit his pipe.

"What do you know about the Shoguns of Japan, Watson?"

"Precious little. Quite the fearsome chaps. Did the old chop-chop on their enemies with their swords, didn't they?"

"Those were the Samurai."

"Oh, well then, I guess I know even less than I thought. Why?"

"They ruled Japan for centuries, but they were disbanded almost forty years ago when the Meiji dynasty was restored. They have not been murdering Christian converts and rendering children orphans for decades. The story given to the Mortons was a fabrication."

"Oh, yes, well that makes sense. But why would anyone, Shogun or Samurai or otherwise, want to kill a young Japanese girl? That tiny girl could not have hurt a flea. What sort of monster would want to hurt her? That does not make sense."

"On that, my friend you are correct."

He fell silent again and returned to his pipe. Reaching down to the floor, he picked up the day's newspaper and began to read.

"The weather," he said, "is clear now but they are calling for light rain this evening."

His reading a weather forecast struck me as absurdly inappropriate.

"It means," he said, "that the Mortons' drive will be soft tonight and that means it is possible that Miss Kisha may try again to leave a message with her tire tracks and scrawl. We shall have to be there to observe her and, if possible, follow her."

"We will not be able to keep up with her," I said. "She will be on bicycle."

"So will we."

It would still be several hours before I had to join Holmes on a nighttime bicycle ride and thus I returned home. Having efficiently completed her tasks for the day, my wife was eager to hear my story and, as always, thrilled that I could once again do my part to help Sherlock Holmes.

"The only problem," I said, after having tried to give as many details as I could remember, "is how could a young woman from Japan have known what 221B stood for and assumed that the Mortons would connect it to Sherlock Holmes?"

"John, sweetheart," she said, with one of those sighs of loving condescension commonly expressed by wives for husbands of very little brain, "Because *you* told them."

"What?"

"You wrote the story about Violet Smith and Cyril Morton. The whole world has read about her in the *Strand*. Maybe, even in Japan, they read it. They saw the names on the certificates and guessed that the Mortons were the ones who could lead them to Sherlock Holmes. *You* did it, dearest. Now, it is damp outside, so please make sure that you put on dry socks and take your service revolver with you. I shall try to stay awake until you get back."

Chapter Three
A Revealing Trip
to the Green Grocer

AT TEN-THIRTY THAT NIGHT, I found myself straddling a bicycle on a residential street in a well-to-do neighborhood. Holmes was doing likewise beside me. I was not as uncomfortable as I had feared. Holmes had managed to obtain two Pedersen bicycles. Unlike the one ridden by the Mortons, these had only a single seat, but it was made of a suspended leather sling, not a small, hard saddle. Thus, it was much gentler in its treatment of the male anatomy.

The glorious spring morning had descended into yet another damp, cold March evening and I was glad of my wool sweater, impermeable ulster, and dry socks. There was nothing about which to make idle chit-chat, and we stood in silence.

"There she is," whispered Holmes at precisely ten forty-five.

A darkly dressed figure on a bicycle was pedaling slowly toward the home of the Mortons. She stopped for a moment at the end of the drive and retrieved what I guessed to be a stick from her bicycle basket. Then she pedaled slowly up the drive, stopped and quickly made markings in the soft ground, and then moved slowly back out again. I could hear the dog barking as she turned and cycled away on the road.

"After her," said Holmes. "But keep back a good distance. We do not want her to see us."

She was moving quite quickly. At the corner of King's Road and Beaufort she stopped, looked back and spotted us. Then she took off like a shot. She was young and athletic, and we were neither. It was a tough slog to keep up with her. We hastened onward at such a pace that my sedentary life began to tell upon me.

But then she suddenly stopped just as she entered a dark patch and Holmes and I braked to a halt under the glare of a street lamp. She turned and looked at us again. From then on, she continued at a pace that was positively leisurely. I was quite befuddled.

"She wants us to follow her," said Homes. And so we did. She soon turned right on Braemerton Street and pedaled south to Glebe Place. She stopped in front of an impressive home and again looked back, seemingly to make sure we had followed. Having seen us, she turned into the drive and disappeared into the backyard.

"Shall we knock on the door and ask to speak to her?" I asked.

"Heavens, no. Had she wanted us to do so, she could have beckoned us several blocks back. No, we must find a way to talk to her but without doing so publicly."

"And just how," I demanded, "are we going to do that?"

Whilst sitting on his machine and propping himself up with his long legs, Holmes slowly extracted his cigarette case, lit one, and took several long draughts before responding.

"We can safely assume that she is working as a domestic. Tomorrow, being Sunday, she will most likely be confined to the house. On Monday, the markets are open, and she will probably be sent to acquire food for the household. That may give us an opportunity to meet her as if by coincidence and chat. Could you, my dear doctor, arrange to be free to do some more bicycling on Monday. I dare say, as both of us get so little active exercise, it shall be a treat. We could use it."

A damp weekend was followed by a glorious Monday morning. I made the necessary arrangements, and at nine o'clock I was once again ensconced on the serviceable bicycle Holmes had obtained for my use. He and I had positioned ourselves on Glebe Place, about a half a block from the house into which our targeted cyclist had been seen entering. At Holmes's suggestion, both of us were dressed as gentlemen so as not to arouse suspicion of the neighbors.

"Were we to dress too casually," he said, "the maids and butlers would be whistling for the police within minutes. This way, they will assume that we are merely aging eccentric cyclists, a species found in abundance throughout the British Isles."

At fifteen minutes to ten, we saw the object of our interest emerge slowly from the drive of the house. She looked around and took notice of us before cycling off in the direction of Cromwell Road. At a green grocer's shop, she stopped, parked her bicycle and entered. We followed her, with both of us picking up shopping baskets at the door, not wanting to appear even more queer than we already did.

We spotted her in the fruit section, carefully examining a bin of costly oranges that had been brought over from Spain. Holmes nonchalantly walked up beside her and, holding his card in his palm, extended his hand in front of her. He spoke slowly and deliberately and hoping, I assumed, that her command of the English language would be sufficient for her to understand him.

"My…name…is…Sherlock…Holmes…do…you…need…my …help?"

She continued to regard the oranges, but a small smirk crept across her face.

"Good morning, Mr. Holmes," she said in perfect English. "It is not necessary to assume that because someone does not have an English face, she does not know the English language."

Then she turned and looked directly at him.

"Please, sir, I must ask you to prove to me that you are indeed Mr. Sherlock Holmes. Please tell me what type of snake killed the doctor in the case at Stoke Moran."

Holmes smiled approvingly at her. "It was a swamp adder, fed on milk, responding to a whistle, and kept in an iron safe. Will that suffice as my *bona fides,* miss?"

She did not seem entirely convinced and kept looking past Holmes and me as if suspecting that someone had followed her. Finally she replied.

"Thank you, sir, for finding me, sir" she said. "Forgive me if I am very frightened. Knowing what I do about you, I assumed you would. I have been expecting you. And good morning to you as well, Dr. Watson."

Holmes spoke quietly but forcefully back to her.

"Miss Kisha, if that indeed is your name, I am assuming that you are in some danger and I assure you that we are here for your protection. Could you please take a few minutes and state your case to me."

"No," she said bluntly. "I cannot. If I am delayed in the least, I will be in trouble. I have only a very limited time to do the shopping and must return to the house by eleven o'clock at the latest. However, as I was expecting you, I have devised a plan. Please take this."

She reached into her pocket and pulled out a sheet of folded paper. Again, her eyes darted around the store.

"It is my regular Wednesday shopping list," she said in a whisper. "This market opens at nine o'clock as does the butcher next door and I arrive here every other day at ten. If you could come well before me and obtain all of these items and have them in a basket by the time I arrive, I will then have time to talk to you. We can meet in the Hereford Arms. They open early for breakfast. Please agree to do so, Mr. Holmes, I beg you. It is the only way I can think of to be free to talk to you without arousing more suspicions. Thank you, sir."

Holmes nodded. "Very well. We shall do that. But before we leave, will you confirm that you are living at 275 Glebe Place and employed there as a domestic servant?"

"No, Mr. Holmes. I am not employed. I have become a slave."

She turned away and moved on to the vegetables. I was prepared to follow her around the store, but Holmes placed his hand on my forearm and shook his head.

"We will follow her plan," he said.

I had a memory of having gone shopping for groceries at some time prior to joining the military several decades ago. However, the greengrocer and the butcher had become foreign countries, and so I did as all married men must do. I beseeched my wife for help.

"John, dear, it is not all that difficult," she said. "*Children* do it for their families all over the world."

"Thank you, darling," I said. "I *know* that children do it, but it has been decades since *I* have done it."

In the name of preserving marital bliss, she agreed to accompany me on Wednesday morning. We took a cab from our home to the high street of Chelsea, arriving in more than adequate time. I was somewhat concerned that Holmes would consider me to have become mentally deficient in having to call upon my wife for assistance. I was disabused of that notion when I saw him exit his cab, followed by Mrs. Hudson.

The two women took the list and explicitly instructed us to go and wait in the pub. Thus, Holmes and I enjoyed the unexpected pleasure of a full English knowing that every item on the list would be procured.

The two of them appeared at twenty minutes to ten, bearing full sacks of meat and produce and nattering on about the outrageous prices charged by merchants in this pretentious corner of London. I suspected that the shopkeepers had been happy to see them off.

At precisely ten o'clock, a young oriental woman entered the pub and furtively looked around. Her face brightened when she saw us, and she walked smartly over to our table.

"*Ohayo gozaimas*, Mrs. Hudson and Mrs. Watson." She bowed deeply to the two of them as she spoke. "I am honored to meet such famous women. I have read much about both of you. Thank you for coming. You have made me feel much safer knowing that you will be helping me."

She sat beside Mrs. Hudson, and for several minutes the three women chatted quietly whilst Holmes openly fidgeted with the cutlery. Fortunately, Mrs. Hudson placed both her hands on tops of the young woman's and spoke needed words of assurance. Then she handed the conversation over to Holmes.

"Time is of the essence," he said. "Please explain your situation to us."

"Yes, Sherlock-san, I shall do so and I shall be both as concise and precise as possible but sparing no significant detail."

She was trembling and took a sip from her cup of tea before starting.

"My name, in English, is Kisha Okada. My family is a very great family from Hakone, in the prefecture of Kanagawa and is blessed to live in the shadow of the sacred Fujiyama. We have been favored by the gods and our ancestors, and we have become one of the leading trading families of Nippon. My cousin, Hatsu, who is more like a sister to me, and I have been fortunate to have been able to study in schools operated by European missionaries and to have learned English since we were children. We have also been privileged to travel to some other parts of the world where our family has business offices. One day, four months ago, a man came to the door of the house we were staying in and informed our governess that he was a representative of Oxford University in England and that he had been given the task of finding worthy students from foreign lands and offering them scholarships to study there. He spoke with great assurance and claimed to have conducted extensive research about Hatsu and me and had determined that we would be ideal recipients of such a scholarship."

"Pardon me, miss," interrupted Holmes. "Was this the same man who brought you to the door of Mr. and Mrs. Morton."

"Yes, Sherlock-san. It was. He said his name was Professor MacDougall."

"Thank you. Pray continue."

"My cousin and I were thrilled beyond words. Our happiness drew a cloud over our judgement for we knew that although we were diligent students, neither of us was considered to be brilliant. Nevertheless, we accepted, and it was a great honor to our parents in front of their neighbors and friends to have their daughters so chosen. My father and uncle arranged our transportation to Cape Town where we were to board a ship and travel to England."

"One of the Castle Line that has the route from the Cape to Southampton?" asked Holmes.

"That is what we had expected. We were met at the train station by a woman who said she was the nurse for the voyage and she escorted us to the docks. The ship was not a passenger liner at all. It was a cargo ship with a small number of cabins for passengers. We thought it strange but the woman was very confident and we believed everything she told us. We boarded and were shown to our cabin and less than an hour later the ship cast off and departed. We were told very firmly that we were never to leave our cabin as it was not safe out on the decks. Food and books to read would be brought to us, and if we needed to use the lavatory we were to bang on our cabin door, and one of the guards would escort us."

"Were the two of you," asked Holmes, "the only passengers?"

"No. We would pass other passengers when coming and going. Eventually, Katsu and I counted six others. They were all young, like us. There were no adults. And we were a mix of colors. There were two boys from India and two girls from Africa and two Dutch girls."

"And all of similar age?" said Holmes. "Did you have anything else in common?"

The young woman paused and looked down at the table. "Please do not think me vain if I say this, but all of us were very attractive. Both the boys and the girls no matter what our race."

"Were you mistreated in any way?" Holmes asked.

"No. The food we were given was European but nourishing, and the nurse came and checked on us once a day. She seemed quite concerned that we remain healthy."

"An interesting detail," said Holmes. "Please, keep going."

"Two men stood guard in the hallway outside the doors to the cabins. Once or twice we opened the door to look out, and they immediately shouted at us to get back in. They were nasty men, and we were afraid of them."

"One day, not long before we arrived in England, we were escorted to the cabin of the man who was the agent for Oxford University, Professor MacDougall. He said that a problem had come up with the scholarships and that we could not be admitted to Oxford for another two years. During that time, we would be placed in situations where we would have to work to cover our expenses. We were shocked and tried to ask questions, but our guards took us by our arms and forced us out of the agent's cabin and back to ours. We were very upset."

"Entirely understandable," said Holmes. "Keep going."

"I cried in my bed about what we had been told. I culd not understand what had happened and my dreams had died. But Hatsu was angry. She did not believe what we had been told and she said she would not let these things happen to us. That night she slipped out of the cabin and placed a note under the door of the other student's cabins. The note said, *The promise of a scholarship was a fraudulent lie. We have been taken from our families and will be sold into service in England. Meet at midnight tonight in Cabin Seven.*"

"And all of you met?" asked Holmes.

"Yes, Sherlock-san. But it was only for a few minutes. We agreed that we had been tricked and that we were the victims of a fraud and that we must try to help each other, but then we were discovered and forced back to our cabins. The next day Hatsu and I were brought to the agent's cabin. He had a large knife and a gun on his desk, and he shouted at me. He showed me that he had complete information regarding our families and said that my little brother and sister would be tortured and killed if I disobeyed or tried to contact the police. He even knew where my grandmother and grandfather lived and said that his men would come and burn their house down if I did not cooperate. Then we were led back to our cabin. We were terrified."

"Were there," asked Holmes, "any other attempts to cooperate with the other students?"

"Yes. The night before we arrived at Southampton a note was slipped under our door. It was from one of the boys who seemed to know something about London. It said: *We must find each other in London. Leave a note with your names and addresses in a crevasse behind the queen's head in the new monument at Charing Cross.*"

"And after you arrived in London, what happened?"

"We were sick at heart. We were paraded from house to house and offered as servants. I honor the work of servants, Sherlock-san, but we had not become servants. We have become slaves and were being sold as if we were no more than beast of burden."

"And the two of you were accepted by the house of Glebe Place. Is that correct?

"Yes, sir. When we saw the names of Miss Violet Smith and Mr. Cyril Morton on their wall when we came to their door, our hopes were raised because we recognized them from the stories about you. But that is not where we ended up."

"Have you been able to make contact with the others through the notes at Charing Cross?"

"Yes. Soon after we arrived, we found a map of London and late at night, Hatsu, and I escaped the house we have been sold to and came to Charing Cross. We found the list of names and addresses and left ours. Hatsu returned several times and compiled a complete list of all of our locations in London."

"And how did you know to contact me?"

"I had read the stories about you in the *Strand*. And amongst the books we had to read on the ship were many old copies. Sailors must be fond of your stories as well."

"They do have a certain dramatic quality to them," said Holmes.

He was about to continue his questions when Kisha looked up at the clock that hung above the bar. She gasped and jumped to her feet.

"I must run. If I am late, I will be given a beating. But here. This is the Friday list. I can meet you again then."

She placed a piece of paper on the table, grabbed the bags of groceries in her arms and almost ran out of the pub. A minute later she ran back in and laid several banknotes and coins in front of us.

"That is for the groceries. And please, Sherlock-san, try very hard to find my cousin, Hatsu. She has been missing for five days. I am very afraid for her."

She turned again and ran out of the pub.

Holmes appeared to be uncharacteristically bewildered. Then he recovered and rose from his chair.

"We can share a cab," he said as he commenced to walk away from the table.

He hailed a growler on Cromwell Road. The rest of us climbed in, and Holmes shouted directions to the driver.

"Charing Cross."

Chapter Four
In Search of Miss Zenani

ONCE WE WERE ON OUR WAY, Holmes looked at me.

"Watson, my dear friend…"

"It is quite all right," I said. "I will look after it when we meet again on Friday."

One of the difficult tasks a medical doctor is required to perform time and again is informing people of the death of a loved one. It never becomes any easier but it has to be done, and I had done so more times than I care to remember. Fortunately, if such a word can be used in this context, the great majority of times the deceased was elderly, and while his or her passing was a sad event for friends and family, it was expected and often served to bring kith and kin together. Far more taxing to the soul were those occasions when I had to tell parents and close friends of the untimely death of a man or woman in the prime of life and worst of all were those times when a child died.

When we met again with Miss Kisha, I would take her aside and tell her of the death of her cousin.

"Thank you," said Holmes. No more needed to be said.

At Charing Cross, the four of us exited the cab and walked over to the monument, the Eleanor Cross, in front of the railway station. It had been erected back when I was in my teenage years and was one of the best-known meeting places in the city. The square surrounding it was busy with the hustle and bustle of pedestrians, and we followed Holmes through the throngs until we were standing at the monument's base.

Holmes was gazing up at it. Following his line of sight, I looked up at one of the statuettes of Queen Eleanor. Behind her head there appeared to be a small dark patch. A moment later, Holmes was climbing up the pillar and retrieving it. He descended and leapt the final yard back to the pavement. We gathered around him as he unfolded a piece of oilskin and extracted a folded piece of paper. On it, written in several different hands, was a list of names and addresses. Most of the students were staying in residences in Belgravia, Mayfair, Chelsea, and St. John's Wood. One of the girls with an African name was listed in a tavern in the East End.

Without waiting for Holmes to ask, I took out my pencil and notebook and carefully recorded them all. When I had finished, Holmes refolded the paper, wrapped it again in the protective cloth, climbed up the monument, and replaced it where it had been found.

Once he had returned to the pavement, I removed the page and handed it to him.

"Thank you," he said quietly. "We have some work to do."

We hailed another cab and, taking a small detour, took my dear wife back to our home and then I carried on with Holmes and Mrs. Hudson to 221B. The long-suffering landlady prepared a pleasant lunch for the two of us which we ate in silence whilst Holmes starred at the list of names.

I broke the silence once we had finished dessert and were sipping coffees.

"Where shall we start, Holmes? "I asked. "One of those addresses is just around the corner in St. John's Wood. Shall we walk over and call on them?"

Although I have been the victim of it for two and a half decades, I will never become immune to the look Holmes gives me when he wishes to convey his opinion that I am hopelessly naïve.

"Truly, Watson, there are times when I wonder if you have learned anything from me over the years. No, my dear friend, we shall not go and call on them. Were I to arrive at their door announcing that Sherlock Holmes wanted to speak to one of their help it would set off an alert that would drive the entire enterprise underground immediately. The owners of the homes who, no doubt, know or should know that they are participating in a criminal fraud will contact the so-called charity straight away and advise them that I am asking questions. Within hours, the young people on this list would be removed to another location and our progress to date will have been for naught."

"Very well then," I said, not wanting to admit that I had been completely foolish. "If we cannot call on them, is there someone who could call on our behalf? Someone who would not arouse suspicions?"

"And did you have anyone in mind?"

Of course, I did not but was loath to admit same. So, I thought for a moment and offered a suggestion.

"What about Mr. and Mrs. Morton? Violet could say that she is recruiting new students for her music lessons and Cyril could offer a free estimate on upgrading the house to the latest electrical services."

Holmes looked vacantly at me and then his blank face slowly changed into a smile.

"Well done, old chap. Quite brilliant. Please forgive my cutting remark of a minute ago. There truly are times when you surprise me."

Had I been feeling candid, I might have admitted that there were times when I truly surprised myself; this being one of them.

***

"Why, of course we will," said Violet Morton. "Between us, we could cover Chelsea and Belgravia tomorrow. Is that not so, dear?"

We had called on the Mortons just after tea time knowing that, as a dutiful father, Cyril would be home in time to spend a few minutes with the children before sending them off for bath and bed.

"A bit of a bother, darling," said her husband. "One of my younger sales lads is usually sent to do that type of work. I really should not be away from the office all day. You never know what is going to happen what with all that is going on now in Europe."

"Oh, Cyril, you must have told me a hundred times that you have the entire firm all so well organized that it pretty well runs itself. And besides, we could use a little adventure now and again. We would be spies for Sherlock Holmes."

As she spoke, I recalled how I had watched when this spirited young woman was being followed by a strange man and she had whisked her wheels round and dashed straight at him. It might not have been the most sensible action to take, but it was certainly not lacking bravado.

She continued her appeal to her perhaps-not-quite-as-adventurous husband.

"Cyril darling, think how chuffed you would be if Dr. Watson writes it up and your name is in the *Strand*."

He smiled and nodded.

"Very well," he said. "I suppose it would be a bit of a spring treat. And the publicity would do the firm a jolly bit of good. You would mention the name of the firm, wouldn't you, Doctor?"

"Of course. You will recall that I did so last time," I said.

"Capital, then. Tomorrow we shall go looking for slaves brought under fraudulent intent. I should be able to have those visits made before noon and back to my office for the afternoon. Capital, yes, quite capital."

"Excellent," said Holmes. "Might I impose upon you again and suggest that we meet here tomorrow to share data?"

We departed. I thought that Mrs. Morton seemed somewhat more enchanted by the opportunity than did her husband, but I was certain that he would perform in a very responsible way. He struck me as that sort of chap.

"Where to now, Holmes?" I asked as we stood on the pavement on a pleasant street in Chelsea.

Instead of answering, he took out his cigarette case, lit one, and began walking slowly in the direction of the intersection. From years of experience with him, I knew there was no point hurrying his answer.

"How would you fancy an excursion to a rather suspect tavern in the East End?" he asked. "The one noted on the list."

"Fancy it? Not in the least," I said. "However, I assume that is where we are off to."

"Yes. If we cannot call on homes in some of the wealthier neighborhoods for fear of being recognized, we shall have to start elsewhere. I expect that I am quite unknown beyond Aldgate.

We hailed a cab at the intersection. Forty-five minutes later, we were in front of *The Mongrel and Manacle* on Whitechapel Road.

We were dressed as gentlemen, and our entrance into what was a working-man's pub caused no end of curious glances in our direction. Several of the men looked up at us with an angry glare of the type a decent and upright man gives to another man who is engaging in immoral pursuits. No sooner had we taken our seats at a table than the barkeep came and sat down with us.

"Not wanting to be rude to you two gents," he said. "Happy to bring you as much ale as you can drink but I would be thinking that you did not enter our establishment on account of our reputation as an ale house."

"Right you are, sir," said Holmes. "We are feeling a little more sporting this evening, and one of our dear friends recommended your fine tavern as a place where a couple of adventurous gentlemen could pass a pleasant hour or two, in exchange, of course, for fair compensation."

He extended his long arm and gave the fellow's back a firm and friendly pat.

The barkeep nodded and smiled.

"As I thought. Happy to be of service. In the back corner, you can see a staircase leading up. If you will take that, then Miss Eliza will meet you upstairs and see that you are looked after."

"I am afraid," said Holmes, "that our interests are quite specific. The recommendation given us was for one particular barmaid, one with very dark skin. The name we were given was a Miss Zenani. Might she be available to chat with us?"

A sly smile spread across the face of the barkeep. "Oh ho. You chaps are looking for a serving of dark meat for your evening meal, are you? Well now, you are a couple of adventurous blokes, aren't you? Yes, Miss Zenani is right out of the heart of darkest Africa she is, and quite the dangerous evening outing. But it breaks my heart to have to tell you that she is no longer to be found here in *The Mongrel and Manacle*. A couple of lads from the association came a fortnight ago and fetched her away. But I am sure that Miss Eliza can fix you up with someone almost as likely to tickle your fancy."

"Oh dear," said Holmes. "That will just not do. We had our hearts set on meeting the new African girl. She has established quite the reputation already, if you know what I mean. Might I ask for your wise and knowledgeable guidance as to where we might find her?" He slipped a pound note across the table to the barkeep as he spoke.

"Well, now, sir," came the reply, "I cannot be certain, and I would not want you thinking that I misled you if what I say is no longer God's truth, but I was told that she could now be found in a fine house at the corner of Gray's Inn and Old Street."

"Ah, yes," said Holmes, smiling. "I am aware of that select establishment, and we thank you for your kind assistance." He left another pound note on the table as he rose to depart.

"What sort of place," I asked once we were back outside on the pavement, "is found up on Old Street?"

"I have never been inside it, but my informants have mentioned it from time to time. It has no name and appears to be no more than a large residence, but it is known as the *House of Torture*. So, it appears that our evening may have acquired a greater risk than I had anticipated. Are you up for it, my friend?"

"In for a penny, in for a pound," I said. "But if I come home black and blue, I will expect you to corroborate whatever account I have to give to my wife."

Chapter Five
A Fool and His Money

THE HOUSE TO WHICH we had been sent was a three-story affair on a corner lot on Gray's Inn Road where it crosses the extension of Old Street that was also known as the Clerkenwell Road. The windows and front door were entirely dark, but in the light from the street lamps, it appeared to be well-maintained. We walked somewhat tentatively up to the front door. There was no knocker, and our banging on it went unheeded. Holmes withdrew a package of Lucifers from his pocket and struck one. In the light from the match, we read a small sign.

```
Patrons are requested to use the
tradesmen's entrance at the back of
the house.
```

We did as advised and walked in through an unlocked door. A well-dressed, handsome young man greeted us, led us to a small parlor and asked if we would like a brandy or something to eat. Holmes thanked him and declined. The chap smiled warmly and bowed as he exited.

"Please make yourselves comfortable, gentlemen," he said. "Madame Selena shall be with you shortly."

The room was very handsomely appointed with good quality paintings and *objets d'art*. The furniture was quite new and comfortable and, somewhere in the distance, someone was playing a piano.

We were not alone.

There were three other chaps sitting and sipping on brandies whilst reading a newspaper or a book. I recognized one of them immediately as one of my former patients and was about to say hello to him when I felt Holmes's hand on my forearm. He leaned in to my ear and whispered.

"No one acknowledges knowing anyone here."

That struck me as odd, but if that were the rule, then I would comply. I picked up a copy of the *Times* and began to read, feeling a small resentment at Holmes for having turned down the offer of a brandy. I could have used one.

Five minutes later, an attractive no-longer-slender woman of a certain age entered the room, picked up a small chair, placed it in front of us, and sat down.

"Good evening, gentlemen," she said quietly. "We have not seen either of you here before. To what do we owe the honor of your visit?"

"We are acting on the recommendation of …" Holmes replied, adding the name of a very significant member of the House of Lords. "He is one of my clients and confidentially informed me that an hour or two in the company of a certain Miss Zenani was an experience not to be missed. The barkeep on Whitechapel Street directed us to your fine house."

"Oh, did Lord Jolly Jimmy send you?" she said, smiling. "Well then, you are most welcome. As to an encounter with Lady Zenani, I am sure that can be arranged. You are warned, however, that she can be very demanding and we take no responsibility for whatever condition you find yourself in when you depart. You do know to leave a small token of your appreciation on the dresser inside the room before you leave?"

Holmes smiled and nodded.

"Splendid," she said. "Now follow me."

She led us out of the parlor and into a dark hallway in which the lamps had been turned down to their lowest setting. I sniffed as we walked and detected the unmistakable smell of good leather. We followed the woman up a staircase so dark that I had to use my sense of touch to know where to put my feet. Doing so was somewhat disconcerting but what I found utterly unnerving were the occasional muffled cries of pain I heard emanating from some other corner of the house.

One the second floor, she opened the door to a large bedroom, indicated that we should enter and wait, and departed. Once inside, Holmes immediately went to the flickering lamp and turned it up. We could now see that in this fairly spacious room there was a large bed with a strong iron headboard and footboard. Attached to the metal columns of the headboard were two sets of police handcuffs that had been wrapped in several layers of velvet. There were two similar sets attached to the footboard. In the corner of the room was a structure of about seven feet in height in the shape of a large X. It had velvet ropes attached to each of the ends of the cross-pieces. On hooks on the wall were hung an assortment of feather dusters, whips, chains, and small, narrow breadboards.

"Merciful heavens, Holmes," I said. "What is this place?"

"You have heard," he said, "that a fool and his money are soon parted? This is one of those places where it occurs."

His answer did not help my understanding, and I was about to demand that he not be so obscure when the door opened.

The woman who entered took my breath away.

She was ... *magnificent*; tall ... as tall as Holmes, maybe taller. Her flawless skin was black, and by *black,* I do not mean the coffee-with-cream color that we are accustomed to seeing in members of the negro race who come to England from America or the Caribbean colonies. I mean *blue-black*. I mean like the African goddess of *The Heart of Darkness*, the one who stood defiantly with her arms outstretched as the white pilgrims drifted down the river. She was clad in only a black leather corset and black underwear and held a coiled whip in her right hand.

She closed the door behind her and spoke loudly.

"I am Mistress Kashama, empress of the Watusi tribe. You will do what I command." She loosed her whip and snapped it hard against the floor.

I was thoroughly nonplussed, but Holmes merely smiled and walked directly to her until his face was in front of hers.

"Good evening, Miss Zenani Masithathu. I am Sherlock Holmes. This is Doctor Watson. We have come to help you escape your situation. Your family in Africa will be protected by the forces of the British Empire."

Her countenance changed immediately from arrogant defiance to shock and fear. She backed away from Holmes and turned as if to run back out the door.

"Stop!" commanded Holmes. "Miss Zenani, we cannot help you and your family unless you cooperate with us. Sit down and listen to me."

The young woman turned back and faced Holmes. Fear was written on her face, but she did as Holmes had commanded and walked over to a chair. I quickly slipped off my suit jacket and handed it to her as I sensed that she was concerned about the immodesty of her body. She nodded to me and immediately pulled it on around her upper body and sat down, using the tails to provide a limited cover to her long, muscular legs.

"Are you truly Sherlock Holmes?" she asked.

"I am."

"How did you find me?"

"I am a detective. That is what I do. And I promise you that no harm will come to your family if you let us help you."

She shook her head. "It is not my family. It is my sister, Makawizwe. We came to England together. They separated us. I do not know where she is, but they told me that if I did not do what they demanded, they would torture her. If they know I am speaking to you, they will harm her. If I try to escape, they said they will kill her."

Holmes looked at the woman in silence for several seconds. The confidence and defiance of a few minutes ago had vanished. She had crossed her arms over her chest and drawn my jacket tightly around her body. Holmes slowly nodded his head.

"I understand. It may be necessary for you to remain here until we have located your sister and can bring both of you to safety. Please, Miss. Time is short. Tell me everything you can that might help us to put an end to the evil deeds that brought you to this place."

She nodded her agreement. "I will do so but they must hear the sound of my whip and your cries of pain several times during the hour, or they will know that you did not come as clients."

"Watson," said Holmes. "Might I prevail upon you to utter an appropriate cry?"

"I suppose I can do that. Give your whip a crack, and I will give it a try."

Without standing up, she shook her whip loose and gave it a few gentle flicks. Then she forcefully reached her hand above her head and brought it down smartly. The whip flew across the room, and the tail of it caught me directly on the front of my leg.

"OOOOWWWW!" I screamed in pain and instinctively leapt to my feet and moved back out of reach.

"Excellent, Watson," said Holmes. "We can do one of those every few minutes."

I stayed back well out of reach. "I am quite sure I can manage without the application of the whip."

"Very well," said Holmes. "Now, Miss, your story please and be concise but do not omit any significant detail even if doing so offends your modesty. Please start with the fraudulent offer that was made to you in your sister. Where were you living at the time? Nairobi? Dar-es-Salaam?"

"No. Durban. We are Xhosa."

"Yes, of course. Your name is from that region. Please then, your account."

"You know my name. My uncle is a prince of the ImiDushane. We are a proud family of warriors. My sister and I are close to the age to be married, and because of our beauty and strength, we have been sought after by many men. But one day a white man came to my father and told him that my sister and I would command a much higher bride price if we were to be educated in England. He claimed that he could give us a scholarship to Oxford University and that we could return in four years and we would be the most valuable brides ever offered within our tribe even if we were somewhat older than the other girls. He said that my father could demand eighty or even one hundred cattle for each of us. My father agreed, and we did not object. We knew that we would be married to a very wealthy man and that our lives would be much better as a result. So, we came on the boat from Cape Town to England."

"When," asked Holmes, "do you realize that you had been defrauded?"

"The little girl from the Orient came to us. We met. Then a note appeared under the door of our cabin. It was from one of the boys who was also on the boat. It told us to leave our names and addresses at Charing Cross. Is that how you found me?"

"It was indeed. Pray, continue."

"When we were taken off the boat, my sister and I were first taken to a terrible tavern."

"The *Mongrel and Manacle*?"

"Yes. There, to our horror, we were told we would have to work as prostitutes. They told us that if we did not do as we were told our families would have very bad things done to them. My sister and I knew that our families would rather die than allow us to be used that way, so we did not cooperate."

"What did you do?"

"I was put in a room and a young man, an English man, entered. He was very well-dressed and seemed thrilled to see me. He immediately began to try to touch me in a way that I knew was not allowed. If any man had even tried to do that in my home, my brothers and cousins would have chased him and caught him and given him a beating he would never forget. But my brothers and my cousins were not there."

"Yes, Miss. You may tell me what happened," said Holmes. "Anything you say will be kept in complete confidence."

"There was no one to help me, so I had to give him a beating all by myself. He had loosened his trousers so I pushed him very hard and he tripped over them and fell on his face. I took his walking stick and knelt on his back and beat his buttocks at least thirty times. He screamed with pain, and eventually the barkeep came and rescued him."

"Yes, Miss. And then?"

"The crazy fool was smiling and laughing. He paid the barkeep another ten pounds and asked when he could come back. The man had lost his mind. At least that is what I thought. Three hours later several very large men came and took me away from the tavern and brought me here. They told me that if I did not cooperate, they would hurt my sister. I was told that I did not have to engage in fornication but that I would have to give beatings to rich Englishmen. And that is what I have been doing. All the men are rich. Some, I am sure, are very powerful in business. Some may even be bishops or priests."

"And," added Holmes, "members of the Privy Council, and captains of industry and second and third sons of the nobility. Yes. Pray, continue."

"One of them came several times in one week and said he wanted to be my slave, at least for an hour and offered to bring me gifts. He seemed like someone I could trust, so I told him to bring me a bicycle and hide it in the shed behind the house. He had four bicycles so he would not miss one. The night he brought it, I waited until late in the evening, and I escaped through a window and cycled back to the tavern."

"Good heavens," I said. "That is exceptionally dangerous for a woman to do alone, especially in the East End."

She looked at me blankly and shrugged. "I put on a man's clothing. White Englishmen do not bother tall men from Africa in the night. They fear us. So, I found the tavern but my sister was no longer there. They had taken her away, and I could learn nothing. I came back here. I have no other place to go, and I am afraid that if I run away, they will hurt her. She is two years younger than I am and not as strong. I am the only family she has here and I must protect her."

"Of course, you must," said Holmes. "I commend you for your loyalty to her."

"I have no choice. She is my sister."

"You have referred to the people who brought you here and who control you as they. Do you have any idea who they are?"

Miss Zenani was silent for a moment, lost in thought.

"The man who tricked my father and brought us here calls himself McDougall, but he is not the *baas man*. There are others, but I do not know who they are. The men who came and took me away from the tavern told the man who owns the tavern that the association was moving me to a place where I would be more valuable. That is all I know."

"Did you have any insight, any guess about where your sister might be?"

"No, but I believe that as long as I stay here and give beatings to foolish men, she will be safe."

That did not make sense to me, nor to Holmes.

"Why do you believe that?" he asked.

She looked up at us, and a sheepish smile crept across her face.

"Sometimes we take advantage of the ignorance of Africa amongst white people. We can also threaten. We can frighten people. I am a foot taller than the woman who runs this house, and I told her that if I heard that she forced my sister to be a prostitute, I would cook her and eat her. She is such a fool that she believed me. As long as I remain here and they are terrified of me, I think my sister will be safe."

Holmes looked at the young woman for a moment and then broke out into a hearty laugh.

"Well done, Miss. Well done. That has to be the most effective threat I have ever heard against the criminal class."

She looked up at him. "If I know that Sherlock Holmes will find my sister and keep her safe your English criminals will not be eaten."

Holmes and I both laughed, and Miss Zenani forced a quick smile. Then she gave me a look and picked up her whip. On cue, I let out a scream before she had time to apply it to my leg again.

"Please, gentlemen," she said. "Do not worry about me. I can look after myself. I am safe here, but I fear for my sister. I dare not run away. Please find her and let me know when you do. When I know she is safe, I will leave this place."

She stood up and gave my suit jacket back to me. We were about to depart when she stopped us. She gave her whip another crack, and I responded with a final loud cry of pain.

"That was good," she said, "but both of you are too pale. You must hold your breath and force your faces to become flushed, or no one will believe that you have enjoyed your time here. And you must leave the money on the dresser."

"Well, Holmes," I said when we were back out on the pavement of Gray's Inn Road, "that was an education. She is quite the young woman."

"Yes," agreed Holmes. "If I ever need a bodyguard, I know who to ask."

"Does Lord J— indeed frequent this place?" I asked.

"There are some things, my dear friend, that it is better if you do not know."

I was quite content with my ignorance, and we started to walk along Oak Street in search of a cab when we heard footsteps coming up behind us.

"Holmes and Watson," came a sharp voice.

We turned to acknowledge whoever it was but did not have a chance to say anything before the overly large fellow quickly spoke again.

"If you two try coming back to this place, you will be leaving in an ambulance."

He quickly turned around and walked away from us.

Chapter Six
The Spies Report

A SURPRISINGLY JUBILANT Mr. Cyril Morton greeted us the following afternoon.

"Thank you, gentlemen," he said. "I have had a splendid day. Far beyond my expectations. Yes, quite splendid."

We had come again to the Mortons' finely appointed city house in Chelsea to receive the reports from Cyril and Violet Morton on the espionage adventures into the homes on the address list.

"I had such an excellent time at the houses in Chelsea and Belgravia in the morning that I managed to squeeze in one more in Mayfair in the afternoon. I never made it back to my office at all. And Violet made it to two places. That makes five in all, Mr. Holmes. We came back really quite chuffed at our accomplishments. You really should consider adding us to your famous list of Irregulars. Mind you, we would have to charge more than a shilling for our services."

Here he laughed happily at his own wit.

"Excellent," said Holmes. "Now then, kindly inform me as to what my newest two spies were able to discover."

"You have no idea," replied Cyril, "how many of these quite lavish houses are in desperate need of completely new electrical services. All of the homes I visited signed contracts on the spot. It was so much more efficient for me to see them myself as I could tell them exactly what was needed, how much it would cost, and when the work could be completed. I am never able to do that when I send out one of my young sales lads. But even without an appointment, I was able to sign them up. It was capital, I tell you, just capital. And my dear wife acquired a new set of quite bright children as her piano students from her first house. The second house was inhabited by Americans, so it is no wonder they were not interested. You know how those people are. What do you think of that, Mr. Holmes?"

I could see that Holmes was not impressed.

"Well done, I am sure," he said. "Now sir, what about the young men and women for whom we are searching?"

"Oh, yes, them," said Cyril. "We found all of them, didn't we dear?"

"Not entirely, darling," said Violet. "In each of the houses, we found a boy or girl from the list although not necessarily those we had expected to find. All are alive and appear to be healthy, although it was somewhat difficult to find a way to chat with them privately. But we were able to do so with a few of them, weren't we dear? And what we learned might be of interest to you."

"I am all attention," said Homes. "Your report, please."

"I took the houses where the names were of the female sex," she said. "It turned out that both of the houses had children and I was able to speak to their mothers about offering piano lessons. The fact that my card had our address here in Chelsea was a distinct advantage as mothers, even those who employ servants whose provenance is suspect are nevertheless concerned for that their children have proper examples set for them by governesses, tutors, and music teachers."

"Indeed, madam," said Holmes. "I am sure they are. Your report, please."

"The first house was the city home of the Earl of Cawdor. He's quite an important fellow, is he not?"

"He serves as First Lord of the Admiralty," said Holmes.

"Well, the maid who opened the door gave me quite the shock. The name on the list for that house was a Dutch girl—a Miss Wilhelmina Mulders—but this girl was not Dutch in the least little bit. She was African and must have been at least six feet tall. She led me into the parlor and offered me tea, just as any good maid would. I had a copy of the list in my purse, and I took a quick look at it, and when she returned with the tea, I quietly asked her if she was Miss Zenani Masithathu. She was quite surprised and even fearful. 'No,' she said very quietly, 'that is my sister. I am Makaziwe Masithathu. How do you know the name of my sister?'

"I quickly told her that I was helping Mr. Sherlock Holmes and that he was trying to make sure that all of the boys and girls on the boat from Cape Town were brought to safety and the evil men who tricked them punished. She told me that she had only been in that house for a few days. I asked if she was in danger and she said that she was not. She told me that in Africa, her family was related to the prince and that she was embarrassed to be working as a maid but that she had no choice unless she was willing to be a prostitute. She feared for what they would do to her sister if she disobeyed.

"But our conversation was interrupted by the lady of the house. We exchanged pleasantries for a couple of minutes and then, the maid having departed, I asked her whether or not she was happy with the service she was receiving from her. She was neither enthusiastic nor critical but defended her choice by saying that it was a mission of mercy and that all of the wages were paid to a charity. I feigned interest, and she gave me the name and address of the charity. Would that be useful to you, Mr. Holmes?"

"Exceptionally. Your first document turned over in your career in espionage. Well done. Did you happen to ask what had happened to the Mulders girl?"

"I am so sorry, Mr. Holmes. I did ask, but all I was told was that she had moved to a house not far from ours in Chelsea. I knew that I should have tried to learn more, but there was no opportunity."

"You did well all the same. Please continue."

"There is not much to report. I met with the children. The daughter was angelic, the boy beastly but that is to be expected when they are being signed up for piano lessons. I shall be paying a visit to the home once every fortnight to give lessons and shall report back to you."

"Excellent. Now then, your second visit. Was it as successful?"

"I fear it was not; neither in my mission as a spy nor in securing more pupils for my piano classes."

"One cannot have complete success all of the time," said Holmes. "Your report, please."

"I had gone another house in Chelsea. The list said that a boy from India had been placed there. I had expected to find a young lad named Rajeev Amla, but he was not there. I was surprised when the door opened and Kisha, the second oriental girl, opened it. After I gasped, I quietly asked her what she was doing here. She knew who I was straight away and became terribly fearful and begged me not to reveal anything. She said that her sister had already vanished and she feared for both of their lives.

"I asked about the boy who was supposed to be at that address, and she said that she knew very little except that she heard from the cook that he had been sent to work as an apprentice to a brokerage in the City.

"I had neither the heart nor the courage to tell her that I had seen her sister and that she was dead. I could not do that in the short time we had. She led me into the front room and quickly told me that she had been under some suspicion from her former master and mistress and that they had contacted the charity and that last night she had been moved to this location. She had no opportunity to say any more before the lady of the house arrived. I explained the reason for my visit and asked if she were interested in lessons for her children. She was surprisingly blunt in telling me that she was not interested. Her answer was well beyond rude and inconsiderate. Mind you, I do believe she was from New York, so I should not have been surprised."

"The names of the masters of that house?" asked Holmes. "Did you note them?"

"Oh yes. *Choate*. I am not sure, but I believe his brother is the American Ambassador, so his relatives receive a nice home here as well. Is that how it works?"

"Most of the time," said Holmes. "Was that all?"

"Well, I was shown the door, but after it closed behind me, I acted on a thought and took a look at the back of the house. My bicycle was leaning up against the back wall."

"Ah ha," I cried. "So, she still has it. Then we should be able to count on her appearing tomorrow morning."

"Let us hope so," said Holmes. "Now, Mr. Morton, sir. Your report."

"Of course, and by crikey, I did have quite a good time of it. At the first house I called on—quite a refined terrace home in Belgravia—I was met at the door by a young woman from India. She was quite confident and refined and led me and offered tea. I very quietly asked her if her name was Beena Kannan. She was, as I had expected, terribly surprised and I told her, *sotto voce* of course, that I knew about her situation and how she had been tricked and that I was arranging for her to be rescued. She was very timorous at first but I succeeded in putting her at ease, and she admitted that I was correct about her situation. Then the lady, Mrs. St. John Brodrick, came by and I explained the reason for my visit. She apologized saying that as she was a woman, she was not at all familiar with the electrical needs of the house but perhaps I could return when her husband was at home.

"Well, I suggested that to save time, perhaps her maid could accompany me through the entire house and I could do my inspection and leave an estimate for her husband's consideration, and she agreed. Now, by the living Jingo, wasn't that clever move on my part?"

"Awfully clever," said Holmes. "Kindly omit the details of your inspection and estimate and tell us what you learned from the maid."

"By crikey, once we were out of earshot she told me a similar story about how her family had been lied to about a scholarship at Oxford. Her father was entirely in favor of her going to England; her being still quite young to be away from home. I would guess that he has a bit of an old fuddy-duddy attitude about the education of women. Not at all progressive like we are here in London. But that she and her mother and sister had prevailed upon him and he had relented. Her story, which I was able to coax out of her as we toured the house, as to the threats made on her should she go to Scotland Yard are quite consistent with what we are hearing. And I should note, Mr. Holmes, the name of the master of the house—I assume you recognize."

"William St. John Brodrick," said Holmes, "is the Secretary of State for War as well as an Irish Unionist."

"Precisely. And this poor young woman had been told that she must listen in on his conversations and find a way to read his documents and mail and make a report to a woman who would come by weekly claiming to be doing inspections for the charity. She was quite forthcoming with me—I must assume that she found me to be worthy of her trust—and she listed some of the items she had seen or heard and passed on. Mr. Holmes, I have prepared a list of them such as I was able to remember but you will see that they were items that concern the Royal Navy and the B.E.F. and such. Just what you might expect from a cabinet minister."

"She said," asked Holmes, "that it was a woman who came by? Not the chap who came to your door and who had recruited them?"

"Quite so," said Cyril. "I suppose I should have asked her more about the woman, but I was rather consumed with preparing my estimate for the house."

"Yes, of course," said Holmes. "Now, kindly continue. The second house."

"Before I move on," said Cyril. "I must tell about how I secured the contract for the electrical work on the house. I spoke to Lady Brodrick and presented a written document, and before she could tell me to wait until she had shown it to her husband, I happened to let slip that her neighbor two doors down had recently had their house upgraded to the latest in services. That was all it took. She signed the order straight away and muttered something about her husband being a penny pincher. I left feeling quite pleased with what I had accomplished."

"Rightly so, I am sure," said Holmes. "Now, the second house."

"Ah yes, quite the strange one that one," said Cyril. "On the list, there was another Indian woman's name, and I expected again that she would have been pressed into service as a domestic worker. However, the maid who answered the door obviously did not come from the lands under the Raj. She was just the common unattractive English working girl. I entered the house, was served tea yet again, and then was quite surprised when two women—one quite young and exceptionally attractive and the other about the right age to be her mother—entered. Both of them were dark-skinned, well, not dark like the one my wife has described, but like all those chaps and women from India, and they were both wearing lovely silk saris and had enough gold jewelry attached to their bodies to finance the Treasury. And the house positively reeked of curry.

"The older woman introduced herself as Mrs. Donald Chakola. You might have run across her husband, an Anglo-Indian of course, and has the agency permits for millions of goods that flow back and forth between England and our jewel of the Empire. She introduced her daughter as Miss Nazneen Jehangir which led me to suspect that the younger woman was not actually her daughter. Her name was on our list, but she did not appear to be in the least coerced into a miserable condition. The older woman went on to explain that the younger one was, in truth, the fiancée of her son, so, her future daughter-in-law would be more accurate. I knew that a different strategy would be called for if I were to be able to speak privately with the young woman. Therefore, recognizing that her name was distinctly from the State of Kerala, I immediately made it known that I was frightfully interested in expanding the business of my firm in that area and that perhaps she might accompany me as I did my inspection and prepared my estimate and answer my questions about the needs for electricity in Thiruvananthapuram, Kochi, and Calicut. The mother was quite quick to say that would be an excellent idea and that should I be looking for someone to be the head of such a venture, her son would be most suitable.

"As I carried out the inspection, I asked, nonchalantly of course, about how the young woman came to meet this family and become engaged to the son. She told me the same story about being offered a scholarship but that when she arrived, she found that there was no scholarship and that she had been acquired, for a significant fee, by a wealthy Indian family and would be forced to marry the son. The family had been quite unsuccessful in finding him a suitable bride in England owing to his unattractive appearance, social clumsiness, and obvious laziness.

"I expressed my sympathy and outrage, of course, and asked if she wished me to take steps to alert the police as to her situation. To my surprise, she told me not to do any such thing. She would have been married off in her home country all the same and that at least here she knew that she would become a part of a wealthy family and that she and her relationship with mother-in-law—a matter of constant conflict amongst Indian marriages—was quite good.

"I was a bit forward and noted, as tactfully as I could, that she was an exceptionally attractive young woman and asked if she was concerned about being to a man who was not at all similarly endowed. She smiled—quite an irresistible smile she had, indeed—and asked me if I had ever heard of the ancient Greek writer Plutarch.

"I had of course—had to read him at university—but I could not, for the life of me, see what he had to do with anything. She asked me if I remembered reading his quite well-known advice: *When candles are out, all women are fair.* Of course, every schoolboy knows that line, and she quickly added 'The same can be said for men.' She was not in the least wanting anyone's help to escape her situation and considered herself to have been favored by the gods.

"I must say, that the whole thing was quite the unexpected. When we had finished the tour of the house, I wrote up my estimate and, even more to my surprise, she did not call on her future mother-in-law to sign it but did so herself. I must admit, that surprised though I was, I again felt quite chuffed about gaining the contract as well as the information you had requested. Mr. Holmes."

"That is," said Holmes, "a surprising alternative to the other situations. Very well, your final report, Mr. Morton."

"That one was quite straightforward. One of the largest houses in Mayfair, but entirely plain—frankly austere—when it comes to furnishings, mind you. It was the city house of George Cadbury. You know the chap; the Quaker who tells us that we must all behave ourselves and then sells us chocolate and is surprised when we don't. However, the name on our list corresponded to the young woman who served me tea whilst I waited for the old fellow to come down. Her name was Lotte, and she was just one of those beautiful blonde Dutch girls whose only role on earth is to make universally plain English girls angry with God. I had only a few minutes to chat with her, but she confirmed that she was working as a maid in this house, but only part-time."

"Did she say what she was doing with the rest of her time?" asked Holmes.

"No. Mind you, I neglected to ask that. I suppose, now that you mention it, I should have. Nevertheless, I did confirm her story; same as all the rest—promised a scholarship and then threatened. Terrified that horrible things will happen to her family back home in the Cape if she informs her employers or Scotland Yard. And, the same routine of having a woman from the charity come by once a week to check up on her and demand a report. Old Mr. Cadbury was quite receptive to upgrading his electrical wiring and lamps and such when I told him that it reduced his likelihood of a fire substantially and that he would more than recover his expense by the long-term reduction in his insurance premiums. So, all in all, an absolutely splendid day."

"What," asked Holmes, "was the girl to report on?"

"Oh, I did not bother getting into that. Old George Cadbury has retired from his role, and his sons now run the shop now. I could not imagine anything that would be of importance. And, the whole lot of them are Quakers, so there is not likely to be even the whiff of a scandal worth starting a rumor over. Although, she did mention that the groom and the garden boy had also been acquired through the charity. But their names were not on our list, so I did not bother asking about them."

Chapter Seven
Taken by Holmes to a Brothel

AS IT WAS NOW well past tea time and on into the supper hour, I invited Holmes to come back to my home and dine with my wife and me. He considerately attempted to decline the offer, saying that it would not be fair to my wife and our cook to arrive without warning after the food had all been prepared. I assured him that the cook would just toss another cup of water into the soup and fetch a smoked ham from the cellar and that it would all be fine.

He surprised me by accepting. I should have known that he had an ulterior motive.

After a pleasant supper during which the three of us discussed and, in our minds, solved many of the problems facing London, the Empire, and the globe, Holmes graciously thanked my wife, pushed back from the table, and slowly lit his pipe.

"My dear Mrs. Watson," he said, smiling coyly. "I must ask of you a favor."

She gave him a friendly sidewards look. "Yes, Sherlock Holmes? And just what would that be?"

"Would you be so kind as to loan me the company of your husband for the remainder of the evening?"

"Perhaps. It would depend on what you are planning to do with him. Anything dangerous?"

"Oh no, not at all. I am planning to take him to a very exclusive brothel."

Both my wife and I burst into laughter.

"Sherlock Holmes," she sputtered, "that might be highly dangerous. My husband is no longer a young man. He might come home at midnight terribly sad, having wasted tens of pounds and with nothing to show for it. Buxom young strumpets can be very intimidating to men of a certain age."

"Ah, there you need not worry," said Holmes. "The brothel I have in mind is only open to men. No women are allowed."

Again, she laughed. I did not.

"He is all yours," she said. "But if he comes home with pinch marks all over his bottom, I shall have to have words with you, Sherlock Holmes."

"I shall do everything in my power to protect that cherished part of his anatomy," Holmes said.

"Excuse me," I interrupted. "As I am the subject of this negotiation, do I not have a say in it?"

The two of them exchanged haughty looks, turned to me and spoke in unison.

"No."

"Where are we going," I demanded once we were in a cab.

"The address is 19 Cleveland Street. It is in Fitzrovia."

"I know where Cleveland Street is, Holmes. It is a perfectly nondescript street of houses. That is the address on the list where one of the boys with an Indian name is living, is it not?

"Precisely."

"Do you think he is a servant in that house?"

"Highly unlikely."

"What is going on there?"

"Think back, please Watson. Do you recall the stories in the press—quickly hushed up—about the telegraph boys and some members of the nobility?"

"Of course, I do. But I thought they had shut that place down."

"Oh no. They closed the doors for a few months but then they reopened. It is all dictated by economics; supply and demand and what not."

"*That* is where we are going?"

"Precisely."

The house on the corner of Cleveland and Tottenham looked every bit as respectable as the house we had visited the previous evening. Again, the windows were completely blacked out with heavy draperies, and again we entered through the rear servants' door.

Once inside, we were in a small unfurnished vestibule. On the far wall was a door and beside it, a small barred window with no glass, much like a teller's counter in a bank. A slight, middle-aged man appeared behind us and looked at us blankly.

"Do you wish lockers, a shared room, or private rooms?" he asked.

"One shared room," said Holmes and he slid several shillings through the bars.

The door beside the window opened, and I followed Holmes through it. On top of another counter were two large, folded white towels and a key, attached to a numbered fob.

"We are in room 23," said Holmes. He began walking down a darkened corridor and into a labyrinth of narrow hallways. He stopped in front of the door with the barely visible number marked on it.

"Just place your towel and hat inside onto the bed," he told me. "We may have to return here later."

I did what he told me to and then followed him around several corners until we emerged into a well-lit spacious parlor. There were at least a dozen sofas scattered through the room, all looking rather new. They and the rest of the furnishings were clean, and all of the woodwork was gleaming. In the room and the hallways lingered a faint odor of bleach. The entire parlor was somewhat cluttered with statuary of various sizes, and the walls were covered with quite good quality paintings. All of the art had one thing in common. It all had a theme of athletes and athletic events in ancient Greece. In the corner of the room was a replica of the famous statue of David by Michelangelo. Critics of that statue had claimed for years that the sculptor had deliberately enlarged the shepherd boy's hands. I was no critic of art, but it occurred to me that whoever made the replica had enlarged more than the lad's hands.

We were not alone.

There were over a dozen other men in the room, and I recognized half of them. Two had come to me as patients to my medical practice. Three were either Members of Parliament or the House of Lords. One was amongst the wealthiest bankers in the City, and the final was a bishop.

Holmes and I had kept on our full evening dress, as had some of the other men in the room. Some, however, were clad only in dressing gowns with their bare calves and feet extending to the carpet. And there were three men whose torsos were entirely bare and who wore nothing but their large towel wrapped around their waist. Most of them were reading a newspaper or a yellow-backed novel, whilst a few were chatting inaudibly with each other.

Several of them recognized Holmes and me and gave us a quick, friendly smile and nod before ignoring us again.

"Holmes," I whispered. "These chaps know who we are. This is madness."

"At ease, my friend. Everything that happens here dare not speak its name. What adult men do behind closed doors is nobody's business but their own."

I was not at all convinced. "Now what happens? How are we to find the Indian boy?" I asked.

"We wait. He will likely find us. Meanwhile, you might take a magazine out of the rack beside you and try not to look so ill at ease."

I extracted a copy of *The Strand Magazine* from the rack, hoping that it might contain one of the stories I had written about Sherlock Holmes. It did not, but there was a short story by a new chap who had appeared recently on the London literary scene, a Mr. Pelham Grenville Wodehouse. It was wonderfully amusing and I was eager to read it through to the end when I felt a kick on my ankle from the boot of Holmes.

Approaching us was an exceptionally handsome young man, dressed in a singlet and athletic shorts as if he were about to run a dash for the school team. He smiled a perfect smile, pushed his long blond hair back over his forehead, and leaned down to speak to us.

"Are you two gentlemen looking for a little company for the next hour or so?"

"We are indeed," said Holmes. "However, I am sorry, but we were not looking for you, my dear boy. I do not wish to hurt your feelings, but we came very specifically looking for a lovely young man by the name of Miguel. Might you know him?"

Holmes slipped a pound note into the young man's hand as he spoke.

"Of course. I would be honored to assist you. Miguel is upstairs. Would you mind following me."

We got up and followed him out of the parlor and up a wide carpeted staircase to the second floor. As we climbed, we were passed by several chaps coming down. They were all clad only in a towel around their waists and a second towel draped around their necks. Their hair and their torsos were dripping wet.

"Holmes," I said. "This place must have a Turkish bath just like the one we enjoy going to off Northumberland."

"Precisely."

"Well, since we have already paid for it, I suggest that we pay a visit there before leaving. You know how a good steaming gives such excellent medicinal results. What do you say?"

"I think not."

"Oh, come now, Holmes. Baths are one of the most democratic places in all of London. One cannot distinguish the building butcher from the sagging banker. And the hard-working bricklayer comes out on top."

"If by democratic," he replied, "you mean that in a bath, all men over fifty look equally ridiculous, I agree."

"Glad to hear it," I said. "Then what possible risk is there to our enjoying it?"

"To your bottom."

I was about to argue with him, but we had arrived at a door on the second floor, and our guide knocked quietly.

"Hey, Mowgli. You have visitors. You have acquired some admirers my darling."

The door opened slowly, and we were greeted in silence by a diminutive, dark-skinned lad who could not have been more than sixteen years old. He looked for all the world like the boy from the illustrations in Kipling's Jungle Book, and I half expected to see a wolf, bear, and black panther lurking behind him.

"Come in," he whispered to us. We did so, and he closed the door. The light was dim, but I could see that he was not quite five feet tall and could not have weighed more than eight stone. He was dressed in a costume of a miniature maharajah with a turban perched on his head. He looked up at us without smiling, his dark eyes resembling a dismal puppy.

I had treated many men and boys during my days of serving under the Raj and I could see immediately that his eyes were somewhat puffy and that both upper and lower eyelids were mildly inflamed. The boy had been crying.

He bowed deeply in front of us and quietly recited his short speech.

"Welcome, Sahibs. I am at your service. You may use me as you wish. What is your desire?"

"Miguel Perera," said Holmes, quietly but forcefully, "my desire is to get you out of this terrible place and safely back to your family."

The boy snapped back from his bow and jumped back so quickly that his turban fell off behind him. His eyes became wide with fear and his face contorted as if ready to break into tears.

"Miguel Perera," said Holmes again. "I am Sherlock Holmes. This is Doctor Watson. Do you recognize our names?"

For some time, there was no response and then a shallow nod.

"We know," said Holmes, "how you and the others were tricked into coming to London, and we are going to help you to escape. Will you let us help you?"

His gaze flicked back and forth from me to Holmes and back again. Suddenly, he ran right at me and threw his arms around my waist. I could feel him trembling.

"Oh please, sir, please. Get me out of here. Get me out of here. Please sir, please."

I put my hands on his shoulders and attempted to gently peel him off of me. He was not about to let go. I let him hold on to me until I felt his trembling subside and his breathing return to a normal rate.

"Miguel," I said. "I am a doctor. If you come with me, I shall tell the men in charge here that you are sick and that I must take you to a hospital before you infect any of the members of the house. Can you pretend to cough?"

"Ah, brilliant," said Holmes. "An excellent plan, my friend."

The boy stepped back from me and sat down on the bed. He head was bowed, and he sat there like that for some time. I could see tears dripping from his face to his legs. He lifted his head and looked at me.

"Doctor, sir, you are very, very kind and I need to get out of this horrible, horrible place. But I cannot go. I cannot."

"Why not?" I asked. "I can tell them that I shall call the ambulance to have you removed. As a doctor, I can give an order like that."

"Oh, sir. I want to go. I want to. But I cannot run away. I cannot go without Rajeev. He is my friend. We came here together. If I run away, they have said that they will kill him. I cannot go until I know that he is safe."

"Is Rajeev here as well?" asked Holmes.

"No. He was at first. But he is very, very smart. He was the best student in our school. They said they had another place they were taking him, but I do not know where it is. I cannot go until I know that he is safe. Please, sir. I want to leave very, very badly, but I cannot."

"We cannot just leave you here," said Holmes.

"You are very kind to say that, Mr. Holmes, sir. But I have been here now for almost two months, and I am still alive. There have been times when I wanted to kill myself, but I am still alive. If I know that Sherlock Holmes is going to save my friend, Rajeev, and then get me out of here, I will have the strength to continue."

Holmes sat and looked at the boy. "I will do everything I can to get you out of here. You are a very brave young man."

The boy merely shrugged. "No, Mr. Holmes. I am not brave. I have no choice."

"Can you tell me who controls your time here?" asked Holmes. "Who is the master of this place?"

"If you are asking me who is the manager of this house, then you can ask for him on your way out. It is no secret. But he is not the master. Every week a man comes here and meets individually with us here, and we report to him. We believe that collects most of the money we are paid. It is he who decides who will work in which house and for how long."

"Is he the same man who met your family and offered you a scholarship?" asked Holmes.

"Oh, no sir. It is not that man at all. He brought us here, but I have not seen him since. There is another man who comes by once a week and demands reports from all of us."

"All of you? But you said that Rajeev was taken away. To whom are you referring.?"

"Oh sir, there are three others beside myself. I do not know their true names but one we call Charlie. He is from China. There is Wee Willie who comes from Scotland, and there is Isaac the Jew. There are four of us, as I said, Mr. Holmes, sir."

"But they did not come with you."

"Oh no, sir. They were already here, sir. Willie and Charlie have been here for much longer than I have but Isaac only arrived a week ago. If you can, Mr. Holmes, sir, you must also try to get them out of here as well."

Holmes appeared to be puzzled by this latest piece of data. We bade goodbye to the lad and departed. I felt sick to my stomach knowing that we were leaving him to the predations of utterly unscrupulous men, but there was nothing we could do further that evening.

"What sort of men," I mused as we were standing outside on the pavement, "would be so vile as to subject a boy to a place like this?"

"They are called criminals, Watson. And the city is crawling with them. That they would do this to a mere child does not surprise me. The greater question is 'why?' You saw how little I paid for us to enter. There is nowhere near enough profit to be made from a portion of the boy's meager wages. Even if there are four of them, it makes no sense."

Holmes lit a cigarette started to pace back and forth. His doing so was interrupted by an exceptionally well-dressed gentleman whose name I can never reveal.

"Good evening, Mr. Sherlock Holmes," said the man, in a near whisper. "I was surprised to see you here, but I welcome your interest."

"Indeed, Lord —," said Holmes. "And why is that?"

"This is one of the few places in all of London where men who wish to exchange alternative affections are free to do so. Some of us suspect that it has been infiltrated by a criminal element. I hope that you are able to vanquish them so that our pleasant pastimes can continue in peace."

Holmes began to reply, but the fellow turned and walked away. Holmes remained in place until he had finished his cigarette and then began to walk north toward Marylebone. After two blocks of silence, he turned me.

"I trust you shall be free to join me tomorrow morning. You will recall that Miss Kisha agreed to meet us again. May I assume that your good wife shall again be willing to find all of the items on the shopping list and that you will meet me in the pub at nine o'clock?"

I assured him that I would be there, whereupon he hailed a cab and held the door of it for me to enter.

"I shall walk home," he said. "I have far too many questions inside my head about this case. Give my regards to Mrs. Watson. Good night, my friend."

He closed the door before I could reply. I would have to wait until the following morning to learn what insights, if any, his furtive brain had been able to untangle.

Chapter Eight
Where Did They All Come From?

THE FOLLOWING MORNING found Holmes and me back in the Hereford Arms and enjoying our full English whilst my wife and Mrs. Hudson again took pity upon us and secured the list of groceries that Miss Kisha had requested. The two of them divided and conquered and within twenty minutes had secured the entire bundle and joined us in the pub.

We had no sooner begun to chat when I looked up and was surprised to see the elegant Mrs. Violet Morton entering the pub.

"I asked her to join us," said Holmes. "She has been useful in the progress of this case, and I may be in need of her further services."

I rose and greeted her and introduced her to my wife.

Only forty-eight hours had passed since Holmes and I had last sat together in this pub, but a flood a data had poured in during that time. Holmes took the opportunity in between mouthfuls of bangers, poached eggs, and grilled tomato to review what we now knew ... and did not know.

"What we appear to have stumbled into, my friends, is a criminal scheme designed to trick susceptible young men and women from around the globe to come to England under the fraudulent promise of a scholarship to Oxford. Once here they are either put into domestic service or into some establishment in which a particular vice is practiced, and their wages are collected in the name of some fabricated charity."

"We do have," I added, "the name and address of the charity, do we not?"

"Oh yes," said Holmes. "For what it is worth, they call themselves *The Royal Leonardo's Homes Benevolent Society* and have an address on St. Peter's Lane in Clerkenwell. I did pay them a visit and discovered that it is no more than a postal forwarding service to which no mail ever arrives nor is forwarded."

"And we know," I said, "the complete names and addresses of all of those who came on the ship from the Cape."

"Not quite, Watson," he replied. "Some of the addresses keep changing and there appear to be other young men and women who are likewise living in forced servitude who are not part of the Charing Cross group."

"Who," I asked, "is moving them around?"

Holmes did not immediately answer and chewed slowly on a morsel of sausage before responding.

"An excellent question, Watson. The fellow calling himself Professor MacDougall was instrumental in the fraudulent recruitment but appears to have handed them over to some other network of people here in London. There have been references to such a group as *the association*. Beyond that, we know little or nothing."

He went on to review the incomplete state of our knowledge. We knew that there were two Dutch girls, Wilhelmina and Lotte, both of whom were listed at addresses in the wealthiest neighborhoods of London. One of the two African girls was serving as a maid whilst the other, Miss Zenani, was giving beatings to men in the house on Oak Street. One Indian girl had been forced to become the fiancé of a young Indian man while the other was a maid in Belgravia. One of the Asian girls who had been presented at the door of Mrs. Violet Morton was dead, and the other was about to arrive and meet with us in a few minutes.

Miguel, the Indian boy we had met on Cleveland Street, had been forced into a dark life of vice and his friend, Rajeev, was apprenticed to a firm in the City but had an address down in Streatham.

In addition to these young people, we had heard of several more who had been enslaved in similar situations.

Having completed his recitation, Holmes reached for his cigarette case and leaned back in his chair as if to reflect. His doing so was interrupted by Mrs. Hudson.

"Mr. Holmes," she said, "it is not my place to interfere in your business, and I have managed not to do so—occasionally with some considerable difficulty, mind you—for quite some time now."

"My dear Mrs. Hudson," said Holmes smiling warmly at her. "I could never have achieved what modicum of success I now enjoy had it not been for your keeping the homes fires burning for all these years. Pray, what are your thoughts on these matters?"

"Well, Mr. Holmes, I was never much of a scholar in school, but I did not too badly in my geography classes. I quite enjoyed learning about those places on the globe marked in red. You know, the colonies of the British Empire on which the sun never sets."

"I am," said Holmes, "as familiar as I need to be with those countries. What it is about them that now come to your mind?"

"Well now, Mr. Holmes. You have told us that there are girls from Japan, and boys from India, and Dutch girls, and girls from India. Is that correct Mr. Holmes?"

"Yes. They are quite the cosmopolitan lot."

"Well, Mr. Holmes. I recall learning in school that those countries are not at all close to each other. Asia and Africa are very large places as is the Indian Ocean. Is not Moscow much closer to London than South Africa is to India? And isn't Japan a long way from anywhere? Now, I may not have had all that many years of school, but it strikes me that one man could not recruit all those boys and girls from all those places in just a few weeks. Would it not take him months to make all those voyages and visit all the families? How did this one fellow do it? There must have been more than one man, but all the stories the boys and girls tell say that it was this Professor MacDougall fellow what found them."

"Ah, an excellent observation, Mrs. Hudson," replied Holmes. He sat for a minute in silence.

"Either there must be more than one Professor MacDougall," he said, speaking slowly and deliberately, "*or* all of those who were recruited must come from the same place. There is no other logical alternative. The young oriental woman informed us that her family name was Okada. My inquiry at the Foreign Office as to the presence of this family's trading company in the Cape was returned positive. The Dutch girls may have a heritage in Holland but are Afrikaans, which explains their presence on the same ship as the others. And the Cape is teeming with Indian laborers and traders and Africans who have migrated from the colonies to the north of the Cape. Thus, it is a reasonable hypothesis that all of the recruitment took place within the Cape Province. The so-called Professor's accent, as reported by you, Mrs. Morton, was like someone from New Zealand. That accent is not far off from the one claimed by those from the south of Africa."

The rest of us nodded and agreed with Holmes's logic. He was about to continue his dissertation when a young man approached our table.

"Begging your pardon, ladies and gentlemen," he said. "But might one of you be a Dr. Watson?"

"I am he," said I, whereupon he handed me a sealed letter envelope.

"If you would not mind, doctor," he said. "Could you please open this and read it before I depart?"

The envelope had my name on the outside but no indication of the sender. I opened it and read it. I felt the blood draining from my face as I did so. I passed it along to Holmes.

It ran:

```
Dear Doctor-san: If you have received
this letter and it has not been opened,
please give the man who delivered it some
money. He is the cook in the house in which
```

I am now kept. Then, please show the letter to Sherlock-san.

    I beg you to accept my apologies. I am sorry that I could not come myself, but last night I learned that my dear cousin, Hatsu, is dead. I am sure that they killed her because of what she had learned and had tried to expose. She had taken her findings to our Member of Parliament because she thought he could be trusted and it is possible that he betrayed her.

    I am now suspected of also having betrayed what we learned about the evil net into which all of us have been trapped. Our lives are now also in danger, and I fear that they may kill all of us like they did Hatsu.

    Please, Doctor-san and Sherlock-san, help us.

    Yours very truly,

    Kishu Okada (Miss)

    P.S. I still have the bicycle belonging to Mrs. Morton. I will keep it safe until she is able to recover it. I am sorry for having stolen it, but I was forced to do so.

I gave the cook some money, and he took the bundle of groceries and departed.

"Good lord," said Holmes, as he passed the letter over to the ladies. "Our time is running out."

He then turned to Mrs. Violet Morton.

"My dear Mrs. Morton. Would it be possible for you to pay a visit to several more houses today in the guise of offering music lessons and, when doing so, confirm the current residence of the remainder of the names on our list? I must warn you that there is a slight possibility of danger in your doing so, but I think it highly unlikely that any one of the parties behind this scheme knows of your role in helping us. Dr. Watson and I would do it ourselves, but we would be recognized straight away, and the game would be up. I would hope that your good husband would not object to my asking you."

"Oh, it did not occur to me to ask his permission. He is at his office all day, and I will try to have all the visits made before he comes home for dinner. What he does not know until then will not bother him."

"Excellent. Please deliver a report to me as soon as you are finished. Now, if the ladies will excuse us, Dr. Watson and I have an urgent call to make."

He was soon on his feet and walking out of the pub. I scrambled to follow him.

"Where are you going?" I demanded.

"Scotland Yard."

Chapter Nine
Report Received, Rescue Planned

"OH, COME NOW, HOLMES," said Lestrade, as we sat in his Spartan office by the Embankment. "There must be a thousand domestic servants and almost as many prostitutes in London who are being treated badly by their masters. I cannot organize thirty or more of my constables to raid the homes of some of the wealthiest and most respected men in the city just because you tell me that their servants are not receiving their full wages."

"This has nothing to do with servants' wages," said Holmes.

"Then what does it have to do with?"

"Treason," said Holmes. "Treason and blackmail taking place within the highest echelons of government and industry."

That got Lestrade's full attention, and he put down his cup of tea and leaned forward on his desk.

"You had better explain that one, Holmes."

"This scheme initially appeared to be one of a malevolent placement agency masquerading as a charity and by doing so skimming a portion of a servants' wages. However, that makes no sense at all. Whatever amount of money can be removed from the low wages of young domestic servants, or even from the payments made to those enslaved in the depths of vice, cannot amount to more than a sweating trifle."

"With that, I agree," said Lestrade.

"The men who pay visits to brothels, particularly those who frequent Molly Houses and Houses of Torture do so, expecting that their peculiar vices will never be exposed. If their interests were to become known, their marriages, positions of trust, and entire futures would be ruined. The merest hint and gossip would be devastating."

"Really, Holmes? Gossip and rumors about what men do once they have loosed their trousers is rampant. If the rumors were to be believed, they would have to be publicized in the Press. Surely, you do not believe that London's newspapers would print such trash."

Holmes's blank expression slowly changed into a condescending smile.

"My dear Inspector, would it help to sell more newspapers?"

Lestrade took another sip of his cooling tea and sighed.

"Right."

Holmes extracted a piece of paper from his pocket and slid it across the table to Lestrade.

"This is a list of the men I observed in only three evenings of visiting houses of vice. Below it is the list of the prominent men into whose homes this gang of criminals has placed their enslaved spies."

Lestrade picked it up and looked at it. His eyes became as wide as saucers, and his mouth issued a low whistle.

"These men," he said, "must be mad. Every one of them has a fortune, a title, or even a bishopric to lose. Some are privy to the most closely guarded secrets of the government. Are they crazy?"

"No. Not at all. The underworld of London operates on an inviolable basis of trust and secrecy. That is why it is such a vulnerable target of unscrupulous criminals. Whilst there may well be honor amongst thieves, it is a rule of thumb that you never steal from an honest man; only from those who have a great deal to lose."

"And you now believe," said Lestrade, "that this young oriental girl had somehow figured all this out and so they killed her."

"That is my current hypothesis. Can you suggest an alternative explanation?"

"No. And now you think the lives of these remaining seven are at risk. Is that it?"

"Precisely."

"And you want me to organize a raid on all these places and get those young people out of there before anything untoward happens to them."

"Precisely. There appear to be even more such enslaved spies, but I have not yet been able to add them to my investigation. I expect to be able to confirm the location of all of these seven by the end of the afternoon. I have a very reliable agent working on it as we speak."

"Right. Very well, then. I will assemble a team of my lads and have them pay a visit to all these places at the same time. Most likely it will be five o'clock in the morning. That's the best time to conduct such an action. Everyone is at home, and the neighbors are not yet peering through their windows."

"Excellent," said Holmes.

"You do know," said Lestrade, "that if none of this is true and we come up empty, there will be hell to pay."

"I consider that to be impossible," said Holmes.

***

Violet Morton arrived at 221B in the late afternoon, beaming with accomplishment.

"Mr. Holmes," she said, "it would not take much to tempt me to give up teaching music and work for you as one of your Irregulars."

Holmes smiled at her and requested that she give an account of her highly irregular day.

"I began with the second Dutch girl, the one named Lotte. Cyril had met her at the home of old Mr. Cadbury, but the address on the list was above a row of shops in Knightsbridge. It turned out to be a small and very select brothel."

"You," I interjected, "entered into a *brothel*?"

"It was entirely safe, doctor. There is a large man with dark skin guarding the door, and only the most respectable men are allowed inside. He assumed that I was recently hired and was exceptionally well-mannered. I had read, I cannot remember where, that exclusive brothels employed piano players, and therefore I spoke with the madam of the house and told her that I was a highly skilled pianist—which, in all modesty, I am, so that was completely truthful—and asked if she might be interested in my services. I said that my dear husband had lost his employment and that I needed to do something to supplement our family income until he found a new situation—which was not exactly truthful but, to be precise, Cyril lost his position as an employee when he assumed full ownership of the firm, so you could say it was at least partly true. She asked me to play something and, while I do not often indulge myself when with Cyril—he does not entirely approve—I have a bit of a passion for the jolly ragtime tunes that are played in the music halls. Not that I would know, but I have read about them. And so, I sat down and banged out *Meet Me in St. Louis, Louie* and *Poor Wandering One.* And then I played and sang that silly song, *I Can't Do My Bally Bottom Button Up.* I confess that I did so quite lustily. Do you know that song, Mr. Holmes?"

"I regret that I am not familiar with it," said Holmes

"Well then, the madam, who calls herself Miss Gizella and she says she is Hungarian but I suspect she is only Irish, loved it and offered me a position on the spot and gave me a tour of her establishment. And, oh my, wasn't it just an elegant set of connected flats. She introduced me to her ladies, all of whom could have won a beauty contest, and in the third room was a Miss Angelique who I could see right off was Dutch. You know, Mr.

Holmes; tall, slender, beautiful blonde hair, sculpted face and brilliant blue eyes. When my tour was over and my wages and hours agreed to—only four hours a day during the lunch hour since I have to be back home for supper with Cyril and the children—I asked if I could get to know some of the other ladies and was encouraged to do so."

"You accepted employment in a brothel?" I gasped.

"Oh, I know, doctor. I shan't be able to honor my agreement and shall send my regrets tomorrow morning. However, it gave me the opportunity to go and speak to Lotte. I went directly to her room and closed the door. I did not have more than a few minutes to speak to her—a client was waiting—but it was enough to confirm who she was and her sad story. It was the same as all the others. Promised a scholarship at Oxford and then defrauded, her family threatened, and made to report weekly to an unknown but quite imposing woman who came around once a week. She now works part-time in the brothel and part-time in the Cadbury house. So, there, Mr. Holmes. That was the first one on my list."

"I commend you on your resourcefulness," said Holmes. "And the next?"

"Not nearly as interesting. I had to take a cab all the way to Streatham. It was the home of a very wealthy old banker, a Mr. Alexander Holder. He is the senior partner of the Holder and Stevenson banking firm. The young butler who met me at the door—in truth he was a secretary to Mr. Holder and not the butler but was answering the door whilst the butler was enjoying his nap—was from India. I told him my name and asked his, and he said that he was Rajeev and that he would take me to see Mr. Holder. Well, he, Mr. Holder that is, has now retired and his sons run the bank, so he was at home during the day. He was very interested in having me provide music lessons to his niece's son who is now his ward. He did not say what happened except that his niece had made some unfortunate decisions in her past, but the little boy was a delight. I followed Mr. Holder up to the second floor—I was somewhat concerned as he is a bit on the heavy side and seemed little accustomed to setting any tax upon his legs—and met his ward, Georgie. We agreed that I would come by once a week on Thursday afternoons and give lessons. I fear I shall have to cancel that opportunity as well. I did not have a chance to engage Rajeev in conversation, but I can confirm that he is living there."

"Excellent work," said Holmes. "We are familiar with Mr. Holder and know his home well. Pray continue."

"The last one was Miss Wilhelmina Mulders. You recall that I had previously gone looking for her, but she had moved and, I was told, she had moved into a house on Elm Park Gardens, which is just around the corner from our city house. It was quite an easy task then to chat with a couple of our neighbors—I picked the ones who are in truth rather annoying busybodies—and ask about a tall blonde girl who I had observed lately and wondered if anyone knew who she was. Well, Mrs. Noseworthy knew straight away who I was talking about and directed me to the home of Mr. and Mrs. Barrowman at number one hundred and three. I believe he has some title, but I cannot remember what it is."

"Baron Brookfield," said Holmes. "He owns several armament factories in the Docklands and in Birmingham."

"Oh, yes. That sounds familiar. Well, I went there immediately and, to my great good fortune, the owners were away for the afternoon, and I was offered tea by Miss Wilhelmina herself. Once I let on that I knew all about her and was working for Sherlock Holmes, she became quite chatty. At first, they said she had to work in a brothel like Lotte, but she told them they would have to kill her first, which would turn her into a very poor investment. So, they told her that she would have to marry Mr. Bentley Barrowman, the son of the industrialist. Now, you would think, wouldn't you, that the unmarried son of a wealthy family must be in want of a wife, like Mrs. Austin told us. But no. It seems that Baron-to-be Bentley is utterly odious. He is highly unattractive and completely lacking in any social graces. When he converses, he tries to be clever and laughs at his own attempts at humor, loudly sputtering 'a-huh, a-huh, a-huh.' His mother frankly describes him as involuntarily celibate and destined to remain that way. It was she who contacted the charity—goodness only knows how she learned about them—and asked if they could arrange a wife for her son. She desperately wants grandchildren and was completely smitten with Miss Wilhelmina. I guess she is hoping that some inherited features can skip a generation and that she will do better with grandchildren than with her only child."

"It has been known to happen," said Holmes.

"Well, Wilhelmina is not at all happy about things and quite desperate. She told me that she had contemplated taking her own life but decided that it would be better to do that after the wedding so that her family could sue for a portion of the estate, or something like that. The wedding is to be a small, private affair a week hence. I promised that Sherlock Holmes would come to her rescue before such a dreadful event. I do hope that was not presumptuous of me, was it Mr. Holmes?"

"Presumptuous? No. It is what I fully expect will happen shortly. But indiscrete? In future, you might be more candid about both your identity and mine. Nevertheless, I shall forward your findings immediately to Inspector Lestrade, and he will be able to orchestrate a raid on all these locations within the next twelve hours."

Chapter Ten
Failure. Now What?

I DID NOT WISH to appear too eager the following morning to learn the good news of the raid by Scotland Yard in the early hours of the morning and, accordingly, I enjoyed a leisurely morning tea with my wife. I had determined that I would take myself over to 221B around eight o'clock and accompany Holmes to Scotland Yard where, I fully expected, we would meet the entire lot of the rescued young people and begin the work of restoring them to their families.

That was not to be.

At seven-thirty a messenger boy came to my door and handed me a note.

```
Watson: Come here at once. The plan has
failed.  Holmes
```

I immediately hailed a cab and within fifteen minutes was climbing the stairs up from Baker Street to Holmes's rooms. I thought I might find him sitting, Buddha-like, contemplating his next move, but no. He was pacing back and forth in the front room, smoking a cigarette. The ashtray contained the stubs of several more that had been lighted and discarded in various states of completion.

"Ah, Watson, so good of you to come," he said without interrupting her pacing. "Take a look at the two notes on the table."

Two pieces of note paper were lying on the table. One bore the letterhead of Scotland Yard; the other had no markings. The first ran:

```
Holmes: Officers paid visits to all
houses at precisely 5:00 am. Not a single
one of the boys or girls was present. Owners
reported that the charity came early last
evening and removed them stating that they
all had an important meeting to attend and
would be returned by 9:00 pm. None were
returned. What is happening?

Lestrade
```

"What happened," I asked Holmes.

"Read the second note."

I did. It ran:

```
Dear Holmes the meddler; Holmes the
busybody; Holmes the Scotland Yard Jack-in-
box:

You have put your annoying nose where it
does not belong and have temporarily
discomfited our enterprise. Cease and desist
at once, or you will be responsible for the
daily death of one of these young men or
women. You know not to doubt our resolve.

Do not attempt to contact us. We will
contact you when we have confirmed that you
will never again intrude in our activities.

You have met your match, Mr. Sherlock
Holmes, and you have lost.

You may think of us as The Association of
the Fittest. We, not you or Scotland Yard,
will rule London.
```

"Merciful heavens," I said. "Who are these people?"

"I do not know," said Holmes, still pacing. "Not yet. But I will not be stopped by their insults and threats."

"Holmes," I objected. "They are not making idle threats. They murdered a young woman merely because she may have learned too much. Their fingers are everywhere already. You have not faced enemies this monstrous since—."

"Since Moriarty," he said, cutting me off. He stopped pacing and picked up his coat, hat and walking stick.

"Kindly come with me. We have to join forces with Lestrade and agree on our next move."

We descended to Baker Street and secured a cab. Once inside, Holmes sat in silence with his fists clenched and his lips moving silently. As we were passing Trafalgar Square, he appeared to relax somewhat and turned to me.

"I assume," he said, "that you could see that whoever they are, they have read your stories in *The Strand*."

"Oh, yes. The names they called you—busybody, meddler, Jack-in-box—they were in one of my very early stories."

"Do you recall who called me those?"

"Certainly. It was Dr. Grimsby Roylott."

"And do you recall what happened to him?"

"A nasty final encounter with his pet swamp adder," I said. "Should I assume that you have something similar in mind for these chaps?"

"Perhaps. I would, however, ask of you, my friend, that you give me a firm kick if you see my pride and anger interfering with the necessary use of cautious reason."

Lestrade was also pacing.

"Who are these people, Holmes?" he demanded as we entered his office.

"I do not yet know."

"Well, they are a bloody well-organized lot. They hauled seven young people out of their homes within a matter of minutes last night. This is not just one fellow peddling boys and girls brought to London as spies and informants. If you do not know who they are you had better find out and fast."

He continued pacing.

"Did you," Lestrade demanded, "receive a message from them as well?"

"I did."

"Let me see it. And you, look at the one that arrived on my desk an hour ago."

Holmes handed him the note that had been sent to 221B whilst he read the one delivered to Scotland Yard and then handed it on to me. It ran:

> Inspector G. Lestrade, Scotland Yard
>
> You have foolishly colluded with Mr. Sherlock Holmes in his interference in our business affairs. Be advised that you must cease and desist immediately. Should you not take this action, know that you will be responsible for the deaths at a rate of one per day of the seven young people currently in our custody.
>
> Furthermore, to compensate us for the inconvenience you and Mr. Holmes have created for us, you are to make payment of £10,000 into a bank account, the specifics of which shall be forwarded in three days, giving you adequate time to procure the funds and no excuse for not doing so.
>
> You must reply to this letter by way of post box number 667 at the Royal Mail Office on Great Portland Street.

> Any attempt to trace the origin of this letter will be discovered and will result in the immediate death of one of the young people in our custody.
>
> Govern yourself accordingly.
>
> The Association of The Fittest

Lestrade and I laid the notes on his desk, and both of us looked at Holmes as if expecting that he would have some brilliant flash of insight.

"Is it correct to assume," he said, "that His Majesty's government—."

"Does not pay ransom or extortion demands?" interrupted Lestrade. "Right you are. Not a farthing. All we would do is increase the moral hazard. What we do with a group like this is to see if they can be broken and take sides against each other. I will send a note back saying if they turn in the one or ones who murdered the girl at Battersea Bridge, we will go easy on the rest of them. Do you have a better suggestion, Holmes?"

"No. Except that we not give away any more time than is necessary. You might wait a day or two before responding. I will need all the time you can secure to try to learn who these people are and where they might have taken their hostages."

"Right," said Lestrade. "I will put a couple of my best men on it. Whoever these rogues are, they are prepared to kill. Best take them at their word when they say they will start killing their hostages. I suggest that you make sure your actions are well hidden."

"Thank you for pointing that out, Inspector," said Holmes. "I have already erred in being overly trusting of the confidentiality kept within the underworld of vice, and with sending amateurs to conduct investigations, enthusiastic though they may have been. I shall not make such errors again. I will be working alone."

Chapter Eleven
I Can't Find Her

OVER THE NEXT TWO DAYS, I saw nothing of Holmes. I assumed that he had most likely donned one of his masterful disguises and was walking the streets of London chatting and eavesdropping in every possible corner that might give some hint concerning this newly emerged criminal network and the location of the seven missing young people.

With great difficulty, I forced the issue from my mind so that I could attend to the needs of my patients and concentrate on my writing accounts of other cases.

On the third day, in the late afternoon, a note arrived from Holmes. It ran:

```
Lestrade's note refusing payment and
threatening the gallows has been
delivered. We await a response. Please
be prepared at a moment's notice to
come.  Holmes
```

I spent the rest of the evening on pins and needles, expecting to be summoned at any moment. At midnight, at the insistence of Mrs. Watson, I agreed to retire for the night. I was making my way up the stairs when there came a terrific pounding on my front door.

"It must be Holmes!" I shouted to my wife and hastened back down the stairs to answer the door.

It was not Holmes. It was Cyril Morton. His face was sweating profusely, his eyes wide with fear, and his collar was loose. The man looked awful. Before I could say anything, he began shouting at me.

"She is gone! They've taken her. I can't find her."

"Good heavens," I gasped, horrified. "Come in, come in. What has happened?"

"Violet has vanished. She's gone. Something must have happened. She was not there at supper time when I came home. I waited and waited, but she didn't appear. Something terrible has happened."

He was in a miserable state of distress. I took the poor man by the arm and led him into the parlor. My wife had joined us and, taking one of his arms each, together we led him to a sofa and more or less forced him to sit down. I sat beside him, firmly holding him in place whilst my wife quickly poured a brandy from the decanter on the mantle.

"Get a hold of yourself, man," I said. "Have you gone to the police?"

"Of course, I went to the police," he said, quite sharply. "At nine o'clock I whistled for a constable and told him that Violet was missing. The numbskull just gave me a pat on the shoulder and told me not to worry. He said that wives go missing for the evening all over London all the time and that they inevitably show up for breakfast."

"Have you contacted Sherlock Holmes?"

"Where do you think I have just come from? I took a cab to Baker Street and demanded to see him. The landlady said that he was not there and had no idea where he was. She had only seen him once in the past three days, she said. I waited until half eleven, and he did not appear. She gave me your address, and that is when I ran from there to here."

He raised his hands to his face, covering his eyes and forehead. His voice was anguished.

"I should never have let her do this. I should never have let her. She has no idea whatsoever about criminals. What was Holmes thinking? How could he have let her go chasing criminals? They are murderers! How could he do that?"

He had dropped his hands and was shouting at me. I managed to calm him somewhat and get a generous snifter of brandy into him.

"What am I going to do, Doctor? What can we do?" He was shouting again. My wife leaned down a spoke into my ear.

"John, a word."

I rose and followed her into the hallway.

"In all the years you have known Sherlock, have you ever seen him unshaven or wearing yesterday's clothes? Has he even left Baker Street without his hat brushed and his boots shined?"

"No. Why? What are you saying?"

"No matter where he is, he will return to Baker Street at some time before morning and bathe and change his clothes. We can go there and wait for him."

That seemed logical and the two of us, again taking an arm each, lifted Cyril Morton from the sofa and led him out the front door to the street. We marched the poor fellow toward the corner where we had a hope of finding a nighttime cab. He did not stop talking. He went on, repeating his story about waiting for Violet to appear, about the hopeless police constable, and vented his anger again at both Holmes and himself.

Dear Mrs. Hudson met us at the door and led us up to the front room of Baker Street. I told her just to ignore us and go back to bed but to no avail. A pot of hot tea and some warm scones soon appeared, filling the tense room with a comforting aroma. Then she sat down with us and joined my wife and me in the meaningless banter that people engage in whilst in great duress and unable to do anything except wait.

We waited ... and waited. Several times, Cyril Morton rose to his feet and started pacing back and forth through the length of the room and just as many times my wife and Mrs. Hudson rose to their feet a few moments later and firmly led him back to his chair.

At three o'clock in the morning, we heard the latch on Baker Street open. Cyril leapt to his feet and ran to the door of the room

"Mr. Holmes! Mr. Holmes!" he screamed. "Get up here!"

I heard Holmes steps first stop and then quicken as he ascended the stairs.

"She's gone. They've taken her!" Cyril was already beside himself and shouting. We managed to get him to calm down and speak coherently. Eventually, the story of Violet's disappearance was told. I watched Holmes's face as he listened. His countenance passed from shock, to fear, and then that steeled look of determination I had observed so many times in the past when he placed his passions under the firm control of his reason.

He turned to Cyril, who had not been at all tactful in the accusations he had leveled at him.

"Mr. Morton," Holmes said. "You have every reason to be angry with me. I erred in sending your wife on a mission for which she was not prepared. I offer you my sincere and humblest apologies. I must, however, beg you to put your emotions aside. Your anger is thoroughly justified, but it is not useful to the task at hand. You, sir, are an engineer and a man of science. I implore you to use your faculties of reason to engage with me on whatever path we must follow to secure the safe return of your wife, as well as the young men and women who are also being held hostage."

"Mr. Holmes!" Cyril bellowed in response. "I do not give a **** about a bunch of immigrants who were duped into coming to England. What I care about is finding Violet. Now!"

Holmes looked at the fellow intently and spoke slowly. "And so you should, sir. I believe, however, and I assume you would agree with me, that reason tells us that the abduction of the would-be students and the disappearance of your wife are most likely to be directly connected to each other. Would you agree, sir?"

After several moments of returning a blank stare, Cyril nodded his head.

"Yes," he said. "That makes sense."

"Then," said Holmes, "it is reasonable to proceed on the hypothesis—until we have evidence otherwise—that they are all being held in the same location. Would you agree?"

Again, Cyril nodded. "So now what do we do?" he demanded.

"Unfortunately, we wait."

"Bloody hell! I am not going to sit here and wait whilst some band of criminals are holding my wife. I will turn London upside down and find them."

"And have them murder her?" said Holmes. "No, sir, I fear that the worst thing you could do is to run out of here like a charging bull and make your intentions known throughout the city. Whoever these people are, they have threatened to kill, and we know that they do not make idle threats. It would appear that the clever and brave young woman, Miss Hatsu, had learned too much about them and she is now dead. It is normal practice for those who kidnap to make contact with those from whom they demand a ransom. Therefore, we wait until they play their hand. We have no other choice."

"How long?"

"These criminals do not strike me as an idle group of layabouts. I expect that we shall hear from them by way of the morning post."

"What if they send a message to my home?" asked Cyril.

"An excellent question," said Holmes. "Allow me to suggest that you write a note to your maid, instructing her to send any message received immediately to this address. I will have it sent straightaway to your home."

"At this hour? That's not possible."

"I beg to differ, sir. Please, prepare a note."

Cyril did as Holmes had told him to. Holmes then placed the note inside an envelope and took it down the stairs. I could hear three sharp blasts on his whistle and knew that he had summoned the closest one of his beloved Irregulars. He soon returned to the room where we were waiting.

"The lad was a bit sleepy," he said, "but he will run the message immediately to your home in Chelsea."

"That is quite a ways to run," I said.

"He has a bicycle. Quite a nice one. A Bianchi from Italy if I am not mistaken."

"What!?" exclaimed Cyril. "Those imported bikes cost a fortune. How can your street urchin own something like that?"

"He stole it."

Chapter Twelve
Proof of Life

THE NEXT FEW HOURS passed painfully. We gave up on idle conversation, and each fell into our chosen mode of silence. Cyril procured a recent novel from the bookcase, *The Call of the Wild*, hoping, I assumed, that it would be exciting enough to engage his tormented mind. I took *The Ambassadors* by Henry James, expecting that it would be sufficiently and reliably boring to put me to sleep. My wife and Mrs. Hudson leaned their heads on the back of the sofa and dozed off. Holmes occasionally paced and otherwise sat in his chair with his long legs folded underneath him, his hand together under his chin with his fingertips touching and his eyes closed.

By seven thirty the sun had come up, and Mrs. Hudson kindly served us a hot, nourishing breakfast which we ate in silence.

At a quarter past eight, there was a knock on the Baker Street door. Holmes immediately descended and returned bearing an envelope in hand.

"It is addressed to you," he said, looking at Cyril Morton and handing him the message.

The distraught husband tore open the envelope and read it. His face paled as he did so and his hands began to tremble. With fingers visibly shaking he handed it over to Holmes who read it and in turn gave it to me. It ran:

Dear Mr. Cyril Morton:

You wife, Mrs. Violet Morton has foolishly been assisting Sherlock Homes in his interference with our affairs. She must never do so again.

This morning she is safe and has not been harmed. We warn you that she will never in her life again be a beautiful woman should you not immediately agree to the following demands.

You will give us your solemn promise that in future you will control your wife and not permit her to engage in activities where she does not belong.

You will make payment of £20,000 to secure her safe return. You must act now to secure these funds. Instructions will be forthcoming for their transfer to us. Your reply is needed this morning to Box 667 of the Great Portland Street Post Office confirming your agreement with these demands.

Should you fail to do so, be informed that whilst you will not become her widower, your beautiful wife's face will be unrecognizable to you.

Govern yourself accordingly,

The Association of The Fittest

Cyril Morton appeared to be in shock. "Who are these monsters, Mr. Holmes? What have you done to them that would make them kidnap Violet and threaten to do such terrible things to her? Do you have £20,000, Mr. Holmes? I do not. What do we do? Tell me! What do I do?!"

He was shouting again and pacing the floor. It took several minutes for him to regain control of himself, whereupon Holmes replied.

"Neither of us needs £20,000," he said. "We only need to appear to be taking steps to obtain it. Please, sir, force yourself to use your reason. These people have revealed to us that they are indeed the same people who have taken the students. They have indicated that they are willing to wait until you have secured the funds. That gives us time and time is what we need. Now, sir, please listen to me. You need to write a note back to them saying that you agree to pay the ransom, but before doing so you must have proof that your wife is alive and unharmed. That is a reasonable demand and standard practice in kidnapping negotiations. Please take a minute now and write such a letter."

Holmes directed Cyril to the desk, and the man sat there in silence, steadying his shattered nerves, before picking up the pen.

"What do I say? What proof do I demand?"

Holmes dictated the letter, stating that Cyril demanded a note written by his wife affirming that she was safe and unharmed. He also wrote that the money would be forwarded by the account of Cyril's firm at the private bank of Holder and Stevenson.

"But I do not have an account with them," Cyril objected.

"It matters not. What matters is that they are led to believe you do."

Cyril shook his head but did as instructed. The letter was written, and Holmes immediately took it down to Baker Street and whistled for another of his reliable Irregulars to take it to the designated Royal Mail office.

He then returned to the room, and himself sat down and wrote a letter. It was somewhat lengthy and took him well over twenty minutes to complete it.

"Take this letter," he said to Cyril when he had finished it, "to Mr. Alexander Holder at his home in Streatham. It instructs him to take whatever measures necessary to secure £20,000 in cash from his bank and to use the shares in your firm as security against the loan."

"My firm is not worth £20,000.," said Cyril. "maybe £15,000 at most. No banker would ever accept such an arrangement."

"He does not have to accept it," said Holmes. "He only has to pretend to accept it and let his actions with respect to your shares become known within his bank. I expect that the people who are behind this crime have established a sufficiently efficient network within the City to confirm whether or not the information we are sending them is true. Mr. Holder will confirm that it is."

"Why would he do that?"

"Two reasons. He met your charming wife when she called on his home to confirm the location of the boy from India, Rajeev. I am sure that, being the fine, old gentleman he is, he will want to cooperate to rescue her. It is part of the settled order of Nature that such an attractive woman should acquire older gentlemen who wish to help her. In addition, Mr. Holder has, in all innocence, aided in the crime by hiring Rajeev, no doubt at a discounted rate. And besides all that, he owes me a favor for services rendered to him many years ago. Now, please leave and return here as soon as you have delivered the note. You should be able to do so within two hours."

Again, we waited.

Mrs. Hudson excused herself and returned to her duties and the landlady of 221B. My wife took a cab back to our home noting that it would be best if she were not present to give me common sense advice before running off with Holmes as it was unlikely to be heeded by either him or me.

That left me and Holmes. After freshening up and changing into some of the clothes I still kept at Baker Street for convenience when I stayed over here, I returned to reading my boring novel. Holmes pulled off of his shelf his compendium in which he kept a record of every serious criminal in London and all their crimes. From time to time I heard him mutter under his breath words to the effects of "Who are they? Who are they?"

It was a full three hours before Cyril Morton returned. When he did, he was clean shaven and had changed his clothes. He was carrying a large case of the size that a musician might be used to carry a trombone, only larger and longer.

"My dear man," I said. "What have you got there?"

"I stopped by our house in Chelsea on the way back here."

"I can see that," I said. "But are you planning to stay here for a month? What all have you packed with you?"

"Violet and I occasionally go on shooting parties. She loves the adventure, and I do my duty to keep her happy. As a result, we own a decent stock of guns. I have brought them with me in case they become necessary. They are cleaned and loaded."

"Great Scott," said Holmes. "We are not going to war. We shall most likely be engaged in lengthy negotiations. You will need all your political skills, not your ability to hit a target."

"Did not someone," asked Cyril, "once say that 'war is the continuation of politics by other means'?"

"No doubt he did," said Holmes. "And no doubt he was not talking about rescuing abducted wives."

"You never know," said Cyril.

Holmes looked as if he were about to argue but shrugged and smiled at the young husband.

"If you say so, sir. However, it would be more helpful if you could give an account of your visit to Mr. Holder."

"Oh, yes, of course. I cannot imagine what hold you have over Mr. Holder, but the old fellow positively leapt at the opportunity to help. He immediately started dashing off memos and instructions to his sons. He even told me that he was not about to let them know, at least not immediately, that the whole exercise was a pretense. He said it would not hurt his sons one little bit to have to wear their guts for garters for a day or two. I had not expected an aging banker to have such an odd sense of humor."

"Excellent," said Holmes. "Our necessary steps have all been taken. So now … we wait."

Once again, I picked up the novel I had been reading. Mr. Morton also tried to read and interrupted himself several times with bouts of pacing. Holmes kept on reviewing his record of crimes and criminals, making constant notes as he did so.

"Will they respond today?" asked Cyril as the hour of five approached.

"Quite likely," said Holmes. "You never know."

Soon, we did know. A knock on the Baker Street door, answered by the ever-faithful Mrs. Hudson, brought another envelope for Cyril Morton to the room. Quite uncharacteristically, Mrs. Hudson remained in the room whilst Cyril read the note aloud. He read:

```
Mr. Cyril Morton: In response to your
request for proof that your wife is alive
and unharmed, please see the attached note
from her to you.

We are pleased to learn that you have
agreed to meet our demands and are taking
appropriate steps to do so. Kindly inform us
when you are prepared to deliver the payment
and we will then issue you further
instructions.

The Association of The Fittest.
```

Cyril let out a sigh of relief.

"At least they have stopped threatening to mutilate my wife."

"I would advise you," said Holmes, "not to believe that they are in the habit of telling the truth. Please, sir. The note from your wife. Is it indeed in her hand?"

Cyril took the attached note and began to read:

My dearest well-engineered stud—

Here he stopped, blushing. "It is from her. It is one of her favorite terms of endearment, in private, of course."

"Of course," said Holmes. "Pray, continue."

I am in peachy keen good health and hope to see you soon. Please direct the remainder of the message to Mr. Sherlock Holmes.

"She has directed this to you," said Cyril to Homes.

"So it would appear. Pray, continue."

Oh, please, Mr. Holmes. Now. Every minute counts. For goodness sake. On you, I is depending. Until you stop, we may be killed. Reverse your investigation. Save us. Each of the boys are in danger. Very great danger. Every one of the girls as well. No one is safe. Believe me, please. Every passing minute is Crucial. ACcept the demands they are making. Leave this case alone. Erase it from your mind. You must do so. Keep from investigating further. Easiest way is to agree to their demands. Never doubt their force. To do so are death. Whatever they demand must be met. Oh, please do not fail us. Other responses will be a disaster. Do not attempt them. Listen to my plea. Eight lives are at risk. You must help us.

Yours until the undertaken undertakes to take you under,

Violet Morton (Mrs.)

Cyril handed the note to Holmes. His face gave a look of bewilderment.

"What is it?" asked Holmes.

"There is something very strange," Cyril replied. "Very strange, indeed. The handwriting is most certainly hers. I can swear to that. The private salutation is also hers as is the schoolgirl's closing. But the body of the letter—her plea to you—is just not her. She never writes like that. Many of these sentences are not sentences at all. She is a stickler for good writing. There is something wrong. They must have threatened her and made her write those words. She would never have done so entirely of her own volition."

"It is a distinct possibility that these words were dictated to her," said Holmes.

He gazed for some time at the letter.

"On the other hand," said Holmes, "the notes sent directly by this Association are all written using correct grammar and stylish syntax. Unless the person who is doing the dictating is someone entirely different to the one who wrote the previous notes, it is difficult to make sense of the departure of writing ability."

"Even if," said Cyril, "someone who had poor command of the language was dictating it, Violet would correct his spelling, punctuation, and grammar. She is like that."

"She may be trying to say something to us," said Holmes. "Please, both of you, keep reading over this note. Keep pondering it and see if you can discern anything in its content that she wants us to know."

For the next hour, the three of us silently read and re-read the message. I tried reading the word from the end back to the start. Then I sounded out only every third word, recalling that a message many years ago was structured in that manner. But my efforts were all to no avail. I was as blind as a mole to any meaning beyond the obvious.

Suddenly, Holmes's posture changed, and the faintest trace of a smile appeared on a mouth the had previously been set as a flint. A minute later he was grinning broadly.

"Your wife," he said to Cyril, "is not only very handsome, she is and exceptionally clever woman. I trust you are aware of that."

Cyril gave Holmes a sidewards look. "Of course, I know she is clever. I would not have married her were she not. What are you saying?"

"Sir, kindly read off to me the first letter of each sentence in the message. Watson, please write them down as he does so."

Cyril picked up the note and began whilst I wrote.

"Including the salutation?"

"No," said Holmes. "Skip that line."

"Very well. Her first sentence begins with the word *oh*. So that means the letter 'o', correct?"

"You have it. Now keep going and do not stop until you get to the end."

"All right. After the 'o' come an 'n' and after that an 'e'. Like that?"

"Like that," said Holmes. "And what does *o n e* spell?"

"One."

"Excellent. Now keep going."

"Will do. After the 'e' comes an 'f' and then an 'o' and then a 'u' and then an 'r.' That spells *four*. So, the first two words and one and four."

"Precisely, now for goodness sake, keep going and do not stop."

"Jolly good. There a 's' and an 'e' and a 'v' and another 'e' and an 'n' and that spells seven. Yes, yes, I will keep going. 'B' then 'e' the 'a' then 'l' then 'e' then 'y' and then 'k', 'e' 'n' 't.'"

"Stop there," said Holmes. "She has just told us where she is"

"One four seven bealey kent," I exclaimed. "But there is no Bealey Road in Kent, is there? Frankly, I cannot think of a Bealey Road anywhere in or near to London."

"For good cause," said Holmes. "There is none, but neither are there many words to use to begin sentences that begin with the letter 'x.' She has alerted us to the anomaly by the misuse of the capitalization of the word *accept*. We may assume that she is telling us to pronounce the first syllable and not the first letter. If we do that, where are we going."

"Bexley!" I blurted out. "Old Bexley Lane. Does not that run out into the country from Dartford?"

"Well done, Watson," said Holmes. "Now, Mr. Morton, keep going. The remainder of the letter is both surprising and disturbing."

"Jolly good. I shall pick up where I left off. The next sentence starts with a 'w' and then an 'o' and another 'o' and then a 'd' and 'l' and 'e' …"

He put the note down and gasped. "Good Lord. Woodley. I cannot believe it. That monster has returned. I thought he was in prison Mr. Holmes for what he did to her years ago."

"He was sentenced to ten years," said Holmes. "If he behaved while in prison, he would have been released after seven. That would be over a year ago. He is back to his miserable life of crime. He must have disguised his appearance effectively, or your wife would have spotted him right off. She did say, did she not, that there was something familiar about him?"

"Do you think," I said to Holmes, "that he is the mastermind behind all of these abductions and the blackmail and the spying on so many people in high places? Woodley?"

"Ah, well done, again, Watson. No, if you were to give Woodley's brain a laxative, he could not fill a matchbox. He is undoubtedly a pawn ... but to whom we do not know."

"Can we go now to Kent?" asked Cyril.

"Yes, we still have time to catch a late train to Dartford. And it might be useful if you were to bring your trombone case with you."

Chapter Thirteen
Spies in the Cold and Dark

WE HUSTLED TO PACK and were soon walking swiftly along Baker Street to Marylebone where we caught a cab. It took us quickly to Waterloo, where we boarded a South Eastern train for Kent. The town of Dartford was just inside the border of Kent, and we arrived in an hour. Before departing, Holmes had burrowed through his piles of maps and atlases until he found an ordnance map of Dartford and the surrounding area.

"The address on Old Bexley," he said, "appears to be about two miles southwest of the townsite. It will be well after dark by the time we get there, but I have packed a dark lantern, and we may be able to walk down the road and discern the house in which our charges are being held."

The last vestiges of twilight were fading from the sky when we disembarked at the Dartford Station. The hotel was close by, and we checked in. To my surprise, Holmes did not rush off in search of our quarry but insisted that we take our supper in the dining room before venturing out.

"Darkness is our ally," he said. "There is sufficient light from the moon to allow us to find and then walk along Old Bexley Lane and we can use the lantern to see the address numbers on the gates.

And Mr. Morton, leave your weapons in your room. Any sound we make will increase the risk to ourselves and the hostages."

By nine o'clock all daylight had gone, but a half moon gave enough light to allow us to see the roadway in front of us. We walked in silence out of the town along Shepherd's Lane and then continued on Old Bexley. I noticed the numbers of the gateposts rising quickly, and I assumed that we would be arriving at 147 within a few minutes. That was not the case. As soon as we had passed the edge of the urban area, the lots became larger and the numbers farther and farther apart. We had walked a full hour before we came to a gate whose post, illuminated with the dark lantern, showed the number we were looking for.

Holmes closed the lantern.

"We must not be seen or heard. The laneway is in almost complete darkness. If you are unsure of which way it turns, look up into the sky. You should be able to see the break in the canopy of the trees against the night sky. Your feet will tell you if you have approached the verge."

It had been many years since I had walked along a country laneway in pitch darkness and total silence. Doing so can be a frightening experience. Every mole and squirrel scurrying in the leaves on the forest floor sounds like a large animal, and a snort or growl from a raccoon renders one certain that a grizzly bear is about to attack. It was not long before I felt Cyril's hand gripping my upper arm as our stealthy trio stole through the forest.

In the dark of night, the lane seemed to go on forever although it was likely less than half-a-mile. We turned a final corner and could see an open field in front of us. At the far end, I could make out a faint glow of light.

"That must be the house," I whispered.

"Most likely," said Holmes. "We may be able to get much closer in the darkness. Please, not a sound."

We followed him along the lane, which was now cutting across the heath and taking us directly toward the homesite. The wind had been blocked whilst we were surrounded by forest, but now it was blowing cold against us. Had we stood still in one place we would soon be shivering. We stopped some fifty yards from the building at an old yew hedge that might once have been the edge of a garden that was now just a tangled mess of overgrown shrubs and untrimmed trees.

"Listen," whispered Holmes.

We did. I heard ... music. Someone was playing the piano and voices were signing.

"That's Violet," said Cyril, a bit louder than was necessary.

"How can you tell?" I asked, sotto voce.

"The song she's playing. It's the *Daisy Bell* song. You know, the one about the bicycle built for two. She bought the music when I bought our bicycle. She knows it by heart. We sing it together when we're cycling. You know it, don't you?"

He began to sing the opening bars of the chorus and was immediately shushed by Holmes.

"Save it for your next ride," said Holmes. "Now take these and see what you can see."

From his pocket, he extracted three compact Royal Navy spyglasses. They were high-powered and extended a distance of nearly two feet. I focused mine and looked directly into one of the front windows of the house.

The curtains were partially drawn, obscuring a clear view of the room. In the gap between them, it looked as if there was a small crowd gathered and standing close together. Once or twice the movement within the group allowed a fleeting glimpse of a piano and the back of a woman seated on a piano stool. From time to time, an adult male stood with his back to the window, stayed there for a minute or two and then departed.

It was cold. All three of us had pulled our coats tightly around us, but we were starting to shiver. I wondered how the prisoners inside the house were managing to stay warm. The answer soon was evident as the back door of the house opened, and a small figure walked from the door to a large back shed. He left the door ajar to give himself some light that shone from the interior into the backyard. He disappeared inside the shed and reappeared a minute later bearing an armful of wood. My guess was that he would have to return in an hour or so once his small bundle had been consumed in the fireplace.

"We cannot stay here much longer," I said to Holmes, my teeth now chattering. "You will have to find some blankets or much warmer clothing if you want to keep observing them."

Holmes reluctantly agreed.

"We can return tomorrow," he said. "We must not rush. They all appear to be unharmed at the moment, and any rash move on our part could spell disaster for them."

"You assume the men with them are armed?" I asked.

"I am certain of it. Did you not see the revolvers in their hands?"

I hadn't, but then I was used to not seeing things that Holmes somehow managed to.

We walked in silence back out the laneway. Once on the road, I attempted to engage Holmes in conversation but he had vanished inside his private thoughts, and I knew from long experience not to disturb him. So, Cyril and I chatted about what we had seen and about what might be a useful strategy for rescuing Violet and the students. If Holmes thought for a second that we might have come up with a good idea or two, we would never know. He said nothing until we were back in the townsite.

Just before we arrived at the hotel, Holmes stopped walking just as we reached the gate of a livery depot. He stood still and gazed and the office building, the yard, and the adjoining barn for about a minute and then stooped down and picked up a small stone from the road. He wound up and gave it a strong throw, landing it square against the door of the barn. There was a loud thud and then silence. He turned away and started walking to the door of the hotel.

Once inside, he spoke to Cyril and me.

"Please, my good fellow, enjoy the remainder of the evening in the parlor and the bar. I have a few things I must attend to."

He turned and quickly went up the stairs to his room. Cyril looked at me as if he expected me to know what Holmes was up to.

I merely shrugged my shoulders and offered to join him for an evening libation. He accepted. He was still terribly anxious about Violet, but he claimed that he was somewhat relieved having seen the back of her head through the window, hearing her play the piano, and knowing that she was still alive and well. Several times, he asked me what I thought Holmes had planned and just as many times I assured him that I was in as complete a fog as he was.

Our glasses of whiskey arrived, and we toasted a wish to the safety of Violet and the students. As Cyril had his glass raised to his lips and was tipping it back, I caught a glimpse out of the corner of my eye of Holmes passing through the hotel lobby. He had undone the earflaps on his familiar hat, and they now covered his ears. He was wearing gloves, and his coat looked oddly bulked as if he had put on at least two heavy sweaters before pulling his coat over them. He disappeared out of the front door of the hotel and into the night.

I did not mention what I had seen to Cyril Morton. He was already sufficiently confused by Holmes, and I was not far behind him.

Chapter Fourteen
A Wave of Crime in Dartford

AT SEVEN O'CLOCK the following morning, I came down from my room to the hotel lobby in search of breakfast. Three people were standing by the front desk carrying on loudly with the clerk. I caught a few words of their energetic conversation before slipping into the breakfast room. Holmes was already sitting at a table in the corner sipping on a cup of tea and reading a newspaper.

"What is all the ruckus for?" I asked him.

He looked at me. "Oh, good morning, Watson. Goodness knows what the locals are jabbering about. No doubt some farmer's prize cow broke loose or some matter of similar earth-shaking importance."

"No," I said, as I took my seat across from him. "I heard them saying that three bicycles had been reported stolen over night."

"Hmm? Three, you say? Oh, my. I suppose that amounts to a crime wave in a place like this. They had better lock up their wives and daughters."

He returned to his tea and reading.

A young lad soon appeared and took my order for breakfast. I asked him about the commotion in the lobby.

"Right, sir. Well, sir, when I first gots here this morning, real early it was, the kitchen staff were saying that two bicycles was stolen. And then a maid sticks her head in and says it was three. A few minutes later it was up to four and just as I comes out, sir, the milkman says that it was five. Now sir, this is a real quiet town, and no one ever steals from anyone seeing as we all know each other, and if you was riding on another bloke's bicycle, you would be spotted right off. So, it's big news here this morning, sir. Gives us all something to talk about. Now, will you have your toast buttered, sir, or plain?"

He took my order and returned to the kitchen.

"Did you hear that, Holmes? Five bicycles stolen last night. No one fellow could do that alone. Must have been a gang from some other town."

"Spaniards," said Holmes.

"What? What do you mean, Spaniards?"

"Roving bands of Spaniards are known for stealing bicycles. Mind you, it could have been Italians. There have been quite too many of them flooding into England of late. Yes, most likely it was Italians."

He had not even lowered his newspaper whilst responding. Obviously, he was not the least bit interested in carrying on a conversation, so I took up another newspaper and waited for my morning meal. Cyril Morton joined us a minute later.

"What is going on in the lobby?" he said as he sat down. "Some chaps in there are arguing about how many bicycles have disappeared. One is saying that five have vanished and another is saying that it was six. Who in their right mind would steal six bicycles?"

"Holmes says it was the Italians. If not them, the Spaniards," I said.

"What? Good heavens. I have been all over both Spain and Italy. They have their own bicycles. Thousands of them. Are you sure it wasn't a group of local Gypsies? What do you say, Mr. Holmes? Probably Gypsies, right?"

"Gypsies," said Holmes from behind the newspaper, "are far too sensible to take bicycles. They much prefer horses, but only if they are a select breed. Gypsies have high standards. Of course, it might have been the Russians. They have no standards at all to speak of ... except for vodka."

The waiter returned bearing my breakfast and took Cyril's order. I asked if he had heard anything further about the bicycles.

"Right, sir. The constable, he comes by just a minute ago. He says that the official number now is eight. All gone in the middle of the night. All from right here in the center of town. No one heard anything. So, there's talk of ghosts and spirits taking the bicycles, sir, seeing as no one heard or saw nothing."

"Well Holmes," I said to the backside of the newspaper. "Are you not going to help these good folks solve their crime of the decade before the entire lot of them start burning witches at the stake?"

"Hmm?" he said, lowering the newspaper. "Why should I get involved in such a trivial local fiasco?"

"Why!? Because having your bicycle stolen may mean nothing to you, but to these folks, it is a serious issue."

Back up went the newspaper. "The bicycles were not stolen. They were merely borrowed. Lord willing, they will all be returned by this time tomorrow."

"Holmes," I said, rather sharply. "What have you done? What did you do last night?"

"I had an excellent sleep. A comfortable bed on a cool night is one of life's simplest pleasures."

"You went out of here before midnight," I said. "I saw you. And you were bundled up as if you were heading for the Arctic."

"The Arctic, you say. My dear doctor, you give me far too much credit. A full night of laying out a plan was the best I could muster. Now, please, both of you, finish up as quickly as possible. We have a full day of reconnaissance ahead of us. I shall meet you in the lobby in half an hour. I have secured boxed lunches from the kitchen and several blankets but do dress warmly."

He rose, and smiled, a little smugly, and departed from the breakfast room.

"What in the world is he up to," asked Cyril.

"I do not know," I said. "But I suspect he has set a plan in place for the safe return of your wife and the seven others."

"How?"

"Blessed if I know. But we are about to find out. Enjoy your breakfast before it gets cold. I will see you in the lobby forthwith. Dress warmly."

"And be armed?"

"A good idea. I will be as well. If you have an extra revolver for Holmes, you should bring it along."

We met up in the lobby. Holmes had a small rucksack on his back, and I brought my doctor's case. Cyril descended the stairs carrying a small sack and with a gleaming new Mauser 98, one of the most accurate and expensive military rifles ever made, strapped to his back.

"You might try," said Holmes to him, "being a little less obvious."

"I will just say that we will be hunting grouse," he replied. "It is a common pastime in this area."

"Ah, of course," said Holmes. "Pardon my ignorance, but when was the last time a hunter went looking for grouse with a military rifle that is the favorite of snipers?"

Cyril looked a bit nonplussed for a moment. "Fine. If you will excuse me, I shall be right back."

He turned and bounded up the stairs, taking several with each leap of his long legs. Two minutes later he returned and this time had not only his rifle but a shining shotgun on his back.

"I suppose that is somewhat better," said Holmes, rolling his eyes.

"They have deer around here as well as grouse," said Cyril. "I shall be prepared for both."

Once out on the High Street, he extracted his ordnance map from his pocket.

"It is daylight now. Therefore, we cannot take the open road as we did last night. The map shows that a watercourse crosses Old Bexley Lane several hundred yards before the gate on 147. The stream runs through the woods and around behind the house where Mrs. Morton and the students are held. There also appears to be an old fencerow running up the hill behind the house. That should be a good vantage point. Follow me."

We walked quickly, inhaling the fresh morning air and rejoicing in the music of the birds and the cold, fresh breath of the spring. Soon we were out of the town and to the junction with Old Bexley Lane. As Holmes had predicted, we crossed a small stream and stepped down from the roadway to follow it.

It was not easy going. The temperature had dropped below the freezing mark the night before and patches of ice had formed. There had been a light fall of snow, and the rocks and banks were treacherous. We had to step carefully over many slippery, wet portions of the stream bed or barge our way directly through the forest. I kept far enough back from Holmes to avoid the branches he had pushed away from swinging back and striking me in the face. Cyril did likewise behind me.

"Would you mind telling us," I shouted at Holmes, "just where the eight borrowed bicycles are to be found?"

"How can they be found? They are not lost."

"Holmes!"

"Very well, if you insist. They are in the shed behind the house."

"And you put them there last night. It must have taken you hours."

"About six. But it all went rather smoothly," he replied as he jumped from one side of the stream to the other and vanished into the thick growth along the edge of the water.

At the base of the hill, I continued my interrogation.

"How did you get them there?"

"The livery master loaned me a horse and wagon."

"The livery was closed."

"How very fortunate. Otherwise, I would not have been able to borrow their transport."

"Was that why you threw the stone at the barn door?"

"Precisely. I was curious as to whether or not there was a dog and needed to wake the old pooch."

"But no dog barked," I said.

"How very curious," he said.

I had what the psychologists call an experience of *déjà vu*.

We trudged on to the top of the hill. As the map had shown, there was an old stone fencerow dividing one side of the hill from the other. At the bottom of the hill stood the overgrown garden, house, and back shed. We bent over to keep out of sight and followed the fence to the summit of the hill. Holmes opened his rucksack and distributed a spyglass and two blankets to each of us.

"Gentlemen, please make yourselves as comfortable and as warm as possible. We need to stay still and watch the house carefully to see if my plan is working."

All three of us sat so that our heads barely poked over the top of the stone fencerow. There was no sign of life until just past nine o'clock when the first wisp of smoke emerged from the kitchen chimney. A few minutes later a second swirl came from the hearth chimney at the front of the house.

"Ah, good," said Holmes. "They should be soon sending someone out to fetch some more wood."

"Who will they send?" I asked.

"I am assuming it will be the one named Rajeev. The one we saw performing the task last night was a male and somewhat larger than Miguel. That could only be Rajeev."

"Then he will see the bicycles?" I asked.

"And the letter with his name, attached to the first bicycle," said Holmes.

"Are you sure he has not already gone back there?" asked Cyril.

"Not unless he flew," said Holmes. "There are no marks yet in the fresh snow."

At half-past nine, the back door of the house opened and a young man, with a blanket draped over his shoulders, came out into the yard. He walked quickly to the door of the shed and entered. It would have taken less than two minutes for someone who did not wish to stay out in the cold to snatch up an armful of cordwood and rush back to the warmth of the house.

Five minutes passed.

The shed door opened and Rajeev stepped out, holding a letter in his hand. He looked first to the left and then the right and then walked to the back of the shed and looked around.

"Come on, Rajeev," muttered Holmes. "Get moving before someone suspects something."

The lad stopped in his tracks for a moment and then quickly stepped back into the shed and returned with his arms laden with firewood.

It was not long after that the door opened again. This time a woman came out and walked to the shed.

"That's Violet," said Cyril. "You might know it. She has to go and see for herself."

"She is clearly in good health and unharmed," said Holmes. "That is a good sign."

"Are you sure," asked Cyril, "that we could not just storm the place and get this whole thing over with?"

"Not unless you want to risk the death of your wife along with several of the children," said Holmes. "At this point, another fifteen hours will not hurt. Time is on our side. I assured them in the letter to Rajeev that we would not put them at risk by rushing in."

"Will they not fear retribution to their families?" I asked.

"I also assured them that the British Empire would take make sure that their families would be safe. For good measure, I added an official seal I borrowed from Mycroft. Remind me to make sure I return it before he notices its absence."

He said no more, and we waited. And watched. And watched. And waited.

Around mid-morning the piano started up, followed soon by singing. Over the next three hours, we must have listened to fifty songs. The first time through a song, it was only the piano. Then the students joined in singing.

"Does she know every song sung in the music halls for the past decade?" I asked.

Cyril sighed. "Her father must be rolling over in his grave, but yes. I am quite sure that had she not married me she would by now be the lead pianist in the Alhambra."

Whilst the music continued, several of the other students took turns going to fetch more wood. Miss Zenani was first, then Miss Wilhelmina, and then the petite Kishu.

Around noon hour, Holmes opened the box lunches.

"Food keeps you warm. Eat up," he said. "We have five hours to go."

Just before five o'clock, Rajeev made another trip to the shed, but this time he returned carrying what looked like several bottles.

"What is he doing?" I said.

"Bringing in the whiskey," said Holmes

"You gave them whiskey?"

"For the guards. There are two of them. Both armed. Last night they took turns sleeping except for the hours between three and four in the morning when both were napping. I was hoping that an ounce or two of good spirits might make it possible for the students not to have to stay awake until that hour to make their escape."

"He was carrying four bottles."

"Very well. Perhaps several ounces. One should not be stingy when wishing to escape unfavorable circumstances."

"Did you tell Rajeev to bring it to the guards?"

"Yes. But to pretend that he discovered it under some firewood on his last load for the evening. That should be around ten o'clock. If it does the trick, the lot of them should be able to sneak out of the house by midnight."

"Do we have to wait here until then?" I asked.

"No. We will have to work our way back through the forest and stream bed before dark if we want to get out of here without breaking our necks?"

"Is it all right to leave them here alone?"

"I should think so. The plan is working. All of them now likely have learned of the presence of the bicycles and my instructions. I had assumed that they had been blindfolded when brought here and thus had no idea where they were or how far from any neighbors. Otherwise, I would not have been surprised if they had walked out already whilst their captors were asleep."

"But Violet," I said, "knew where she was."

"Indeed, she did," said Holmes. "Remind me to ask her how she learned that."

Chapter Fifteen
Two are Missing

IT WAS HALF SEVEN before Holmes was satisfied that we could depart. We were all stiff and famished, made all the worse by the smell of curry wafting up from the kitchen of the house. Cyril was loath to leave the site where his beloved wife was being held captive, but Holmes reminded him that Violet would have wished him to have a decent supper and not get a chill.

In the twilight, we walked back down the hill, through the forest and back into the town. I should not have been surprised, but still, I had not expected to encounter two police wagons on the High Street and then to enter the dining room of the hotel and see Inspector Lestrade sitting and waiting for us.

"Holmes," he said. "Please tell me that you have not sent for me to come to Kent because some gang of petty thieves stole a bunch of bicycles."

"Ah, has that made the news in London already?" asked Holmes.

"Bloody right, it did. Right smack in the middle of page nineteen just before the prices at the cattle auction."

"I fully expect, my dear Inspector, that what is about to transpire tonight will mark the opening salvo in a battle that may be the most newsworthy of either of our careers and that the specifics thereof will never become known to the Press or the Public."

"That important?"

"You have my word."

"Right. Very well, then Holmes. How long do my men and I have to wait around here?" asked Lestrade.

"At least until midnight. No later than four o'clock in the morning. As soon as the students are all safe, you can go and arrest their captors."

And then the entire group of us sat in the hotel lounge and waited. And waited.

At midnight, Holmes got up, wrapped a blanket over his shoulders, and went and stood out on the porch. The two police constables dozed off in the hotel's armchairs with no objection voiced to them from Lestrade. Cyril got up and started pacing.

At somewhere around half past midnight, Holmes burst into the room. He was grinning from ear to ear.

"I hear them," he said.

The lot of us leapt to our feet and scrambled out to the porch of the hotel. I could also hear the sounds of chatter, and whoops and laughter coming down the High Street. Soon they appeared. One by one they pulled up to the pavement in front of the hotel and dismounted. Some of them ran straight to the waiting police constables and threw their arms around them. It was a joy to see their faces beaming, some even with tears streaming.

I counted them off. Kishu … Miguel … Rajeev … the two Dutch girls … the second African girl, whose name I could not remember. Six had arrived. There were two missing.

We waited. No more arrived.

"Where is Violet?" shouted Cyril. "Where is she?"

He had grabbed one of the Indian boys by the collar and was shouting at him.

"Sorry, sir. Sorry, sir," Miguel was saying to him. "Mrs. Morton could not come. We are very, very sorry sir. She told us we must go without her. So sorry, sir."

I stepped in and removed Cyril's hands from the lad.

"What happened, Miguel?" I asked.

"Oh, uncle Doctor, sir. When it was time for bed, doctor, sir, the men said that they had received a message to lock Mrs. Morton in a room because she was far too valuable now to let anything happen to her. That is what we heard. They took her and put her in the maid's room and put a padlock on the door. We could not undo it, sir. We tried. We tried very, very hard, but we could not get her out. We had to be quiet so that the men would not wake up. We could whisper to her, and she told us that we must escape as planned. She said that her husband and Sherlock Holmes would come for her. She made us promise to leave without her. That is what happened, doctor, sir."

I gave the young fellow a pat on the back and looked out over the lot of them as they parked their bicycles along the porch. Then I grabbed Miguel by the collar.

"Where is Zenani? She is not here. Is she coming? What has happened to her?"

"Oh, uncle doctor, sir, Zenani refused to leave if Mrs. Morton was left behind. Her family are warriors, she said, and have been put on earth by God to protect those who are weaker. She said she had no choice but to stay behind and protect Mrs. Morton, sir. That is what she told us."

"Good heavens, Miguel. You are a smart young man. Those beliefs are nonsense and superstition. Could you not convince her that there was nothing to be gained by putting two lives at risk?"

The boy gave me a very odd look and spoke quietly.

"Doctor, sir, forgive me. Maybe you are brave enough to take sides against Zenani. I am not."

I could not argue with his logic.

One of Lestrade's constables took the students inside the hotel and arranged for them all to have a late snack and a bed for the night. The local constable had arrived and was already busy trying to sort out the vanishing and returning bicycles. Holmes, Lestrade, Cyril, and I convened on the porch.

"Gentlemen," said Holmes, "I fear that another covert visit under cover of darkness is in order. This time, weapons may be required."

The four of us climbed into the back of one of the police wagons, and Holmes directed the driver to take us out of the townsite and to the gate of 147 Old Bexley Lane.

"Mr. Morton," said Holmes to Cyril. "I must apologize again to you. I should have expected that pretending to arrange to pay a ransom for your wife would render her a much more valuable captive. Please, believe me, sir. I should have expected that to happen, but I failed to."

"That is very decent of you, sir," said Cyril as we bounced along out of the town. "But when I heard that Violet had made the rest of them promise to leave without her, I somehow knew that she would be all right. No reason, just what I felt. Must confess, I am more than a bit proud of her."

"And rightly so," said Holmes.

Once we reached our destination, we got out and retraced the steps Holmes and I had taken the night before down the dark drive to the house.

By now it was two o'clock in the morning and clouds were obscuring the moon, rendering the outline of the house only a dark mass against the horizon. We stopped at the edge of the tangled garden. There was no light and no sound coming from the house. We whispered to each other.

"Do we storm the house?" asked Cyril.

"Can we enter without being heard?" said I.

"It is always best," said Lestrade, "to take action without violence of any sort. Certainly best for those being held captive."

We slowly approached the house. In complete silence, Holmes tip-toed to the front door and tried the handle. It was locked. In silence, he gave a push to several of the windows but they were also fully secured. We began to circle around to the back of the house being careful to put our feet down slowly and gently so as not to make a sound. Then we stopped.

A light went on in the front room. The glimmer of it reflected through the lower floor and could be seen in all of the windows.

We heard footsteps … a man's. They were moving from the front of the house back to the kitchen. Another lamp was lit. The footsteps went thundering up the stairs to the upper floor.

"Bill! Wake up!" came a shout from inside. "They're gone!"

"That was Woodley," said Holmes. "I remember his voice."

Soon, we heard a string of loud, vile oaths and profanities.

Both men were now storming back and forth through the house and up and down the stairs.

"Bring the two of them out here!" shouted Woodley.

The window through which I was peeking gave a limited view of the kitchen. The second man, who Woodley had called Bill, was now in the kitchen and bending over the door to the maid's room. The door swung open, and he charged inside. A second later he came out, roughly dragging Violet Morton behind him. I could hear Cyril gasp and felt him stiffen.

"Easy, Cyril," I whispered. "Force yourself to use your reason."

"I have none left," he whispered back.

Bill had forced Violet into the dining room and out of our sight. We could hear the shouts of the men and the muffled voices of Violet and then of Zenani.

The shouting and the muffled replies continued for several minutes. Lestrade began to move toward the back door, followed by Holmes. He gestured for Cyril and me to follow. We were about to break down the door and barge in, guns in hand.

Two gun shots came from within the house.

"Dear God," cried Lestrade, "they've shot her. Now! Come. Break down the door!"

"No. Don't," said Cyril.

The three of us turned and looked at him. The fool was positively smiling. He turned around and started walking toward the front of the house.

"What are you doing?" shouted Lestrade in a stage whisper.

Cyril continued walking, turned his head back to us, and in a normal speaking voice said, "I am going to pay a call on my utterly fabulous wife."

We caught up to him as he was ascending the steps to the front door.

"Are you mad?" said Lestrade. "If they hear you, they could shoot her again. Or both of them. Stop. Now."

"Inspector, you are a police officer," Cyril said. "and Doctor, you served in Her Majesty's armed forces, right? Tell me, gentlemen, what was the caliber of the shots you just heard?"

None of us spoke. He continued.

"Let me be more specific. Did you hear the loud *bang!* of a full-sized revolver?"

We had not. The shots we heard were more like a *pop!* or perhaps a *snap!* of a small caliber handgun.

"The men," said Holmes, "only had standard revolvers. Where did the 22-caliber pistol come from?"

"From Violet's handbag," said Cyril. "Now, if you will excuse me, I expect she will appear at the door."

He approached the door and then stopped.

From with came a loud, anguished scream of pain. It was a man's voice. The scream turned into a horrifying shriek of terror and then stopped.

Cyril turned back to us. "I do not think it likely that Violet inflicted that."

I suspected that I could guess who had.

Cyril then raised his hand and knocked three times on the door, followed by a pause, and then twice more.

We heard footsteps from inside and then the unbolting of the door. It opened, and the tall, queenly Mrs. Violet Morton was smiling at her husband.

"Why hello, darling," she said. "Not the best outing we have ever had together, but we shall just have to make do. Please come in. I'll put on the kettle for you and your friends. There's a bottle of whiskey left as well."

She gestured for us to enter the house. We followed her into the dining room. Zenani was standing there, holding a revolver in each hand and pointing them at two men who were crumpled up on the floor. One of them was holding his arm, his faced contorted with pain. Both were bleeding from their kneecaps.

"Darling," said Cyril, "did you shoot those poor chaps?"

"The gun went off," she said, "and they must have jumped in front of the bullets."

"What about the chap with the sore arm?"

"Oh dear. He was foolish enough to try to reach for his own gun after catching a bullet in the knee."

"Foolish, darling?"

"Yes, dear. He was standing beside Zenani when he did so, and somehow his arm is no longer attached to his shoulder socket. Foolish man."

Holmes approached Woodley and bent over.

"Good morning, Mr. Woodley," he said. "It has been a while since I exchanged blows with the greatest brute and bully in South Africa. Although I do believe that the last time we met, you had also just been shot. You must be more careful in the future."

Woodley glared up at him, his eyes blazing in anger. He swore several times.

"Your days are numbered, Holmes. They are much more powerful than you could ever imagine in your worst nightmare. They will be the masters of you and of all of London."

I bound up the wounds of Bill and Woodley and we loaded them into the back of the police wagon along with the six of us. Just before we were ready to leave the house, Holmes jumped out of the wagon and ran to the backyard. He reappeared a minute later, wheeling the two remaining borrowed-not-stolen bicycles.

Chapter Sixteen
Still at Large

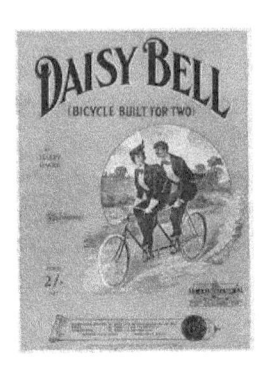

THE EVENTS I HAVE RECOUNTED in this story took place just over one year ago. Since that time, several significant changes have taken place in the lives that were affected.

With the help of the Holder and Stevenson private bank and with the support and encouragement of his fabulous wife, Cyril Morton sold his most of his shares in his firm for a value far above what he had thought they were worth. Together with their children and governesses, the Mortons have gone on a safari adventure in East Africa, to be followed by a visit to the Great Wall of China, Japan, and America.

Oxford University was not willing to accept any of the students unless they endured the lengthy, full application process. However, Cyril Morton approached his friends, the elite and very wealthy socialists, Sidney and Beatrice Webb, and secured entrance for five of the students in their new university, the London School of Economics.

Miss Nazeen elected to stay in the home into which she had been placed and to marry the son of Mrs. Donald Chakola. Together, she and her mother-in-law have become a formidable partnership, and the only stipulation made by Sherlock Holmes and

Inspector Lestrade was that she must promise not to spy on her father-in-law. She recently gave birth to a son who is not entirely unattractive.

Miss Zenani did not go to any university. By the time the trial had ended, the newest hotel in London, the Ritz on Piccadilly, had opened and she became a permanent resident in one of their best suites of rooms (for which extra sound-proofing had been installed). During the weekdays, between the hours of ten and four, a constant stream of highly-placed gentlemen from the clubs on Pall Mall and St. James, can be seen entering her suite and leaving an hour later, flushed and smiling.

Sherlock Holmes continues in his mission of ridding the world of evildoers and I do my bit to assist him when needed. Our work is far from over. The homes into which the young spies had been placed are all now much wiser and will, we hope, never again cut corners by taking in servants placed by fraudulent charities. At the time of writing these words, however, we are still tracking down other enslaved students from foreign countries who were recruited and placed by Woodley and his superiors.

The murderer of the lovely, unfortunate Hatsu Okada is still at large. A team of very expensive barristers and solicitors defended Woodley and Bill, and they were given sentences of a mere three years, less time already served.

Immediately after we departed from the town of Dartford, Holmes paid a visit to the well-known estate agent on Pall Mall who had arranged the lease of 147 Old Bexley Lane. He was informed that the short-term arrangement had been paid in advance in cash. The names on the documents turned out to be fictitious. The name of the Member of Parliament to whom Miss Hatsu had gone, seeking assistance, however, is known. The identities of the members of the criminal organization, who somewhat arrogantly call themselves *The Association of the Fittest*, remain concealed. Their tentacles undergird all of London and, as you will learn in the coming story, extend beyond the borders of England and all the way to the New World.

This case, with more features of interest and more possibility of development than Sherlock Holmes had originally expected, proved to be the prelude to the next.

Historical and Other Notes

Between the years of 1870 to1910, Victorians/Edwardians embraced the bicycle and millions of people, mostly but not always young, took to the open road. Cycling was enjoyed for the healthy exercise it provided as well as the social aspects. Clubs and associations abounded and bicycle outings were highly popular. It liberated the working class from having to find employment within walking distance, and it became the highly controversial symbol of the emancipated adventurous young woman.

While today we associate the word *Victorian* with prudery and strict adherence to restricted morality, the late 1800s and early 1900s in London were anything but. There was a vast underworld of prostitution and gay enterprise. The Cleveland Street Scandal of 1889 involved underaged telegraph boys serving a prostitutes for wealthy Englishmen and was quickly hushed up. You can Google it. Throughout London, there were several *Molly Houses* where gay men could meet and enjoy each other's company. And the reference to the *House of Torture*—an Edwardian center of what we now refer to as BDSM/kink practices—at the corner of Gray's Inn and Old Street is also historical.

The locations noted are generally historically accurate, as are most of the individuals named. Woodley and Holder have been transferred from the Canon.

The Cape Province—the present day Republic of South Africa—was under British control following the Boer wars, and had become a destination for immigrants from all over Europe, Asia, and other parts of Africa.

The posters shown at the start of each chapter in this story were used to promote cycling during the late Victorian/Edwardian era. The French had the raciest, but the English were definitely the most racist.

A NEW SHERLOCK HOLMES MYSTERY

THE ADVENTURE OF THE PRIORESS'S TALE

CRAIG STEPHEN COPLAND

The Adventure of the Prioress's Tale

A New Sherlock Holmes Mystery

Chapter One
Boys Will Be Boys

"WATSON," SAID HOLMES ONE DAY at breakfast from behind the morning newspaper. "You are a man of medicine. I need your opinion. Is it biologically possible for the male of our species to commit crimes too heinous to imagine before reaching its eighteenth year?"

"Certainly," I replied in a distracted manner, being engrossed as I was in writing out an account of one of our more recent adventures. "Some even younger."

"Allow me to be more specific. Is it conceivable, in the farthest reaches of medical science, for a group of a dozen boys to act in concert to inflict unspeakable atrocities upon a similar number of girls? Your medical opinion, please."

I put down my pen.

"Honesty, Holmes. I think you picked a point. Surely, you do not believe that those boys had anything to do with the disappearance of the entire team of girls in Dover."

"It is much too early, and there is far too little data to form any hypothesis. I am merely observing that the possibility that they were abducted by the young males with whom they were fraternizing cannot yet be ruled out."

"Come now, Holmes," I objected. "Are you being reasonable in your assessment of the boys in question?"

"The *boys in question* are in their middle to late teen years. When speaking of such creatures, the word 'reasonable' belongs on another planet. The male of the human species at that time in its life does not possess a brain that functions according to reason. He is merely an inchoate mass of animal spirits."

The story that elicited Holmes's questions and cynical observation was on the front page of every newspaper in England and had already appeared in the press of the Continent and America.

Four days ago, the field hockey teams from the very select St. Mary and St. Martha School for Girls had gone on a beach holiday as an end-of-the-year reward for their excellent season. Their coach and a couple of their teachers had taken them to a pleasant holiday park beside the Channel, just outside of Dover.

As fate would have it, in the site not far from them, a group of senior boys from the all-male Berean Christian Academy in Reading was taking a similar beach holiday. Inevitably, the boys and the girls made contact with each other. Details of what took place after that are contradictory, but it seems that on the second night, twelve members of the girls' senior team colluded to meet after midnight with a similar number of boys. To add to the thrill, they agreed to cycle with cover of darkness to the great Dover Castle. They would meet inside the castle keep and, under the full moon on the night of the solstice, wait and see if the ghost of the headless drummer boy would appear on the ramparts. The prospect of having young spines tingled in mixed company was too intoxicating to be missed.

It is unclear what next took place. The boys all swear that they did indeed meet with the girls and spent a couple of hours chatting and giggling together. However, at two o'clock in the morning, according to the boys, the girls all departed on their bicycles. The boys stayed for another hour smoking cigarettes together in flagrant violation of the rules of their school. Then they cycled back to their campsite and crawled into their bunks.

At roll call the next morning, all of the boys reported, somewhat bleary-eyed. Their headmaster and their teachers were none the wiser.

At the girls' site, the twelve did not. They had vanished.

Not one of them could be found. Their beds had not been slept in.

The girls from the junior team, who had not been allowed by the older ones to join them on their clandestine outing, were questioned. They unanimously informed their teachers and coaches that their older tent mates had snuck out after midnight to meet the boys but had never returned. Every one of the younger girls denied having any idea what had happened to them.

By the noon mealtime, they had still not appeared, and concern for them became intense. The staff of the girls' school paid a visit to the site of the Berean Christian Academy and demanded a meeting.

The pastor, Reverend Reuben Edwards, who served as the headmaster of the Academy, refused to believe that his boys could have committed so grievous an offense. He responded to the insistence of the staff from the girls' school and called all the boys to assembly. Any boy who might have committed such a terrible offense was asked to identify himself. The culprits, being honorable schoolboys all, stepped forward, prepared to take whatever punishment was their due. They confessed that they had, indeed, flagrantly violated the rules of their school, brought dishonor and shame to their families, and placed a black bar sinister across the escutcheon of their Academy.

But they claimed, without a single waiver, that they knew nothing about the missing girls.

The staff of both schools questioned and cross-questioned every one of them individually, but no explanation was forthcoming. Some of the lads displayed severe anxiety on hearing about the disappearance of the girls as it seemed bonds of affection between certain of the boys and the girls had developed in the haunted hours under the full moon.

The local police were then contacted and a cursory search of the holiday park and the townsite was undertaken. Nothing was found.

The twelve did not appear for the evening meal. The intensity of worry increased markedly.

The following morning there was still no sign of them. The police assumed that they had been kidnapped for the purpose of levying ransom, but no demand had been received.

Word had leaked out to the press. Several ambitious reporters from the London papers arrived in Dover and tried to secure interviews with the students from both schools even though they had been explicitly requested not to and to speak only to the staff.

By noon of the second day, in spite of the unceasing efforts of the local constabulary and the staff and students of both schools, there still was no sign.

An appeal for reinforcements was sent from the local police in Dover.

At three o'clock that afternoon, constables from throughout Kent and neighboring East Sussex converged on Dover, established a grid pattern and began a systematic search. Every train from London that arrived at the Priory Station disgorged yet another mob of reporters from every newspaper in the country, and by nightfall, the representatives of the Press in America and the Continent had made their presence known. Every room in every hotel and guest house in Dover had been claimed, and the good citizens of the town could not dare venture forth from their houses without being overwhelmed by a pestilence of reporters and men with cameras.

But there was nothing to report.

A deep sense of alarm had enveloped Dover and was spreading like an infection across England.

The staff of the schools had wisely brought all of their charges together into one compact area and with the assistance of the local constables cordoned it off to protect their students from the rapacious Press. The older boys—the culprits and now leading suspects—had been confined to their tents but the younger boys and girls had, under the circumstances, been allowed to engage in sports and games. The line, however, was drawn at mixed bathing, which remained strictly prohibited.

It was now the following morning—a sultry summer morning, common late in June—and Holmes and I were sipping our breakfast coffee together. My dear wife, Mary, was attending meetings in the West on behalf of a charity to which she devoted many days of her time and rather than fend for myself in our home in Little Venice, I moved, as I often did, back into my old familiar quarters on Baker Street.

"Have they requested your services yet?" I asked Holmes.

"Of course not."

"Why 'of course not?' It is terrifying to think what might have happened, and no one appears to know anything. Just the type of situation when they call on you."

He put the newspaper down and lit a cigarette.

"I am only consulted on cases that involve a serious crime which Scotland Yard finds itself, as it often does, incapable of solving. To date, no crime has been declared. However, by this time tomorrow morning, if the lost have not been found, you may expect that Inspector Lestrade will be ringing our bell."

For the past twenty-five years, I have known and observed my unique friend, Sherlock Holmes. Beneath the thin veneer of his practiced nonchalance and disinterest, I could tell that his mind was already roiling with a burning desire to be brought in to work on a complex and unusual case that was worthy of his full powers. I was not surprised when we rose to retire for the night, to see him making a stop at the bookcase and pulling down his copy of Baedeker's *Guide to Kent*. By morning, he would have memorized every map and piece of data for all of Dover and its hinterland.

I spent the next day at my medical practice but managed to step out to the street every two hours to obtain the latest edition of the newspapers. With each new report, the speculations of what had happened to the girls became more lurid and sensational. What I noted, however, was the reported arrival of distraught and angry family members in Dover. The parents (or their lawyers) and older siblings of the missing girls were understandably terribly distressed. Those of the Academy boys were furious, not so much at their sons for their misbehavior, but at the local police force who had kept the primary suspects under guard at the campsite and refused to allow their parents or the Press to speak to them.

I fully expected that the next day would find Holmes and me on our way to join the pandemonium.

Both Holmes and I rose early the following morning and quickly ate our breakfast. As Holmes had predicted, our bell on Baker Street was rung at a few minutes past seven o'clock.

"Mrs. Hudson," shouted Holmes, "would you mind terribly letting in Inspector Lestrade?"

The good woman, who never tired of finding small ways to be of assistance to her now famous boarder, could be heard descending the stairs. What I heard next was puzzling. Mrs. Hudson at first said nothing, and then I thought she was speaking in quiet tones of consolation. After that, I heard steps coming slowly and deliberately up the stairs. I rose and walked over to the top of the staircase. Below me, I could see Mrs. Hudson with her arm around the waist of another woman, helping her up one stair at a time. The woman was dressed in the habit of a Catholic nun.

Chapter Two
Nunsense

MRS. HUDSON ENTERED THE ROOM. The nun was with her, leaning heavily on her arm and moving with short, unsure steps. Her well-formed face was seamed with lines of trouble, and her complexion was leaden. The eyes which in better times must have shone bright blue were moist, surrounded by puffy reddened eyelids.

The sister was led by our faithful landlady toward the empty sofa, but before she turned around to be seated, she dropped to her knees in front of the cushions. Her forearms rested on the sofa with the whitened fingers of her hands intertwined. Her face was buried in her wrists and we could see her body shaking. Intermittent with her sobs, I heard the partial mumbled words of the familiar *Hail Mary*. The typical response of Holmes or me to such a dramatic entrance would be to force a good stiff ounce or two of brandy past the lips of anyone so incapacitated. For obvious reasons, that did not seem appropriate.

To her eternal credit, Mrs. Hudson knelt down beside her on the bear-skin rug, placed her near arm across the sister's shoulders and put her other hand on her wrist. For the next five minutes, both of them remained in that position. Slowly the distraught nun raised her head, and Mrs. Hudson responded by assisting her to her feet.

"Come dear," she said. "There's a pot of tea in the kitchen and some scones and honey. Come now."

She led her back through the room and into the kitchen. At first, I could hear only Mrs. Hudson's soft muffled voice, but after several minutes another voice joined her.

A full fifteen minutes passed before the two of them returned, walking independently of each other. The sister, still pale but more or less in control of herself, nodded toward Holmes.

"Please, forgive this weakness, Mr. Holmes. I am terribly overwrought. This good lady has been a godsend and has helped me to recover a little."

Holmes and I rose to our feet, and Holmes responded.

"Given what you must now be going through, Prioress Priscilla, your fortitude is most admirable. I had not expected you to call but am honored that you did. Please make yourself comfortable and provide me with all possible information concerning the events in Dover."

She took a slow step toward the table and placed her hands on a hardback chair. She turned it around and put it down directly in front of Holmes. The two of them sat down, facing each other. She closed her eyes and drew several deep breaths.

"The St. Mary and St. Martha Girls' School wishes to retain the services of Mr. Sherlock Holmes," she began, now somewhat more in control of her speech and posture. "May I continue on the understanding that you accept?"

"You may do that, Prioress. However, I must advise you that if Scotland Yard also wishes to retain me for the same situation as you do, they must be given priority. As their case will be almost identical to yours, that should not be a concern. Do you accept that proviso?"

"I do."

"Excellent. Now, please give an account of the events that took place in Dover to the best of your knowledge. You may assume that we are aware of all material facts that have been reported to date. Kindly, state your case."

"Mr. Holmes," she said, her voice quiet and deliberate, "I beg you to understand that for myself and all of the staff of my school, this is not merely a *case*. It touches on the very essence of our purpose in this life. We believe that Almighty God has placed us on this earth at this time to work as His servants in forming the characters of the young women committed to our charge and guiding them to become all He intended them to be. The disappearance of our girls has penetrated us to the dividing of soul and spirit."

"And I assure you, Sister Priscilla," Holmes replied, "that we shall treat the situation with corresponding gravity and intensity of effort. Pray, continue."

"Thank you, sir. If you have read those accounts, then you know what happened to the team of girls. I was not in Dover for the beach holiday camp but back here in London looking after the rest of the students and teachers. I went to Dover as soon as I received the news and have stayed there, without sleeping, until I decided to implore you to help us. Last night I took a very late train back to London."

"And have," said Holmes, "no doubt read this morning's papers. So, you are aware that the police have now stated that foul play is suspected."

"Yes, and that possibility horrifies me beyond words. Imagining what terrible things, fates worse than death, may have been visited upon my girls, is destroying my soul. There is, however, one very significant additional piece of information which makes the situation all the more desperate but that has not been released to the Press. I expect that it will become known within a few days if the girls remain … remain … unaccounted for." She had begun to tremble slightly on those last words but paused, briefly clutched her rosary, and continued.

"This, Mr. Holmes, is a list of the names and family addresses of the girls on the team."

She reached inside her habit to a hidden pocket, extracted a folded piece of paper, and handed it to Holmes. I moved so that I could read over his shoulder and as I read I felt my eyes growing wider and my mouth opening slightly in disbelief. The girls whose names were on the list, they who had so recently vanished without a trace, were, every one of them, the offspring of the singularly most powerful, the wealthiest, the most influential in all of England. Not a single one of the addresses was diminished by a street number.

"Merciful heavens," I gasped. "If any one of these girls were kidnapped, her captors could demand a king's ransom. Why, half of them are from noble families. And look. Three of them have fathers who are in the Cabinet."

"Four," said Holmes.

"It was my understanding, Prioress," he continued, "that your school was affiliated with the Roman Catholic Church yet three-quarters of these families are not of your religious persuasion."

"That is correct, Mr. Holmes. We try to the best of our humble ability to operate on the basis of enlightened and all-embracing principles. As far as we are concerned, all of the girls are daughters of the Church. We consider members of the Church of England and its global Anglo-Catholic Communion to be merely our brothers and sisters who have temporarily lost their way."

"I see three here," said Holmes, "who are neither Anglican nor Catholic, but adherents of Protestant and reformist sects. There is even one who is from a well-known family of religious enthusiasts."

"The deserving daughters of *all* families should be given the same opportunity to become Marys or Marthas—either exemplary wives and mothers whose value is above rubies or, should they choose not to marry, to become all their Heavenly Father created them to be and fully capable of accomplishing anything any man is able to. It is for that reason, sir, that we have reached the zenith of the most highly sought-after schools for girls in England."

"A reputation well-earned," said Holmes. "Permit me to ask, however, if the members of this team of girls are from such important families, why did you not have anyone protecting them? Surely, you must have known that there was a risk of their being abducted."

"We did, and I believed we had taken appropriate measures. In addition to my Assistant Head-Mistress, Sister Evangeline, they were accompanied by their coach, Miss Charlotte Cooper, and by their German master, Mr. Wilhelm Steiger, who has had extensive military experience. The directions given to them required at least one to serve sentinel duty during the night. Due to a misunderstanding between Mr. Steiger and Miss Cooper, it appears that this duty was not performed adequately."

"Would that be the Miss Charlotte Cooper who has won several Wimbledon championships and represented Britain at the Olympics?" asked Holmes.

"It is indeed, Mr. Holmes. She is an exceptional athlete and coaches both our tennis and our hockey teams. She is a source of inspiration to the girls at Mary and Martha."

"And also deaf," said Holmes.

The Prioress paused before responding.

"That she is. She has been that way for the past ten years. It does not in the least impair her performance as a teacher and a coach. As long as you face her directly when speaking, she is fully capable of understanding everything you say to her."

"Excellent," said Holmes, "I have more questions, but before we continue, please tell me what it is you are expecting me to do?"

"To find them ... just find them ... and bring them back safely."

Still pale and weary, Prioress Priscilla appeared to have recovered a bit and was now sitting upright and speaking with quiet confidence. She struck me as a woman who was used to giving polite but firm instructions and having them followed.

I will never know what Holmes's response might have been. We were interrupted by a forceful ringing of the bell at Baker Street, followed immediately by a round of loud knocks.

Inspector Lestrade had arrived.

Mrs. Hudson scampered down the stairs to let him in.

"I apologize," said Holmes, "for the delay. Scotland Yard has just entered the fray, and I suspect that they are about to make the same request of me as you have just done."

Lestrade marched into the room and stopped when he saw the nun.

"You must be from the girls' school," he said, not waiting even for a civil round of introductions.

"I am," she said.

"Good. And have you just hired Sherlock Holmes to find your lost hockey team?'

"I have."

"Well, I just saved you his fee. He will be working for Scotland Yard. But that should not matter as we have the same demands as you do."

"That is quite acceptable to us," replied the sister.

"Splendid. But you will have to live with the fact that it shall be me who yanks on his chain, not you. Agreed?"

"Inspector, I do not *yank* on anybody's chain, sir; least of all, Sherlock Holmes's. And forgive me if I tend to believe that your *yanking,* as you call it, takes place mostly in your mind."

Holmes and I both could not conceal a smirk at that one. Lestrade turned somewhat reddish.

"I shall be ready for both of you within an hour," said Holmes. "Mrs. Hudson will attend to your needs whilst I send off several notes and then pack."

"Half an hour," barked Lestrade. "You can send your wires from Dover. We need to get moving. You would not believe the fire that has been put up my backside on this one. And now that you're on this case, Holmes, consider that you have one up yours as well. Marching orders came from the Office of the Home Secretary himself."

Holmes nodded to him and turned to me. You are joining us, my dear doctor?"

"I would not miss it."

The London Evening Star

Final Edition, Saturday, 24 June, 1905

Were Tender-aged Girls Violated Before Being Abducted?

American Pastor Says His Boys are "innocent as lambs." Are They?

By: Jack Breaker

The *Evening Star* has discovered that the twelve lovely young girls, all of whom were brilliant students and splendid athletes, had met with some of the boys from the Berean Christian Academy earlier on Tuesday afternoon and agreed, whether under threat from the boys or not is not known, to meet with them in the keep of Dover Castle.

This newspaper does not wish to disturb the sensibilities of our readers, but we all know why young men try to have maidens meet with them in dark haunted places under the full moon during the summer solstice. Were their intentions honourable? Only the most naïve, perhaps like the American pastor, Rev. Reuben Edwards, the headmaster of the boys' school, are foolish enough to believe that they were.

According to the story told by the boys, they said goodbye to the young ladies of the St. Mary and St. Martha Senior Girls Hockey team around two o'clock in the morning. We can only imagine what the boys might have done to them under the full moon after the hour of midnight that forced the girls to flee, leaving the boys behind.

"If anyone touches a hair of my dear little sister's head," said Mr. James Royce of the Fallendale estate, "he will have to deal with me and I shall be merciless." Other parents and family members expressed similar vows.

Satisfied that a heinous crime had taken place, the local constabulary have asked for the involvement of Scotland Yard and we expect that the Yard's indefatigable investigator, Inspector G. Lestrade, will take over responsibility for solving the crime.

"The boys from the Christian Academy are the primary suspects," is what we expect Inspector Lestrade will announce upon his arrival in Dover. "Scores of hardworking policemen are desperately searching for any sign of the girls," he will no doubt report. "Our thoughts and prayers are with their families at this time," is what he has said on similar occasions in the past.

The *Evening Star* will continue to bring its readers the most current reports, regardless of how shocking they may be, as long as this crisis remains critical.

Chapter Three
Dover Souls

ONCE WE WERE OUT of 221B and on to the pavement of Baker Street, I acquired another handful of newspapers that the newsboys were hawking.

The *Times* and the *Telegraph* reliably reported on the few facts that were known at the time. Added to the accounts were comments from interviews with the parents, older siblings, and other relatives of the missing girls. Emotions were running high, and the statements made revealed a fully understandable state of anxiety.

The account in the *Evening Star,* a relatively new broadsheet newspaper that was struggling to attract more readers, left me appalled.

"Good heavens," I muttered. "They have nothing new to report, and so they are making things up. Inspector, did you truly say these things?"

He gave me a sidewards look. "Was the reporter who wrote that nonsense named Jack Breaker?"

I looked again at the byline and confirmed his assumption. "You are familiar with him?"

"The Yard considers him below a sewer rat."

We climbed into the police carriage that Lestrade had waiting for him and bounced our way quickly to Victoria. Both Holmes and Lestrade scribbled texts of wires to be sent and handed them to a constable when we reached the station.

Twenty minutes later found Holmes, Prioress Priscilla, Lestrade and me in a cabin on the SE&CR, pulling out of Victoria and on our way to Dover. I encouraged the sister, who appeared to me to be utterly exhausted, to catch a short nap on the way. Unfortunately, Holmes was having none of that and made use of the time by respectfully interrogating her.

"It would be helpful to know," he said, "about the character of these twelve girls. Are there any insights you can disclose to us that might be useful in discerning what happened to them?"

"Would you kindly be more explicit, Mr. Holmes?"

"What he's asking you, Sister," interrupted Lestrade, "is are these girls of yours on their way to being Florence Nightingales or Cora Pearls? Are they budding young Pamelas or Shamelas? Are they saints or trollops? Sorry if I must be blunt but we do not have time to beat around the bush."

"Inspector," she replied. "I have spent the past twenty years guiding the lives of young women. I have yet to meet one who did not embody something of all of the alternatives you have suggested. Every one of those girls is both a sinner and a saint, as am I, as are you, as are we all."

"Right. Very well then, I shall be more explicit. Could your team of girls have been forced against their will to meet with the boys?"

Sister Priscilla said nothing for a minute and starred at Lestrade as if he had become a simpleton.

"And just how, Inspector," she asked, "might a group of boys manage to do that?"

"I can't imagine."

"And neither can I."

"Right. Well then, did these girls ever do anything like this in the past?"

"They are a very highly-spirited group and exceptionally competitive and given to outbursts of independence. Have they ever broken school rules or come in after curfew? Yes, of course they have. Have they ever snuck out for hours in the middle of the night? Never."

"Why not?"

"Because, Inspector, they all knew full well that had they so flouted the rules of their school, their team would have been disbanded. Winning the cup for their division was of paramount importance to them. For that reason, they usually behaved themselves."

"But you were not surprised to learn that they had set up a rendezvous with some boys in the middle of the night once they knew that there was nothing you could do now to punish them?"

"No, Inspector," the Prioress answered after a long pause. "I was not. In my twenty years of teaching young women, I have never encountered a more brilliant, more athletic, more determined, or more willful group. They are quite an unusual lot."

Lestrade said no more and Holmes took over the questioning.

"May I assume that for each of these girls, your office has an extensive file?"

"We do."

"And did you think to bring those files with you to Dover?"

"I had one of my staff bring them yesterday."

"Excellent," said Holmes. "We shall have to have unrestricted access to them."

"Of course."

"And have you collected all of their belongings from their tents? We will need to examine them as well."

"That is understandable."

"Now then, have you had an opportunity to speak directly to this Reverend Reuben Edwards fellow?"

"I have."

"May I assume that you took the measure of the man?"

"He is an upright and honorable man and quite devoted to his church, his school, and the boys under his care."

"Prioress Priscilla," said Holmes. "I will rephrase my question. Kindly disclose to me your *candid,* unvarnished and entirely truthful impression of this fellow."

She gave Holmes a hard look, and he gave it right back.

"It is difficult," she said, "to have entirely charitable feelings towards someone who firmly believes that only those of his particular religious persuasion are going to Heaven and that all the rest of Christendom, especially those who are faithful members of the Catholic Church, are destined to spend eternity in Hell. The fact that he claims to have received this insight directly from the Almighty does not endear him to me."

"I am not asking you to tell me whether or not you liked him. I would have assumed that you might not. I am asking you to give me your assessment of his character. Is he to be trusted?"

"He is a man of the cloth, and I must assume he is truthful. He has said that he knows nothing about what happened to my girls and I have no reason to doubt his word."

"Ah, but what about his boys? Do you trust them?"

"I have not had an opportunity to speak to them. And even if I had, I have no experience in contending with the minds, souls, and bodies of boys. I would have no idea where to start if I were to have to determine that they were lying to me. With a young woman, I could tell in an instant. But not boys."

Holmes let up with the questions for a few minutes, during which time the Prioress let her head fall back onto the padded top of the seat in which she was sitting and promptly fell asleep.

We did not wake her until the train pulled into the station in Dover. As she slumbered and Holmes reviewed his *Baedeker's Guide,* Lestrade and I exchanged newspapers and amused ourselves with stories about the success in the West End of Baroness Orczy's *The Scarlet Pimpernel* and the opening of G.B.

Shaw's *Man and Superman*. Mrs. Emmeline Pankhurst had led a demonstration at Westminster for giving the vote to women, and France and Germany were once again at each other's throats and rattling their sabers over the last remaining corner of Africa—Morocco—to be put under the colonial control of a European power. After a few cursory readings, I set the papers aside. Nothing else in their pages remotely compared with the immediate concern for the lives and well-being of twelve English schoolgirls.

Chapter Four
Poor Orphan Boys

AS WE STEPPED OFF THE TRAIN onto the platform of the station in Dover, an unpleasant thought occurred to me.

"Holmes," I said, "we have no place to stay. Dover has been overrun with the Press, families of both the boys and girls, and the shamelessly prurient. There is not a hotel room to be had within miles."

My question was answered by Sister Priscilla.

"Rooms for you and the Inspector have been arranged at the boys' orphanage."

"The orphanage?" I asked. "It will hardly do to have us put orphan boys out of their beds."

"The Sisters of St. Vincent," the Prioress said, "who operate the orphanage were not pleased with the idea either until I told them that it would be for Sherlock Holmes. Then they assured me that their boys would be fighting over the opportunity to boast that Sherlock Holmes had slept in their bed."

"Right," said Lestrade. "And what do they think of having an inspector from Scotland Yard using their pillow? Probably not so keen on that, are they?"

The Prioress looked straight back at Lestrade and forced a smile. "It will likely give them nightmares, Inspector, but I am sure that the damage will be temporary. Now come, the three of you. If we walk quickly, we may be able to get to the orphanage before being spotted by the Press. Please follow me."

"Right," muttered Lestrade. "Fortunately, Scotland Yard can commandeer a room in the hotel by tomorrow. Shame that a private detective cannot do that, Holmes."

The sister led us briskly for several blocks through the streets of the singularly unique city of Dover, *the gateway to England.*

Outwardly, Dover appears to be like many other established towns of England with a cluster of traditional buildings, narrow streets, an assortment of churches, a parade of shops hawking their wares, and all dominated by a massive ancient castle.

Behind that façade is a town unlike any other. Back and forth through the docks of Dover passes the populace of the entire globe. Every color, tongue, and creed enters England by way of Dover and just as many leave and voyage to the Continent. You will observe the captains of industry, and commerce, the medalled generals of every nation's army, sailors innumerable, missionaries and clerics of all faiths and creeds, as well as those you suspect to be fleeing from the police in some town a thousand miles away. Of late, with the nasty pogroms sweeping across the Czar's Pale of Settlement, there have been tens of thousands of Jews. Most, wisely, only stay briefly in England before setting sail for America, determined to make a new life for their families.

As we passed the pubs and shops where this cacophony of humanity was entering and exiting, it seemed to me that any one of a dozen bands of foreign sailors and thugs could be candidates for crimes of kidnapping, murder, and violations too unseemly to name. Holmes and Lestrade had their work cut out for them.

The St. Vincent de Paul buildings were adjacent to the Catholic Church a few blocks from the station and a stone's throw from the foot of the steep Castle Hill. Each of us was given a separate room. Mine was small but spotlessly clean and contained only a single cot with a thin mattress, a writing desk and chair, and a crucifix. The window afforded a pleasant view of Dover Castle. Whoever the lad was who had been forced to vacate his Spartan room, he was not living in luxury.

Having deposited my valise in my room and quickly washed up in cold water, I departed and found Holmes and Lestrade waiting for me in the hall. Holmes was holding an envelope, which he handed over to me. The insignia on the corner was of His Majesty's Government. I opened it and read. It ran:

Sherlock: Imperative that you drop all other matters and devote your skills entirely to finding the missing girls. There is far more at stake than the future of a hockey team.

Also: what do you know about a group calling itself The Order of the Fittest?

I await your reply.

Mycroft.

I handed it back to Holmes and expressed my indignation.

"Honestly, Holmes, can there be anything more important to your brother than the very lives of these young women?"

He nodded. "I know Mycroft well enough to be certain that he is as concerned for the missing girls as we are. I read this note as saying not that there is anything more important, but that there is something else, a grave concern to His Majesty's Government *as well as* their lives. As to what it is, and any connection to the pretentious *Order,* I have not the foggiest."

"Neither do I," added Lestrade.

The three of us descended to the entry of the orphanage and were greeted by a tall, older man in a police uniform.

"Welcome, gentlemen," he said "Allow me to introduce myself. I am Chief Constable Albert Pughsley of Kent County, formerly of the Royal Navy and now serving in Dover. I am glad of your assistance."

I observed his face. It bore the deep lines etched by years looking out over the sea. He struck me as a man who had been to every port-of-call I could name and many I had never heard of. He had the air of a man to be taken seriously

Lestrade responded to him, speaking as if scripted in a memo from his office. He said some flattering things about the local forces, all the while subtly making it clear that Scotland Yard was now in charge of the investigation.

The Chief Constable listened with studied politeness before replying.

"To be frank, Inspector," he said, "I learned a long time ago that there is no end of what can be accomplished as long as no one cares who gets the credit. At the moment, I am far more concerned about the lives of twelve young women than what appears in the newspapers. And let me warn you, sir, that as soon as the Press learns that Sherlock Holmes and Dr. Watson are here, they will be all over us. Now then, time is pressing. Allow me to suggest that I provide you with such information as we have whilst we walk up to the Castle."

"Is the Prioress not coming with us?" I asked as we departed from the orphanage.

"I asked about her," said the Chief Constable. "She's asleep, and her sisters say that she needs to stay that way. You can catch up with her later."

Dover Castle is one of the largest in the British Isles. The road leading up to it rises steeply from just above sea-level at the port and works its way through several switchbacks until it passes under the narrow archway at the gatehouse and through the great curtain wall, some four hundred feet above the town.

"It was reported," I said, "that they all came here on their bicycles. That is a very steep push all the way up here."

"They are young," said Pughsley.

Having huffed and puffed our way to the summit, we were now standing in the castle keep at the foot of the steep stairs that led to the top of the walls. We followed the policeman up.

"This is where those lads and lassies met," said the Chief Constable.

The view from the ramparts is exhilarating. We had arrived on a clear day and could easily see the coast of France on the far side of the Channel. It did not surprise me that on a moonlit night, with the summer breeze blowing in from the sea, a group of students might have found the experience irresistibly seductive.

"We have interrogated the boys," said Pughsley. "They admitted that some of them went for walks with the girls along the ramparts. Some went exploring other passages within the castle. Maybe a kiss or two was stolen here and there, but they all swear that nothing untoward happened beyond that."

"And do you believe them?" asked Lestrade.

"Well, yes. We did everything to them but put their testicles in a vice, and they kept to their story. I don't believe that a dozen lads can all lie consistently. They must be telling the truth."

We walked on into the castle itself. As the sun was still high in the sky, light was streaming into the halls and chambers of the enormous old stone structure.

"If I may ask, Constable," said Holmes. "Are there no guards posted in the castle at night? Is it open to anyone who wants to enter? Surely, there must be countless men whose character is suspect and who might carry out all sorts of misdeeds in such a location."

"Well, yes and no, Mr. Holmes. There is nothing of value left in the castle to guard. As to people wandering around and committing foul deeds, you have a point there. The town is chock full of sailors from all over God's good earth. For those fellows, we have come up with a means of keeping them out of here at night, and though imperfect, it has been working rather well for several decades."

"And how do you do that," asked Holmes. "without posting a guard?"

"The ghosts look after that for us, Mr. Holmes."

"The ghosts?"

"Yes, sir. Have you ever known a single sailor from anywhere who is *not* superstitious?"

"I cannot say that I have."

"Neither have I. And that's why we make sure that we keep having sightings of the headless drummer boy, and King Harold with an arrow in his eye, and heretics who were burned at the stake and still on fire. Ordinary folk, even those who have lived in Dover all their lives, are afraid to come up here at night. No telling what might happen to them."

"With respect, Constable," said Holmes, "your strategy does not appear to have worked on the young and adventurous."

"Aye, right you are on that one, Mr. Holmes. I guess we failed. We had not seen that one coming."

From the ramparts, the officer led us into the main castle edifice. Most of the rooms and chambers were well lit by the afternoon sun steaming through the windows, but the hallways and passages were dark, requiring the aid of the electric torch the officer from Dover had brought with him. The enclosed areas were dank and musty, and there were puddles of water here and there on the floors. The walls throughout the building were of bare stone and brick, except for the occasional piece of rusting, corroded iron that protruded from them. At one point along the tour, just as we were about to descend, the Chief Constable stopped and commented.

"The boys confessed that they had led a few of the girls into the darkened areas where not even a glimmer of moonlight could be seen. One lad even admitted to taking a girl down into the dungeon. There may have been a bit of the hanky-panky going on, but all the boys insist that every one of the twelve girls departed on their bicycles and did not return."

"Did you," asked Holmes, "find anything in the rooms or passages that suggested the girls did return here?"

"No, not really, Mr. Holmes. We found the odd candy wrapper and wrappings from meat pies and such, and there were a few articles of women's clothing … undergarments mainly."

"Indeed?" said Holmes. "Do you not deem them significant?"

"No, not really. You see, occasionally some of the local women of the evening bring their customers, sailors mainly, up here for whatever business transactions they choose to carry on. The darkness adds to the thrill, and the fools pay a premium to think that there are ghosts all around them. Most of the pieces of clothing we found were of a size that would be far too large for a young athlete. So that is why we reached our conclusion, Mr. Holmes."

After a half an hour of poking through the score of rooms, wings, and floors of the castle, the Chief Constable led us back out into the open keep.

"If I may," said Holmes, when it was clear that our inspection of the building was over, "can you be sure that you inspected every possible corner? These ancient buildings are rather famous, are they not, for secret rooms and hidden passages?"

"Aye, so they are," replied the Chief Constable. "But every town in England is blessed with an association of old teachers, soldiers, clergy, nurses, and librarians and their ilk who consider it their life's work to carry out research and debate on the most minute and trivial aspect of their beloved local history. Similar associations meet and argue about arcane details of Shakespeare or Lady Jane Austen. I assume, Mr. Holmes, that you are familiar with such groups of local citizens."

"I am and consider them to be a complete waste of perfectly good minds and imaginations that could be used for the betterment of society."

"Well now, you may have a point there, sir. Mark my words though, if the stories of your cases as recorded by the good Doctor here keep on being as famous as they are, someday some flock of eccentrics will gather to debate and feud all about you."

"Such a prospect," said Holmes, "is as unappealing as it is unlikely."

"Perhaps," replied the Chief Constable. "But that is neither here nor there today. What matters is that we have such a group here in Dover who have devoted their waking hours to learning and arguing about every imaginable detail of Dover Castle. So, we enlisted their help. They made maps of every room and passage in the Castle, and they came and led my men all through all of them, and gave free lectures along the way. There was not a square inch missed."

"Well done," said Holmes. "What is next?"

"That's it for the building," said the Chief Constable. "I will take you now to the tunnels."

The London Evening Star

Afternoon Edition, Friday, 23 June 1905

Were Our Girls Kidnapped by White Slavery Arabs?

"I cannot bear to think about it," says older brother of missing little sister.

By: Jack Breaker

Have you been recently to the National Museum? Have you seen the unspeakable evidence witnessed in person by the famous Italian artist, Giulio Rosati? He secretly recorded unimaginable scenes of depravity so European Christian nations could see what continues to happen to this very day —the licentious selling of white Christian young women to wealthy old Mohammedans?

Is that what has happened to the missing girls from St. Mary and St. Martha?

During the past three hundred years, Arab pirates off the Barbary Coast have kidnapped over ONE MILLION Christians and sold them into slavery. It is a well-known fact, confirmed by ninety-six percent of scientists, that men with darker skin are irresistibly attracted to woman with lighter skin, and especially to the young, soft, virginal white skin of Christian girls from European countries. Within the hallowed halls of our universities, scholars have given these women a scientific name, *The Cicassian Beauties*.

What happens to them after they have been kidnapped? You only have to look at the authentic paintings in our great National Museum to answer that question and the answer is terrifying. Rosati's recording of the heathen events at *The Picking of the*

Favourite or *The Inspection of the New Arrivals* leaves nothing to the imagination (Caution: responsible God-fearing parents will not allow their children to see these paintings). Beautiful white Christian girls are stripped naked and paraded in front of rich old Arab men. After prayers to Allah, a price is agreed upon and a girl from a good family in France, Holland or England is sold like a piece of livestock and enters a harem. If she is lucky, her family will find the money, sometimes after selling everything they own, to pay a ransom. By the time she is returned to the loving arms of her weeping mother and heart-broken father, the damage done to her body and soul may be too unspeakable to name.

As readers of this newspaper already know, twelve girls, whose names their school refuses to release (for what reason, they did not say) disappeared the night before last from Dover Castle.

A local police officer, who cannot give his name for fear of retribution, admitted to this reporter that a boat could easily dock in many places in Dover, load a cargo of bound and gagged English girls and sail away under cover of darkness. By now they could already be in Tangiers.

The Evening Star and this reporter pledge to our readers that we will leave no stone unturned in our relentless pursuit of these unfortunate girls. Additional information will be disclosed with each edition.

When the safety and honour of innocent, Christian English girls is at stake, we must all do our part.

Chapter Five
Tunneling Down

I REMEMBERED READING about the caves and tunnels of Dover as a schoolboy. Up and down the coast, there was said to be no end of subterranean cavities, some made by Mother Nature and others manmade. They had been used by pirates and smugglers since time immemorial. I knew they existed but had no idea how extensive they were. I was about to learn.

"This way," said Constable Pughsley. He led us back out of the keep to a cutaway in the side of the hill.

"You're a tall one, Mr. Holmes," he said as he opened a small door. "Mind you don't bump your head."

Again, we depended on the light from his electric torch as he led us into what he called the *Casement Tunnels.*

"This entire corner of Kent," he informed us, "is on top of an enormous layer of chalk. It is soft, and so it can be carved out easily. There were always caves along the coast, but back when England was afraid that Emperor Nappy was going to cross the Channel and invade, we sent over two thousand troops to Dover to protect us. They had no place to house the soldiers safely, so they dug out tunnels and put them down here. Now, our boys didn't take too kindly to digging themselves, so they used prisoners we had captured in France and put those *sans-culottes* chaps down here and made them dig."

We followed him into the darkness along a long, inclined ramp. In the light from the torches, I could see that the walls were covered with brick and mortar, rising to an arch, a foot or two above our heads. We kept walking and walking. The air was close and damp and smelled distinctly of dead rats.

"Merciful heavens," I said as I ducked my head one more time to avoid hitting it against a protruding piece of brickwork. "How far do these go on?"

"Oh, there's a couple of miles of them, counting here under the castle and up on the heights to the west. But we're quite certain that there is no one hiding in here."

"And how," asked Holmes, "can you possibly be sure of that?"

"Well now, Mr. Holmes, we reasoned it this way. The girls departed on their bicycles and did not come back to the castle, right? So, the girls would have to bicycle, slow and careful on account of the steep slope, back down the road. Now then, it was possible that somewhere along the road a band of men, gypsies perhaps, could have been waiting. And maybe they forced them into the tunnel. Are you with me on that, Mr. Holmes?"

"I am. Pray, continue."

"Well now, that was our first theory. So, that's what we checked first. But there were no bicycle tracks to be seen on the road as it has a hard surface. But nothing stopped and turned off the road, and nothing was taken into the tunnel. Furthermore, nothing was found inside the tunnels."

"Are you quite sure," asked Holmes "you have checked the entire warren?"

"Well now, Mr. Holmes, those same old blokes and grandmothers who study the history of the town and castle are also fascinated by the caves and tunnels. So, we have maps of every inch of every tunnel, and we have checked out every miserable stretch of them. The old folks themselves came and helped us and there is not a soul in the Kingdom who knows those tunnels better than they do. But just to assure you, sir, that's why we're now taking you to see for yourself, sir."

We crept on through the dark, narrow passages and then encountered several larger rooms which had been used for barracks or for storage of food and ammunition. They were not nearly as suffocating as the tunnels. However, we did not see evidence that anyone had been there in the recent past.

Once back in the open fresh air, Holmes turned to the Chief Constable.

"Sir, I thank you for sharing your knowledge with us. However, with respect, allow me to ask why, if you were already certain that the girls could not possibly be secreted in the castle or the tunnels, did you bother to use hours of precious time leading us through them?"

"Well now, Mr. Holmes," replied the Chief Constable, "we knew from your reputation how thorough you like to be, so we thought it would be efficient if we immediately helped you eliminate the obvious possibilities from your list. You see, sir, there's a rule we use in doing our investigations. It goes, *once you have eliminated all other possibilities …*"

I bit my tongue and said nothing.

"If they are not in the castle or the tunnels," demanded Holmes, "Where do you propose they are?"

"Well now, Mr. Holmes, it is a serious mistake to hypothesize before you have sufficient data, but with that caution in mind, and admitting that we are as ignorant as we were three days ago, we would be thinking that those girls are no longer in Dover. Best theory we have right now, is that they are not even in England. We're suggesting that they must have been abducted and taken across the Channel. Mind you, maybe they have run off to Paris or the south of France of their own accord. They are quite the high-spirited lot we've been told and nothing in the way of cries or struggle was heard. For all we know they might be carousing up and down the *Rive Gauche* whilst you and I have been gasping and sloshing our way through those miserable tunnels."

We walked quickly, occasionally trotting, back down the steep switchback from the heights to the townsite. Our next stop would be the St. Vincent's orphanage to retrieve Prioress Priscilla and pool whatever data was now available to us.

She met us at the door.

"You have visitors, Mr. Holmes," she said. "There is an entire committee waiting to talk to you. They are greatly agitated and they are not the type who like to be kept waiting."

"The parasitical Press?" I asked.

"Worse," she said.

Chapter Six
Discounting the Viscount

"MR. SHERLOCK HOLMES, we need a few minutes of your time."

A tall, stately, young man advanced toward us as we entered the common room of the orphanage. He cut quite an impressive figure and had an air of polished aristocracy about him. He was not only scrupulously dressed as a gentleman, but his suit and accessories announced bespoke from Saville Row. His handsome face was impassive as he stepped in front of us, blocking our way. Gathered behind him, the ladies seated and the men standing, were another seven people, every one of whom looked as if they might own a city house in Mayfair and an estate or two in Sussex. I thought I recognized several of them from photos in the society pages of the weekend newspapers.

"I am Viscount Fallendale," the fellow said. He did not extend his hand to greet us nor offer a card.

"Good afternoon, sir," replied Holmes. "I have had the privilege of assisting your father, Gerald. Your mother was Agnes was she not, before she passed away? And your step-mother is the quite famous Mrs. Isabella, of Trentino. It is a pleasure to meet you, sir. To what do I owe the honor?"

If the viscount was affronted by Holmes's informal response, he was disarmed by the all-innocence look on his face. After a brief pause, he replied.

"We," he said, gesturing to the people behind him, "are a committee appointed by the families of the missing girls and the imprisoned boys. We were pleased to hear that you are here in Dover and working on the case. Allow me to introduce my fellow members."

He then proceeded to point first to the women present and then the men. I counted three with noble titles, a member of one of the wealthiest banking families, the wife of a famous Admiral of the Fleet and two Americans, one was a lawyer, and the other was distinctly Jewish.

Holmes nodded graciously to each member in turn whilst Lestrade, the Chief Constable and I stood back and observed.

"With the exception of two families," the young Viscount began, "and they will be joining our ranks quite soon, all of the families of the boys and girls are now in Dover. Most of us have taken rooms at the Lord Warden Hotel. I am sure, Mr. Holmes, that you can appreciate how very deeply we are concerned about the fate of our children."

"I can indeed. It is most understandable."

"Very good then. We have expressed our concerns to the highest levels of His Majesty's Government and insisted that all available resources be requisitioned forthwith and instructed to leave no stone unturned in the search for the missing girls. We are also taking steps through our barristers and solicitors to have the boys from the Academy released from their imprisonment."

"Again, sir, quite understandable."

"Understandable, yes. But not nearly enough. As soon as we learned that Mr. Sherlock Holmes had arrived in Dover, we took steps to have Scotland Yard informed that from henceforth you will be working for our Committee and that the police should relinquish their contract with you. Is that agreeable to you, Mr. Holmes? I give you my word as a gentleman that your fee will be increased several fold from what the policemen could have paid you. Is that also agreeable to you, Mr. Holmes?"

"No."

Holmes added nothing to his reply while the Viscount looked at him as if expecting something more. Holmes returned the look with an expression of practiced pleasantness on his impassive face.

"I beg your pardon, Mr. Holmes. Did you not understand what I just said?"

"Of course, I did. What part of 'no' did you not understand?"

"Now look here, Mr. Holmes, I gave you my word as a gentleman—."

"Tut, tut, my dear fellow," Holmes interrupted, in his blandest voice. "I gave *my* word as a gentleman to Scotland Yard that I would provide my services to them. As a gentleman yourself, you cannot expect another gentleman to go back on his word. Hardly that."

Whilst the young lord was searching for words, Holmes continued, now speaking past him to the assembled committee.

"Members of the Committee, please let me assure you that I shall make use of whatever skills I may possess to resolve this terrible situation. I give all of you my word that I shall work tirelessly until the missing girls are safely returned to their families."

Adding a small dramatic flair, Holmes placed his hand over his heart, as if by doing so the veracity of his pledge was enhanced.

"As to the boys from the Academy," he continued, "they are in no danger and thus are not my concern. You are much better off working through your lawyers with respect to them. I may wish to ask you questions about your family and will inquire for you at the Lord Warden. Now, if you will excuse us, we have a pressing engagement to attend to."

Our egress was blocked by a now angry Viscount Fallendale. He brought his face within a few inches of Holmes's and spoke quietly.

"Look here, Holmes," he said. "I had expected that you would know how to act when your services are requested by your betters."

"Oh dear," said Holmes. "I will try to remember your advice should I happen to run into any such people."

"Holmes! I am warning you. We will not be trifled with. Do not dare to cross us."

Holmes smiled at him, turned away and walked toward to the main door of the orphanage. As we followed, we were accosted by an attractive younger woman who was a member of the committee.

"Please, Mr. Holmes, a word. I promise not to keep you."

Holmes looked more than a little annoyed but, being a gentleman, he stopped and turned to her.

"Yes, Miss Brunel. What is it? Please be prompt."

She smiled at him. "I respect your integrity, sir. Thank you."

"Is that all you have to say?"

"No, sir. My younger sister is amongst the missing girls."

"I am sorry to hear that. You must be very worried."

"No, Mr. Holmes, I am not."

That took all of us by surprise.

"I beg your pardon, Miss," snapped Holmes. "Then what is it you possibly have to say to me?"

"Just to suggest to you that you should not be in haste and should work as thoroughly as you consider necessary. I have no fear for their safety and well-being and neither should you."

"That is an inexplicably bizarre statement coming from a sibling. Explain yourself, please, Miss."

"I attended all of the girls' hockey games over the past few months."

"So did their coaches. What of it?"

"Are you familiar, Mr. Holmes, with the mythological tribe of warrior women known as the Amazons?"

"Of course, I am."

"Compared to this team of girls, those Amazons are Tinkerbells."

"Kindly abandon your metaphors and speak plainly."

"What I am telling you, Mr. Holmes, is that the senior girls' hockey team is the fiercest collection of young women I have ever known. They refuse to lose. They take no prisoners. And God help the poor sods who have taken them hostage. If I can assist you in any way by providing data about them, you may call for me at the Lord Warden. Just ask for Myrina."

Chapter Seven
Our Newest Irregulars

WE OPENED THE DOOR of the orphanage to exit to the pavement and stopped in our tracks. Facing us was a crowd of men all dressed somewhat alike in workmen's caps and ill-fitting suit jackets. For a brief moment, I imagined them standing there holding torches and pitchforks, but they were merely holding notebooks and pencils or standing behind camera tripods and chomping on cigarettes. The Press had found us.

"*Mr. Sherlock Holmes. Did Scotland Yard bring you in because they were incompetent one more time?*"

"*Mr. Holmes. Is it possible that our girls have been abductified by the White Slave Traders?*"

"*Dr. Watson. The girls were such fierce athletes that some medical experts have said they must have been boys in disguise. Can you confirm that?*"

"*Chief Constable Pughsley. Some of those American boys are Jews. Could the girls have been captured and forced to convert?*"

The barrage of questions came at us like a maelstrom. Another dozen of the same nature followed those I have recorded above. I dared not attempt even a one-word response to any of them.

Fortunately, the Chief Constable strode forward and held up his hand until the rabble fell silent.

"Gentlemen of the Press," he said. "I will be issuing a statement tomorrow morning at nine o'clock at the police station. I look forward to speaking with you at that time. That is all. Good day, gentlemen."

He turned around and walked back into the safety of the orphanage. We followed, closing the door behind us.

The constable gave his head a shudder. "Angels and ministers of grace defend us," he said. "I will make my way through the corridors to the church and exit by way of the rectory. My suggestion to you chaps is that you remain protected inside the orphanage until the supper hour has passed. Those reporters will have to attend both to filling their stomachs and filing their stories. They will disperse within an hour or so."

I had been rather looking forward to a pleasant tea and supper in the hotel dining room and felt that prospect disappearing from my grasp. "And where," I asked, "are we then to take our tea and supper?"

"The Sisters of St. Vincent here will find something," said Pughsley. "They manage to keep their boys looking healthy. I am sure they will be able to give you a decent bowl of stew."

He retreated back through the orphanage and Holmes, Lestrade and I found a small sitting room just off the entrance hall where we could consider our next round of actions. Whilst sitting there we heard the committee of parents make their way out the door and into the waiting maw of the Press.

An hour later, we were sitting at one end of a long refectory table. In front of each of us was a thick, plain crockery bowl and plate, a tin mug and a set of well-used cutlery with forks that once-upon-a-time might have had parallel tines. We shared the dining hall with sixty boys ranging in age from seven to mid-teens. They were all chattering amiably and casting no end of glances at us. I could hear our names being spoken repeatedly.

Sister Miriam, the headmistress of the St. Vincent orphanage, stood up in front of the boys and waited until they stopped their noise, whereupon she recited a grace. When she had finished, she came and sat beside us, and the din from the hall full of boys returned.

Over the next hour, we endured the hard benches and noise of St. Vincent's refectory and devoured a nourishing bowl of stew unaccompanied by anything that remotely resembled a glass of claret. Whilst the atmosphere in the town of Dover was tense, nothing could dampen the spirits of boys who laughed and hooted and hollered throughout the supper hour. Several of them carried out serving duties and brought trays to our table, with two of them pausing to boldly ask, "Are you really Sherlock Holmes?"

Holmes assured them that he was while the headmistress took the opportunity to interrogate us on all sorts of issues in the current news of the day. What did we think about that awful massacre in St. Petersburg when the Czar sent troops against the peasants that had been organized by the brave Father Gapon? And how could we account for the thrashing the Japanese had given to the Russian navy? What was Kaiser Bill up to riding his white horse through the streets of Tangiers proclaiming Germany's support for Moroccan independence? Did any of us believe that women should be given the vote or did we consider Mrs. Pankhurst to be a hopeless idealist? And would the motor cars and lorries ever replace the reliable horse-drawn carriages delivering mail all over the Empire?

We responded to the best of our ability but as the dessert course was being served I noticed that Holmes had lost interest in the conversation and had directed his gaze across the roomful of boys.

"Sister Miriam," he said, interrupting Lestrade's analysis of the latest model of motor car, "might I ask a few questions about your boys?"

"Why certainly, Mr. Holmes. I can tell you that none of them had anything whatsoever to do with what has taken place here in Dover—the missing girls, I mean. Every one of them was asleep in his bed all night long. Of that, I am certain. One of us does the rounds every half hour through the night to make sure."

"Yes, of course. That thought had not crossed my mind at all. What I was wondering was how they might react if I were to ask a select few of them to help me in our investigation."

"You mean, sir, to help you like your Irregulars do?"

"Precisely. What would they do?"

"Commit murder," said the Sister.

"I beg your pardon, Sister."

"I can assure you, Mr. Holmes. That they would be prepared to murder each other to have the chance to become one of Sherlock Holmes's Irregulars."

The three of us laughed for the first time in several days.

"Well then," continued Holmes, "perhaps we could come up with a fair means of selecting a few of them. Are there any of them who have been particularly well-behaved this term?"

"None."

"None, Sister?"

"Not a single one of them, Mr. Holmes. They are boys. Their souls and spirits are good-hearted and brave as they come, but as soon as our backs are turned, they are up to no end of mischief. The older they become, the more incorrigible. It is all I can do to keep the merchants and local police officers away from them. We love them all but …well … they are boys. What would you expect?"

A smile was slowly spreading across Holmes's face.

"How many boys are in the senior class?"

"Nine."

"Excellent. I could not hope for a better reference. I will take them all."

The London Evening Star

Afternoon Edition, Saturday, 24 June 1905

Is So-Called "Christian Academy" Really a Zionist Front?
American Pastor Admits that He Admits Many Jews to His School

By: Jack Breaker

Only a few months ago, in the picturesque small Russian town of Dubrossy, a handsome young Christian boy, Michael Rybachenko was murdered. The Russian police, acting on information from reliable sources, immediately arrested ten people, five men and five women, all Jews and charged them with the horrible crime. And why did they do it? "They used his blood," said the local chief of police, "to make their matzo."

    A similar murder took place in Bohemia in 1899. Agnes Hruzova, a beautiful, hard-working nineteen-year-old seamstress was abducted whilst walking home through the forest. When she did not return home, her friends began a desperate search that ended in the horrifying discovery of her violated body. Her throat had been cut, her blood drained, and much of her clothing torn away. The crime was solved when the police arrested the Jewish vagrant Leopold Hilsner and accused him of killing the innocent Christian girl so her blood could be used in ritual Jewish sacrifices.

    The most famous account of the sacrifice of Christian children for secret Jewish rituals was recorded by the great English poet, Geoffrey Chaucer and appeared in *The Canterbury Tales.* Was it a coincidence that the story was called *The Prioress's Tale?*

The Evening Star has also uncovered evidence that the Berean Academy, a so-called Christian School run by American religious enthusiasts may, in truth, be a front for the training of promising young Jewish men. Is it possible that these young men, like the Jews in Dubrossy and Bohemia, abducted an entire team of virginal Christian girls for sacrifice in secret Jewish rituals?

Lest readers of this newspaper, who may be sympathetic to Jewish concerns, have any doubts, we can also report that this reporter has seen, with his own eyes, a copy of a secret Russian document called *The Protocols of the Elders of Zion* in which the Zionist plans are disclosed for bringing the entire Christian West under Jewish control and forced to participate in traditional blood sacrifices.

The American clergyman, Rev. Reuben Edwards (it could not be established which American seminary gave him his degree, if any truly did) of course vehemently denies any such allegations. But we must remember, so did Leopold Hilsner.

Chapter Eight
Spies Go to Work

THE GOOD SISTER ROSE from her place and walked over to the table where her senior boys were loudly finishing their dessert. I watched as she gave them a stern look and demanded silence, whereupon she leaned down and spoke to them. Several mouths fell open, and nine sets of eyes became as wide as saucers. Quick glances were made in our direction.

"They will meet you in the common room in half an hour," said Sister Miriam when she returned to our table.

"May I assume," asked Holmes, "that these lads are quite familiar with Dover and the regular activities and people of the town?"

"Every blessed square inch; the actions public and private of every citizen; and no doubt countless things of which I do not wish to be informed."

Half an hour later, we assembled in the common room. In front of us stood nine boys, all at attention and all of them having washed their hands and faces, tucked in their shirts and brushed their hair.

"At ease, Irregulars," announced Holmes. Then he began to issue his marching orders. Beginning the following morning, all of them would be assigned to various locations throughout Dover. They were not to draw attention to themselves and must try to avoid being noticed. They would each be issued a small notepad and pencil and were to record anything that appeared out of the ordinary. Note was to be made of the times that anything unusual happened. Under no circumstances should they exaggerate anything so as to try to make themselves seem more important than they were. Most of them would find the day boring, but there was to be no shirking of duty and no abandoning their posts except for short periods to attend to bodily necessities.

All of them nodded vigorously in agreement with each instruction. Once Holmes had finished his instructions, he gathered the boys around a study table and spread out a map of the town. Willy and John were assigned to patrol the castle hill; George and Tommy the docks; Art would have the High Street and Freddy the railway station. The east end of the town and the road leading to the bay and the holiday parks was given to Charlie and the west end and the high fort to Bert. That left just one lad, Jimmy, the smallest of the lot and one who could easily have been mistaken for a boy several years younger.

"Jimmy can take his gully," shouted one of the bigger lads.

"Yeah, let Wee Jimmy guard his precious stream and valley," said another.

I looked at the small towheaded fellow and noticed that he was blushing and fixing his gaze at the floor.

"Jimmy," I said to him quietly. "Come aside; a word with you."

"Do not let them bully you just because you are small," I said. "You have every right to be assigned one of the important posts as any of them do. Where is it that you would like to be posted?"

He shrugged. "I'll take the gully, sir. It's only fair."

"What is fair about it? That doesn't seem fair at all to me," I said.

"It a bit of all right, sir. The rest of them are ticked because Sherlock Holmes is staying in my room and sleeping in my bed and they're jealous. So, it is only fair that I just be a lookout in the gully. Besides, sir, it is where I go in my spare time, and I like it there."

I patted the little chap on the head and sent home back to the table. Holmes completed his assignments and confirmed that they would all report in before supper the following day.

"It is my custom," he said, "to pay my Irregulars a tuppence a day—"

"No," interrupted Sister Miriam. "That would not be fair to the younger boys. These young men will carry out their task for the sole reward of serving their country and the cause of justice. You will all agree to that, won't you boys?"

Again, they all nodded howbeit less enthusiastically than earlier.

"Excellent," said Holmes, "but it would be appropriate to give some reward for work well done. If all of you carry out your assignments conscientiously, Dr. Watson has agreed to purchase a new football and a new rugby ball for St. Vincent's. All the boys, young and old, may enjoy its use."

That was news to me but it brought murmurs of approval from the troop and an approving nod and smile from the headmistress. One of the boys was bold enough to suggest that they could start their postings straight away and work until dark. Holmes considered that offer but declined, saying that they all needed to get a full night's rest before they began their espionage the following morning. I suspected that the entire lot of them were not likely to fall asleep the least bit early.

"Pray tell, Holmes," I said after the boys had departed. "What is it that we are going to do all day tomorrow whilst the orphan boys are doing their spying?"

"We shall meet with the other boys, the ones from the Christian Academy and their headmaster. I trust that both of you will be able to join me."

"I am free to do so," I said.

"I am not," said Lestrade. "Not because I am not interested in those boys' reports. Quite the opposite. But Holmes, you know whose families those girls are from. The heat I am getting from Westminster and the City is enough to singe the hair on my toes. So, I have three more men coming down from London with files on every one of those Academy students and their families and their school and their Pastor Headmaster. They are still our primary suspects."

"By which," said Holmes, "I take you to mean your *only* suspects?"

"And do you have any others?" demanded Lestrade.

"With so little data to go on, I have no choice but to suspect everyone and no one," said Holmes.

"What do you mean, *no one*? Don't talk nonsense, Holmes."

"It remains a possibility, my dear Inspector, that the girls vanished of their own accord. I admit, it is farfetched, but at the moment it cannot be ruled out. But do try to come and join us for supper tomorrow and hear what my spies have to report."

"I'll be there," said Lestrade, followed by a harrumph and his departure out of St. Vincent's and to the room he had commandeered in the hotel.

Chapter Nine
A Christian School?

"GOOD MORNING, MR. HOLMES. You are an answer to my prayers."

"If that is so, Reverend Edwards," said Holmes, "I fear your prayer list is distinctly lacking in ambition."

"No siree, Mr. Holmes. I have been in deep prayer all morning beseeching the Lord to send a miracle that would deliver us from the trials and tribulations that have fallen upon my students. I got up from my knees only a few minutes ago, and here you are already. It is undeniable proof that God knew my need and answered my prayer before I even asked. That is truly a miracle, sir."

We were standing in front of a large holiday tent, and the gentleman we had just encountered was a tall American in his late forties. At one time in the past, he was likely a lanky, handsome young man but the years had added several stone of unflattering weight and subtracted most of his hair. Even though it was a hot day and we were meeting him in a holiday park by the sea, he was dressed in a dark suit and clerical shirt and collar. I have precious little knowledge of theology, but it struck me that if the best miracle that the Almighty, who had created the universe *ex nihilo,* could manage this morning was the timely appearance of Sherlock

Holmes and me then perhaps He was not overly moved by the good reverend's orisons.

Holmes responded in a gracious manner as required for his purposes.

"I am honored to be so chosen, Reverend. Since the good Lord has, in His wisdom, revealed the miraculous purpose of my visit to you and not to me, perhaps you would enlighten me as to what you and He are expecting?"

"Well, Mr. Holmes. That's real easy. I need you to find those girls or at least figure out what happened to them so I can get these blasted British coppers and Press off the backs of my boys."

"Clearly, you are quite entirely convinced that your boys not only had nothing whatsoever to do with the disappearance of the girls but know nothing about it. Is that correct, Reverend Edwards?"

"Absolutely. Could not be more certain of that if the good Lord wrote it in stone in front of me. These boys have been put through hell during the past few days. They've been grilled by the police over and over again and hounded by the vermin of your English Press. The police won't let them leave this site even in the custody of their parents or guardians. It is all I can do to try to keep their spirits up. They are no angels and were most assuredly overtaken in a fault, but they are good boys. They don't deserve what they are going through."

"And what, if I may ask, have you and your boys been doing to try and solve the mystery? Anything?"

"Well, Mr. Holmes, I have been spending hours in prayer."

"Splendid. However, I happen to be a firm believer in the practice of *ora et labora*. Would you not agree?"

Holmes's reference to the Benedictine Order went sailing over the head of the American pastor.

"What I am suggesting," Holmes said, "is that you might put your boys to work to assist in the search."

"Well, that would be real good if the coppers would let them do that. But so far, they have been told they cannot leave the site here. It was all I could do to have them allowed outside of their tents."

"I believe I may be able to assist in that matter. I shall speak to the police officers and see what can be arranged. I expect that these lads would be of greater assistance if put to work than if confined to this site. Before taking any action, however, would you kindly furnish me with a list of the names of the boys who ventured out that night and met with the girls?"

The reverend hesitated before answering. "Mr. Holmes, sir, I don't know if I can do that. You see it has been a struggle to keep the names of the boys away from the Press; otherwise, their families would be hounded to death. I'm sure you can appreciate that."

"I do, and I respect your concern. However, unless you believe that the Almighty has arranged the miraculous appearance of someone who cannot be trusted to keep a confidence, I suggest that you have faith in me. Whatever reputation I am privileged to have has been secured by my never having betrayed the privacy of any client, and your boys are not about to be the first."

"Hmm ... well, all right, Mr. Holmes."

He turned and entered his tent and came back bearing a single sheet of paper.

"This is all of them. An even dozen. All from the senior class."

Holmes looked over the list, and I watched as his brow furled.

"Four of these boys have Jewish names and two are from Hindu families. I had understood that your school was for Christians."

"We are a Christian school, Mr. Holmes. We are founded on Biblical principles and believe in the inerrancy of the Holy Scripture. Those scriptures teach that the Jews are God's chosen people and that they are part of His divine plan before the Rapture can take place. As to other creeds, we follow the injunction of our Lord to 'suffer the little children.' Therefore, we welcome them all into our midst and give all due respect to the practices of their faith."

Holmes carried on, giving eschatology a pass, and we followed the headmaster to the tent line where he called his students to assemble in front of us. He began by instructing every boy to close his eyes and bow his head whilst he delivered a long, audible prayer. Holmes and I remained open-eyed as did most of the boys. We caught several of them looking at us and winked back. They had no idea who we were, but that small act of shared impudence established an unspoken camaraderie between us and the lads we were about to interrogate.

Having finally ended prayer, Rev. Edwards introduced us to the twelve schoolboys. Upon hearing the name of Sherlock Holmes, their faces lit up, and they tussled amongst themselves when asked to form a line and wait their turn to speak with us.

Over the next three hours, Holmes and I met individually with them. My exceptional friend had long ago discerned that all people, regardless of their age or station in life, were far more likely to be guileless and candidly forthcoming when spoken to respectfully. He adhered to this practice whilst cross-questioning the boys, yet he did not fail to ask them very direct questions, even those touching on matters that caused a few of them to blush. Nevertheless, they all responded—some hesitantly—with unvarnished answers. Holmes thanked every one of them, sincerely reminding them that they had helped with his investigation, and gave them a friendly clap on the shoulder. They left our presence feeling more than a bit chuffed.

The problem was that not one of them provided any additional insight into what happened to the girls. As we had been informed by the local officers, every one of them confessed to having disobeyed their school's rules and participated in the rendezvous, but nary a one of them knew anything about the girls after they departed on their bicycles from the castle keep.

"Well. Holmes," I asked after he had finished with the final boy. "Are they telling the truth or have they all brilliantly conspired and colluded?"

He sighed in response. "Unfortunately, they must be telling the truth. It is not without reason that successful criminal gangs seldom engage more than five people. Once the membership surpasses that mark, one of them is bound to be disloyal, break the bonds, and seek his own reward at the expense of his partners. A group of a dozen quickly falls apart. Such is human nature. These lads are all sticking to their original story even though there would be a considerable reward to be had if the truth were otherwise and one of them were to inform on the rest. We shall have to look elsewhere for useful data."

"You told the clergyman that you would arrange to have the restrictions of their freedom loosened. Shall we find the Constable now and do that?"

It was a hot, sultry day and in my medical opinion, I was quite certain that all the lads needed to enjoy a refreshing swim and an informal game of football.

"We shall," said Holmes. "But first, let us walk over to the girls' campsite and see what we can learn from the staff and the younger girls."

The site where the girls from St. Mary and St. Martha were camped was only a hundred yards farther in the holiday park. We walked along a path through a copse of trees to reach them.

The site where they had been camped was completely empty.

Chapter Ten
Banned Books

WE IMMEDIATELY TURNED around and walked quickly back into Dover town. At my insistence, we stopped briefly at the police station and spoke to the Chief Constable. He agreed to send one of his officers out to the holiday park with instructions that the boys were now free to enjoy the beach and the football pitch as long as they did not leave Dover.

Then we proceeded directly to the orphanage to demand of Sister Miriam if she had any knowledge of what had happened to the staff and students from the girls' school.

It would only be a minor exaggeration if I were to report that Sherlock Holmes stormed into the orphanage and demanded to speak to the headmistress. We were directed to the common room in which we had met earlier with the new band of Irregulars. Seated around the room were Sister Miriam, Prioress Priscilla (still looking drawn and weary), a full-bearded, older, blond-haired, blue-eyed gentleman, and a woman I recognized from the society and sports pages of the press, Miss Charlotte Cooper, the famous athlete who had taken the Venus Rosewater Dish at Wimbledon several times and was now employed as the coach of the girls' hockey team.

Sister Miriam looked up at us as we entered.

"Good afternoon, gentlemen. I am terribly sorry, but you have missed the lunch meal. Shall I have the kitchen prepare sandwiches for you?"

I was about to answer in the affirmative as my stomach had confirmed what the sister had said when Homes, to my digestive disappointment, turned down the offer and proceeded straight away to the matters at hand.

"Prioress Priscilla," he said, "where have your students, their tents and their belongings gone? Are you not aware that the police now consider this to be a serious crime and the removing of evidence and witnesses is against the law?"

"I am quite aware of that, Mr. Holmes. Keeping the younger girls here was extremely distressing for them, and I have sent them back to London with instructions that they should be released to their families for the summer. Their well-being is my responsibility and surpasses any fine points of the law. All of the bedrolls and belongings of the older girls have been retained and are stored inside one of the rooms here in the orphanage. You or the police are free to go through everything if you wish."

"Prioress," said Holmes, this time more than somewhat sharply, "the removing of evidence connected to a crime without the explicit permission of the police is itself a crime."

She took a slow sip of her tea and sighed. "Oh, dear. I do not think the police will arrest me, Mr. Holmes. Nothing has been removed. Mr. Steiger will take you to the storage room. If you have any questions, I will be back here for tea at five. Until then, I shall be spending the time in prayer and meditation and do not wish to be disturbed."

For a moment I was sure that Holmes was going to reply with the same admonition from the Benedictine Order that he used when speaking to the American reverend but he caught himself and merely nodded slowly.

"And the files on the missing girls?" he asked.

"Are there as well."

Holmes turned toward the blond gentleman. "Mr. Steiger, if you would please," he said.

The German master rose and with erect military posture and steps began to walk out of the room.

"*Bitte, Herr Holmes. Folge mir,*" he said, and we obeyed.

In the small storage room that was adjacent to the kitchen, the German gestured first to a set of shelves in which were stacked a dozen rolled and tied bedrolls.

"These are the beddings of the girls. You may find all their clothing, toiletries, and belongings. Should you need further assistance, do not hesitate to ask.""

Then he pointed to a small table, on top of which was a pile of files. "The informations of all the girls. *Auf Wiedersehen, meine Herren, haben Sie einen schönen Nachmittag,*" he said and left the room.

"Watson, would you mind," Holmes said, "examining the bedrolls. You are a doctor and a married man and far more at ease than I am in inspecting the personal items of the female sex. But do make a complete record of everything. I shall busy myself with the files."

For the remainder of the afternoon, the two of us poked and pored over the files and the belongings of the missing girls. One by one, I untied the bedrolls and laid them out on the floor. Inside them, I found various articles of clothing, including bathing costumes, jumpers, light cotton skirts, and blouses. Each girl also had and several pieces of undergarments, some of which were practical and appropriate to a girl in her late teen years and a few that struck me as fitting only for a married woman to wear to entice the amorous affections of her husband.

All of the girls, not surprisingly, also had numerous items of reading material. I recalled my own years of camp life when, during the long evenings of the summer solstice, I would lie in my bed and read.

Within the bedrolls, I noted a copy of *Jane Eyre,* every schoolgirl's favorite, two of the recently published and wildly popular *Rebecca of Sunnybrook Farm,* and one of Conrad's *Nostromo,* no doubt being read by a young woman with literary ambitions. Most of the materials, however, were magazines. To my delight, I counted four copies of *The Strand,* each of them containing a different one of my stories of Sherlock Holmes. One young woman had an entire set in which were the sequential chapters of *The Hound of the Baskervilles.* Other girls had brought copies of *Union Jack, The Idler,* and *Isis,* this last one being a satirical effort by students at Oxford. I was not surprised to find a few dog-eared penny dreadfuls featuring the blood-warming stories of Dick Turpin and Black Bess, Sweeney Todd, and Varney the Vampire.

At four o'clock, Holmes put down his last file and requested that the two of us now compare notes. I understood this to mean that I was to report on what I had found and so I did. Naming each of the girls in order, I listed off the items I had found along with a reasonably detailed description. Holmes listened carefully, jotting notes in the corresponding files and then reaching out his long arm toward me so that I could hand him the pages I had made for each girl.

For another half hour, he perused the files again cross-referencing them with the notes. With nothing left for me to do, I picked up a copy of *Rebecca* and had become thoroughly engrossed in it when Holmes interrupted my imaginative wanderings in the far reaches of the State of Maine.

"Come," he said, rising from his chair, "Our good Prioress will have returned by now and I have somewhat to say unto her."

He hurried down the hallway, with me at his heels, and back to the common room. The same cluster of people we had left earlier in the afternoon had gathered there for tea. Holmes strode into the middle of the room and gave the Prioress a hard look and, without apologizing for his lack of manners, broke into their conversation.

"Prioress, I have questions for which I need immediate answers. I trust I will receive your full cooperation."

"By all means, Mr. Holmes."

"You told me that these girls were highly loyal to each other and lived and worked together in an exceptionally unified way, or words to that effect, did you not?"

"I did."

"From their files, I detect a serious split between two factions."

"Do you?"

"Yes. Of the twelve girls on the team, the records of nine of them show a litany of violations of school rules and disciplinary actions that were taken against them. Three of them, however, have not a single black tick against their names and numerous citations for voluntary service to the school and their churches. I assume that you are fully aware of this."

"I am."

"Prioress, for the past quarter century, I have dealt not only with countless individuals but also with all manner of groups, associations, unions, families, and guilds. I have yet to find one in which such a sharp division of character between two factions does not result in enmity and the forming of clearly marked opposing parties. I have every reason to believe that such a situation must exist within your team of hockey players."

"Your conclusions, sir, are very reasonable and altogether wrong."

"Please clarify that remark."

"Do you happen to remember the positions the three girls—those whose comportment has been impeccable—play on the team?"

I watched as Holmes closed his eyes and turned over the pages of the files that he had lodged in his memory.

"Alice Cadbury," he said slowly as if reading from a page that he had retrieved from the recesses of his brain, "is the Midfielder, Edith Booth is the Left Wing, and Sarah Akers-Douglas is the Right Inner."

The Prioress then stood up and took a few steps until she was standing in front of the young woman I recognized as Charlotte Cooper, the finest woman tennis player in England.

"Mrs. Sterry," she said, addressing her by her married name, "would you please describe the three players Mr. Holmes has just named. Were you able to understand what he said?"

The coach stood and moved until she was standing squarely in front of Holmes. She was an attractive woman in her mid-thirties, and even under her modest clothing, I could detect a powerful set of shoulders. I assumed that she, being deaf, chose to stand facing Holmes in order to read his lips as he spoke.

"Those three players," she said, speaking loudly, as is common among those whose hearing is poor, "are the three highest goal scorers on the team. They are also the best attackers in the entire league. They are fierce competitors and never hesitate to charge fearlessly into a melee. Even when they are cut and bleeding, they will never let up. The team could not have won the cup without them, and they are admired and respected by all the other players. The three of them have been given the name of "The Saints" by the other girls but it is a title of affection and adoration. Is there anything else you wish to know about them, sir?"

"No. Your explanation is quite reasonable."

"It may be of interest, Mr. Holmes" the Prioress added, "for you to know that at the beginning of the Michaelmas term last fall, our school hired a new music master. She is an exceptionally talented and spirited African woman from the American city of New Orleans. She introduced our choirs to a hymn from her homeland that is all about the saints who go marching in. The girls' hockey team adopted it, somewhat irreverently, as their theme song and chant it loudly before, during, and after their games. It is another mark of the exceptionally strong unity that prevails amongst in spite of the significant differences in their characters. Does that help to answer your question, Mr. Holmes?"

"It does. Permit me to move on to a much more serious matter."

"As you wish."

"Dr. Watson made a complete record of all of the items that were enclosed by the girls' bedrolls. On average each of them had six or seven books, magazines, yellow back novels, penny dreadful, or serious novels."

"That is not surprising, Mr. Holmes. Girls of that age tend to be voracious readers."

"Three of the girls, however, only had two pieces of reading material. Those three girls also were the ones with by far the highest list of rule violations and disciplinary actions recorded in their files."

"Is that so?"

"What is *so,* Prioress Priscilla, is that you deliberately removed several items from their bedrolls. Why did you do that?"

Looking Holmes directly in the eye, she replied. "Mr. Holmes, in today's world, until a young woman is fortunate enough to be married or acquire an income and assets of her own—an achievement with which far too few are blessed—the only fortune she has is her reputation. Such a precious thing can be taken from her in an instant as the result of the most insignificant indiscretion. I do not wish that to happen to any of my girls and as a result, I have withheld certain items from your examination."

"Your actions are understandable and obviously well-intentioned. They also constitute a flagrant breaking of the law. I will give you my word that I will not violate a confidence. However, if you do not turn those materials over to me immediately, I shall whistle for the nearest set of constables to come and search your rooms until the absconded items are found. I not only cannot promise that local policemen will maintain a similar iron-clad confidence, I would not count on it happening for a minute. Now, it is your choice."

For a minute, she said nothing and simply fixed Holmes with a withering stare. Then she quietly replied, "That is not a choice at all, Mr. Holmes. Please wait here, and I will bring the items to you."

She departed and returned within five minutes, bearing three small canvass sacks, each of which had a baggage tag attached to it that bore the name of one of the girls. She deposited them on the table in front of Holmes. He opened the drawstrings on each the sacks and removed the contents, making three displays of books and magazines. As he laid the items out, I felt myself blushing.

The Prioress's rationale was immediately and overwhelmingly apparent.

Spread out in front of us was a collection of the most outrageous publications of our age. There were several well-worn old copies of *The Pearl, The Oyster* and *Milady's Boudoir* along with complete editions of *Dracula, Fanny Hill, Tom Jones, My Secret Life* and *The Romance of Lust.* To my dismay, the Prioress had also chosen to confiscate issues of the *Strand,* and two copies of a similar magazine from America, *The Boston American.*

Sherlock Holmes glanced dispassionately over the collection without displaying any trace of emotional response. The German master, Herr Steiger, had become wide-eyed in astonishment. Apparently, the Germans either did not indulge their imaginations in such concupiscent pursuits or, if they did, could not imagine that an English schoolgirl would also do so. The only one who seemed amused was Charlotte Cooper, on whose face I detected a trace of a smile which she quickly forced herself to conceal.

I asserted my position as a gentleman of the medical profession and informed the Prioress that I concurred with her actions in trying to protect the reputations of her girls and assured her that such records as I would make would use abbreviated codes that would be decipherable only by Holmes and me. I could not, however, resist one matter on which I took issue with her selections.

"Truly, Prioress Priscilla," I said, "there is nothing harmful in either the issues of the *Strand* or the *Boston American.*"

"The copies of the *Strand* which I removed, Doctor, do not contain any of your fine accounts of the work of Sherlock Holmes in his commendable battle against the forces of evil. There is, however, an article promulgating the forbidden practice of communicating with the spirits of the dead. Such practices are proscribed by the Church as well as being the domain of charlatans. Our girls are better off not being exposed to them."

I thought that was taking things a bit far, but I could see some reason in her position. But I could see none in her removing of the American magazine.

"The leading story in that issue," I said, as I had recently read it myself, "is a fine account of how a brilliant scientist used his intelligence and reason to break out of a prison. He had been locked up in Cell 13, if I recall, and managed to escape. Surely, that is neither dangerous nor offensive."

"Of course not, Doctor. But the final story in the issue claims to be a memoir of a woman who voluntarily submitted herself to the ownership of a wealthy man, was violated and physically punished, and claims to have enjoyed the experience. Not only is such an account utterly abhorrent but it was clearly written by a man, and indeed by a horrible cad with a vile imagination. There is no possibility that any woman would ever descend to such depths of depravity."

I had only read the first few paragraphs of that story and, having found the quality of writing so amateurish, I did not continue. I did, however, agree with the sister's assessment.

I made my notes and handed to Holmes for insertion into the girls' files. He was about to resume his questioning when we were interrupted.

"WE FOUND THEM!"

The American clergyman burst into the room and loudly and triumphally repeated his claim.

Chapter Eleven
Girls on Bicycles

THE SISTERS AND THE STAFF issued shouts of joy.

"You found the girls?" demanded Holmes. "Are they nearby? Are they safe?"

"No, no," explained the clergyman. "But we know what happened to them. My boys found their bicycles."

"Be more specific," said Holmes.

"After I told my boys that they were free to go for a swim, they all did. There is a small beach at St. Margaret's Bay, just past the holiday park. Being fine, modest, young gentlemen, they stepped into the bushes to change into their bathing costumes and came upon twelve bicycles. Right off, they knew who they must belong to. Boys have a brilliant memory for bicycles, and they could identify several of them as the ones ridden by the girls when they met."

"That says nothing about the current location of the girls," said Holmes.

"Well now, I would say it does, Mr. Holmes. "At the far end of the beach is a small dock but the water is deep enough for a private ferry to land. Those girls must have cycled down to the beach after they left my boys and hid their bicycles and boarded a boat. Maybe they were forced. No one can say for sure. But it is a plain as the nose on your face, Mr. Holmes. Those girls are nowhere near Dover now. Those coppers can turn their attention to the south of France, or Paris, or they could even be in Russia by now. You can come and see for yourself and then I expect you will agree with me that all restrictions must now be lifted."

"Please take us there straight away," said Holmes. Then he turned to the sisters and school staff who were quickly gathering up the printed materials on the table before the intruding American could see them.

"I will return and would appreciate an opportunity to continue our conversation."

"Of course, said Sister Miriam. "The supper hour is almost upon us. It will be over by the time you return. Shall I have the kitchen organize a few sandwiches for you to take with you."

"A wonderful idea," I said quickly, before Holmes could decline the offer. Having missed lunch, I was not about to lose my second meal of the day. The bicycles would still be there ten minutes later. Holmes paced back and forth impatiently whilst we waited for the kitchen to deliver two box lunches. I ignored him and chatted with the righteous but amiable American chap about his school.

Once we had been generously provisioned, we set out from the orphanage in the direction of the Back Road that would take us up along the top of the magnificent White Cliffs of Dover. The prioress and the girls' coach elected to join Holmes, Rev. Edwards and me as we walked quickly toward the site.

"I would hope," said Holmes to the clergyman, "you have not disturbed the site. Your boys know how important that is."

"Well now," he replied, "I am real sure that my boys would be careful, but I cannot speak for the police."

"The police?"

"Before coming to find you, I stopped in at the police station and let the local man and that fellow from Scotland Yard know what we had found. They were out the door before you could say *Jack Robinson*."

Holmes grimaced.

Soon we were standing at the edge of the cliffs and looking out over the Channel toward the coast of France. A private ferry would need only a few hours to chug its way from here across to a private dock outside Calais. The more I thought about that possibility and what might have happened to the girls had they been forced to board and taken to France, the more my appetite was diminishing.

One hundred and fifty feet below us was a small stretch of secluded beach that was a favorite of bathers who enjoyed the bracing cold water on a hot summer day. We traversed our way back and forth down six stretches of precipitous switchback path until we were on the beach. At the far end, I could see a cluster of police officers and several small bodies who I assumed were students from the American school. As we trudged up the sand and pebbles, I observed a small man emerge from the woods. He was somewhat stooped and had narrow shoulders and upon seeing us, turned in our direction and stood still. Inspector Lestrade had already arrived at the scene and was waiting for Sherlock Holmes.

"The bicycles," said Lestrade, "are where they were found back in the copse. You can examine them if you want. They have not been closely scrutinized. I told the local officers to wait for you."

"Thank you, Inspector," said Holmes. "That was very decent of you."

"Decency has nothing to do with it. I want this case solved and fast. Do you have any idea what families those girls come from?"

"I have seen the list," said Holmes.

"I suppose I should have expected that. Very well then, get to work."

Holmes and I entered the cluster of trees and bushes that stood at the base of the cliffs. In a small clearing, several local policemen were standing guard over the bicycles, but they permitted us to pass. Respectfully and politely, they did not permit the Prioress and the girls' coach to join us.

"These ladies," said Holmes, "will be able to give positive identification to the bicycles. Kindly let them join us."

Lestrade gave a nod to the constables, and the four of us passed through their barrier.

"Prioress Priscilla and Mrs. Sterry," said Holmes, "please move in as close as you can without disturbing the ground immediately adjacent to the bicycles. Now then, can you state for certain that these are the bicycles of the missing girls?"

The nun turned to face the coach directly and repeated Holmes's instructions slowly so that they could be understood by one who had lost her hearing. The coach nodded and spent less than a minute walking back and forth along the perimeter. She turned to the Prioress, but the nun indicated that she should give her answer to us directly.

"Gentlemen, these are the bicycles of the girls' hockey team. I have seen them at our practices all this past year. If you wish, I believe I can tell you which girl rode which bicycle."

"That will not be necessary, madam, and I thank you for your assistance," said Holmes.

He then turned to Lestrade. "Did you observe any evidence in the surrounding area?"

"There are footprints leading up to the dock, but it has been several days since the disappearance and this beach and dock are used by all kinds of people, mostly the temporary residents of the holiday park. The ground from here to the dock is covered in pebbles and does not readily accept footprints."

"As I have seen," said Holmes. "Pity."

For the next twenty minutes, Homes moved systematically through the bushes and then the pathway leading to the dock. Having done so, he returned to where the two women and I were waiting.

"I require a completely candid answer, ladies. Is it conceivable that this entire team of girls could, of their own volition, board a vessel on a lark in the middle of the night to run off to Paris or some such similar adventure?"

"No," said the coach.

"Inconceivable," said the Prioress.

"Might some of them?" asked Holmes. "Perhaps with some prompting in letters from the outside world?"

The answer to that question came a bit slower.

"It is not beyond belief," said the Prioress, "that the same three girls in whose bedrolls were found the offensive reading materials might have taken themselves on a jolly jaunt to Paris. I wish I could claim the contrary, but I cannot."

"Thank you for your candor," said Holmes. Then he turned to the coach.

"Mrs. Sterry, what would type of shoes would the girls have been wearing if going for a vigorous bicycle ride?"

"Their plimsolls, the same as they would wear during a game."

"As I thought," said Holmes. "Thank you."

Those were his only questions, and the four of us began our trek back to the orphanage, leaving Lestrade and the other officers to make sense of the abandoned bicycles.

Holmes and I walked together, out of earshot of the Prioress and the coach.

"Did you," I asked, "see tracks made by girls' plimsolls? Was that why you asked about them."

"No. There was not a single mark. That is why I asked. Now, several days have passed, and there has been quite a bit of foot traffic at the site, and the ground is not conducive to leaving footprints, but it is curious nonetheless."

It also struck me as curious that the girls would carry their bikes down to the beach rather than hiding them somewhere along the top of the cliffs. I was quite certain that if the thought had occurred to me, it would also have done so to Holmes.

By the time we returned to the orphanage, the twilight was fading, and I was ready to retire to my small room. Holmes appeared to be of the same mind, and he would doubtless spend whatever time he could before going to sleep in intense mental exercise.

We were met in the hallway by Sister Miriam, the headmistress. She handed Holmes an envelope that bore the mark of His Majesty's Government. Holmes opened it, read it and handed it to me. It ran:

Highest priority. Must remain confidential.

Sherlock: Have received news of discovery of the bicycles and agree that girls are almost certainly not in England any longer.

The Cabinet has had further communication from Paris claiming that the girls are being held captive there by the organization calling itself The Order of the Fittest.

They are demanding that that His Majesty's Government publicly declare its support for the Kaiser and his demand that Morocco remain independent. That would place Britain in direct opposition to France and goes against current policy.

The threat is that the girls would either be killed or sold into slavery in the Orient if we do not comply.

Necessary that you abandon Dover immediately and begin investigation in Paris to try to locate captors and girls.

Imperative that you make arrangements to travel straight away.

Mycroft.

I gave the note back to Holmes who proceeded to stand still and stare at it for several minutes.

"Very well, then," he said. "we shall be off to bed and shall catch the morning ferry across to Calais. Thank you, Sister, for your kind hospitality and thank the lads who gave up their beds. Our time here apparently is over."

We bade her a good evening and explained that we did not require any further tea or food and were on our way to our rooms.

"Please, gentlemen," she said. "Have you forgotten? You asked the Irregulars you appointed to be prepared to give their reports before supper. They have been waiting now for four hours for you. They would be so terribly disappointed if you were to ignore them. Could you please meet with them briefly?"

"I am sure we can," I said quickly, before Holmes could object. If the girls were no longer in Dover, it would be no more than a meaningless formality to hear their reports, but if the nine of them had given us their entire day, the least we could do is give them an hour to listen to them.

The London Evening Star

Morning Edition, Tuesday, 27 June 1905

GIRLS BICYCLES FOUND!

"They are long gone from England," admits Scotland Yard.

By: Jack Breaker

As a result of the determined work of the reporter for *The Evening Star* and several other earnest members of the Press, twelve bicycles belonging to the missing girls have been discovered in a secret location on a hidden beach just outside Dover. Scotland Yard and the local Kent County Police admit that they did not move fast enough and it is now a sure thing that the girls have been taken out of England.

"If they have been kidnapped to Paris," vowed Viscount Fallendale, the distraught older brother of one of the girls, "I will go there myself and get them back. I would risk my life to save my little sister."

In the tense surroundings of the Lord Warden Hotel, this reporter delicately posed questions to the parents. They expressed similar feelings, saying that they would spend whatever it cost to bring their "babies" home. These families are not without means. One of them has made the princely offer of Five Thousand Pounds to anyone who can rescue his daughter and added an additional One Thousand Pounds if in doing so they were able to aid in the arrest and conviction of the culprits.

Is Scotland Yard finally willing to admit that they are up against a formidable criminal mind? The famous amateur detective, Mr. Sherlock Holmes, has been seen (in spite of his disguises) in Dover. Reliable sources have informed this reporter that he may be sent to France to try to find the girls, before it is too late.

Chapter Twelve
Flushed with Success

THE NINE BOYS WERE SPRAWLED out across the chairs and sofas in the common room and leapt to the feet when we entered. I could tell that Holmes begrudged the waste of time that the reports now constituted but, out of his sense of duty and fair play, he rose to the occasion and demanded that each of his Irregulars stand and deliver his report.

Willy and John went first and reported on the activities they had observed on the Castle Hill. They took several minutes to account for every quarter hour of the day but in the end had observed nothing more than the comings and goings of the Press and their interviewing of each other. George and Tommy had not only watched the docks but had diligently counted every man, woman, and child that had passed through the gates and, to the best of their ability, ascribed to each of them their assumed nationality and standing. It was a fascinating study of England's immigration and emigration, but there was nothing out of the ordinary.

Freddy reported on the railway station and noted the high number of strangers who were arriving in Dover, most of them, he assumed were either from the Press or members of the boys' and girls' families. The former were loud and cheaply dressed, the latter were the opposite on both counts. Art noted that there seemed to be considerably more than the usual food carts coming from the grocers' buildings and moving up and down the High Street and beyond to the various hotels, guest houses, restaurants, and up the Castle Hill.

Charlie and Bert gave full reports from the West Hill and the eastern edge of the town but admitted that there was nothing unusual in what they observed and insisted that no one could have passed by them unseen.

That left just one boy, Jimmy, the small, shy lad who had agreed to take on the vigil of the stream and gully. He came forward and stood in front of Holmes and me and appeared very ill at ease, saying nothing.

"Come now, Jimmy," said Holmes. "We haven't all night. What did you see today?"

"Mr. Holmes, sir, I was in the gully all day."

"Yes, Jimmy, that is the post you were assigned."

"I like spending my free time there, sir."

"You told us that yesterday. What do you have to report?"

"Except after a rain, sir, the stream is always clear, sir. On hot days I can drink from it, and there's days I have even sat right in it to cool off, and I will be dry by the time I come home, sir."

"A pleasant pastime," said Holmes. "And did you do that today?"

"No, sir. I was frightful hot in the middle of the day, and I was about to cool off but I couldn't."

"And why was that, Jimmy?" asked Holmes, his impatience now only thinly concealed.

"Because of what I saw in the stream, sir,"

"Fine, Jimmy. What did you see?"

The boy now squirmed, cast a few furtive glances over to where the other boys were sitting and snickering, and clenched his fists.

"Turds."

That brought a roar of laughter from the rest of the boys and a barrage of rude, off-color comments. Sister Miriam rose and stood in front of them and demanded silence.

"George," she ordered, "I heard what you said. Now come and stand here and put out your palms."

George winked at his colleagues, and stood with both palms out and facing up. From somewhere within her habit, the sister withdrew a leather strap and gave him a hard, stinging lash on each hand. He winced, but then turned and grinned back at his peers, who gave him friendly punches to his shoulders. The outcry was now diminished to a buzz of whispers.

Holmes returned to Jimmy and now appeared interested in the small fellow's report.

"Expand on what you said, Jimmy," he told him.

"Yeah, Jimmy," came a voice from the cluster of bigger boys. "Were they pebbles or boulders?"

That brought another round of laughter and a strong rebuke from Sister Miriam, who threatened that the next one to speak out of turn would forfeit his role as an Irregular. That shut them up.

"There were some pebbles," Jimmy stated, answering the question that had not come from Holmes. "No boulder turds, no long sausages either. Mostly just regular turds."

"Yes. Keep going," said Holmes.

"They all came in a mass. Lot of them, and then there were none for a long time and then another mass. Whilst I sat and watched, there were three floods of them. About two or three hours apart."

"Are there houses farther up the valley?" asked Holmes.

"No, sir, there's only the woods. And it can't be from the deer, sir. I seen deer turds and they don't look the same, and the deer do it in the woods, not in the stream. These were people turds, sir."

Holmes was now intensely interested.

"That is indeed a report that is truly unusual, Jimmy. Well done. It is too dark now to inspect the valley and stream but at first light tomorrow, we shall do so, and you shall lead us there."

Holmes then turned to the rest of the boys who were no longer snickering.

"If any of you wish to join us first thing tomorrow, you would be welcome. You will be the world's first Irregular Turd Brigade."

That brought howls of laughter, and even the sister and coach joined in. The laughter and comments too crude to be recorded continued as the boys made their way up to their rooms for the night.

First light at the time of year so close to the solstice came before five o'clock in the morning. The night chill still hung in the air, and the Sisters had arranged cups of cocoa, sweet buns, and fruit for the boys who had volunteered for the Turd Brigade. All nine of them were present, bright-eyed and bushy-tailed.

"Jimmy," said Holmes, "please lead the brigade to the site of the mysterious floating turds."

The tiny fellow was not accustomed to leading anyone, but Holmes put his hand on his shoulder and directed him to the front of the column. We crossed around the south front of the Castle Hill until we reached the eastern side of it. At a bridge over a small stream, Jimmy departed from the roadway and descended into a shallow gully. There as a well-worn path along the far side of the watercourse and in single file we worked our way uphill. As we did, the gully became deeper, cutting into the slope of the Castle Hill. The sunshine would not reach the valley floor for another two hours, and there was a distinct damp chill in the still air. The vegetation was lush, with an abundance of the spring woodland flowers gracing the bases of the trees and the edges of the stream. The distinct pungent smell of damp earth and wet forest was not at all unpleasant.

About one hundred yards from where we had departed the roadway, Jimmy stopped and looked up at Holmes.

"It was here, Mr. Holmes, sir. I was sitting on that rock there and thinking about cooling off when I spied them. It was right here, sir."

"Excellent." Holmes turned and addressed the column of Irregulars.

"Sturdy Turdsmen," he shouted and was met with cheers of approval. "The location of the place where the turds entered cannot be lower down the stream from this point. It must be above here. Therefore, the column is to proceed upstream, but at each thirty paces another one of you must stop and take that place as your post. There are twelve of us altogether so we shall be able to spread out along the course of the stream for well over a quarter mile. You are to keep your gaze fixed on the stream and the first person to spot the armada of turds is to shout."

"What are we to shout?" asked Freddy.

Without missing a beat, Holmes replied. "Once more into the breeches!"

We spread out along the course of the stream. Holmes remained at the lowest point, and Mrs. Sterry and I led the boys upstream, dropping one then another off at the prescribed intervals until only the coach and I were left.

"Would you mind, Dr. Watson," she asked, turning to face me directly, "if the two of us worked together. I can play tennis without hearing properly, but I find that being alone in Nature in silence very disconcerting."

Even though I was old enough to be her father, I was flattered by her request. There are few things that surpass the pleasure of an interesting conversation with an exceptional—and beautiful—young woman.

"Tell me, Doctor Watson," she began after the two of us had found the least uncomfortable rock on which to perch, "what was it like to grow up so long ago before they had motor cares and telephones? Did ships still move only by sail when you were a boy?"

For the next hour, I reluctantly recounted life during the Dark Ages and was relieved when she began to ask questions about my past adventures with Sherlock Holmes. I had just started into an account of the treacherous race down the Thames as Holmes and I pursued the diabolical Jonathan Small and his dart-blowing Islander when a cry went up farther down the valley.

In addition to the battle cry Holmes had provided, we could hear shrieks of "Crikey, it's a flood of them!" and similar expressions, most of which are not suitable to be recorded,

We rose and began to hurry our way down to where the first siting had taken place. By the time we reached the critical location, the upstream boys had arrived and were chatting merrily with the primary observers.

"You sure?" demanded one of them, but he was silenced by the arrival of the downstream sentries who were each claiming more numerous sightings of much larger objects.

"Your attention, Irregulars!" shouted Holmes above the din. "You must spread out into the forest. You are looking for the source of the attack. Most likely it will be an old sewer pipe. Off you go."

Within five minutes, one of the lads had found the source. Holmes and I were soon looking down on a small crevasse in the forest floor at the back of which, obscured by mud and undergrowth, was an ancient drainage tile. A small dribble of effluent was still trickling from it and flowing from there into the stream.

Holmes smiled. "I do hate to disappoint you, my dear doctor, but we shall not be going to Paris. That theory was merely a blind and won't do. It appears that the missing girls may still be here in Dover and could be held in captivity somewhere in the labyrinth of tunnels and flushing a bucket now and again."

The London Evening Star

Evening Edition, Thursday, 29 June 1905

Not All Missing Girls are "Angels" Confesses Prioress Headmistress

Could they have run off to Paris of their own accord?

By: Jack Breaker

The Evening Star has discovered that it is possible that not all of the missing girls may have been the paragons of ladylike virtue that English citizens were led to believe.

This reporter was privileged to secure an exclusive interview with another senior field hockey team member who played against the team from St. Mary and St. Martha. That student, who we will not identify out of respect for her age and family reported that, "Those girls were insane. They would stop at nothing to score a goal or defend their goalkeeper. They terrified us. It was like we were facing a dozen mad women who had escaped from Bed'lam."

Where did this highly inappropriate behavior come from? Again, through diligent investigation, your reporter has learned that the entire team—yes, THE ENTIRE TEAM—recently participated in the parade led by Mrs. Emmiline Pankhurst and her new radical organization, The Women's Social and Political Union. That organization has been called by the esteemed Bishop Johnson-Godsboddy, "the most diabolical association of furious, angry harpies to ever have attempted to disrupt the divine order of the Universe."

At a recent rally, Mrs. Pankhurst called not only for giving all adult women the vote but for complete equality of women and men, a completely impossible political change that this newspaper opposes and will always oppose.

Where would such a bizarre policy lead us? It will lead, among other things, to the conscripting of equal numbers of men and women into the Royal Navy and forcing them to share the very cramped sleeping quarters that our brave sailors now accept. And we all know what that would lead to.

Unthinkable ideas like these may have been planted in the fertile minds of these young women whilst attending Mrs. Pankhurst's rally. Did she lead these girls into vain thoughts of emancipation? If so, might that have led them to run off en masse from the loving families and parents and assert their freedom on the streets of Paris. If they have done so, *The Evening Star* will find them and attempt to put some common sense back into their young heads.

Chapter Thirteen
The Arse Door

HOLMES CONGRATULATED THE BOYS on their fine work and sent them back to the orphanage. Reckoning that the ancient drainage tile had been laid in a reasonably straight line, he, Mrs. Sterry, and I worked our way through the trees and undergrowth up the hill until we were standing in the cleared area near the top of the north-eastern slope of the Castle Hill. It had been a steep climb and Holmes, and I were huffing and puffing by the time we reached the top. Mrs. Sterry was not.

"The chamber," said Holmes, "in which the girls are being held must be somewhere under this portion of the castle grounds."

"But why," I asked, "did it not appear on the maps? Why wasn't it found when they searched?"

"That we do not know. However, our next task is to find it."

"But even all those retired hobbyists knew nothing about it," I said.

"True, but it is possible that my newest Irregulars do."

An hour later we were back in the orphanage common room with the maps of the tunnels laid out on a table and the boys who had been so useful to us all gathered around and looking at them.

"What is missing?" asked Holmes.

"Not much," said Willy. "The maps are right good, sir. All the tunnels and rooms we know of are there. Only thing I don't see is what we call the a*rse end door."*

Several of the other boys nodded and muttered their agreement with his assessment.

"And just what," asked Holmes, "are you referring to?"

"It's on the back side of the hill, sir. The main entrance to the tunnels is by the front approach to the castle but on the backside is a small door that's all overgrown and never used, but it still opens and leads into the main tunnels. We call it the arse door because it's on the back side."

"Of course," said Holmes. "We shall have to inspect it, but you are certain that there are no rooms or chambers under the far slope that are not shown on the map?"

"Can't rightly say for sure," said Willy. "There's stories about lost tunnels and rooms all over the Dover coast. No one knows what might be true and what might be legends, but we have been playing in the tunnels for years, sir, and we haven't seen any such secret room."

Holmes again thanked the boys and dismissed them. I had run over to the High Street and purchased the promised new football and rugby ball, and they were about to be put to use.

"We need to pay a visit to the arse door," said Holmes, "and then, I fear, we shall have to go exploring the tunnels again."

Mrs. Sterry was quite adamant that she would accompany us. "If we do find the girls," she said, "they will know and trust my voice. They have all heard it a thousand times from the sidelines. They do not know you and may be fearful of strange men."

"There is, madam," said Holmes, "a serious possibility of running into danger."

"I can run much faster than either of you," she said and came with us.

With electric torches and a map of the tunnels in hand, we walked back up the Castle Hill and over the top to the eastern slope. At precisely the place the boys had marked on the map for the hidden entrance, we found a low, narrow door. Bushes grew in front of it making it impossible to see unless you were right on top, but it was easily accessible once we were facing it. What was more revealing, however, was what we distinctly observed on the narrow path leading to the door.

"Cart tracks," said Holmes as he knelt down to examine them. "There are several sets but all from the same wheels. The freshest were made as late as last night and, given the depth and width of the wheelbase, I would say by a donkey cart. You can observe the small hoof prints as well. Someone is making regular deliveries by way of this door."

"Somebody," I said, "could be bringing food and water and other necessities to them. Shall we lie in wait for the next delivery and then pounce on him? That way we can be sure of catching at least one of them."

"I think not," said Holmes.

I gave him a look that said that I wanted that one explained.

"It would be wise to stand watch over this site until we can confirm what is being delivered and by whom. If they are receiving daily provisions of food and water, it would be highly reasonable to conclude that they are still in acceptable health and are not in immediate danger on that score. I suspect that whoever is carrying out the deliveries in merely a local grocer contracted to do so. Apprehending him would give us little additional data and would certainly tip our hand to those behind the abduction. At this time, they imagine that their ruse of pretending to be in France has worked. It is best that we allow them to continue to think their red herring has tricked us until we know precisely where the girls are being held."

"Are you going to apprise Lestrade and the local officers about the deliveries and what we found this morning in the stream?" I asked. "We did rather bang on about how we were all working together."

"And Mr. Holmes," said Mrs. Sterry, "I am a trusted employee of the school. I am bound to inform Prioress Priscilla regarding the true location of our girls."

Holmes was not comfortable with what the two of us had brought up.

"Yes, yes," he said. "Of course, you are right. We must do that. My hesitation comes from my years of seeing that once a fact is known by several people, it invariably spreads to many more very quickly, ceases to become a secret, and any advantage it might have given over the criminal is lost. Permit me to propose a plan of action that preserves both our integrity and our advantage."

"We are listening," I replied before thinking that it might not be the most sensitive reply when one of the two of us was deaf.

"Very well," said Holmes. "Let us wait a bit before telling them and continue our quest in the tunnels immediately. We will carry out a thorough exploration of the labyrinth and *then* take our information to our associates. Would that be acceptable?"

Both the coach and I nodded our agreement and followed Holmes through the door and into the maze of darkness. I pulled the small door closed behind us lest any of our adversaries happen to pass by. Soon the air became heavy and damp and the only light was from our torches. The passage we had entered was lined with dark brick and only wide enough for one body at a time to move ahead.

"This tunnel is not on the map," I said. "Should we be following Ariadne's example and unwinding a ball of thread or some such precaution in case we get lost?"

"Excellent, Watson. Fortunately, there is an abundance of pieces of chalk on the ground. I have one in hand and will be making discreet marks on the wall as we move. I suggest that the two of you do likewise."

Holmes led the way, and I noticed that he was constantly looking down to the floor of the tunnel trying to see if there had been any tracks or other marks left by those making the deliveries.

There were none. The floor may have been chalk, but it was still sufficiently hard to resist imprints from normal footwear. Plimsolls would be untraceable.

The tunnel followed a straight line for about fifty yards, which should have brought us into a conjunction with the main tunnel system but all that we came to was a dead end. We had passed no passages leading to the left or right, and now it seemed that our efforts had been for naught.

"Deliveries are not made to *cul-de-sacs,*" said Holmes. "We must have missed a secondary passage."

We retraced our steps but found none, and we returned to the solid wall that had blocked our way. We were at a loss.

"Mr. Holmes," said Mrs. Sterry. "Here. This may be a door."

She was shining her torch onto a patch of wall, completely covered by brick. It was obviously just a part of the wall, and nothing looking like a door could be seen.

"Feel it," she said. "Put your hand on it and then put your hand on this part of the wall."

She demonstrated by putting her hand, with fingers spread out on one patch of brick and then on a second patch a couple of feet away.

Holmes and I both did, but I could tell nothing.

"What am I supposed to feel?" I asked, shining my torch in my face so that she could observe my lips as I spoke.

"When you are deaf," she said, "frequencies sensed through touch become your ears. This first piece of wall has a very faint vibration whilst the second has none. Try it again but this time put your hand on the brick, bring your face close and hum."

We did as she told us.

"Yes, there is a difference," I exclaimed. "The small section reverberates. The main stretch beside it does not."

"Brilliant," said Holmes as he was already examining the designated piece of wall with his glass. He put the glass away and grasped one of the bricks that appeared to need its mortar repointed, and he pulled it out. The brick was no more than a thin slice, and only one end of it pulled away from the wall. I heard a distinct click and a small door opened in front of us.

"The brick on the face of the door," said Holmes, "is only a thin veneer but finished to resemble all the other expanses of wall. There is a metal sheet behind it on which the slices of brick have been affixed. Come."

As we stepped through the opening, I noticed that the other side of the small door had also had a thin brick veneer affixed to it, rendering the opening almost impossible to detect. Once I shone my torch around the space we had entered, it was obvious how well the hidden door had been concealed. We were in a section of one of the main tunnels, a stretch that Holmes and I had walked through recently and that the local historical eccentrics had inspected for decades without ever noticing the disguised door.

I was momentarily pleased with my recognition of the space we had entered, and then I became dismayed. Far from discovering the chamber in which the girls were held, we had merely returned to a part of the tunnel complex that had already been thoroughly explored. We had accomplished nothing.

Even in the dim light provided by the electric torches, I could read the same perplexed thoughts on the face of Sherlock Holmes. Then he relaxed into a thin smile.

"Watson," he said, "you do not have a very refined ear from music, but if I were to hum the note of the A below middle C, do you think you could hum the same note?"

"I suppose I could."

"Excellent. Then we shall do so and strongly. Whilst we do so, we shall walk slowly along the tunnels with our faces close to the walls. Mrs. Sterry will accompany us and place her hands on the brickwork and try to feel for any vibrations that might indicate another similarly constructed doorway."

"Do you believe that there is another such door leading to a secret tunnel?"

"I am counting on the lack of imagination of whoever constructed these tunnels and assuming that if they found a way to make a door disappear once, they will have done it twice, or maybe more so. It may be in vain, but we can give it a try; unless you have a better suggestion."

I did not, and the two of us began to hum loudly whilst Mrs. Sterry placed her flat palms one after the other, foot by foot, along the walls. We moved slowly and methodically, checking off each stretch of the tunnels on the map as we progressed. We worked our way first down one side of a tunnel and the back along the other side. After a full two hours, I was giving up hope and worried that the batteries in our torches might give out. I was becoming increasingly suspicious that Holmes's plan was hopeless. And besides, I was getting quite bored with plodding and humming.

As fate would have it, we had returned to the small door through which we had entered the larger tunnel. We had initially turned to our right, and now we started a search moving to the left. We had gone no more than ten yards when Mrs. Sterry stopped and began to move her hands all over a stretch of brickwork.

"Here," she said. "Look here."

Holmes and I both stopped the tedious humming and began to look for the telltale hairline cracks the would establish the edge of a section of a wall that opened.

"Ah ha!" said Holmes. He ran his finger from the floor to a point six feet up. "There is the crack. Now let me see if I can find the handle."

A moment later he gripped the end of one of the pieces of brick veneer and pried it away from the wall. There was a loud, hollow click and the section of wall swung out toward us.

Holmes was positively beaming as he hopped through the doorway and started down a tunnel that was similar in dimensions to the section we had just explored. There was no need to mark our way as the tunnel continued in a straight line and, as best I could reckon, on a bearing of due north. The floor, however, seemed to be rising at a gentle gradient of about four percent. At around the thirty-yard mark, it took a ninety-degree turn to the right and continued in an easterly direction.

"This is good," said Holmes in a whisper. "We are warm. It is coming into line with the drainage pipe."

After another thirty yards, the tunnel suddenly opened up into a chamber of forty feet square with a ceiling that was higher than what we have been walking through. We stopped and, in the silence, I thought I heard something.

"Holmes? Do you hear what I think I hear?"

"Yes. I hear … singing. The tunnel must continue beyond here and whilst we must not get our hopes up too soon, it appears to be leading us to the girls."

"Mrs. Sterry," I said turning to face the coach. "Can you feel the vibrations. It's the girls, and they're singing.

She stood completely still for several seconds and then broke into a broad smile.

"Yes. I feel them."

We flashed the light of our torches along the opposite wall looking for a continuation of the tunnel but did not immediately see an opening. So, we made our way over to that wall and began to move along it slowly.

We stopped.

I was deafened by the loud, ear-shattering retort of a revolver firing. A bullet struck the wall just above our heads sending fragments of brick down on our faces and into our eyes.

Chapter Fourteen
Blame the French

MY MILITARY TRAINING responded reflexively. I dropped immediately to the floor, pulling both Holmes and Mrs. Sterry with me. In doing so, I dropped my torch, and once I was prone, I started to wiggle my way towards it.

"DO NOT MOVE!" came a command from behind us. "There is a gun pointing at you, and you will be shot, all three of you, if you so much as move a muscle."

Then there was silence.

"Are you going to introduce yourself?" asked Holmes. "No need to forget your manners."

There was no answer. My torch, still turned on but lying a couple of yards beyond my reach, gave sufficient light to the room that the three of us were exposed. Whoever held the gun was not.

"Whoever you are," said Holmes, "you cannot just stand guard over us forever. Do speak up."

From a dark corner of the room came a reply.

"Mr. Sherlock Holmes, Dr. John Watson, Miss Charlotte Cooper, my name is unimportant. I am merely the hired spokesman for an exceptional order of brilliant and powerful people who seek to make this world the best place possible for the best people. This is the second time, Mr. Holmes, that you have discomfited them and they are not at all pleased with you. You were observed entering the tunnels by the northern door, and your shrewd detection of the passage was also recorded. Your cleverness, sir, is to be your downfall. You will now serve as the one who will convey the demands of the captors of the school girls to the highest powers in England. Your reputation for honesty and incorruptibility will now serve to *their* benefit."

"And if I refuse?" said Holmes.

The disembodied voice answered. "That is not a tenable position. For each day you delay, starting with the day after tomorrow, one of the girls will be executed. I advise you not to even consider the possibility. Is that understood, Mr. Holmes?"

"Understood. Very well then, what are your demands?"

"One: that His Majesty's Government immediately issue a statement supporting the continued independence of Morocco and opposing the claims of the French to extend the hegemony over it. Two: that a public statement be made that His Majesty's Government will undertake a review of their *Entente Cordial* with the French, so recently and foolishly entered into."

"And if those demands are refused?" asked Holmes.

"This tunnel has been mined with explosives. If the demands are not agreed to, the tunnel will be blown up, and the beloved daughters of the most powerful men in England will die a slow and miserable death from thirst and starvation. Kindly do not bother responding to what you have just been told. You need to leave this tunnel now and deliver these demands. If you do not, I will have to shoot you and your companions. Now leave, Mr. Holmes."

The three of us slowly stood up and began to walk back out of the chamber. Mrs. Sterry suddenly turned around and faced the far wall.

"M AND M GIRLS!" she screamed. "HURRY! HURRY! SPIT! SPOT!" and then clapped her hands twice. After a second of silence, her shout was responded to by a distant roar of joy echoing back through the tunnel.

The deafening bang of the gun again filled the chamber and fragments from the ceiling rained down on us.

"Do not dare do that again," said the voice. "You will regret it if you do."

We walked in silence until we had exited through the concealed door and were back in the main tunnel.

Holmes was lost in concentration. I could almost hear the wheels of his exceptional mind whirring with one plan of action after another. I looked over at Mrs. Sterry who, to my surprise, was glowing. She noticed my questioning look and grabbed my arm with both hands.

"They are alive, Doctor. It is my absolute conviction. They are all together, and they are alive."

Yes, I thought to myself. They are, but they may not be for long. I feared that the government would not bend an inch in agreeing to the demands. The *Entente* with France had taken years to sort out and upon being signed had been hailed as a great accomplishment with the promise of long-lasting peace between two countries—indeed, two empires—that had spent the better part of the past five centuries at war with each other.

"Yes," I replied, "they are alive, and they are here and not in France. But they are very much in peril."

Being deaf, she had not heard the demands and threats. I turned to face her and repeated what we had been told. Mrs. Sterry now walked in pensive silence until we had exited the tunnel by way of the main door and were standing back outside the castle.

"Doctor Watson," she said. "If these men who have taken the girls captive were to hurt any one of them, the rest would become a deadly swarm and kill him. They are fiercely loyal to each other, and I mean to the point of death. That is who they are."

Part of me wished that I had had the opportunity to watch them play field hockey, but that would have to wait for a better day. I turned now to Holmes.

"Well my friend," I said. "What now?"

"We shall have to inform Lestrade and the Prioress. Like Mrs. Sterry, they will be relieved to know that the girls are alive and in England but heaven only knows what bumbling course of action they will now take."

We departed the castle and this time Holmes and I did go immediately to inform both the police and Mrs. Sterry went in search of the Prioress.

"How many guards do they have," demanded Lestrade. "Are they armed? Who are they? Did you recognize any of them? Did you see any evidence of dynamite? How can you tell if the tunnel back to the girls has explosives in it?"

For these and many other questions, we had no definite answers. Nevertheless, Lestrade, Chief Constable Pughsley and the other police officers were visibly relieved to learn that the girls were alive and still in Dover.

"It's none of my business," said Lestrade, "but frankly, I wish Whitehall would tell the Frenchies to get out of Morocco. The British Empire needs to control that stretch of the Mediterranean. Maybe the Cabinet will come to their senses and agree to the demands. That would make our job a whole lot easier. And the girls would be back to their families in a few days, all safe and sound."

"And what do you suppose is the likelihood of that happening?" asked Holmes.

Lestrade sighed. "About bloody zero. Well then, what are we going to do to foil this nonsense. And if any one of those girls ends up dead, Scotland Yard will be called incompetent for the next decade. Mark my words on that."

"I do not expect that to happen," said Holmes. "I am sure there is a way to put our brains and imaginations to work and come up with a way to beat these rascals."

"You think so, do you? Well, would you mind terribly, Mr. Holmes, telling me what it is?"

"Not yet."

"Bloody hell! Why not? If you know something, then I need to hear about it and now!"

"I cannot enlighten you, my good Inspector, because I do not yet know what it is. Now, if you will excuse me, this case has some exceptional points of interest and I must take time and contemplate the conundrum."

Holmes and I returned to the orphanage. I tried once to engage him in conversation but to no avail. He was lost in his thoughts, and we continued in silence. Upon reaching the St. Vincent's buildings, he went immediately to small room he had borrowed from Jimmy, and I did not see him again until the next meal time.

"Congratulations, Mr. Holmes," said the Prioress as we were served yet another bowl of stew, enhanced this time by a small clump of fresh vegetables. "You found them. We cannot thank you enough."

Holmes turned to her. "Thank you, Prioress. Permit me to remind you, however, that the contributions of your remarkable coach, Mrs. Sterry, were critical to the discovery and that the task is far from over. The girls are still in peril."

"Surely, Mr. Holmes," the Prioress responded, "the Home Office, the Foreign Office, and Scotland Yard will all assign their best and brightest now and work out some sort of solution."

"I fear that they will do exactly that."

He returned to his silence. The rest of us chatted on and speculated concerning the next steps the powers that be were likely to take. We had just begun on our desserts when a telegram boy arrived and delivered an envelope to Holmes. He read it, grimaced, and handed it over to me. It ran:

To: Mr. Sherlock Holmes

From: G. Lestrade,

    Chief Inspector, Scotland Yard

Scotland Yard and His Majesty's Government express their profound gratitude to Mr. Sherlock Holmes for his success in discovering the location of the kidnapped girls from the St. Mary and St. Martha School.

As the task assigned to you was to find the missing girls, we can now confirm that that task has been accomplished satisfactorily. Therefore, by this notice, we are concluding our Agreement for the use of your services. Full payment of your standard fee will be forwarded within thirty days. Kindly submit a record of your expenses for reimbursement.

We thank you again for your excellent service. Please note that all the boys from the Christian Academy have been released and will soon be on their way back to Reading.

I could feel the eyes of the rest of the table watching me as I read, and to allay their curiosity, I handed the note on to the Prioress.

"Wonderful news," she exclaimed.

"Pardon me, Sister," I said. "I see nothing wonderful at all. Your girls are still in grave danger, and Sherlock Holmes has been removed from the quest for saving them. What is wonderful about that?"

"It is wonderful, Doctor, because he will now be working for me, which, if you will recall, was my initial request when we met in London. His task will be to secure the safe return of my girls. May I assume, Mr. Holmes, that you are in accord with my decision?"

The London Evening Star

Afternoon Edition, Thursday, 29 June 1905

MISSING GIRLS FOUND!

Finally, Scotland Yard locates the hockey team but can they be rescued?

By: Jack Breaker

Acting on a tip from a fellow diligent and dedicated reporter, Scotland Yard finally recognized the foolishness of thinking that the missing girls were in France and searched in the maze of tunnels under the great Dover Castle.

All of the girls are there and are alive and well. It turns out that they were not, as first suggested by official sources, abducted for immoral purposes but are being held by a group who describe themselves as patriots fiercely loyal to the British Empire who are passionately opposed to the expansion of French power next door to British Gibraltar.

The only demand they are making before promising the safe return of the girls is that the Foreign Office let the world know that Great Britain supports the rational demand of Kaiser Wilhelm II, the grandson of our dear departed Queen Victoria, that Morocco remain independent instead of allowing it to become a colony of France and its harbors used to shelter the French navy.

This demand is eminently reasonable and should be acceded to by the mandarins at the Foreign Office. British citizens must ask ourselves, "Do we truly trust the French?" For the past five hundred years, the only answer to that question is a profound NO!

The Evening Star is calling upon our readers, the intelligent and informed citizens of England's green and pleasant land, to join us in this crusade. BRING OUR GIRLS BACK AND GIVE THE BOOT TO THE FRENCH!

Let your Member of Parliament know today.

Chapter Fifteen
Not Still Going Strong

WHETHER IT CAME from the local officers, Scotland Yard, or one of the mandarins in Whitehall will never be known. Whatever the source, the news of the discovery of the girls in a secret tunnel under Dover Castle appeared in the morning edition of *The Times*. Also revealed were the demands and threats of the group who were holding the girls. As *The Times* was known as a serious and responsible newspaper, the populace assumed the story was true and they, along with scores of reporters, once again swarmed the castle keep and the steps of the St. Vincent's orphanage.

Holmes and I were sitting in Jimmy's little room reviewing what we had learned and swapping ideas for our next step when Sister Miriam knocked on the door.

"Gentlemen, I am sorry to disturb you, but the inspector from Scotland Yard has requested that you come to the door. I must warn you that there are at least a dozen reporters who have followed him."

Lestrade was waiting at the front door. Behind him stood a phalanx of uniformed constables. Lestrade must have handpicked them for they all seemed to me to be on the young side. Except for the Chief Constable, there was not a weathered face amongst them.

"It appears," said Lestrade, a sheepish smirk on his face, "That we require one more piece of work from you, Holmes. Kindly come with us now and show us where the hidden door to the secret tunnel is located. We cannot find it."

Holmes nodded, and he and I fell into line behind Lestrade, and the dozen police officers formed an impenetrable blue wall keeping the Press at bay.

Like a parade of laborers, we wound our way through the streets of Dover and up the Castle Hill road until we reached the cutaway in the hill that held the main door to the tunnels. Several of the curious local townspeople had watched from their windows and decided to join us. Looking behind me, I could see the entire motley crew of our orphan Irregulars scampering along at the end of the line.

Lestrade turned and faced the crowd.

"Now hear this!" he shouted. "This is a police operation. All the rest of you are to stay well back. Anyone interfering shall be charged with obstructing the police."

He was met with questions shouted by a few of the reporters which he duly ignored.

We entered the dark tunnel, now somewhat lighted by electric torches of the constables. The local folks and the Press had no lights to guide them, and many of them dropped off as we penetrated farther and farther into to bowels of the Castle Hill. By the time we reached the stretch of wall in which the secret doorway was located, only a few intrepid reporters and members of the parents' committee were still behind the constables, but behind them was our troop of Irregulars whose laughter and raucous jibes at each other could not be extinguished by their constant falls and stumbles as they staggered along in the darkness.

Without saying a word, Holmes walked up to the brick wall and reached for the one slice of brick that served as a door handle, pulled it away, and swung the door open.

To our shock and amazement, the space behind the door was lit up by a lantern. A man was standing there, dressed to the nines, much like the striding chap who had recently appeared on bottles

Red and Black Whiskey claiming to have been born in 1820 and still going strong.

"Good morning, gentlemen," he announced in a loud theatrical voice. "Allow me to introduce myself. My name is Dabney O'Dowd. Some of you no doubt recognize me from my highly praised performance as Iago in last summer's outdoor theater in Blackpool. Let me begin by assuring you that I have had no part in any criminal activity, no more than I was responsible for the deaths of Desdemona and Othello. I am merely the hired spokesman for a loyal group of English citizens who are so deeply and passionately concerned for the future of the Empire that they have been driven, with no choice, to such unpleasant tactics as the temporary sheltering of these fine young daughters of England with the hope that some sense will be brought into the minds of the Members of Parliament and the Prime Minister and his Cabinet.

"I have been chosen," he continued in stentorian voice, "to serve as the humble intermediary and to convey to the fine order of men loyal to the Empire, your willingness to meet their demands. After which, the girls will be released unharmed."

"Prove to us that all of them are still alive," demanded Lestrade.

"A most reasonable request," said O'Dowd, "and one that was rightly expected."

He turned and shouted back into the tunnel.

"Miss Alice Cadbury, will you please come forward."

From the dark recesses of the tunnel, a strapping young woman appeared. The light beams from several electric torches were directed to her face. She reflexively squinted in pain and the beams were lowered. Her face was marked with patches of grime, her hair was a mess, and her clothing somewhat disheveled, but otherwise she appeared to be in good health and was walking confidently.

She looked around at the people standing in front of her, and her eyes settled on Mrs. Sterry. They smiled at each other and exchanged a thumbs up gesture.

"Miss Cadbury," intoned the actor. "Please tell this gathering of fine people how you and the other girls are getting on."

She gave him a look a disdain and turned to the crowd.

"We are all alive and in good health. We have received adequate food and water and have not been beaten or physically harmed. Beyond that, we are prisoners, confined to a dark chamber and sleeping on the bare floor but we do have blankets. What else is there to say?"

"Nothing at all, my dear," said O'Dowd. "And as a gesture of goodwill from those loyal citizens who have had to confine you, I can announce that you are now free to leave your temporary prison and rejoin your family."

Again, she gave him a look of utter contempt.

"Don't be an ass. I am not about to leave my team."

With that, she turned around to walk back into her prison.

"Ah, such a brave girl," said O'Dowd and patted Miss Cadbury on her backside as she passed him. That was not a wise move.

In a lightning move, she swung around and smashed her right fist into his face. He staggered back against the wall. She continued on her way back into the tunnel, and the crowd let out a spontaneous, sustained cheer.

O'Dowd had his hand to his mouth and nose, and soon blood started seeping from behind it and dripping down his white cravat and red suit jacket. In that state, he motioned for Lestrade to come forward and the two of them fell into a quiet conversation that I could not hear. I assumed that Lestrade, being as he was an experienced, veteran police inspector, was negotiating for more time. O'Dowd, handkerchief still to his face kept shaking his head.

Finally, Lestrade stood back and turned his head slightly and nodded.

In a unified rush, four of the young police officers ran past O'Dowd. A split second later, Charlie, one of the orphan Irregulars broke out of the crowd and followed them.

Another two constables moved forward, grabbed O'Dowd's arms and snapped a set of handcuffs on to his wrists. A look of horror came over his face, and he turned and screamed down the tunnel.

"NO! NO! STOP! It will explode. You will die!"

Nothing happened.

From the back of the crowd, one of the reporters broke past the police line and also ran into the tunnel.

"NO, YOU BLOODY FOOL!" O'Dowd shouted. "You're a dead man!"

Again, nothing happened ... and then it did.

A thunderous explosion blew out of the tunnel door. A cloud of dust and brick fragments came with it. O'Dowd and the officers holding him were knocked off their feet, and the rest of us grasped for our handkerchiefs or sleeves to avoid breathing in the thick dust.

Coughing and sputtering, we all staggered back to our feet.

"You fool! You stupid fool!" screamed O'Dowd at Lestrade. "Your officers are all crushed, and your girls will die!" His mouth was open, and horror was in every lineament of his face.

"Take him away," Lestrade ordered his constables. They lifted and dragged O'Dowd through the crowd, using their bodies to protect him from the hands of the few members of the parents' committee who had made it all the way to the secret door in the tunnel. Otherwise, his eyes might have been scratched out and his face beaten to a pulp by the gauntlet of enraged parents and siblings through which he had to pass.

A cluster of constables formed around Lestrade and plowed their way through the crowd. At first, the reporters shouted questions at him, none of which were at all respectful. The parents chimed in until we reached the entrance of the tunnels and emerged into the daylight. There, the other parents and curious local citizens were still waiting. Information was exchanged informally, and the din of shouts and questions died as the tragedy of what had taken place settled on the crowd. The parade back down the hill and into the town was akin to a funeral procession. No one spoke.

Chapter Sixteen
The Problem of Cell 13

IT WAS A VERY GLOOMY lot that sat around the common room an hour later. Holmes had installed himself in an armchair, drawn his long legs up underneath his torso, closed his eyes and brought his hands together, fingertips touching. On his darkening face, only his lips occasionally moved. Twice he stood up, paced the room and stared earnestly out the window for several minutes before returning to the Buddha-like pose.

The Prioress had retreated into the adjacent church to pray, leaving Sister Miriam, Mrs. Sterry, Mr. Steiger, and me to descend into despair.

"How long, Doctor," asked Sister Miriam, "can they survive?"

"Without food, up to four weeks. Without water, four days. If the temperature in the chamber falls, they could die overnight. Fortunately, it is summer, and they have blankets, so that is not likely. Miss Cadbury said that they had been provided with water, which leads me to fear that they do not have a source of it where they are. That could become very dangerous."

That was the end of our conversation.

Two hours later, Constable Pughsley came by.

"Thought you folks might like to know that they found a mining engineer in town and he's taken a look at the collapsed tunnel."

"Yes," I said. "What did he say?"

"It's not good. The entire complex is cut into chalk, and is not particularly stable. Not like cutting into granite. Dynamite is out of the question; it could cause the entire maze to fall in. The tunnel will have to be cleared by hand and then reinforced every yard. The old brickwork held it up for all these years, but it has collapsed."

"How fast can they move," I asked.

"There is only enough room for three or four men to work alongside each other. Even if they work in shifts around the clock, they will not be able to move more than five yards a day."

"Merciful heavens," I sighed. "It was at least thirty yards from the door back to where we were shot at. God only knows how much further it is beyond there."

"As I said, it is not looking good."

He gave me a friendly pat on the shoulder and a nod to the others before departing.

We returned to our silence. The late afternoon passed into evening and we ate our dinner in shared misery.

It took me a long time that night to fall asleep. I was worried sick about the dreadful prospects facing the girls and utterly depressed over the death of the policemen, Charlie, and the reporter. Somewhere around one o'clock in the morning, I finally fell asleep.

I was awakened at five by a pounding on my door.

"Watson!" Holmes was shouting from the other side. "Come. There is a longshot but we have to take it."

In a trice, I was in my clothes and out into the hall.

"Come. We shall have to find Prioress Priscilla."

I followed him as he rushed down the stairs and into the kitchen, where the cook staff had started to prepare breakfast for the boys.

"Where is the Prioress?" he demanded. "Where is she? We must see her immediately."

"Sir," said one of the cooks, "she is in the church. She has spent the night in prayer. We never disturb her when she is at prayer, sir."

Holmes ignored the caution and turned and nearly ran through the building until we entered the church. The light of the early morning summer sun was already streaming through the stained-glass windows. In the glow, I could see Prioress Priscilla kneeling against the communion rail.

"Prioress Priscilla! Come! This instant!" Holmes shouted.

She looked over at him, clearly shocked. The sacrilege of interrupting a nun whilst at prayer had not bothered Holmes one bit.

"Really, Mr. Holmes—"

"Do not argue! Come! Now!"

"What is it?"

"Go and get those three canvass sacks in which you placed the forbidden reading material and bring them to the common room. Immediately!"

"Mr. Holmes—"

"Just do it! Now!"

She glared at him but acquiesced and a few minutes later appeared back in the common room bearing the three sacks. Holmes, somewhat rudely, grabbed them from her and dumped the contents out onto the table. He rifled through the books and magazines and selected two items—the copies of the *Boston American* magazine that had been deemed unfit for young minds to absorb. He thrust one of the copies into my hands.

"Watson, quickly. Re-read the first story. Read quickly but carefully."

I opened the magazine to page five, on which I found the title, *The Problem of Cell 13* by an American writer, Jacques Futrelle. I had never heard of him before.

I was not at all sure what Holmes was up to, but I learned long ago to simply be quiet and do what he told me once he had entered into one of his searing, intense states. And he was in one now.

I sat in one of the armchairs and quickly re-read the fictional story of Professor Augustus F. S. X. Van Dusen, or, as the press liked to call him, *the thinking machine.* The story was highly engaging and not overly long.

Whilst we read, Holmes was constantly jabbing at the text with a pencil and muttering to himself. I carefully underlined a few excellent sentences and plot devices that I thought I might borrow for my future efforts. It took both of us around twenty minutes to finish the story, during which time Sister Miriam and Mrs. Sterry came and quietly sat down in the room along with Prioress Priscilla, but they were giving us very queer looks.

"Are you finished?" asked Holmes.

"I am," I replied.

"Do you see the little light it throws upon the mystery of the girls imprisoned in the Dover tunnels?"

"I suppose so, but do you believe that any of them would think of catching a rat and using it as a means of communicating with the outside world? That was quite a unique action by this professor fellow."

"If they have read this story, then it should come to them."

He then turned to the girls' coach.

"Mrs. Sterry, is it likely that any of the girls on the team would be frightened by a rat?"

She looked at him as if he had descended from another planet.

"No."

"Would they hesitate to kill one using only a rock or a shoe if they had to?"

"Perhaps for two seconds but after that, the rat would be a goner."

"Excellent. What if they had to capture a live rat and hold it in their hands."

She paused before answering that.

"Half of them might shy away from that, but the others would do it if for some reason they had to. Why in the world are you asking me about rats?"

"Because there is a possibility—not a strong one, I admit, but a possibility all the same, that they may copy what they read in this story and use one to communicate with the outside world. Now then, Sister Miriam, would you mind terribly organizing my Irregulars straight away. I have great need of them."

"I can do that, sir, but I will have to wake them up, and they will not have had any breakfast. They might be somewhat cranky and uncooperative."

"Yes, yes. Well then promise them ... oh, good heavens, I don't know ... promise them two extra rashers of bacon and a treat of peaches and cream if they get to work forthwith. Would that do it?"

"And a piece of chocolate?"

"If that is what it would take, then by all means. I will meet with them on the steps outside the front door. The chill morning air will get their blood moving."

Twenty minutes later, our eight newest Irregulars—Charlie was missing—were standing, shivering a little, in the morning sun on the pavement outside the St. Vincent buildings. There was an odd mixture of bleary-eyed somnambulism and chattering excitement bouncing around within the group.

"Come with me, lads," said Holmes. "We have to return to the spot where you found the drainage tile."

He set the pace at a forced march, and the boys hustled and skipped to keep up. Mrs. Sterry brought up the end of the line. We followed the road to the small bridge, descended to the stream—now re-christened *Jimmy's Creek*— and began working our way up the hill, through the trees and bushes. In the early morning, all of the vegetation was wet with dew, and soon my trousers had become damp and clammy as were the shorts and socks of the boys. But not one of them complained. Whinging does not elicit much sympathy amongst boys who had had already lost their parents and faced hardships that most of us have never, thank heaven, had to endure. So, onward and upward we trudged.

Ten yards below the spot where the drainage tile had been found, Holmes had the boys stop and form a line, standing apart from each other by the distance of the outstretched arms when the fingertips could barely touch. He moved the line over until they were nearly twenty yards to the left of the stream bed and roughly parallel to it.

"Now then lads," Holmes said to them, "you are not looking for turds this time. You are looking," Holmes continued, "for a small piece of paper, most likely folded, on which there will be a message, probably addressed to either Mrs. Sterry or Prioress Priscilla. You will keep your distance from each other and will move very slowly forward, carefully looking at every inch of the forest floor as you pass. When you come to the stream, cross over it and continue doing the same thing on the other side until I tell you to stop. Is that understood?"

In the story, the professor had, on a wager, allowed himself to be locked up in Cell 13 of a major prison in New England. He had brilliantly unwound a long stretch of thread from his clothing, attached one end of it along with a message to the leg of a captured rat and then set it free in an old sewer pipe. As he expected, the terrified rat ran through the pipe until it reached the open field beyond the prison wall. One of the boys who was playing baseball in that field found the envelope and, with the promise of a reward for doing so, delivered it to the professor's accomplice, leading eventually to his escape. Holmes was banking on the girls' trying the same ploy. It was a long shot, a *very* long shot, but it was within the realm of possibility.

On Holmes's command, the line began to move slowly. Once or twice a shout went up, but whatever one of the boys had observed proved not to be what we were looking for. This continued until they reached the stream, crossed over it and carried on the same distance on the other side. Holmes halted the search and had the line move up the hill, keeping the distance between each of the Irregulars. They turned around and now moved slowly back toward the stream, crossed it and moved back until they were in line with where they had started.

Again, Holmes moved the entire line up the hill, and they methodically turned around and started the dragnet moving back toward the stream.

The line had shifted up the hill three times, and still nothing had been found. I was losing hope and prepared to suggest to Holmes that we call off the exercise when a cry went up.

"I've got it!"

That was immediately followed by, "I've found one too!"

And then a third, "Me too!"

"Brilliant," shouted Holmes. "Bring them here."

Three notes, apparently identical in content, were handed over to Holmes. He gave them a cursory glance and looked over to Mrs. Sterry.

"My dear coach, your girls are even smarter than the professor. They wrote out three copies, using the principle of redundancy to greatly increase their odds of success. Now, what do they have to say?"

He read one and handed the others to Mrs. Sterry and me. Mine read:

To whosoever finds this note. Please deliver it to either Sister Priscilla or Mrs. Charlotte Sterry of the St. Mary and St. Martha School and you will receive a generous reward.

Dear Headmistress and Coach: We are all alive but have no source of food or water. If our attempt to reach you has been successful, you will find a thread in the dry drainage pipe not far from where you found the note. N.B. Not the wet sewer pipe.

Please find a way to get water to us as soon as possible. We have very little.

Yours very truly,

The Senior Hockey Team

The London Evening Star

Morning Edition, Monday, 3 July 1905

DEATH OF A FEARLESS MARTYR

Heroic reporter sacrifices his life bravely trying to unearth the truth.

By: the Editors

It is with deep sadness that *The Evening Star* reports the tragic death of our intrepid young reporter, Mr. Jack Breaker.

In the final heroic act of his all-too-short life, John David Breaker raced past the obstructions of Scotland Yard in his passionate quest to bring the truth of the story of the kidnapped girls of Dover to the eyes of the citizens of Great Britain. As he ran down the tunnel under Dover Castle, attempting to reach the trapped girls, the tunnel collapsed. No doubt, his dying regret was that he could not file his story on time.

"Like so many of our reporters," said Osmond Mosley, the publisher of *The Evening Star*," Jackie was concerned for only one thing – the truth. Our thoughts and prayers are with his friends and family."

"Our brother," said his older sister Elizabeth, "always put his concern ... ahead of everyone and everything else in life."

The terrible event took place yesterday in the dangerous depths beneath the castle where Jack Breaker and his other colleagues in the British Press had discovered the entrapment location of the missing girls. Common sense, a commodity of which Scotland Yard is in short supply, had dictated that the powers that be should negotiate with the captors and work to resolve the crisis peacefully to the benefit of all concerned. Ignoring Mr. Breaker's advice, several police constables stormed the tunnel, leading directly to its collapse and the death of our reporter.

In recognition of the example set by the exceptional young man, *The Evening Star* has established a bursary for those students who wish to follow in his footsteps so that they may pursue their rigorous studies at Kent University. Readers wishing to be a part of this eternal memorial may send their contributions care of the editor.

Chapter Seventeen
The Morse Concerto

```
MORSE CODE

A •−          J •−−−      S •••
B −•••        K −•−       T −
C −•−•        L •−••      U ••−
D −••         M −−        V •••−
E •           N −•        W •−−
F ••−•        O −−−       X −••−
G −−•         P •−−•      Y −•−−
H ••••        Q −−•−      Z −−••
I ••          R •−•
```

"IRREGULARS!" HOLMES SHOUTED. "One more task. There is a second drainage tile, and it should be close to where the notes were found. Please look for it."

"No need, sir," replied one of the lads. "It's right here, sir. We saw it when we were looking for the notes."

"Well done!" shouted Holmes. Then he turned to Mrs. Sterry and me.

"Come now; we have to find that thread and make use of it."

"Holmes," I said. "Are you not forgetting something? Your Irregulars."

"Oh, yes. Thank you, my dear doctor. Irregulars! Gather round."

He extracted a five-pound note from his wallet and entrusted it to George with instructions to take the gang of them after lunch to the dining room of the Lord Warden Hotel and order a round of peaches and cream."

That brought a round of whoops and laughter.

"Oh, Mr. Holmes, sir," said George. "They would never let the likes of us past the door of that hotel. It's only for snoots and snobs. Not for us orphans."

"Ah, that is a shame," said Holmes. "In that case, you will have to go to the pub and ask for the same thing. There should be enough money for two servings each."

That brought a cheer, but then Bert spoke up.

"Mr. Holmes, sir. That is right good of you, sir. But it don't seem right for us to be eating peaches and cream when Charlie is missing and could be dead."

That comment threw a wet blanket over the troop and elicited a sympathetic reply from Holmes.

"Well spoken, young man. Very well, then. The money is entrusted to George. The celebration will be postponed until Charlie has been found and restored to your ranks. Then all of you may go and celebrate."

The lads nodded their agreement and began their descent back down the hill.

We bent over to look at the second drainage tile but could not see anything that looked like a thread. I got down on my hands and knees and tried to peer up the pipe but could see nothing. Holmes also looked with the same result.

"Doctor," said Mrs. Sterry, "hold this and give me your hand."

I looked up at her, and to my shock, she had removed her blouse and was handing it to me. Her shoulders were bare and her torso was covered by only her corset. She sat down on the sodden soil with her back to the opening of the tile drain. Grabbing my hand with her left hand, she leaned back until her bare shoulder abutted the tile. Then she inserted into the drain what had to be one of the most finely sculpted, muscled arms as I had ever seen in my years of medical practice. She kept adjusting her prone body until her triceps had vanished into the pipe.

"HALLOA!" she shouted. "I've got it!"

Slowly, she wiggled her body back away from the open tile until her fingers appeared. Clasped in them was a dark line which she pulled on very slowly and handed it up to me.

I pulled on the line until it was taut. Holmes had his glass out and bent over to take a look at it.

"Brilliant," he said. "They have braided the line with three threads instead of one to increase its strength. Once again they have bested that Professor."

Mrs. Sterry now pulled her blouse back on whilst I stood and held the braided line. I was holding it taut when it suddenly gave a sharp jerk and was pulled out of my hand. I picked it up straight away and gave two sharp, small tugs on it. My action was answered by two tugs from the other end.

"Look," I said. "One of them is on the other end. But how can we communicate with them? Can we tie a note to the line like they did?"

The answer to my question came from the other end of the thread. I felt a small tug followed by a two-second pause and then another two small tugs in quick succession. Then came a pause of some five seconds, followed by three tugs, each followed by a two-second pause. The tugs and varying pauses continued and a few seconds later, I shouted at Holmes.

"It is Morse code! One of them knows Morse code. They are sending us a message."

"That must be Florence Fawcett," said Mrs. Sterry. "She is just like her mother, Philippa. She excels in everything."

"Holmes," I said. "Get out a pencil and notepad and take this down. Dash, dot, dot, space, dash, dash, dash, space, dash, dash, dash, dot. Another space. Now dash, dash, dash. Space. Dot, dot, dash. Now they've paused."

My time in the military was decades ago but when one is required to learn a code on which your life and those of the men you are treating depends, you learn it rather well and do not forget.

"She is asking ... *do you*. Here comes more." The next tugs and pauses spelled out the words *know Morse code*. I immediately tugged and paused back *dash, dot, dash, dash, pause, dot, pause, dot, dot dot.* Yes!

Over the next few minutes, they confirmed that the entire team was safe but had only a few bottles of water. I assured them that help was on the way but did not dare disclose that it might be a week or more before the workmen could clear the tunnel. I then looked over at Holmes.

"What do I tell them now?"

"Tell them to wait for one hour. That is all they need to know at this time. We have to get down to the town and purchase a spool of fishing line and then a spool of piano wire. The braided thread is not sufficiently strong to serve as a continuing means of communication."

I did as he had requested and bade Florence Fawcett and her teammates a temporary goodbye, assuring her that we would be back soon. The three of us then jogged and stumbled back down the hill and through the vegetation until we were back at the road.

Finding fishing line was easy enough. There were several anglers' shops along the edge of the water beside the ferry docks. Piano wire was a greater challenge. I asked the wizened fellow behind the desk in the shop where we purchased our fishing line if he knew where one could find such wire.

He gave me an odd look in response. It would seem that fishermen do not often engage in piano repair. But he was helpful all the same.

"There's a shop up on Norman Street what tunes and repairs pianos. German. Named *Opper*. He can help you."

We hurried north the few blocks to a small shop off York Street. The sign hanging outside the shop read *Opper Knockity Piano Tuning and Repairs*. We went inside and before Holmes could ask for a spool of piano wire I let my curiosity get the better of me.

"Your name, my good man," I said to the somewhat stooped fellow behind the counter, "does not seem German to me. Where are you from?"

"*Guten Morgan,* I am from Stuttgart," he said, looking at the three of us, "and my name is Johann Schwartz."

"Why, then, do you call your shop something completely different?"

"Because I only tune once," he said, grinning.

Holmes and Mrs. Sterry burst into laughter. I could not see what was so funny.

"We need a spool of your piano wire," said Holmes.

"*Ja,* what gauge is it you want?"

Holmes, Mrs. Sterry and I looked at each other. We had no idea.

"Average thickness would be quite acceptable," he said.

"*Was ist* average? You mean wire for Middle C?"

"Yes, whatever you use for Middle C would be quite acceptable," said Holmes.

"*Wie viel,* how much is it you need? Ten feet? Twenty feet? How many strings are broken?"

The three of us huddled together. "What do you say, Holmes? The far side of the hill cannot be more than fifty yards away from the tile. Should that be enough?"

"Yes, I should think so. Fifty yards should do the trick."

He was about to request that amount when Mrs. Sterry placed her hand on his arm.

"Then you will need one hundred yards. If you wish to attach anything to the wire, you will need twice the distance if they have one end of it and you attach something at the other and then they pull it through."

"Oh, yes," I said. "Yes, one hundred yards."

I turned to Mr. Schwartz.

"About one hundred yards if you can spare it."

"*Was!* Why you need so much?"

I could not think of a reasonable reply but Mrs. Sterry, with a straight face, calmly replied.

"It has to be very loud, sir, because I am deaf."

Mr. Schwartz looked at us as if to say we were all completely mad, but nevertheless it would be a significant sale, and so he disappeared back into his shop and reappeared rolling a spool of tightly wound wire.

"This is new spool. Comes from Turino, so one hundred meters. Will that do?"

"That would be jolly good," I assured him, and Holmes counted out the pounds needed to pay for it.

"Wait *eine Minute,*" he said. He went back into his shop and fetched a short piece of pipe.

"Now you can carry it. There is no charge."

We stuck the pipe through the center hole of the spool and Holmes and I each took one side of it. It was heavy and awkward to carry, but we managed until we reached stream bed at the base of the hill. First Holmes slipped, dropping his end of the pipe and allowing the spool to fall off and roll into the stream and a few minutes later I did the same.

"Put it down, both of you," ordered Mrs. Sterry.

We did, and she immediately withdrew the pipe, handed it to me, hoisted the spool up onto her powerful shoulders, and began marching up the hill. I made a mental note that for gentlemen in their mid-fifties, an Olympic tennis player can be a very useful accomplice.

At the drain pipe, Holmes first attached the fishing line to the thread, and I sent a message in code back to the girls telling them to pull gently until they observed the line. Slowly the thread disappeared into the tile, followed by the much stronger fishing line. Holmes measured off each yard as it progressed.

When the number was approaching fifty, I began to despair, thinking that the last thing I wanted to do was to have to run back to Mr. Schwartz and buy more wire. Fortunately, at fifty-two yards, just a few feet short of fifty meters, the movement stopped. Holmes then carefully attached the fishing line to the piano wire, and I sent a message telling them to start again with their gentle pulling. They did and stopped just shy of fifty meters.

Chapter Eighteen
Surveying the Situation

"SO FAR, SO GOOD," said Holmes. "That will suffice to pull objects through the drain. Our first task is to try to find a way to get drinking water to them. Might I ask the two of you to wait here and send and receive messages to the girls whilst I run back into the town to obtain some vessels we can fill with water and send through the pipe."

He descended the hill, and for the next hour, Mrs. Sterry and I sent and received several messages in Morse code by way of tugs on the wire assuring the girls that help was on the way and rescue was imminent.

"Should we let their parents know that we are in contact with them?" she asked me.

I pondered that one. The obligatory, decent thing to do would be to allow the girls and their parents to speak to each other. It would assuage the incredible tension and worry that all of them were now facing. However, it would also bring a mob to the drainage tile site with a dozen families all demanding to send messages to their daughters, something I knew Holmes would wish to avoid.

"Yes, we should do that," I said. "But could we wait until tomorrow? After we have sent them drinking water and such?"

Holmes reappeared bearing a canvas sack from which he extracted several *piccolo* bottles and a half dozen test tubes.

"The hotel," he said, "fortunately had a bin of these individual Champagne bottles, and a local chemist agreed to part with a few of his test tubes. Would you mind, Watson, filling them up with water from the stream and putting the cork stoppers in them?"

I found an accessible part of the stream, taking care to make sure I was upstream from the first drainage tile, and filled both a bottle and a test tube. We first secured a bottle to the piano wire and sent a message to the girls to try to pull it through.

The wire began to move, and the bottle vanished into the drain. Slowly and surely the wire moved until some fifteen yards had been absorbed.

Then it stopped. I could feel the recipients continuing to tug gently, but it was clear that the bottle had hit an obstruction and I pulled the wire back. Then we tried with the test tube. This time it moved nearly half way to the chamber in which the girls were trapped, but then it too stopped. The tugs exerted on the far end became stronger, and suddenly the wire began to move again. I smiled happily until the wire stopped moving and I assumed the tube of water had made its way to the girls.

Then a message came back.

The test tube had broken. It also was too large to clear whatever detritus, corners, and other obstruction blocked the way. Perhaps a rat could make it all the way but a cylinder full of water could not.

"If they have held on to some of their water supply," Holmes asked me, "how long can they survive?"

"Perhaps a week, if they ration what they have carefully, but not likely much longer."

In the limited space alongside the stream, Holmes paced back and forth for several minutes, and then he stopped and gazed up toward the top of the hill.

"Come," he said, "There are more ways of killing a cat than choking it with cream."

He turned and began back down the hill. The two of us obediently followed.

"Watson, my good fellow," he said over his shoulder as we made our way yet one more time through the bushes and stream bed. "Kindly drop in to the Police Office and inform the Constable of the drainage pipe and wire. We can be certain that he is familiar with Morse code and can sit there and send messages back and forth between the parents and their daughters."

He then stopped and turned around so he could speak to Mrs. Sterry.

"Could you, my dear, return to the hotel and round up the parents and take them to the drain tile? Thank you."

"And where," I shouted, "are you going?"

"To find a land surveyor. I shall meet you back at the orphanage in an hour."

Two hours later, I was waiting in the common room along with Mr. Steiger and Sister Miriam. I had apprised Chief Constable Pughsley of the piano wire and means of communicating with the girls. Mrs. Sterry had let the parents know about it as well and one of them unfortunately had informed the Press. As a result, the reporters swarmed the hill and were no doubt interfering with the messages back and forth between the parents and their children and asking every mother how she felt when she first learned that her daughter was safe. Prioress Priscilla and Mrs. Sterry had joined the crowd on the hill.

Holmes finally appeared and with him were two men. One was carrying a surveyor's tripod over his shoulder and bearing a small theodolite case in his free hand. The other had a Gunter's chain slung over his back and was girded with a belt bearing a plumb bob, spirit level, and other assorted instruments and tools.

"Permit me to introduce Mr. Alexander Maxwell and Mr. Walter Murray, both graduates of the Queen's College in Glasgow and members of the Surveyor's Guild of England."

Mr. Steiger and I stood to greet them, and they politely walked over to Sister Miriam, whom they, being residents of Dover appeared to know.

"These fine chaps kindly agreed to take time away from their task of working on the foundations for the new pier and assist me in the quest to save the girls. We still have several hours of daylight, so please take note that we are going to determine exactly where the girls' chamber is located under the castle hill and find a way to alleviate their situation."

"Might I join you, *Herr* Holmes?" asked Mr. Steiger. "Although I serve only as the girls' German master, I spent years in the army when I was a younger man and am quite familiar with the techniques of mapping and surveying."

"I would be grateful for your assistance," said Holmes.

With the parents and the Press all up by the drainage tile, the way was clear for us to approach Dover Castle. Several constables guarded the cutaway door and the site had been transformed into a construction zone. Beams and timbers necessary for reinforcing the tunnel were piled up outside the door, and a cartload of them was being taken into the tunnel whilst we came up to it. Another cart emerged from the tunnel bearing a load of bricks and large chunks of chalk that had been cleared away from the collapsed passage.

"Can you start your work here?" asked Holmes of Mr. Maxwell.

"Aye, we can do that," he said and took several minutes to set up and level his theodolite. After that, our progress was painfully slow as we had to make way for the workmen who had been hired by Scotland Yard to clear the tunnel. But slowly we took the measure of every stretch. Mr. Maxwell held one end of the chain whilst Mr. Murray had the other, and they recorded the precise distance from the corner to another. Using the theodolite, they noted the angle of every corner and any change in elevation.

Mr. Steiger assisted numerous times by holding one end of the chain along with the plumb bob so that the distance could be recorded precisely even though the floor level was undulating. By the time we had finished the task and arrived at the entry to the collapsed portion of the tunnel, it was well into the early evening, and Holmes declared that our day's work had been quite long enough.

Unlike the boys who had been conscripted to join Holmes's Irregulars, the men from the survey firm could not be compelled to begin work at first light before having their breakfast. Thus, we agreed to meet at nine o'clock the following morning.

Regardless of such an agreement, I was awakened not long after sunrise by a banging on my door.

"Watson, please get up and come quickly," came the familiar voice from the hallway outside my room. "We need to get back to the tunnel. Bring your torch."

Chapter Nineteen
De Mortuis Nil Nisi Bonum

I ROSE, BATHED at the hand basin, and dressed in a matter of minutes. Holmes was pacing in the hallway and began walking toward the entrance of the orphanage the moment he saw me. He was carrying a cold chisel in one hand and had a small hammer tucked into his belt.

"Merciful heavens, Holmes. What is it this time?"

He did not immediately answer but stopped to light up a cigarette and then began walking quickly toward the Castle Hill.

"When the tunnel exploded," he finally said, "do you suppose whoever caused it to happen trapped any of his own men inside with the girls?"

"No. That would have been unthinkable, and besides, the girls would have said something about it in the messages we have exchanged with them on the piano wire."

"Precisely. Now then, do you suppose they would have buried and killed their own men in the collapse?"

"Highly unlikely."

"Precisely."

"Would one of the kidnappers or anyone working for them have exploded the tunnel and knowingly buried himself whilst doing so?"

"Impossible."

"Precisely."

He said no more as we ascended the hill and came to the main entrance to the tunnel. A couple of sleepy-eyed constables were standing guard and were understandably surprised to see us. They recognized Holmes and waived us through.

The tunnel was filled with piles of objects related to the clearing of the debris and the reinforcing of the walls and ceilings and a unit of the workers who had been assigned to the night shift were busy trying to extend the tunnel through to the chamber in which the girls were trapped. Oil lamps had been set up all through the tunnel, rendering my torch redundant.

"What a blind beetle I've been," said Holmes once we had arrived at the door to the secret tunnel, "I should have drawn my conclusion much earlier; it is so obvious. Of course, there is nothing so obvious as a fact that is hiding in plain sight. But if the explosion succeeded in trapping only the girls and burying the policemen—"

"The constables made it through," I interrupted him. "So did Charlie. My apologies, Holmes. I forgot to tell you that. They transmitted that to Mrs. Sterry and me during the exchange of messages after you went to find the surveyors."

"What about the reporter? Wasn't he the man from the *Evening Star?*"

"Oh, I neglected to ask, and they made no mention of him."

Both of us chose not to dwell on that matter for fear we would violate the principle of *nihil nisi bonum* and express an uncharitable sentiment.

"Be that as it may," said Holmes. "The conclusion I have reached is that the explosion could only have been set off by someone standing outside the tunnel door."

"You mean one of the crowd who had followed us?"

"Precisely."

"Do we have any way of knowing who all was there?"

"I suspect," said Holmes, "that if we queried the constables—they are all local chaps—and the Irregulars and one or two of the townspeople, we should be able to come up with a reasonably complete list although memories can never be entirely relied upon. But let us leave that until later. Now, take a look at the base of the wall."

He was indicating the corner where the base of the wall met the chalk floor of the tunnel.

I got down on my hands and knees to observe and whisked away a pile of dust and fragments left behind by the explosion and the clearing work.

"There is a seam of caulking mortar all along here," I said. "If you brush the dirt and dust away, it looks quite fresh."

"Yes, it does," said Holmes. "Now, let me see what might be hiding behind it."

Taking the hammer and cold chisel, he gently tapped away at a small section of the seam.

"Ah ha! As I suspected. Look here, Watson."

Underneath the mortar were two black wires, covered in gutta-percha.

"These," I said, "were just installed very recently. They look new."

"They are and if we follow this seam back away from the door, the ends of them should appear."

Some forty feet back, the fresh caulking ended, and about six inches of two black wires was visible. The ends of both pieces had been stripped, exposing the copper wire under the gutta-percha.

"The explosion was set off by an electrical charge," said Holmes. "All someone had to do was to touch these two ends together, and the circuit would be complete. I warrant that sometime in the next few days, one of these workmen will come upon a large dry cell battery somewhere under the rubble. An agile fellow could have connected the two ends of the wires using his shoe to bring them into contact with each other. No one would have noticed."

"What sort of twisted fiend," I said, "would have stood here, waited until the constables and Charlie were in the tunnel and they set off the explosion knowing that in doing so he was burying them alive?"

"We are," said Holmes, "doing business with a band of ingenious but ruthless villains. Now, though, we have to postpone uncovering them and save the girls before they die of thirst."

Nine o'clock found us back at the tunnel entrance having had breakfast and coffee and prepared to move ahead with the surveyors. Again, the very useful Mr. Steiger had kindly offered to assist us.

"Good morning, gentlemen," said Holmes to the surveyors. "I assume you are quite prepared to retrace all the angles and measurements you made yesterday but to do so on the surface rather than underground."

Walter Murray looked at Holmes with condescending disdain. "Are ye daft, mon? We shall do no such thing, Mr. Holmes."

"I beg your pardon. That is what I hired you to do, and you agreed."

"Aye, we'll do what you're paying us to do, but do you no recall any of your trigonometry, Mr. Holmes?"

Many years ago, I made a list of all the areas of knowledge that Holmes was and was not aware of. I was not sure, but to the best of my recollection, while his expertise in chemistry was profound, trigonometry and the other branches of mathematics did not even make it on to the list.

"I fear I do not."

"Auch, mon. If the entrance door is Point A and the door to the secret tunnel is Point B, and we have the exact distances and angles of every zig and zag in between, all we had to do last night was sit down and make the calculations and we can run a straight line from A to B. Do you follow me, Mr. Holmes?"

"Not entirely, but I am sure you are right, so kindly lead Dr. Watson and me to the location on the top of the hill that lies directly over top of the door to the secret tunnel."

Twenty minutes later, having set up their theodolite, aimed it at the calculated angle and measured off the distance with their chain, the two Scots pushed a marker into the soil at the exact place on the surface that sat directly above the entrance to the tunnel.

"There's your door, sir," said Mr. Maxwell. "Now, you will have to try to recall where you went from there until you reached the spot where you say someone took a shot at you."

Holmes and I paced out what we remembered as the distance and directions we had taken once inside the now collapsed tunnel. The surveyors noted our estimations and marked spots on the ground that showed the limits from side to side and how far. A square of ground about five yards wide and seven yards long was pined.

"Aye, and now," said Alex Maxwell, "what is your best guess as to the size of the room in which someone shot at you?"

It had been dark in there, but both Holmes and I recalled that it might have been around forty feet square. Again, markers were place in the ground but were added to the first square to make a significant larger plot. Finally, we guessed at the distance and direction of the portion of the tunnel we never entered whence came the sound of the girls' cheer. It sounded like more than thirty yards and, since sound echoes in a hard-walled tunnel, it might have been as far as fifty yards away and we could not know if that part of the tunnel was straight or curved.

"There, gentlemen," said Mr. Maxwell, "is your plot. Somewhere under that is the chamber the girls are stuck in."

He was pointing to a parcel of roughly half an acre, longer than it was wide, that stretched down and away from the crest of the northern slope of the hill.

"Thank you, my good chaps," said Holmes. "You have been exceptionally useful. Now all I have to do is find a well driller in Dover and have him set his rig up here and we can start to drill. If we work methodically, we should be able to find the chamber within the next two days."

"Nay," said Mr. Murray. "You canna be doing that, Mr. Holmes. Perhaps you can have a rig up near to the top of the hill but you don't dare move one too far down."

"And why not?"

"Do the sums and the subtractions, sir. The main entrance is forty-four feet below the crest of this hill. We measured the difference in height as well as distance. You went up eleven feet between the entrance and the door to the collapsed tunnel. You said that the stretch you walked in that part also had a wee bit of a climb to it. So, you had better add on another five or six feet. That drops your distance from the crest of the hill to the floor of the girls' chamber down to twenty-three feet. Are you with me, sir?"

"Yes, of course. Keep going."

"Aye, well that chamber, if it is like the other rooms carved out of this hill, will have a ceiling a some eight to ten feet high. Now you're down to fourteen feet. Will ye take a look at what happens to the hill as you move north. It slopes down. By the time you reach the far end your own eye can tell you that you have descended at another eight feet; maybe nine. There's a layer of overburden of at least four feet. Are you with me Mr. Holmes? What it means is that the layer of chalk the forms the ceiling above any room that far away is only a foot or two thick. Put a stream driven drilling rig on top of it and start chugging away and the whole thing could cave in. Your girls would be dead before you could get them out. Do ye see what I'm saying to you, sir?"

"How can we drill down on that section of the hill?" asked Holmes.

The two Scots conferred with each other for a minute and then Mr. Murray answered.

"There's a fellow by the name of Abner Friesen who has a farm up outside East Langdon. He's one of the odd Mennonite zealots that have no truck or trade with anything mechanized. We know that he has an old well-drilling rig that is powered by a horse walking in a circle around it. We did a job for him a couple of years back and are on good terms. Would you like us to go and ask him to bring his rig and his horse down here and drill the lower part of the hill."

"I would be most grateful for any such assistance," said Holmes. "How quickly could you have him here?"

"If we go now, we can be to his place by late this afternoon. He's a handy fellow and could have his rig down here by the end of the day tomorrow. He could be starting to drill by the day after tomorrow."

"I will go with you," offered Mr. Steiger. "That man's native tongue will be German."

Chapter Twenty
Drilling Down

ONCE BACK IN THE TOWN CENTER, we reported to Inspector Lestrade and, as Holmes had promised, brought him up to date on what we had accomplished so far.

"Well done, Holmes," the inspector said. "Please move with alacrity on your drilling. I shall keep the workers digging and reinforcing around the clock. If you find the chamber within the next few days, we can keep the girls alive. If not, we will need the tunnel cleared to bring out the bodies. And as soon as you have the opportunity, do try to find out who the madmen are behind this horror."

We were referred to a modern well driller, a Mr. Mark Carpenter, who had been drilling boreholes throughout Kent for the past forty years. At first, he dismissed our request stating that he was fully booked for the next four months, but when we told him the reason for our urgent need, he agreed to have his rig and steam-powered drive unit up the hill by the following morning.

Mr. Carpenter, his son, Gary, and his men arrived on the hill with his drilling rig by late morning the following day. They set up the 'A' shaped tower with a long pole supporting each of the four corners of the structure, laid out the necessary assorted bits, pipes, grabs, and fishing tools, hooked up the small steam engine unit and started to work.

"It won't take long," he said. "Chalk is the softest rock in all of England. We can bore ten feet an hour at least."

By the supper hour, he had drilled over forty feet … and found nothing. There was no possibility that the chamber was below that level, so he extracted his drill and moved it fifteen yards to the left.

"We can start her up again first thing tomorrow morning," he said as he and his crew cleaned their equipment and departed for the night.

Three days had now passed since the explosion in the tunnel. Those trapped inside were now almost certainly out of water. While some caves in other parts of England had water dripping down the walls, it was not without reason that people spoke of something being *as dry as chalk*.

By noon the following day, the Carpenter crew had drilled two more holes without finding the chamber. They kept moving systematically along the crest of the hill but could only start down the slope a short distance before they would enter the zone where the vibrations from their engine and pounding drill might cause the ceiling to collapse.

Mr. Abner Friesen had appeared that morning as well, bringing with him two other men from the small community of Mennonite faithful who lived in the area. Wilhelm Steiger joined them, and they all carried on, conversing in German. Mr. Friesen and his brethren quickly set up his ancient but simple rig at the lowest part of the parcel and started leading his draft horse around and around in circles, causing the gears to mesh and the drill to turn slowly. It moved downward at a fraction of the speed of the powered one, but it was nearly silent as it did so, casting off not a single vibration.

At the end of that afternoon, the Carpenter team shouted and we raced over to see what they had found. They had not found an empty chamber, but the grab was bringing up chunks of brick.

"We're in the tunnel," said the drilling master. "I can try another hole tomorrow morning in line with this one, but that will be as far as I can move the rig down the hill."

The following morning, the powered rig was moved down the hill in line with the hole that had detected the tunnel. They moved it as far as we dared and started up the motor. This would be the last hole they could bore using the steam engine.

The Mennonite team moved up the hill in line with the team coming down, but they could drill no more than one hole a day.

The Carpenter drillers found more brick. The Mennonites found nothing. Night fell, and we returned to the orphanage.

This would be the girls' fourth day without water. The parents continued to gather around the drainage pipe sending and receiving messages. Almost all of the messages that came that day from the girls mentioned their thirst. By the end of the day, desperation had set in.

We breakfasted early the next morning and arrived at the hill by half seven. The Carpenter's rig was gone, but the Mennonites were already hard at work and had been there since five o'clock. By eleven o'clock their first hole had been completed, and they had come up empty.

"We can do one more," said Abner Friesen. "Maybe two more if we have some lights."

They only needed one more.

At four o'clock that afternoon, the draft horse suddenly started trotting. Resistance on its harness had disappeared. Mr. Friesen leapt in front his horse, grabbed the bridle and forced it to halt. He removed the rig harness so nothing would move and then he and his neighbors along with Mr. Steiger slowly extracted the drill from the hole. They fed a fishing tool down the cylindrical hole. He looked up at us and smiled.

"Someone is tugging on this. *Ja.*"

The fishing tool came back up. A handkerchief was attached to its claw.

Holmes lay prone on the ground with his face directly over the hole and shouted.

"Hello down there! How are you?"

A young woman shouted back. "We are all alive, sir, but if you wouldn't mind, could you send some water down. We're a bit parched. I'm afraid."

"On its way."

"Can we pour water down?" asked Holmes of Mr. Friesen.

"*Nein.* The hole will collapse and close. We have to push the casing down to secure it. You cannot use it before the casing is in place."

He and his colleagues methodically picked up a length of casing and slowly and carefully put it in place and forced it down into the hole. Then another and then another.

While they were doing this task, I had walked back down the front of the hill, found the workers crew in the main tunnel and had them help me bring up several buckets of clean water. One of the younger workmen ran down into the town and returned bearing a garden hose. By the time I returned to the drill hole, the parents and Press were thronged around it. The Prioress and Mrs. Sterry were with them.

"Did you let them know about the drilling up here?" I asked Holmes.

"I am innocent. The girls sent the news via piano wire."

The hose was fed down the hole, a funnel stuck in one end, and water slowly tricked into it. One of the fathers who, if judging by his clothes and shoes, was a wealthy man, ran up to the Mennonite farmers, spoke some high-sounding words of thanks and praise, and held out and a handful of what looked like ten-pound notes to Mr. Friesen.

The old Mennonite looked at him in obvious anger.

"*Wir haben das nicht für Geld gemacht,*" he said and turned and walked away.

"Mr. Friesen, sir," said Holmes to the old farmer. "A word if I may."

"*Ja.*"

"What, sir, it the largest auger you have that can drill into this ground.

"*Einen halben Meter.*"

"Watson," he said to me. "Could the torso and hips of a young woman, with her hands stretched out above her head, pass through a tube that is about eighteen inches in diameter?"

"As long as she is not overweight, I see no reason why not?"

"I think we can count on the fact that not a single member of this team would fall into that category, especially since they have now gone several days without food."

"You want to pull them up?" I asked.

"Yes. The fellows clearing the tunnel will still need another week or two. We could have the girls out of there in a couple of days if we can drill down to them."

"As long as none of them gets stuck part way. But what about the police officers?"

"Ah, yes. Those young chaps. I fear they will have to wait for the tunnel."

He returned to speak to Mr. Friesen.

"Sir, if you could drill a shaft using your largest auger, we could get the girls out and back to their families much more quickly. Would that be possible, sir?"

"*Herr* Holmes. *Ja,* this is possible but can you give me one day? This morning the wife and children had to milk my cows so we could be here at sunrise. Let us have a day to make arrangements for our farms, and we can be back and drill a big hole."

"That, sir, is more than I can ask for," said Holmes.

The Mennonites left their rig in place and led the draft horse back down the hill. The parents of the girls, the wives, and mothers of the young police officers, and goodness knows who all else were crowding around the drilled hole. There was considerable chaos as people jostled to shout messages down the pipe, send food and items of clothing, and occasionally pour another installment of drinking water. After an outbreak of shouting, the Prioress stepped up beside the pipe and took charge.

Holmes took my elbow and leaned into my ear.

"There is nothing more we can do here today. We can return in two days and see if we can extract the girls."

"And Charlie?"

"Ah, how could I forget. And Charlie."

We returned to our now quite familiar common room. A sealed letter was waiting for Holmes. He opened it, read the contents, and handed it over to me. It ran:

Mr. Sherlock Holmes:
We appear to have underestimated your cleverness.
Do not make the mistake of underestimating our determination to see our goals achieved.
Although you have discomfited our scheme for abducting the girls, do not assume that this round has ended.

The Order of the Fittest

"Somebody," I said, "is not happy with you, my dear Holmes."
"I did not care a fig for their happiness. What does alarm me is that they are observing our every move."

The London Evening Star

Evening Edition, Friday, 30 June, 1905

What Does the British Public Know About Mr. Sherlock Holmes?

Is he truly who he claims to be? We wonder.

By: the Editors

In its quest to find the missing girls, Scotland Yard has once again, at taxpayer's expense, hired the well-known (thanks to the sensationalized stories about him in the *Strand)* amateur detective to help them.

Their doing so begs the question, what are we paying inspectors at Scotland Yard for if we must also hand over the money from the pockets of hard-working citizens to pay for the exotic habits of this amateur detective?

Yes, he has had some remarkable successes. Mind you, his dear friend, the writer, Dr. J. Watson, only tells writes about his accomplishments and not his failures. Because of that exceptional bias, the public has not learned what this reporter and *The Evening Star* learned this morning.

It is possible that Mr. Sherlock Holmes is related by blood to the notorious murderer, Dr. Henry Howard Holmes. As reported in this newspaper, this monster of a man is believed to have killed twenty-seven people in a path of bloodshed that runs through Philadelphia, New York, Chicago, Minneapolis, and Toronto. He was finally tracked down and arrested by the fearless Pinkerton Detectives and hanged.

The family name of Holmes is not all that common and most who bear that name are at the very least distantly related to each other. Is it just a coincidence that this villain was a doctor, like the closest friend and Boswell to Sherlock Holmes, Dr. J. Watson, and that both doctors are also highly paid writers? Is it just a coincidence that the final murders committed by Dr. H. H. Holmes took place on St. Vincent's Street in Toronto, a house that is located within a block of another man from Toronto, Mr. Meyers the Bootmaker, who also has a close connection with Sherlock Holmes, as disclosed in *The Hound of the Baskervilles.*

It is a scientifically proven fact that there is only a very fine line between the psyche of those men who commit crimes too foul to name and those men who have nothing else to do in their lives but try to catch the murderers. Dr. Watson has, perhaps in a moment of candour, revealed that Sherlock Holmes has admitted that he would have been a brilliant criminal had he not chosen to be a detective instead.

No one is accusing Mr. Sherlock Holmes of anything untoward. We are only suggesting that, considering the high fees paid to him out of the public purse, a review be conducted of his activities to determine if the British taxpayer is truly receiving value for his money.

Chapter Twenty-One
Over the
White Cliffs of Dover

DURING THE SUMMER days at the beginning of July, the sun rises before five o'clock in the morning over the English Channel and, on a clear day, the rays of light emerge from the coast of France and illuminate the great White Cliffs of Dover. It is a glorious sight and makes a fellow feel proud and blessed to be an Englishman.

    That was how I felt as we made our way up to the top of the Castle Hill on that splendid morning. If all went well, by the end of the day, the entire team of kidnapped girls would be rescued and returned to their families. And one must not forget the impish Charlie who would be back with his pals. The hefty police officers would have to wait a few more days but even if their living conditions were miserable, they would have adequate food and water and would return as a select group of heroes in this pleasant corner of Kent.

    By half five that morning, Holmes, Prioress Priscilla, Mrs. Sterry, and I were all gathered at the top of the hill. We were far from alone. Inspector Lestrade, the Chief Constable, and a dozen policemen were there as well. The wall of blue uniforms was holding back the crowd of parents and older siblings and the Press who were already jostling back and forth to be in the front row watching the Mennonite farmers attach their largest auger to the ancient drilling rig. The force needed to cut a much larger cylinder into the ground required two draft horses and these massive beasts were put into harness and soon began to plod their weary way around and around in a circle as they drove the mechanism that caused the auger to work its way into the soil.

"We cannot do this quickly," said Mr. Abner Friesen to whoever was within earshot. "It will take at least six hours. You all may as well *nach Hause, gehen.*"

No one took his advice.

Holmes, however, gave me a tug on my sleeve and did the same with Inspector Lestrade.

"Come," he said to us. "There is another task at hand. We can return here well before the first girl is pulled up."

An hour later found the three of us having had a hot breakfast with the boys of St. Vincent's and sitting in the common room facing our beloved Irregulars. Holmes had secured an easel, a square of blackboard, and a stick of chalk with which he could draw.

"Now my fine Irregulars," he said to the boys. "You must throw your minds and memories back to a few days ago, to the time just before Charlie ran into the tunnel and it exploded. Can you all do that? Close your eyes if you have to, but take yourself back there."

Most of the boys closed their eyes. A couple of them squinted tightly as if by doing so they might enhance their memories.

"Excellent," said Holmes, "Now, open your eyes and look up here."

On the easel, he had drawn a line across the top. "This line represents the wall of the tunnel and about here was the secret door. I was standing here, Dr. Watson was here, the police were here, here, and here …"

With each person or group named, he made a mark on the board. By the time he finished, he had marked the location of all of the different parties with the exception of his Irregulars. Therefore, he turned to them and asked, "When you arrived, you were all at the back of the line. Now, can you remember where you were at the exact time of the explosion?"

Tommy spoke up. "Mr. Holmes, sir, we had all moved up. We wanted to see what was happening, so we wiggled through the crowd until we were all near the front."

Holmes paused, and I sensed that he had not received the answer he had hoped for.

"Then did none of you happen to see who was standing *here*," he asked, pointing to a place that would have been at the back of the crowd and up against the wall, the location that the villain must have stood as he touched the wires together and brought about the explosion.

"No sir," said Tommy. "Like I said, sir, we were all up to the front by then."

"None of you were still at the back?" Holmes asked again.

"No, sir."

Then came a quiet voice.

"I was."

Once again, all heads in the room turned and looked at Wee Jimmy.

"Were you, now?" said Holmes. "Could you show me on this board about where you were standing when the explosion happened?"

Jimmy came hesitantly to the front of the group. This time there was no jibes or insults, and the rest of the boys sat in respectful silence.

"I was standing right here," he said and put a mark at the very back of the crowd.

"Excellent, Jimmy. Now did you see who was standing *here,* against the wall? Most likely he was a stranger and not either one of the parents or one of the local folks from Dover who joined us. Can you describe what he looked like?"

"Aye, sir. But he weren't no stranger, sir."

"No, then who was he?"

"It were the German, sir, the teacher what's been with you and the doctor all along."

Lestrade, Holmes and I looked at each other in shock and disbelief.

"Where is he?" demanded Lestrade.

Giving a quick thank you to Jimmy and the other boys, the three of us immediately rushed up the stairs to the room that Mr. Steiger had been using. The door was open, and we barged in.

He was gone. The room had been cleaned out.

"I will send out a bulletin immediately," said Lestrade.

Holmes sighed and sat down on the bed.

"My dear Inspector, we are only a few hundred yards from the ferry dock. He is long gone."

For several minutes, the three of us said nothing. Then Holmes rose and forced a smile.

"Come, we may as well enjoy some good news. They should be almost ready to start pulling the girls up."

Two hours later we were standing back on the northern slope of the hill and watching as Mr. Friesen and his crew carefully installed the last of the casings into the large hole they had bored into through the earth to the chamber in which the girls and the young constables were trapped.

I had brought my doctor's bag along with me in case any of them needed immediate medical attention, but I was also worried about the effect that the sunshine would have on eyes that had been in darkness for several days. Therefore, I had also prepared thirteen strips of cloth that could be used as blindfolds and organized a row of closed four-wheeler carriages with shades on the windows so that the girls could all remain in a darkened space until they were ushered into a curtained room at the hotel. There, their eyes could become accustomed slowly to the light.

Chief Constable Pughsley, drawing on his years in the Royal Navy, had a coil of thick rope and had fashioned a harness that could be wrapped securely around the slender bodies and used to draw them up without cutting into their flesh.

When the last of the casings was dropped into place, the Prioress stood over the hole and shouted instructions to the girls. The prospect of having to be blindfolded did not sit very well with them as they wanted to see their families straight away.

"Tell them," said Mrs. Sterry, "that if they damage their eyes they will never be able to see a ball clearly again and that will be the end of their playing hockey."

That put an end to that problem, and the harness was lowered. The young constables down there helped the first girl tie herself into it and, with her arms stretched above her head to diminish the diameter of her body, she was slowly raised up. A crew of police officers under the direction of the Chief Constable slowly and carefully pulled up on the rope, making sure that there were no sudden jerks and slippages.

First, two somewhat grubby hands emerged from the pipe, and then a set of arms and then a head and face of a young woman, Her eyes were covered, but she was grinning from ear to ear.

"It's Gillian!" shouted a woman in the crowd and the first of the waiting mothers ran up to embrace her daughter. Her father and other members of her family soon were clustered around her, giving hugs and kisses and leading her by the hand to the interior of a carriage.

One by one, the girls emerged and were lovingly claimed by their joyful families. The Press crowded around them even to the point of shouting questions through the windows of the carriages, but they were generally ignored.

As a doctor, I have observed over the years the reunions and intimate meetings of members of families, and it is indeed a sight that restores one's faith in humanity. The tears of joy and the sobs of relief cannot be faked. It was a thrilling experience.

The last body to be hauled up was Charlie, also blindfolded. There was no family to meet him.

However, Sister Miriam was there, and as soon as he heard her voice, he threw his arms around her. She peeled him off and led him by the hand over to Holmes and me.

"Charles," she said to us, "wishes to thank you for rescuing him and apologize for his misbehavior in running into the tunnel when he should not have."

"Well now," I said. "Young man, you have had quite the unpleasant adventure. I trust it will be a lesson to you not to disobey instructions."

He turned his face up to me and could not conceal an impish smile.

"I learned my lesson, Doctor Watson. But it was not so bad down there. I had twelve girls all wanting to look after me, and the constables were splendid. Officer Jerry told me that if I kept my nose clean, I could become one myself in a few years. I am going to do that, Doctor. That's what I'm going to do."

We bade goodbye to the Irregulars of St. Vincent's and thanked them for their service. Sister Miriam took us aside as we departed the building and were about to walk to the train station. We thanked her again for her hospitality and support, and she responded in kind.

"It is I who must thank you, gentlemen. You have given my boys the adventure of a lifetime. They will be talking about it all summer."

"My newest Irregulars were exceptionally helpful," said Holmes. "but now their lives will go back their regular routine."

"Yes, Mr. Holmes. They will continue to explore the White Cliffs of Dover and Jimmy will go to sleep in his own little room again."

Chapter Twenty-Two
Unstylish in Plimsolls

WE RETURNED to London.

The newspapers continued to report on the story and the rescue of the constables who were still trapped in the chamber. Two days after our departure, the workers who were clearing and reinforcing the tunnel came upon the body of the reporter, Jack Breaker. Miraculously, he was comatose but still alive. He was immediately removed and taken to hospital where it was reported that he was in very rough shape, with several broken bones, but expected to make a reasonable though painful recovery within a few months.

Both of us concealed any unkind thoughts that might be considered *schadenfreude* but Holmes did mutter something about divine justice.

At the end of that week, I received a note from Holmes asking me to drop in to 221B at the end of the day as Inspector Lestrade would be coming by to chat about the continuing investigation into the kidnapping. By the time I arrived, the two of them were sitting in the familiar front room where Holmes and I had passed so many hours in years gone by.

"Ah, Watson," said Holmes as I entered. "Our good Inspector has just informed me that the constables who were trapped in the tunnel have been rescued. All in good condition. Their eyes will have adjusted by tomorrow, and they will be back on the job the day after."

"Oh, that is good news," I said. "Quite the villainous plot, wouldn't you say? I would never have thought that old German chap would have been the mastermind behind such an outrageous villainy. Or do you think that silly actor, O'Dowd was part of it?"

I had expected an affirmation of my comment, but instead I received condescending looks from both of them.

"Come come, Doctor," said Lestrade, "you have not concluded that *they* were behind the whole thing, have you?"

Actually, I had been somewhat under that impression but requested, as I had done many times in the past from Holmes, that I be respectfully enlightened.

"The first thing you need to know," said Lestrade, "is that Mr. Dabney O'Dowd is under arrest and charged with aiding and abetting. *And* he has secured a team of defense lawyers. *And* would you like to know which firm from the Temple is representing him?"

"Who?"

"Dewey, Cheetham and Howe."

"But that is the most select firm in the country. How could some summer stock actor afford them?"

"Thank you, doctor, you have just proved my point," said Lestrade.

"What about the old German fellow?"

"I have," said Lestrade, "assembled a rather extensive file on Mr. Steiger. He only started teaching at the school at the start of the term. Before that, he lived in Bonn. He retired two years ago after a very successful career working for the Kaiser."

"What did he do?" I asked.

"Intelligence. Very senior."

"Then why do you not think he was behind all this?"

"The demands," said Holmes, "for action by His Majesty's Government did not come from Dover. While Steiger was staying in St. Vincent's along with us, Whitehall and the Cabinet were receiving messages sent from London and Paris from this group who call themselves the Order of the Fittest. We are proceeding under the assumption that Steiger had been quite strategically hired by them and shrewdly placed in the school. This plot to kidnap the girls and use them to force the hand of the government was in the works for several months and refined during the visit to Dover. The opportunity to abduct them came with the midnight visit to the Castle."

"But how could anyone have expected that?"

"Once Steiger had been identified to the public as a suspect," said Holmes, "one of the boys from the Academy came to Scotland Yard with some very useful data. He informed them that Mr. Steiger had casually made their acquaintance at the holiday park and engaged them very cleverly in chatting about the girls. He reminisced in the congenial way that older men do about his golden days in college in Heidelberg and his glorious adventures after dark when the members of his Westphalian House would meet up with some of the barmaids after dark in a local ruins and all the good times they had had together. He very slyly planted the seed in their minds for the rendezvous in haunted grounds of Dover Castle."

"Quite the clever fellow," I said.

"Indeed," said Holmes. "His years in espionage were useful, but most likely he was only a highly skilled and well-paid mercenary in the pay of this mysterious Order."

"Do we know who they are?" I asked.

"Regrettably, no," said Holmes. "However, the good Inspector has retained my services to find them, expose them, and put them out of business."

"And might I be so bold as to request that I accompany you from time to time and record your exploits?"

"As long as—"

He was interrupted by the ringing of the bell at the Baker Street door. I looked at Holmes, and he responded with a shrug and upturned palms. We heard Mrs. Hudson descending the stairs and waited, wondering who would be calling at this late hour in the afternoon without having made an appointment.

Mrs. Hudson entered and dispelled our ignorance.

"It is a young lady, Mr. Holmes. She said she is one of *the girls* and requested … no, it would be better to say that she *demanded* that she see you."

"Did she offer a card?" asked Holmes.

"No, sir, but she did give her name. She is Miss Edith Royce."

"Then please, show her up."

I had seen this young woman only for a brief second when she emerged blindfolded, dirty, and disheveled from the cylinder that had been drilled into the Castle Hill. However, what immediately popped into my mind was the fact that her name had been attached to one of the canvas sacks of forbidden reading material that the Prioress had been forced by Holmes to submit to us.

We stood as the young lady entered the room. Her appearance was far removed from a week ago. Now she was dressed in the finest fashion of the day for a woman of her age, and her rosy cheeks and lovely face were the picture of youthful health and beauty.

She walked confidently toward us and in a warm—dare I say, flirtatious—smile, greeted we three gentlemen of advancing years.

After a few words of greeting and chat about the experience she had endured, Holmes began his questioning of her before even requesting her to state her case and reason for the visit.

"Miss Royce, kindly inform us as to what took place in the castle keep after midnight on the night your vanished."

"It was really just an adventurous lark, Sir. Nothing untoward happened. The boys from the Academy were all very sweet, and we had some lovely laughs and so forth. Nothing you would not expect when a team of girls meets up with a nice group of boys. One or two names and addresses were exchanged and—"

"Miss Royce," interrupted Holmes. "I do not care what happened between your team and the boys. What happened *after* two o'clock when you departed from the keep?"

"Oh … yes … well … *that*. We were all together on our bicycles and had worked our way slowly—it is a very steep slope—and had just passed the door in the cutaway that leads into tunnels when suddenly we were stopped by a group of men who shone their torches and lanterns in our faces. They were carrying guns and knives and told us that if we made a sound, they would do unpleasant things to our bodies. We were somewhat upset. It was not a comfortable time for us."

"Continue."

"They were a rough looking lot, and we could smell the rum on them from several yards away. They told us to get off of our bicycles and enter the door to the tunnels. Perhaps we should have fought back. We can be somewhat adversarial, you know. But, as they say, discretion is the better part of valor, so we did as we were told. From there they led us quite some distance to the chamber in which you found us. What else do you want to know?"

"Did you recognize any of them?"

"One or two were sailors we had seen earlier in the streets of Dover, but we did not know who they were. We assumed that they were all a gang of local ruffians. After they took us back into the chamber, they took turns standing guard over us, four at a time. They all departed about an hour before the explosion. That is quite all I can tell you about them, Mr. Holmes."

"Very well, kindly tell us why you have slipped out of your family's city house in Mayfair, telling no one of your plans, and came to speak with me this afternoon."

As a result of my years of working alongside Sherlock Holmes, I was not surprised by his assertion. I had also observed that although Miss Royce was very well dressed, in a striking violation of the rules of fashion her feet were shod with plimsolls.

These soft-soled shoes allowed for noiseless footsteps. It was for that reason that the wags had begun to call them *sneakers*.

If she was curious concerning what Holmes had said, she did not show it. In a very composed manner, she smiled and responded.

"I came to thank you, Mr. Holmes. And, of course, you as well Dr. Watson, and you too, Inspector Lestrade. We know that you took great risks in finding us and rescuing us and we are all very grateful."

She smiled again with one of those smiles that I was sure would prove dangerous if not ruinous to any number of young men in the years to come.

Holmes was having none of it.

"You are quite welcome. Now kindly get on with it. What is the true reason for your visit?"

"Oh, yes, well, in addition to expressing my gratitude, I have some very good news to impart to you that I thought you might enjoy hearing."

"Capital. Then speak it."

"Our right defense player, Jane Holdernesse, is a very dear friend of mine."

The young woman she named was related to one of the wealthiest families in England, one for which Holmes had delivered valuable services in the recent past. However, she was also one of the trio of miscreants who had a very improper library of unspeakable reading material.

"Yes, what about her," said Holmes, his impatience emerging.

"Sir, four years ago, her little brother, Nigel, took a terrible fever and died. It was devastating to her. She loved him dearly."

"I am sorry to hear that. What has it to do with anything?"

"She took quite a shine to Charlie and has convinced her family to adopt him."

She announced this fact with a beaming smile and I could not help responding.

"That's wonderful news. Charlie will go from an orphan to a gentleman. Splendid!"

I must confess that the prospect of Charlie joining in an unholy alliance with Miss Jane left me wondering what havoc her parents might have brought upon themselves.

"Nice to hear," said Holmes. "Is there anything else?"

"Oh, yes. Some more good news. Did Mrs. Sterry ever tell you about the attackers we call *the saints*?"

"She did."

"Oh, good. Well, Sarah Akers-Douglas, our right inner, ended up somewhat smitten with Jerry, one of the constables. She returned to Dover to be there when he was rescued and came striding out of the tunnel. Yesterday, they announced their engagement. Isn't that brilliant?"

"How," asked Holmes, "can two people fall in love in complete darkness?"

That question elicited a coquettish smile from Miss Royce and even a small giggle.

"Really, Mr. Holmes, you must know that if it is true *when candles are out, all women are fair,* by the same measure, in the darkness any man can be an Adonis."

Even Holmes had to smile at that one.

"And one more thing," she said. "I believe you met Miss Myrina, Edith's older sister, did you not?"

"We did. What of her?"

"Well, sir, whilst she was staying at the hotel she met a very handsome major, one of the Coldstream Guards, and they are now wonderfully in love with each other. Isn't that just fabulous, Mr. Holmes?"

Holmes had lost his patience, and he reasserted his cross-questioning posture.

"Enough of the good news, Miss. It was thoughtful of you to inform us of what we would have heard from other sources within a few days. Now, what is the true reason for your visit?"

She sat up straight and assumed a posture of composure. Her clenched fists and whitening knuckles betrayed her.

"I understand that whilst in Dover you met my older brother, Viscount Fallendale."

"We did. He was terribly concerned for your well-being."

She did not respond verbally to that remark, but the tiny smirk was unmistakable.

"During the Trinity term, he came thrice to visit me at school," she said.

"Yes?"

"He had never done that before."

"The final term," said Holmes, "is critically important to your future and it is understandable that, in the interest of your family, he would be concerned for your performance. You do, if I may be blunt, have a reputation for being, shall we say, independently minded."

"My grades are the second highest in all of my classes. Only Florence Fawcett is ahead of me. I have already had confirmed acceptance at Cambridge."

"Your brother must be quite proud of you."

"No, Mr. Holmes. He hates me."

"Those are very strong words, young lady."

"Are they? Well, let me add to them. I feel the say way about him."

"That is an unfortunate situation between a sister and a brother."

"A *stepbrother*, Mr. Holmes. His mother died when he was twelve years old, and Father married my mother four months later. For reasons that are both emotional and financial, he resents my existence."

"That is regrettable but not unheard of amongst families in which matters of inheritance loom large. But what has it to do with his visits to your school?"

"He hardly spoke more than a few words to me each time."

"Many young men his age are busy in the City or with matters of government and industry. Perfunctory family visits are quite common."

"He is a complete idler. He spends his time at his club, or the racetrack, or watching sporting events, or trying to seduce barmaids."

"Then perhaps he was merely eager to get back to his preferred pastimes."

"On each occasion, Mr. Holmes, he also met with Mr. Steiger, the German master."

That got the serious attention of all three of the men in the room.

"Did he?" said Holmes. "And might that have been out of concern for your grades in the course?"

"I chose to learn Spanish and Italian, not German."

"Yes, Miss. Anything else?"

"Yes. Three weeks ago, I was back at our city house for a visit. Around tea time, I was walking past Brown's, and I saw him entering along with another man. They both went into the dining room. Three days ago, that man's picture was in the newspaper in connection with our abduction."

"And was he identified?"

"Yes. It said his name was Dabney O'Dowd. He was the one that Alice said she punched in the nose. The newspaper reported that he had been charged with aiding and abetting in our abduction. My stepbrother knows him."

"That is of singular interest, Miss," said Holmes. "Pray tell, if we wanted to have a friendly chat with your brother, where might we find him? At his club, perhaps?"

"Yes. He's probably there now. He belongs to the Tankerville on Pall Mall."

Holmes now gave the young woman a very stern look and spoke slowly and deliberately.

"Do you understand the consequences of what you are doing in implicating your brother in your abduction?"

She nodded. "I do." There was no smile and her face had paled.

"And you will swear to me that what you are saying is true and that you are not in any way fabricating anything out of adversarial feelings toward your brother?"

"I swear," she whispered.

"And that you may be called upon to give evidence against him in a court of law?"

"I'm ready."

"And that if found guilty of engaging in criminal activity, he could spend years in prison."

Again, she nodded. "That would be … good."

Chapter Twenty-Three
Tested at the Tankerville

SHERLOCK HOLMES HAD BECOME a well-recognized figure on the streets of London, as had I. Usually, if we entered a club on Pall Mall or St. James, we were greeted with cheers, and the members were always eager to engage us in unholy conversation about the nefarious criminal activities of our great city. Our welcome was decidedly cooler if we were accompanied by the Chief Inspector of Scotland Yard.

The Tankerville had acquired a reputation over the years as a favorite of those men whose lives and activities ran a bit close to the law. Well-off toffs who were too fond of their cards, or of women other than their wives, or both could be found there on any given evening. It was, as you may recall, the club of choice of Colonel Sabastian Moran.

We entered and were greeted with warmly by the porter who immediately changed his expression when he saw Lestrade coming in behind us.

"Yes, gentlemen," he said, *sotto voce,* as we stood by the porter's desk.

"If you would not mind, sir," said Holmes. "Is there a private room available? We need to have a word in confidence with Viscount Fallendale? Just tell him that he has visitors."

Without a word, the porter led us to a small private meeting room on the second floor.

"Wait here, please," he said. "I shall bring the Viscount."

A few minutes later we heard the loud obstreperous voice of the young noble. I suspected that he was somewhat into his cups.

"Bloody hell," he was shouting at the porter. "I was holding the best hand I have had all night. Why did you not tell them to wait?"

He entered the room and looked at us. His countenance clouded over and he and fell silent.

"Good evening, Viscount Fallendale," said Holmes without getting up. "Please be seated. We need to ask you a few questions, if you don't mind."

"Oh, do you now? Has no one ever taught you that it is proper form to make an appointment?"

"No," said Lestrade. "That lesson does not apply to Scotland Yard."

"Fine, then go ahead and ask your questions. I have a game to get back to, and you are interrupting it."

He sat down in one of the chairs, sloped his way to the floor and crossed his arms over his chest.

"We want," demanded Lestrade, "to know about your membership in a criminal organization that calls itself the Order of the Fittest and its treasonous work on behalf of the government of Kaiser Wilhelm."

With one of those instantaneous blinks of fear that flashes across the face of a man who has been caught out, the Viscount betrayed his surprise. He recovered almost immediately.

"The Order of *what?* Oh, let me see now ... I know about the Order of the Garter, the Order of St. John, the Order of Mike and Georgie, and the Thistle, and, of course, the Phoenix. But I do not recall hearing about ... what did you call it? ... the Shittist?"

"The *Fittist,"* said Lestrade. "And I will advise you that if you are willing to cooperate with us in dragging this group of villains to the bar, the law will go lighter on you when you are convicted of participating in it."

"Oh, *puleese*, mister policeman, do try not to be so bothersome and boring. Now, if that is not all you have to talk about, kindly excuse me. My fellow lords are waiting for me at a very rich table."

He stood up and turned toward the door.

"No," said Lestrade. "You are not excused. I am informing you that your presence is required tomorrow morning at Scotland Yard at 9:00 am. If you do not show up, a police carriage will come to your residence and compel you to attend. You may bring a solicitor with you if you wish. Good day, sir. You are now excused."

Viscount Fallendale gave a look of contempt to Lestrade and left the room.

"Do you," Holmes asked of Lestrade, "wish me to be present when you question him?"

Lestrade paused before answering.

"I think not, Holmes. No disrespect, of course. But there are times when we question someone when it is better that outsiders not be present. That way no one can ever ask you what took place, if you know what I mean. Please, no offense intended."

"And none taken. Do let me know if you acquire significant data from him."

"Shall do."

At noon the following day, my curiosity had gotten the better of me, and I walked over to Baker Street to find out if Holmes had heard back from Lestrade. Just as I approached the door of 221B, a police carriage pulled up, and Lestrade stepped out. He saw me and gave a nod, but his face was blank.

It was all I could do not to ask him about his interrogation but courtesy required that I wait until Holmes was present. We both entered the front room where Holmes was sitting in his usual chair and puffing on his usual pipe.

"A pleasure," he said, "to welcome both of you. Please, do have a seat. So good of you to come over after your meeting this morning, Inspector. How did it go?"

"Not at all well."

"Oh, dear. What happened?"

"He did not appear."

"Did you send your men to get him?"

"Of course, I did. Hopkins went off immediately with two constables. Fallendale has rooms at Brown's, and they went there straight away."

"And did they find him?"

Oh, yes. They found him all right. Found him quite easily. He was in his bedroom ... still dressed in his evening clothes ... and stretched out of the floor."

Holmes paused as the realization of what Lestrade had said sunk in.

"You are saying that he was dead?"

"Very. A bottle of cyanide was on the dresser table."

"He took his own life?" asked Holmes.

"That is what will appear in the papers tomorrow. Poor chap was terribly glum after the strain of his dear sister's abduction and his loss in a high stakes card game."

"Yes ... and?"

"Hopkins concluded almost immediately that it was set up. The hotel cleaning staff reported that they had never seen the bottle and would certainly have noticed. The night desk clerk said that Fallendale came in before midnight, quite drunk and that two other chaps were with him. All three went up to his rooms and but the two men came back down no more than ten minutes later. Hopkins could not smell any trace of cyanide around his mouth but saw a red puncture mark on his wrist. Looks like someone who knew what he was doing poked a needle into him and he was likely dead in two minutes."

"Any initial hypothesis?" asked Holmes.

"I would say that whoever he was colluding with knew that he would sing like a canary this morning to save his own hide and did not want to give him the chance."

"That seems a reasonable insight."

"Well, Holmes, since this is the second time you have foiled one of their ventures, I would say it is also *reasonable* to conclude that they are not feeling very kindly towards you, my friend."

"I agree, quite reasonable."

"The let me add one more. We, and more specifically *you,* Mr. Sherlock Holmes, have not heard the last of them."

Historical and Other Notes

Dover Castle is one of the largest medieval castles in England. Fortifications on the heights of Dover, looking out over the English Channel, were in place since time immemorial but the construction of the castle as it now exists started during the reign of Henry II (1154 – 1189). It was expanded and strengthened on numerous occasions after that and particularly during the Napoleonic era when an invasion from France was expected.

It is haunted. The ghost of the headless drummer boy has been seen and heard by many reliable witnesses whose sanity and probity surely is not in doubt.

Tunnels and caves all along the Dover coast have existed forever. As noted in this story, the tunnels were extensively expanded first by English troops and then by forced labor of the French POWs during the years of Napoleon. These tunnels were further expanded during World War II. The Evacuation of Dunkirk, *Operation Dynamo,* was planned and operated from rooms within the tunnels. However, that era is beyond the dates of this story.

The *Entente Cordiale* was signed between Britain and France in April 1904 and formally put an end to hundreds of years of conflict. The complicated diplomatic negotiations leading to its signing were led by the French in an attempt to draw England to the French side in the growing tension with Germany. Part of the *Entente* included the agreement by Britain that the French could annex Morocco with no objection from the British as long as France agreed that English hegemony could extend over Egypt.

For understandable reasons, the Germans did not like this arrangement. In March 1905 the First Moroccan Crisis took place when Kaiser Wilhelm II had his yacht stop in Tangiers and he proceeded to ride through the city, proclaiming German support for the independence of Morocco and for keeping the French out of it.

The diplomatic dispute escalated to the point that troops of both France and Germany were massed along their shared border. The Germans appealed to Britain to join it in supporting Moroccan independence, which did seem to some to be in Britain's interest as it would keep the French away from the strategic Straits of Gibraltar. Britain, however, stuck to its recent commitment to the *Entente Cordial* and offered no support to Germany. It was a tense time throughout Europe and evoked strong reactions from many parties.

Some of the characters in the story are drawn from the history of the time. Mrs. Charlotte Sterry (née Cooper) was an exceptional athlete who won Wimbledon several times and took the gold medal in women's tennis in the 1904 Olympic Games, the first gold medal to be awarded to a woman in Olympic history. At age 26, she became deaf but continued throughout her life to be a champion of women's sports. There is no record of her ever having met or assisted Sherlock Holmes but considering her indomitable spirit, it is reasonable to imagine that she might have.

Wilhelm Steiger served under Bismarck and during the early days of Kaiser Wilhelm and rose to the head of intelligence services. Whether or not he sold his services during his retirement is unknown.

The Sisters of St. Vincent de Paul opened an orphanage for boys in Dover around 1883. The buildings were adjacent to the St. Paul's Catholic Church. The Sisters provided charitable services on the site to many orphans, children with special needs, and destitute mothers for decades after that. The operations ended in 1993.

The Dover locations listed in the story are generally accurate. There is, however, no valley or watercourse on the eastern slope. I made that one up.

Horrific acts of anti-Semitism and outrageously false blood libel stories were common throughout Europe from the time of Chaucer, who included one as *The Prioress's Tale* in *The Canterbury Tales*. The stories continued right up through the Holocaust. Let us hope and pray that they have now been left behind.

While doing research for this story, I came across what is known as Betteridge's Law of Headlines. It states: Any headline that ends in a question mark can be accurately answered with the word *No*. I gratefully acknowledge the insight.

Beginning in the late 1800s and continuing to the present day, various individuals and groups have attempted to use the concept of evolutionary biology and natural selection—the 'survival of the fittest'—to account for human individual and social behavior. The uses made of the writings of Charles Darwin, Herbert Spencer, and other scientists and historians have, for the most part, been benign even if illogical. Unfortunately, they have also been used to justify a host of malevolent practices including slavery, colonization, mass sterilization, class segregation, opposition to racial miscegenation, white supremacy, and eugenics. These ways of thinking have been labelled 'Social Darwinism' by those who condemn them.

When I was a young high school student, my older brother (now Dr. James Copland) purchased several paperback books through a mail-order house. One of the was *The Adventures of Sherlock Holmes*. Another was a compilation of mystery stories and included the still famous *Problem of Cell 13* by Jacques Futrelle.

That story has been reprinted time and again and regularly appears in anthologies and lists of the greatest mystery stories ever. It was originally published in the *Boston American* in the fall of 1905. I have been just a little unfaithful to the historical publication date and moved it to the spring of that year.

When the promising author, Jacques Futrelle, was only thirty-seven, he met a situation from which he could not escape and was lost on the *Titanic*.

The genesis of this story was the near disaster and miraculous rescue of the boys' soccer team in Thailand in late June and early July 2018. The last of the boys and their coach were being pulled out of the caves as I sat down to draft the plot.

About the Author

In May of 2014 the Sherlock Holmes Society of Canada – better known as The Bootmakers – announced a contest for a new Sherlock Holmes story. Although he had no experience writing fiction, the author submitted a short Sherlock Holmes mystery and was blessed to be declared one of the winners. Thus inspired, he has continued to write new Sherlock Holmes Mysteries since and is on a mission to write a new story as a tribute to each of the sixty stories in the original Canon. He currently writes from Buenos Aires, Toronto, the Okanagan, and Manhattan. Several readers of New Sherlock Holmes Mysteries have kindly sent him suggestions for future stories. You are welcome to do likewise at: craigstephencopland@gmail.com.

More Historical Mysteries by Craig Stephen Copland

www.SherlockHolmesMystery.com
Copy and enter links to on links to look inside and order

Studying Scarlet. Starlet O'Halloran, a fabulous mature woman, who reminds the reader of Scarlet O'Hara (but who, for copyright reasons cannot actually be her) has arrived in London looking for her long-lost husband, Brett (who resembles Rhett Butler, but who, for copyright reasons, cannot actually be him). She enlists the help of Sherlock Holmes. This is an unauthorized parody, inspired by Arthur Conan Doyle's *A Study in Scarlet* and Margaret Mitchell's *Gone with the Wind*. http://authl.it/aic

The Sign of the Third. Fifteen hundred years ago the courageous Princess Hemamali smuggled the sacred tooth of the Buddha into Ceylon. Now, for the first time, it is being brought to London to be part of a magnificent exhibit at the British Museum. But what if something were to happen to it? It would be a disaster for the British Empire. Sherlock Holmes, Dr. Watson, and even Mycroft Holmes are called upon to prevent such a crisis. This novella is inspired by the Sherlock Holmes mystery, The Sign of the Four. http://authl.it/aie

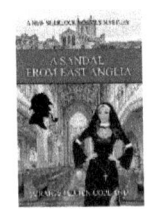

A Sandal from East Anglia. Archeological excavations at an old abbey unearth an ancient document that has the potential to change the course of the British Empire and all of Christendom. Holmes encounters some evil young men and a strikingly beautiful young Sister, with a curious double life. The mystery is inspired by the original Sherlock Holmes story, *A Scandal in Bohemia*. http://authl.it/aif

The Bald-Headed Trust. Watson insists on taking Sherlock Holmes on a short vacation to the seaside in Plymouth. No sooner has Holmes arrived than he is needed to solve a double murder and prevent a massive fraud diabolically designed by the evil Professor himself. Who knew that a family of devout conservative churchgoers could come to the aid of Sherlock Holmes and bring enormous grief to evil doers? The story is inspired by *The Red-Headed League.*

http://authl.it/aih

A Case of Identity Theft. It is the fall of 1888 and Jack the Ripper is terrorizing London. A young married couple is found, minus their heads. Sherlock Holmes, Dr. Watson, the couple's mothers, and Mycroft must join forces to find the murderer before he kills again and makes off with half a million pounds. The novella is a tribute to A Case of Identity. It will appeal both to devoted fans of Sherlock Holmes, as well as to those who love the great game of rugby.

http://authl.it/aii

The Hudson Valley Mystery. A young man in New York went mad and murdered his father. His mother believes he is innocent and knows he is not crazy. She appeals to Sherlock Holmes and, together with Dr. and Mrs. Watson, he crosses the Atlantic to help this client in need. This new story was inspired by *The Boscombe Valley Mystery.*

http://authl.it/aij

The Mystery of the Five Oranges. A desperate father enters 221B Baker Street. His daughter has been kidnapped and spirited off the North America. The evil network who have taken her has spies everywhere. There is only one hope – Sherlock Holmes. Sherlockians will enjoy this new adventure, inspired by *The Five Orange Pips* and *Anne of Green Gables.* **www.SherlockHolmesMystery.com**

http://authl.it/aik

The Man Who Was Twisted But Hip. France is torn apart by The Dreyfus Affair. Westminster needs Sherlock Holmes so that the evil tide of anti-Semitism that has engulfed France will not spread. Sherlock and Watson go to Paris to solve the mystery and thwart Moriarty. This new mystery is inspired by, *The Man with the Twisted Lip,* as well as by *The Hunchback of Notre Dame.* http://authl.it/ail

The Adventure of the Blue Belt Buckle. A young street urchin discovers a man's belt and buckle under a bush in Hyde Park. A body is found in a hotel room in Mayfair. Scotland Yard seeks the help of Sherlock Holmes in solving the murder. The Queen's Jubilee could be ruined. Sherlock Holmes, Dr. Watson, Scotland Yard, and Her Majesty all team up to prevent a crime of unspeakable dimensions. A new mystery inspired by *The Blue Carbuncle*.

http://authl.it/aim

The Adventure of the Spectred Bat. A beautiful young woman, just weeks away from giving birth, arrives at Baker Street in the middle of the night. Her sister was attacked by a bat and died, and now it is attacking her. A vampire? The story is a tribute to *The Adventure of the Speckled Band* and like the original, leaves the mind wondering and the heart racing. http://authl.it/ain

The Adventure of the Engineer's Mom. A brilliant young Cambridge University engineer is carrying out secret research for the Admiralty. It will lead to the building of the world's most powerful battleship, The Dreadnaught. His adventuress mother is kidnapped and he seeks the help of Sherlock Holmes. This new mystery is a tribute to *The Engineer's Thumb*. http://authl.it/aio

www.SherlockHolmesMystery.com

The Adventure of the Notable Bachelorette. A snobbish nobleman enters 221B Baker Street demanding the help in finding his much younger wife – a beautiful and spirited American from the West. Three days later the wife is accused of a vile crime. Now she comes to Sherlock Holmes seeking to prove her innocence. This new mystery was inspired *The Adventure of the Noble Bachelor*. http://authl.it/aip

The Adventure of the Beryl Anarchists. A deeply distressed banker enters 221B Baker St. His safe has been robbed, and he is certain that his motorcycle-riding sons have betrayed him. Highly incriminating and embarrassing records of the financial and personal affairs of England's nobility are now in the hands of blackmailers. Then a young girl is murdered. A tribute to *The Adventure of the Beryl Coronet*. http://authl.it/aiq

The Adventure of the Coiffured Bitches. A beautiful young woman will soon inherit a lot of money. She disappears. Another young woman finds out far too much and, in desperation seeks help. Sherlock Holmes, Dr. Watson and Miss Violet Hunter must solve the mystery of the coiffured bitches and avoid the massive mastiff that could tear their throats out. A tribute to *The Adventure of the Copper Beeches.* http://authl.it/air

The Silver Horse, Braised. The greatest horse race of the century, will take place at Epsom Downs. Millions have been bet. Owners, jockeys, grooms, and gamblers from across England and America arrive. Jockeys and horses are killed. Holmes fails to solve the crime until… This mystery is a tribute to *Silver Blaze* and the great racetrack stories of Damon Runyon. http://authl.it/ais **www.SherlockHolmesMystery.com**

The Box of Cards. A brother and a sister from a strict religious family disappear. The parents are alarmed, but Scotland Yard says they are just off sowing their wild oats. A horrific, gruesome package arrives in the post, and it becomes clear that a terrible crime is in process. Sherlock Holmes is called in to help. A tribute to *The Cardboard Box.* http://authl.it/ait

The Yellow Farce. Sherlock Holmes is sent to Japan. The war between Russia and Japan is raging. Alliances between countries in these years before World War I are fragile, and any misstep could plunge the world into Armageddon. The wife of the British ambassador is suspected of being a Russian agent. Join Holmes and Watson as they travel around the world to Japan. Inspired by *The Yellow Face.* http://authl.it/akp

562

The Stock Market Murders. A young man's friend has gone missing. Two more bodies of young men turn up. All are tied to The City and to one of the greatest frauds ever visited upon the citizens of England. The story is based on the true story of James Whitaker Wright and is inspired by, *The Stock Broker's Clerk.* Any resemblance of the villain to a certain American political figure is entirely coincidental. http://authl.it/akq

The Glorious Yacht. On the night of April 12, 1912, off the coast of Newfoundland, one of the greatest disasters of all time took place – the Unsinkable Titanic struck an iceberg and sank with a horrendous loss of life. The news of the disaster leads Holmes and Watson to reminisce about one of their earliest adventures. It began as a sailing race and ended as a tale of murder, kidnapping, piracy, and survival through a tempest. A tribute to *The Gloria Scott.* http://authl.it/akr

A Most Grave Ritual. In 1649, King Charles I escaped and made a desperate run for Continent. Did he leave behind a vast fortune? The patriarch of an ancient Royalist family dies in the courtyard, and the locals believe that the headless ghost of the king did him in. The police accuse his son of murder. Sherlock Holmes is hired to exonerate the lad. A tribute to *The Musgrave Ritual.* http://authl.it/aks

The Spy Gate Liars. Dr. Watson receives an urgent telegram telling him that Sherlock Holmes is in France and near death. He rushes to aid his dear friend, only to find that what began as a doctor's house call has turned into yet another adventure as Sherlock Holmes races to keep an unknown ruthless murderer from dispatching yet another former German army officer. A tribute to *The Reigate Squires.* http://authl.it/akt

The Cuckold Man Colonel James Barclay needs the help of Sherlock Holmes. His exceptionally beautiful, but much younger, wife has disappeared and foul play is suspected. Has she been kidnapped and held for ransom? Or is she in the clutches of a deviant monster? The story is a tribute not only to the original mystery, *The Crooked Man*, but also to the biblical story of King David and Bathsheba. http://authl.it/akv

The Impatient Dissidents. In March 1881, the Czar of Russia was assassinated by anarchists. That summer, an attempt was made to murder his daughter, Maria, the wife of England's Prince Alfred. A Russian Count is found dead in a hospital in London. Scotland Yard and the Home Office arrive at 221B and enlist the help of Sherlock Holmes to track down the killers and stop them. This new mystery is a tribute to *The Resident Patient*. http://authl.it/akw

The Grecian, Earned. This story picks up where *The Greek Interpreter* left off. The villains of that story were murdered in Budapest, and so Holmes and Watson set off in search of "the Grecian girl" to solve the mystery. What they discover is a massive plot involving the re-birth of the Olympic games in 1896 and a colorful cast of characters at home and on the Continent. http://authl.it/aia

The Three Rhodes Not Taken. Oxford University is famous for its passionate pursuit of learning. The Rhodes Scholarship has been recently established and some men are prepared to lie, steal, slander, and, maybe murder, in the pursuit of it. Sherlock Holmes is called upon to track down a thief who has stolen vital documents pertaining to the winner of the scholarship, but what will he do when the prime suspect is found dead? A tribute to *The Three Students*. http://authl.it/al8

The Naval Knaves. On September 15, 1894, an anarchist attempted to bomb the Greenwich Observatory. He failed, but the attempt led Sherlock Holmes into an intricate web of spies, foreign naval officers, and a beautiful princess. Once again, suspicion landed on poor Percy Phelps, and once again Holmes has to use both his powers of deduction and raw courage to not only rescue Percy, but to prevent an unspeakable disaster. A tribute to *The Naval Treaty.* http://authl.it/aia

A Scandal in Trumplandia. NOT a new mystery but a political satire. The story is a parody of the much-loved original story, *A Scandal in Bohemia*, with the character of the King of Bohemia replaced by you-know-who. If you enjoy both political satire and Sherlock Holmes, you will get a chuckle out of this new story. http://authl.it/aig

The Binomial Asteroid Problem. The deadly final encounter between Professor Moriarty and Sherlock Holmes took place at Reichenbach Falls. But when was their first encounter? This new story answers that question. What began a stolen Gladstone bag escalates into murder and more. This new story is a tribute to *The Adventure of the Final Problem.* http://authl.it/al1

The Adventure of Charlotte Europa Golderton. Charles Augustus Milverton, was shot and sent to his just reward. But now another diabolical scheme of blackmail has emerged centered in the telegraph offices of the Royal Mail. It is linked to an archeological expedition whose director disappeared. Someone is prepared to murder to protect their ill-gotten gain and possibly steal a priceless treasure. Holmes is hired by not one but three women who need his help. http://authl.it/al7

The Mystery of 222 Baker Street. The body of a Scotland Yard inspector is found in a locked room in 222 Baker Street. There is no clue as to how he died, but, he was murdered. Then another murder in the very same room. Holmes and Watson might have to offer themselves as potential victims if the culprits are to be discovered. The story is a tribute to the original Sherlock Holmes story, *The Adventure of the Empty House.* http://authl.it/al3

The Adventure of the Norwood Rembrandt. A man facing execution appeals to Sherlock Holmes to save him. He claims that he is innocent. Holmes agrees to take on his case. Five years ago, he was convicted of the largest theft of art masterpieces in British history, and of murdering the butler who tried to stop him. Holmes and Watson have to find the real murderer and the missing works of art --- if the client is innocent after all. This new Sherlock Holmes mystery is a tribute to *The Adventure of the Norwood Builder* in the original Canon.

http://authl.it/al4

The Horror of the Bastard's Villa. A Scottish clergyman and his faithful border collie visit 221B and tell a tale of a ghostly Banshee on the Isle of Skye. After the specter appeared, two people died. Holmes sends Watson on ahead to investigate and report. More terrifying horrors occur and Sherlock Holmes must come and solve the awful mystery before more people are murdered. A tribute to the original story in the Canon, Arthur Conan Doyle's masterpiece, *The Hound of the Baskervilles* . http://authl.it/al2

The Dancer from the Dance. In 1909 the entire world of dance changed when Les Ballets Russes, under opened in Paris. They also made annual visits to the West End in London. Tragically, during their 1913 tour, two of their dancers are found murdered. Sherlock Holmes is brought into to find the murderer and prevent any more killings. The story adheres fairly closely to the history of ballet and is a tribute to the original story in the Canon, *The Adventure of the Dancing Men*. http://authl.it/al5

The Solitary Bicycle Thief. Remember Violet Smith, the beautiful young woman whom Sherlock Holmes and Dr. Watson rescued from a forced marriage, as recorded in *The Adventure of the Solitary Cyclist*? Ten years later she and Cyril reappear in 221B Baker Street with a strange tale of the theft of their bicycles. What on the surface seemed like a trifle turns out to be the door that leads Sherlock Holmes into a web of human trafficking, espionage, blackmail, and murder. A new and powerful cabal of master criminals has formed in London and they will stop at nothing, not even the murder of an innocent foreign student, to extend the hold on the criminal underworld of London.

http://authl.it/al6

The Adventure of the Prioress's Tale. The senior field hockey team from an elite girls' school goes to dover for a beach holiday … and disappears. Have they been abducted into white slavery? Did they run off to Paris? Are they being held for ransom? Can Sherlock Holmes find them in time? Holmes, Watson, Lestrade, the Prioress of the school, and a new gang of Irregulars must find them before something terrible happens. a tribute to *The Adventure of the Priory School in the Canon*. http://authl.it/apv

Contributions to The Great Game of Sherlockian Scholarship

Sherlock and Barack. This is NOT a new Sherlock Holmes Mystery. It is a Sherlockian research monograph. Why did Barack Obama win in November 2012? Why did Mitt Romney lose? Pundits and political scientists have offered countless reasons. This book reveals the truth - The Sherlock Holmes Factor. Had it not been for Sherlock Holmes, Mitt Romney would be president.

http://authl.it/aid

From The Beryl Coronet to Vimy Ridge. This is NOT a New Sherlock Holmes Mystery. It is a monograph of Sherlockian research. This new monograph in the Great Game of Sherlockian scholarship argues that there was a Sherlock Holmes factor in the causes of World War I... and that it is secretly revealed in the *roman a clef* story that we know as *The Adventure of the Beryl Coronet*.

http://authl.it/ali

Reverend Ezekiel Black—'The Sherlock Holmes of the American West'—Mystery Stories.

A Scarlet Trail of Murder. At ten o'clock on Sunday morning, the twenty-second of October, 1882, in an abandoned house in the West Bottom of Kansas City, a fellow named Jasper Harrison did not wake up. His inability to do was the result of his having had his throat cut. The Reverend Mr. Ezekiel Black, a part-time Methodist minister and an itinerant US Marshall is called in. This original western mystery was inspired by the great Sherlock Holmes classic, *A Study in Scarlet.* http://authl.it/alg

The Brand of the Flying Four. This case all began one quiet evening in a room in Kansas City. A few weeks later, a gruesome murder, took place in Denver. By the time Rev. Black had solved the mystery, justice, of the frontier variety, not the courtroom, had been meted out. The story is inspired by *The Sign of the Four* by Arthur Conan Doyle, and like that story, it combines murder most foul, and romance most enticing.

http://authl.it/alh

www.SherlockHolmesMystery.com

Collection Sets for eBooks and paperback are available at *40% off the price of buying them separately.*

Collection One http://authl.it/al9
The Sign of the Tooth
The Hudson Valley Mystery
A Case of Identity Theft
The Bald-Headed Trust
Studying Scarlet
The Mystery of the Five Oranges

Collection Two http://authl.it/ala
A Sandal from East Anglia
The Man Who Was Twisted But Hip

The Blue Belt Buckle
The Spectred Bat

Collection Three   http://authl.it/alb
The Engineer's Mom
The Notable Bachelorette
The Beryl Anarchists
The Coiffured Bitches

Collection Four   http://authl.it/alc
The Silver Horse, Braised
The Box of Cards
The Yellow Farce
The Three Rhodes Not Taken

Collection Five   http://authl.it/ald
The Stock Market Murders
The Glorious Yacht
The Most Grave Ritual
The Spy Gate Liars

Collection Six   http://authl.it/ale
The Cuckold Man
The Impatient Dissidents
The Grecian, Earned
The Naval Knaves

Collection Seven   http://authl.it/alf
The Binomial Asteroid Problem
The Mystery of 222 Baker Street

The Adventure of Charlotte Europa Golderton
The Adventure of the Norwood Rembrandt

Collection Eight http://authl.it/at3

The Dancer from the Dance
The Adventure of the Prioress's Tale
The Adventure of Mrs. J. L. Heber
The Solitary Bicycle Thief

www.SherlockHolmesMystery.com

If you enjoyed these stories or if there are ways it could be improved, please help the author and future readers by leaving a constructive review on the site from which you obtained the book. Thank you. Much appreciated,

CSC

Do you subscribe to Kindle Unlimited/Prime/KOLL?

If so, then you can borrow ALL New Sherlock Holmes Mysteries ALL the time for FREE.

Copyright © 2018 by Craig Stephen Copland

All rights reserved. No part of this book may be reproduced or transmitted in any form or by any means, electronic or mechanical, including photocopying, recording, or by an information storage and retrieval system – except by a reviewer who may quote brief passages in a review to be printed in a magazine, newspaper, or on the web – without permission in writing from Craig Stephen Copland.

The characters of Sherlock Holmes and Dr. Watson are no longer under copyright, nor are the four original Sherlock Holmes stories that inspired these pastiche stories.

Published by:

Conservative Growth Inc.

5072 Turtle Pond Place,

Vernon, British, Columbia, Canada